Follow the lives of Laurel's "forever friends" Toddy and Kit in the remaining novels of the *Orphan Train West* trilogy:

Homeward the Seeking Heart

Vivacious, mischievous Toddy is left at Greystone by her actress mother. Toddy's exuberance attracts Mrs. Vale, a wealthy widow who seeks a companion for her invalid granddaughter, Helene. Toddy soon wins their hearts, yet feels unworthy because of her background. Not even the love of Chris Blanchard can provide the self-esteem she needs. Is Toddy's yearning for a place to belong only an elusive dream?

Dreams of a Longing Heart

Kit goes with a farm family, where she becomes a hired girl/mother's helper for the mother of five sons. Just when the future looks bright, Kit must choose between faithfulness and opportunity. Her decision leads to unexpected blessings, terror, and love.

BY Jane Peart:

Homeward the Seeking Heart
Quest for Lasting Love
Dreams of a Longing Heart
Scent of Heather
Sign of the Carousel

QUEST FOR LASTING LOVE

JANE PEART

Fleming H. Revell
A Division of Baker Book House Co
Grand Rapids, Michigan 49516

Scripture quotations in this volume are from the King James
Version of the Bible.

Library of Congress Cataloging-in-Publication Data

Peart, Jane
    Quest for lasting love / Jane Peart.
      p.   cm.
    Sequel to: Homeward the seeking heart.
    ISBN 0-8007-5372-0
    I.   Peart, Jane. Homeward the seeking heart. II.   Title.
PS3566.E238Q4   1990
813'.54—dc20   90-40569
                                      CIP

Copyright © 1990 by Jane Peart
Published by Fleming H. Revell
a division of Baker Book House Company
P.O. Box 6287, Grand Rapids, MI 49516-6287

ISBN: 0-8007-5372-0

Sixth printing, May 1993

Printed in the United States of America

To the *real* "riders" of the orphan trains, the over 100,000 children who were transported by train across the country to new homes in the Midwest, from 1854 to the early twentieth century, whose experience and courage inspired this series.

QUEST FOR LASTING LOVE

1

Boston
December 1888

Something dreadful was about to happen. Laurel just knew it. Mama had seemed strange all morning. In fact, Mama had not seemed like herself for weeks. Watching her mother move slowly about the small rooms they rented upstairs in Mrs. Campbell's big, dark house, Laurel was newly alarmed.

For weeks now, even when she was playing tea party with her dolls, Laurel often felt her mother gazing at her. When Laurel looked up, she would see a sad expression on the beautiful face, and the dark, violet-shadowed eyes would be glistening with tears.

Frightened, Laurel would ask, "Why are you crying, Mama?"

Then her mother would quickly gather Laurel up into her arms and hold her, saying, "Nothing, my darling. Everything will be all right, you'll see."

But things were not all right, Laurel knew, and day by day she could feel that little knot in her chest grow tighter. Something was wrong.

Her mother gave piano lessons on Tuesday and Thursday afternoons, and Laurel always played quietly in a corner of the room while the students fumbled through their scales and the simple pieces they never seemed to get quite right. Usually after the last pupil left, her mother would sit at the piano and play lovely, rippling melodies, filling the room with harmony. A welcome relief after two hours of missed keys and sour notes.

Lately, however, when the lessons were over, her mother closed the piano lid with a deep sigh. Then, pale and exhausted, she would lie down on the narrow sofa, one arm flung over her eyes. Laurel would come over and sit on the cushions behind her and gently stroke her forehead.

"What would I do without my little nurse?" her mother would say with a weary smile.

Sometimes she drifted into a shallow slumber, waking with a start, two bright spots of color in a face otherwise drawn and white.

"Oh, my, Laurel, our supper will have to be fashionably late this evening."

At mealtimes they pretended that the simple fare of bread, tea with milk, and a piece of fruit for Laurel was a sumptuous affair fit for royalty. Her mother would be Queen Lily and Laurel would be Princess Laura Elaine, which was her *real* "christened" name, after her two grandmothers.

Laurel did not know her grandmothers. Her mother told her that they both lived "a long way off," but someday she would meet them.

"Someday, when all is forgiven—" her mother would murmur when Laurel asked when. Laurel did not understand. But she was so happy with the life they had together, she did not trouble herself with wondering about much else.

But more and more, things had been disturbingly different. She had awakened in the night several times to the sound of her mother's weeping— weeping that would often turn into a frightening paroxysm of coughing. Stiff with anxiety, Laurel, in her own small bed, would hug her doll Miranda. Hearing her mother get up, she would awaken to see her throw a shawl over her long, drifting nightgown and huddle in the chair by the window, trying to smother her hoarse racking cough.

It was one afternoon soon after a particularly bad night when the coughing had lasted a long time that her mother had left Laurel with Mrs. Campbell to go to the doctor.

Laurel liked staying with Mrs. Campbell, who was fat and jolly and cooked for the boarders who lived in her other rooms. She was usually in her large cheerful kitchen where she always seemed to be stirring something and where all sorts of wonderful things simmered on the stove, filling the air with delicious odors.

She pushed a little stool over for Laurel to stand on beside her at the big, square, scrubbed pine table and let her help roll out the biscuit dough. Then she showed her how to take a small glass tumbler, dip it into flour, and cut out the round shapes to be put on the baking sheet and placed in the oven of the big, black iron stove.

They were thus happily occupied when Laurel's mother returned. Mrs. Campbell took one look at her and pulled out her oak rocker for her to sit. Then she filled her blue kettle with water from the kitchen pump and placed it on the stove to boil.

"There now, rest a bit and I'll have a nice cup of tea for you in a minute. You look that worn out, Lillian." Then in a low-ered voice and with a furtive glance at the child, she asked, "Is it bad, then?"

Laurel's mother leaned her head against the high, fan-shaped back of the chair and nodded wordlessly. Laurel wiped her floury hands on the large apron Mrs. Campbell had tied around her, got down from the stool, walked over and climbed up into her mother's lap. Her mother nestled her close, resting her chin upon Laurel's soft dark curls, and answered Mrs. Campbell's question.

"Yes, Mrs. Campbell, very bad, indeed, I'm afraid. I shall have to make plans—" Her voice drifted away weakly.

"If there's anything I can do to help—"

There was something in Mrs. Campbell's response that made Laurel cuddle even closer to her mother, winding her little arms around her mother's waist, breathing in the sweet, violet scent of her. She felt an inner trembling. That dark thing she had felt hovering over them crept nearer.

Before she was even fully awake, Laurel heard the steady pattering of rain against the windows and felt her mother's hand gently stroking her hair.

"Come, darling, you must get up."

As Laurel sat up, sleepily rubbing her eyes, she saw that it was still dark outside.

"Is it nighttime?" she asked, watching her mother's slender figure moving about in the lamplight, setting the table for breakfast.

"No, precious, it is very early in the morning. But we both have to go somewhere, and I am fixing a special breakfast for us. Cocoa for you and the last of the coffee for me."

Even though her mother was being especially cheerful and gay, Laurel felt that queasy sensation stirring deep inside. Was this the day the dark unknown thing was going to happen?

The feeling was so strong Laurel could not really relish the surprise treat of sticky buns or the creamy hot cocoa.

But it wasn't until her mother had brushed her hair for an extra long time, carefully winding each curl around her fingers then tying them in bunches with velvet ribbons on both sides of her head, that she told Laurel what it was.

"You know, darling, Mama has not been feeling too well lately and the doctors tell me I must have a long rest if I want to get strong and healthy again. So, I have to go away to a place in the mountains where they can take care of me and help me get better. And you are going to stay at a nice place with a lot of other little girls and boys whose mamas are sick or away—" Here her voice broke and she hugged Laurel to her. Laurel felt the wetness of tears on her mother's soft cheek and she clung to her in sudden panic.

"But I don't want to go anywhere without you, Mama!"

"I know, my darling, but it will only be for a little while. I will come as soon as I can and get you and we will be together again. I promise!"

In stunned disbelief Laurel watched her mother pack a small valise with all her neatly ironed clothes—the dresses with the embroidered yokes, the pinafores, the white cotton chemises, panties, ruffled petticoats trimmed with crocheted edging, all handmade so lovingly for Laurel.

Then Lillian took off the gold chain and locket she always wore from around her own neck and fastened it around Laurel's.

"I want you to wear this until I come for you, Laurel." She pointed out the intertwined swirled letters on the heart-shaped front. "See these? They spell out our initials. The L.M. stands for Lillian Maynard—my maiden name—and the P.V. is for your father—Paul Vestal. It's important for you to remember that, Laurel," she said. "Your father gave me this before we were married, since he couldn't afford an engagement ring. But I always loved it." Then she opened the locket to show the pictures inside. One was of Lillian herself when she was a young girl with her dark hair falling in curls around her shoulders; the other picture, of a handsome, dark-eyed young man. "This is your precious papa, Laurel."

Laurel could not remember her father. He had been killed in a tragic accident, knocked down by a team of runaway horses when he was crossing the street on his way home one snowy evening when Laurel was just a baby.

"Now, remember, Laurel, don't take this off for any reason, until I come."

After that her mother buttoned her into her velour coat with the scalloped cape that she had fashioned for her only the month before. After she tied Laurel's satin bonnet strings under her chin, she kissed her on both cheeks. Then, hand in hand, they went quietly down the stairs of the sleeping house and out into the dark, rainy morning. At the street corner they found a cab and sad-looking horse, its driver bundled into a muffler, his chin on his chest, a battered stovepipe hat slipping forward on his brow.

Lillian squeezed Laurel's hand and said with a hint of the old gaiety in her voice, "This is going to be quite an adventure, darling. As long as we have to go, we're going in style."

"Where to, lady?" The driver roused himself with a jerk.

"Greystone," Lillian told him as she helped Laurel mount the high, rickety steps into the cab.

"You mean the County Orphanage?" he barked.

"Yes," Lillian said and this time her voice quavered.

Inside, she put her arm around Laurel, drawing her close. The ancient gig swayed and jolted over the cobblestone streets through the dreary morning drizzle, jogging slowly up a steep hill. All the while, Laurel felt the chill creep in through the cracks of the old vehicle, into her very bones, and she shivered, leaning into her mother. They did not speak on the way, just clung to each other.

Finally the cab jerked to a stop in front of a stone fortress-like building.

The driver opened the roof flap and hollered down. "Greystone!"

Laurel's mother grasped her hand tightly and, after getting down herself, lifted Laurel down. Then she said to the cabbie. "Wait, please. I need to ride to the train depot."

Still holding Laurel by the hand, she mounted the steps. At the massive, double door, Lillian gave the metal doorbell a twist. Her mother was holding Laurel's hand so tightly it hurt her fingers, but even so she did not want to let go.

Finally the door was opened by a tall woman. She seemed to loom over them, making Laurel's mother seem smaller, more fragile than ever.

"Yes?" She regarded them with narrowed eyes, waiting for Laurel's mother to speak.

When it came, her voice seemed thin and faint. "I'm Lillian Vestal, I've come to....This is my little daughter—"

"Ah, yes, Mrs. Vestal. We were expecting you." The woman stretched out her hand toward Laurel, who drew back. Then she spoke crisply to Laurel's mother. "It is best you leave now, ma'am. The children are at prayers and will be going into breakfast. There will be less of a fuss if you say goodbye here."

Laurel's hand clutched her mother's convulsively. She felt the sick rise of nausea into her throat. "No, no," she tried to say, but the words wouldn't come out.

Her mother bent to hug her, whispering, "You must be a brave, good girl, my darling. I will be back soon. Very soon."

"Come along, child." The voice in the doorway was firm.

Lillian pried Laurel's hands from around her neck, murmuring soothing words as Laurel felt herself being pulled out of her mother's embrace. She heard a smothered sob and turned to reach out again for her, but Lillian had already started down the steps.

At last she heard her own scream shrill through the air. "Mama! Mama! Come back!"

At that moment Laurel was picked up bodily and thrust through the door. When she heard it slam behind her, she wriggled out of the confining arms that held her, flung herself sobbing against the thick impenetrable door, and pounded her tiny fists against it.

2

Greystone Orphanage

All her life Laurel would remember the bewildering change from her life with her mother to that at Greystone. Numbed with shock, she moved like a little sleepwalker, unconscious of the stares of the other children, the worried frowns of the orphanage staff. Unresponsive, she allowed herself to be placed in line for meals, but barely touched her food. Eyes lowered, she did not respond to friendly overtures, merely nodded yes or no if asked a direct question.

Only her big, dark eyes reflected the pain caused by the abrupt transfer from the small, warm, sheltered world she had shared with her adored mother to the large, impersonal institutional life of Greystone.

For the first two days Laurel was at Greystone, she got up in the morning at the rising bell like everyone else. Then she dressed, put on her coat and bonnet, went down the main stairway and planted herself on the bottom step, her arms folded across her chest, her mouth set stubbornly.

"My mother is coming for me," she stated flatly and shook her head at any request to come away. Miss Clinock wisely rejected the use of any disciplinary action on the part of the other matrons or having Laurel physically removed from her post.

On the third day, however, the Head Matron herself approached Laurel.

"Laurel, your mother left you with us while she is in the sanatorium getting well," Miss Clinock intoned. "But until then, she expects you to try to be happy here with the other children, to be obedient and do as you are told. Now, come along, Laurel," she said firmly and held out her hand. "You want us to give your mother a good report of you when she *does* come, don't you? You wouldn't want us to have to tell her you had been a naughty girl who wouldn't mind, would you?"

Tears turned Laurel's eyes into glistening coals. She didn't want Mama to be disappointed in her. Slowly she got up, lifting her chin bravely, but refusing to take Miss Clinock's outstretched hand.

"Come along, then, there's a good girl," the woman said and led the way upstairs to the third floor dormitory.

Rows of small iron cots lined the long room. Beside each bed was a small chest, on which was an enamel pitcher and washbowl. Next to that a wooden stool. As Miss Clinock entered with Laurel, two dozen heads turned and all the little girls momentarily stopped tidying their cubicles.

"Get on with your duties, children," Miss Clinock spoke crisply. Her eyes roved around the room, then spotted the one narrow cot left unmade, its blankets tossed back, the pillow rumpled. "Come along, Laurel," she said and made straight for that one.

"Kit," Miss Clinock addressed a girl with smooth brown braids, who was pulling up the covers of her own cot next to Laurel's. "Will you please show Laurel how to make her bed and put her clothes neatly away?"

The girl turned around, glancing at Laurel with a shy smile. "Yes, ma'am."

"Every morning before prayers and breakfast, Laurel, your bed is to be made, your nightclothes put away." Miss Clinock spoke directly to Laurel. "Starting today, you will wear the Greystone uniform like the rest of the girls in Third."

"But my *mother* made *my* clothes! She wants me to wear these," protested Laurel, her lower lip beginning to tremble.

"We will put the things your mother made for you away carefully, Laurel, so that they will be ready for you when she comes. But while you are at Greystone, you will wear what the other girls wear," Miss Clinock said decisively.

Then she told Kit, "After things are put right here, Kit, take Laurel to Mrs. Weems in the Sewing Room to get a uniform." With that directive, the Head Matron left.

Laurel plumped down on the end of her cot, chin thrust out, arms folded again. She felt a gentle tug on the bedclothes underneath her as Kit began pulling them straight.

"Come on, I'll show you how. It's really easy," she said in a low voice.

A tear rolled slowly down Laurel's cheek. She didn't uncross her arms to free a hand to brush it away. Then she felt Kit's arm go around her shoulder. "I know how you feel," Kit whispered. "I felt the same way when I first came here. But you get used to it, honest."

"I'm not going to stay here," Laurel said as if trying to convince herself. "I don't have to. My mother is coming for me. *Soon!*" She squeezed both eyes shut tight, letting the tears flow unchecked.

"So is *mine!*" piped up a cheerful voice and Laurel opened her eyes to see a smiling little face with a tip-tilted nose pushed right up to hers, round blue eyes staring at her inquisitively. "Any day now." She reinforced her statement with a little nod and bounce as she popped herself down on the bed beside Laurel.

"And so is my *da,*" chimed in Kit, adding her declaration to theirs. "At least, as soon as he gets a job."

The three looked at one another appraisingly. In that moment of mutual affirmation, some kind of bond was forged. As yet it had not been tested, but the foundation for friendship was laid. Each of them, in her desperate bid to believe that she was different from the other children at

Greystone, found hope alive in at least two other hearts. By associating with the other two who also were determined to cling to that hope, her own was bolstered.

No three little girls could have been more different in appearance, personality or disposition, yet they became inseparable as the weeks turned into months and their status as "temporaries" inevitably changed.

If it had not been for the other two, Laurel would have found it even harder to adjust to Greystone. The overall drabness of the routine, the cheerless halls, the grinding daily routine of life was brightened a little for her by the companionship of Toddy and Kit.

The three sat at the same table at mealtimes, sought each other out during recreation. Kit was protective, shielding Laurel from some of the older children who were prone to bully the younger, shyer ones. Toddy, though small, was spunky and with her gift for mimicry often turned a potentially ugly playground incident into a comedy with herself as the clown.

During the weeks that followed, Toddy, Laurel and Kit grew closer. It was at night, when the lamps had been taken away, and she lay in her narrow little bed alone that Laurel felt most keenly the reality of her situation. Would her mama never come? she asked herself over and over, fingering the delicate chain of the locket she never removed from her neck. This anxious question would start the tears and the choked sobs. It was then the friendship of the three counted most.

Their cots were side by side in the vast dormitory and, when any one of the three was suddenly gripped by a terrible longing for comfort, her little hand would grope between the cots to find the others' extended in silent understanding.

Their ages varied by a matter of a year, but when tested, it was found they were at the same grade level. Kit, the eldest of the trio, had already had a year of schooling and had kept up her reading skills by reading to her little brother Jamie. Laurel's mother had taught her at home and Toddy, though the youngest of the three, had learned to read from playbills and theater posters, sheet music and railroad schedules.

Separately they had suffered the most traumatic experience in life. Together they helped each other survive by reassuring themselves and each other that soon their parent would come to get them, take them away from Greystone.

After the first long week, Laurel received a letter from her mother. A note, actually. Lily had written:

> My darling little girl,
> This can be only a few lines. They want me to rest and don't allow me to write more than this. I am getting better every day. Soon we'll be together again. Don't forget to be a good girl and say your prayers every day, especially for your loving mother.

Enclosed was a picture postcard with the words SARANAC LAKE SANATORIUM identifying a low, rambling rustic building surrounded by pine trees with porches all along the front. Lillian had drawn a tiny arrow to one of them, printing above it, "This is where I sit out in the sun and fresh air every day."

Laurel looked at the picture, trying to imagine her mother on the small porch. Then she put the letter and picture under her pillow. She unfolded it and read it so many times it became creased and worn around the edges.

Every week Laurel laboriously printed a letter to her mother with her version of daisies, her mother's favorite flower, drawn carefully down the border and on the flap of the envelope. Then she gave it to Miss Massey to address and mail.

Laurel never forgot the day that Miss Massey took her by the hand and led her into Miss Clinock's office.

"Sit down, Laurel, I have something to tell you," the Head Matron said. In her hands were two envelopes which Laurel immediately recognized from the daisies on them—the same daisies she always drew on her letters to Mama.

However, there was something else printed in bold black letters across the front. She could not make it out, so Miss Clinock held up the letter so Laurel could see. Slowly Laurel spelled out D-E-C-E-A-S-E-D. DECEASED.

"Do you know what this word means, Laurel?" Miss Clinock asked kindly.

Laurel shook her head but her heart began a drumbeat that felt as if her chest were exploding. "No, ma'am," she replied in a hoarse whisper.

"It means, Laurel, that your mother is dead."

Dead! Dead? Laurel did not know what *dead* was! Mrs. Campbell's old cat had died, she remembered, and once she had heard Mrs. Campbell tell a visiting neighbor while pointing a thumb at Laurel, "The child's father is dead." But Mama had always told her her Papa was in Heaven with the angels. Did that mean—

Laurel could neither move nor speak. She simply sat there, glued to the straight chair opposite Miss Clinock's desk.

"Are you all right, Laurel?" prompted the Head Matron. "Do you understand what I just told you?"

Suddenly everything got very bright and hot. The room tilted crazily and the pictures on the walls swayed. Laurel saw Miss Clinock rise from behind the desk and start toward her, but her approaching figure began to blur and wobble.

A roaring started in Laurel's ears, getting louder and louder as she felt herself pitch forward, plunging into a whirling black hole. The next thing she knew she was lying down, with both Miss Clinock's and Miss Massey's worried faces leaning over her. One of them propped her up.

"Here, Laurel, sip this," Miss Massey said, holding a glass of water to her lips.

Laurel never remembered too much about the next few days. Somehow they passed in a kind of gray fog. Toddy and Kit were always nearby, but it was as if she were alone. Other people were only vague images to her, while, awake or sleeping, she seemed to see her mother's face everywhere.

She was never sure when the realization actually took hold that her mother was gone forever. Lillian would never come so that they could go home together. In fact, Laurel had no home to go to—except Greystone. She had become just like all the other children. An orphan.

When Laurel was told she was among the children from Greystone who would be traveling west on the Orphan Train, her first reaction was fear of the unknown. But as soon as she knew Kit and Toddy would be going, too, it was all right. Toddy's excitement was contagious and soon Laurel was looking forward to the day when they would meet Reverend and Mrs. Scott, representatives of the Christian Rescuers and Providers Society, and their escorts on the trip west.

The children were given small cardboard suitcases in which to pack their few belongings to take with them on the long trip to their new lives in the Midwest.

To her dismay Laurel discovered she had outgrown all the lovely, handmade smocked and embroidered clothes her mother had made for her. So she had to accept the small wardrobe given to each girl for the journey. The garments were serviceable, if plain—a warm merino dress of dark blue, two cotton pinafores, one to wear and one to keep clean for the stops in the rural towns where the adoptions would take place, two changes of underwear, chemises, pantaloons, two petticoats, three pairs of cotton stockings, and a flannel nightgown. All the girls were issued a warm coat and bonnet and a new pair of high-top black boots with two sets of laces. All these were purchased from contributions made to the Rescuers and Providers Society by interested donors.

But as she packed, Laurel slipped into her suitcase one of the finely tucked and lace-edged camisoles her mother had made. Even if it didn't fit, it had come from beloved hands. Besides her locket, it was the only thing Laurel had left of her life before Greystone.

3

Meadowridge

On a glorious spring Sunday Dr. Leland Woodward drove his small black buggy into the cleared area between the Community Church and Ryan's pasture. He sat for a minute, the reins slack in his hands, listening to the voices floating out from inside the white frame building.

Smiling, he hummed along with them. "Blessed assurance, Jesus is mine! Oh, what a foretaste of Glory Divine—" It was one of his favorite hymns.

He knew he was late arriving for the eleven o'clock service, but he'd had to go home first to bathe, shave and change. He had been out most of the night delivering the Storms' new baby. But he didn't feel tired. In fact, he was exhilarated. Helping bring a new life into the world always gave him a boost that lasted for days. That is, if there weren't complications.

And everything had gone splendidly this time. Irma Storm was a healthy young woman who'd had no problems giving birth to a fine baby boy. Her husband Tom was a happy man. That made four sons for the Storms. Good for a farmer. In the next few years, Tom would have his own crew of harvesters come haying time! Leland chuckled. Children—that's what life was all about really. Suddenly the expression on his lean, handsome face saddened and unconsciously he sighed.

He ran his hand through his thick, prematurely gray hair, then reached for his hat on the seat beside him, put it on, gave the brim a snap, and got down from the buggy, his movements agile for a man nearing forty. Leland tethered his mare to a nearby tree, close enough to the fence so she could reach over and nibble some of the long meadow grass.

Mounting the church steps, he walked inside. One of the ushers saw him and greeted him. Leland dismissed with a gesture the offer of assistance to show him to a seat, but took the hymnal he was handed, then stood for a moment at the back looking around.

He and Ava used to have a regular pew they sat in every Sunday, but that was when—Leland checked another sigh. Ava didn't attend church with him nowadays. Hadn't for nearly two years. Folks seemed to understand and yet maybe he should insist. Maybe it would help. Even seeing the children filing out for Sunday school before the sermon might jolt her from her malaise. But nothing really seemed to help.

His eyes made a quick search for an empty spot. It was better to sit near the door. That way, if anyone should need to send for him during the service, he could slip out without disturbing the congregation or start any buzzing speculation among them as to who might have taken sick or had an accident. Or been shot!

Leland suppressed a wry smile. When he had first arrived here right out of Medical School, Meadowridge was only a mere twenty years away from its roots as a raw mining town. Often he'd had to patch up the rowdies who had gotten into some Saturday night fiasco or other, and a few times some fellow got "trigger happy." Mostly ended up shooting his own foot. But that was a long time ago. Things had settled down quite a bit since then. When the women and children came, schools and churches and houses were built. Decent family folk wanted a decent town to live in, and farming became more popular and productive than searching for gold in the hills that rimmed the pretty valley.

Leland saw a seat at the end of the row in one of the last pews and moved toward it with his light, springy step. Everyone occupying that bench shifted over one to make room for him, nodding and smiling a greeting. The town's only doctor was well liked.

The last of the opening hymns sung, there was a general murmuring of voices, rustling skirts, and shuffling of Sunday-shined shoes, as the congregation settled in for one of Reverend Brewster's sermons. Leland sat back, folded his arms, ready to be instructed, inspired or exhorted. He was in a for a surprise, however because the Reverend was even now announcing a guest speaker.

"Mr. Matthew Scott of the Christian Rescuers and Providers Society is here with a message today that I think will have special meaning for all of us. Living as we do in this beautiful, peaceful valley, surrounded by rolling hills, bordered by a river that gives us our pure water, abundant fish, refreshment and recreation, sheltered in our comfortable homes, lacking nothing in the way of food or clothing, we are apt to forget there are people in this world so unfortunate as to be without any of these necessities." Reverend Brewster paused significantly.

There was an uneasy stirring, glances exchanged among the parishioners as if wondering what their pastor had in store for them.

"I am not speaking only of grown men and women, but of innocent little children as well—abandoned, some of them left to fend for themselves on the streets of a great city—like New York or Boston. Ah, but I shall let Mr. Scott, who knows these sad stories better than I, tell you from his eyewitness experience of this deplorable situation. Mr. Scott, I turn the pulpit over to you."

A tall, thin young man stepped up to the lectern. He had tousled, rusty-brown hair, wore wire-rimmed glasses, and his scrawny neck rose out of a stiff, high collar that seemed too big for it. He looked like a timid, bookish college student.

But when he began to speak, his voice was rich and full and he spoke with an earnest fervor and dramatic depth.

There was not a dry eye in the crowd when Mr. Scott had finished. There were the sounds of sniffles, throats being cleared, and noses being blown throughout the church building. Mr. Scott took off his glasses and wiped his own eyes before he made a last statement.

"I feel sure this appeal has not gone unheard in this community. I know the plight of these children I have described has touched some of you. If that is the case, perhaps you will then be led to open your homes to one or possibly two of these abandoned and orphaned children, to share your warm hearth, your affection, your good examples of Christian charity.

"The Christian Rescuers and Providers Society is dedicated to placing the right child in the right home. We do have certain requirements for the welfare of the child, and to help the adoptive family. Our main goal is to provide these poor lost children with Christian homes in which to be nurtured, trained up in the way they should go, to become God-fearing, law-abiding, self-supporting human beings. The alternative that awaits such children, it grieves me to mention, may be a life lived on the streets, forced into crime and degradation at an early age with the inevitable result— incarceration in one of our nation's prisons. Need I say more? I feel sure your generous hearts will respond. Anyone who may be interested in talking with me further, please see me after the service. I will remain as long as there are questions."

Leland swallowed hard. He had felt an increasing stricture in his throat as Scott had spoken. In spite of his outwardly impersonal professional manner, Leland Woodward had a tender heart that was easily touched, and he had been greatly moved by this talk.

He rarely showed his emotions, however. Even in the great tragedy of his life, the death of his little daughter from diphtheria at the age of seven, he had maintained a stoic composure. It was his grief-stricken wife to whom the sympathy had flowed. Perhaps feeling that a doctor was accustomed to dealing with death, people assumed he could cope with Dorie's death. Many homes had been ravaged by the terrible epidemic that had swept through Meadowridge at that time. They did not know Leland tortured himself that he might be to blame for his little girl's death. Had he somehow brought the infection home to his own child? No one could comfort him for no one knew the depth of his sorrow, his self-scourging, his guilt.

So many came to mourn with Ava. And one by one they had come away shaking their heads. "Her heart is broken. She'll never get over it."

Leland wondered if she ever would. It had been nearly two years since they had lost their only child. Now Ava scarcely ever left the house. She never came to church, saw friends, involved herself in any of her old activities, the things she used to enjoy.

Leland knew his wife was in what was clinically called "melancholia," a depression so deep nothing seemed to be able to lift the dark cloud of sorrow from her.

She had kept Dorie's room untouched. The child's dolls, toys, playthings and books remained as though she might come running in from school at any minute.

Leland knew it was unhealthy. Everything should be put away, given away, swept out of sight. It only aggravated his wife's condition, kept her moored in the same desperate state of inconsolable sadness. But he, though a man of medicine who brought healing to others, was helpless to help the one he loved so dearly.

Leland saw the line of church members forming to meet Mr. Scott. They were clustering around him, asking questions, finding out more about the Orphan Train that would be coming west and would be making a stop in Meadowridge.

He hesitated, turning his broad-brimmed gray felt hat in his hands thoughtfully. Better not to act precipitously. Certainly, he would have to talk to Ava first.

Was it too late to reach her? He missed desperately the sound of a child's voice, laughter in the house, of running feet on the stairs. Would Ava consent, could she accept another child into her life, one who needed her?

He thought of the charming girl he had married—her laughing hazel eyes, her sparkling smile and happy nature. Was it possible she could be that way again? Maybe a child could bring it all back.

Was it worth suggesting? Worth bringing all the old wounding memories to the surface? Then he thought of the darkened room where his wife spent most of her days, staring out the window, or wandering into the bedroom with the white wicker furniture, the dollhouse and bookshelves of fairy tales that had belonged to the little girl who was gone.

It couldn't go on. Something would change. Ava would break—Leland shuddered unconsciously. No, he had to do something, take some action before it was too late. Ava could slip over the brink, and he would have lost not only his daughter but his beloved wife as well.

He would wait until just before the Orphan Train was due to come before he pressed for a decision. In the meantime he would gently persuade her to start thinking about it. Ava loved children. She was made to be a mother. Unfortunately nature had made it impossible for her to bear another child physically—but in her heart? Surely that gentle, caring heart was able to love another child.

In the meantime he would sincerely seek God's will in the matter. Leland had always asked the good Lord for guidance and direction in his life. And so far, he had never failed to get it.

4

Laurel saw her face reflected in the train window as if in a mirror. She stared out into the darkness as the Orphan Train sped across the prairie through the night.

With her finger she began to spell out her name on the gritty surface of the windowsill. "LAUREL VESTAL."

As she wrote, she formed the words silently with her tongue: "My name is Laurel Vestal." The metallic clickety-clack of the train wheels along the steel rails seemed to repeat them. *Laurel Vestal, Laurel Vestal, Laurel Vestal.*

Laurel moved, shifting her position on the hard coach seat. Her head felt hot and she leaned it against the cool glass of the window. Her throat was scratchy, too. Noticing she looked slightly feverish, Mrs. Scott had made up two of the seats into a bed earlier than usual so Laurel could lie down.

"You'll feel better in the morning," Mrs. Scott said, tucking the blanket around Laurel's shoulder. "We can't have you sick when we get to Meadowridge, now can we? Who would want to take a sick little girl home with them?"

Even though Mrs. Scott had spoken teasingly, it worried Laurel. Who, indeed, would want to take her home anyway? Because it was the first time Laurel had not been surrounded by other children for weeks, she allowed her secret fears to emerge. It was the secret fear of all the children on the Orphan Train, really, although nobody talked about it. What if nobody wanted her? No family adopted her?

Laurel closed her eyes and wished—the old wish, the one that never came true. She tried to wish herself back to the little flat on the top floor of Mrs. Campbell's house, tried to hear her mother playing on the piano, tried to recall the melodies of her favorite pieces—"Annie Laurie" or "The Robin's Return"—feel that warm, sweet security of her mother's presence again.

She sighed, a sigh that came from deep inside. If only she had Miranda to cuddle. Why hadn't she remembered to carry her doll with her that last morning when she and her mother had left the apartment?

Laurel blinked, trying not to cry. Her mother had said there would be lots of toys to play with where she was going. But at Greystone the toys had to be shared with everyone, and there were never enough to go around. Besides, none of the dolls could replace her beautiful Miranda. Most of them were worn, battered, the wigs gone, the paint chipped off their faces.

Unconsciously Laurel's hand moved to her neck, fingering the chain and locket that held her mother's and father's pictures. She had promised Mama she would never take it off. At least "until I come to get you." Recalling her mother's words, Laurel felt angry.

Why had her mother not told her the truth? About Greystone? About how sick she was and that she might die? Now, Laurel could not halt the tears. They rolled down one by one and, as she brushed them away, they made sooty streaks on her cheeks.

What had become of all their things? Her books, her doll's bed, the little china tea set that had belonged to Mama herself when *she* was a little girl? The piano and the painting her father had done that hung over it, the one of the lighthouse at Cape Cod? When they hadn't come back, had Mrs. Campbell taken everything up to her attic?

Once Laurel had gone there with Mrs. Campbell when she had lugged up some big boxes that some tenant had left behind. Laurel remembered Mrs. Campbell saying, "You just never know when a person may show up again. And as long as I've got the room, why not? Poor Mr. Lonergan might have had a spell of bad luck, or been hit over the head and lost his memory or something, who can tell?"

Mrs. Campbell was an avid reader of the kind of newspaper that printed the dramatic catastrophes of life in lurid detail. Laurel had a vivid picture of the woman, sitting in her kitchen rocker with the newspaper spread open, clucking her tongue and shaking her head as she read out loud some of the headlines of the stories printed on its pages: "Excursion Boat Capsizes, All on Board Perish," or "Fire Ravages Building, Frenzied Tenants Leap to Their Death."

Mrs. Campbell had probably packed all their belongings neatly and carried them up to her attic. That thought gave Laurel a little comfort.

Just then the mournful sound of the train whistle hooted shrilly as they approached a crossing. Laurel huddled further into the skimpy blanket and pressed her face against the window, peering out eagerly. Laurel liked it when the train slowed a little going through a small town and she could see lights like little yellow squares in the houses they passed. They looked so inviting, so cozy. She tried to imagine who lived there, what kind of family, how many children, what they were doing. Maybe a mother knitting, a father smoking a pipe, children playing on the floor, maybe a baby in a cradle nearby. She would try to imagine what it would be like to be inside—safe, happy, secure.

The familiar longing gripped her heart, bringing on that uncomfortable, choking sensation, a kind of emptiness, that started in the pit of her stomach and spread slowly through the rest of her.

Behind her, Laurel could hear the other children's voices as they finished up a game they were playing. Above all the others, Toddy's voice taking the lead, giving orders. She was glad Toddy was her friend, and Kit. It was Toddy who had come up with the plan of how the three of them could stay together, be adopted in the same town at least. At first, Laurel thought her idea was wrong, like telling lies. But then Toddy had explained it was just like being in a play! And it was the only way they could be *sure* they wouldn't be separated. Of course, Mrs. Scott had scolded them when she discovered what Toddy had coached them to do—Kit, dragging her leg as if she were crippled; Toddy, crossing her eyes and twisting her face into the most awful grimace, and Laurel, hunching one shoulder higher than the other as she walked.

Even though they had gotten into trouble for doing it, Laurel was glad it had worked. There was only one more stop on the trip. Meadowridge. Here they would all find homes. Here, in the same town where they could go to school together and see each other often. That was important. Without Toddy and Kit, Laurel didn't know what she would do.

Unconsciously, Laurel shuddered. She dreaded having all those grown-ups staring at her at every train stop. Trying *not* to get adopted had been bad, but now that she wanted to be adopted, it was even scarier.

The day after tomorrow, they would be in Meadowridge. Mrs. Scott had shown them where it was on the map she had pinned up on the wall. She said it was about the pleasantest town she had ever seen, that she would like to live there herself instead of in Pennsylvania where she and Mr. Scott lived.

Laurel's eyes began to feel heavy. She was sleepy. She pushed the lumpy pillow under her head and closed her eyes. No matter what, even if it *was* scary, it was better being on the Orphan Train on its way to Meadowridge and being adopted—than staying at Greystone and being an *orphan!*

5

"Just to make sure no one's coming down with some contagious disease with which a whole family could be infected," Dr. Woodward had volunteered to give each of the Orphan Train children a brief physical checkup before he or she was "placed out" in one of the adoptive homes. Reverend Brewster, on the advice of Mr. Scott, had suggested it might be a good idea.

On the morning of the Orphan Train's arrival, Leland stopped at the door of his wife's darkened sitting room, and stood there for a moment frowning. Then, striving to sound cheerful, he spoke. "It's a beautiful day, my dear. Why do you have the shutters closed and the curtains drawn? Let me open them, let in some of that lovely sunshine," he urged and started to move toward the windows.

"No, please, Lee," she protested, raising a fragile hand. "I have a slight headache. The glare bothers my eyes."

Leland halted then went over to the chaise lounge where Ava Woodward lay. He lifted her thin wrist in his fingers, automatically feeling for her pulse. He placed his other hand on her forehead but it felt cool to his touch.

"Do you think you'll feel better later? Well enough to accompany me to the train station? The Orphan Train is due in at one o'clock."

"Oh, no, Lee, I couldn't." Ava shook her head.

"But the child—don't you want to help me choose?" he persisted gently.

"No—" she murmured. "It was your decision—"

Leland checked a quick spurt of irritation. "But we discussed it thoroughly, my dear, and you agreed."

"Because you wanted it so, Leland." Ava sighed deeply. "You can be very persuasive."

Leland felt his fists clench. "Ava, if you had any doubts about this, you should have expressed them when I first brought up the subject, not wait until *now*...the very day the children are coming."

Her fingers picked at the fringe of the shawl wrapped around her frail shoulders. She did not meet his pleading eyes.

"I've had the room made ready," she said meekly.

But your heart, is it ready? Leland asked mentally, gazing down at his wife.

She raised her head and, seeing his beseeching look, reached for his hand. "Be patient with me, Lee. It will take time—"

"It's been two years, my dear. It's time we got on with our lives." He paused. "A child is what this house needs now. You said so yourself—"

"I know, Lee. I thought I was ready. But, now, I don't know—" her voice wavered uncertainly.

Leland tried to control his impatience. He took out his watch and consulted it.

"I have to make house calls. I'll be back by noon. Please, dear, make the effort to come with me to the train. It would mean a great deal to me. And to the child."

He leaned down and kissed her on her cheek, then left the room and the house in an agony of indecision. Maybe it had been a mistake to talk Ava into taking one of the Orphan Train children. Perhaps a terrible mistake.

But down deep, Leland didn't think so. He felt it was the right thing. At any rate he was committed now. He had written the Rescuers and Providers Society that he and his wife would take a child into their home. He had stipulated a boy. A boy, he felt, would be easier for Ava than a little girl. It would be too hard for her to accept another little girl... after Dorie.

Like most men, Leland Woodward had always wanted a son. Dreamed of having one. A lad everyone would call "Doc's boy," to ride along in the buggy with him when he made house calls. He planned to get him interested early in science, buy him a microscope, send him to one of the best medical colleges, and then when he got his degree, he could go into practice with his father.

Leland had adored his little daughter, but still had longed for a son. When it was definite Ava and he would never have another child of their own, Leland had put away his dreams of a son to follow in his footsteps. But now that possibility had arisen once more. An adopted boy he could bring up as he would have his own son. It could all still happen.

In spite of Ava's resistance, Leland felt fairly sure that once the boy was in their home, she would come around. Yes, Leland reassured himself, he had made the right decision.

At twenty minutes before one o'clock, Leland arrived at the Meadowridge Church Social Hall—alone. When he had returned home after making house calls, Ava was still lying on the chaise, now with a cologne-dampened cloth over her eyes. She felt too indisposed to go with him, she whispered. Knowing it was useless, he had not argued.

But while he arranged his makeshift office, adjusting the window blind for more light, filling a glass tumbler with wooden tongue depressors, Leland's mind was troubled. Suppose Ava really did not want a child. Evidently she had made herself ill over the prospect. What should he do now? He supposed another home could be found for the boy. He had not signed anything legal; he could explain to the Scotts—

Leland had no more time to consider the problem because the door of the Social Hall opened and there was a rush of voices as a crowd of people entered. Soon he was busy peering down little throats, checking ears, listening to the thrumming of dozens of healthy little hearts.

As one child after the other filed into this temporary medical facility, Leland felt that old yearning for a child grow stronger. Each child whose clear eyes he looked into, each pink tongue he depressed, each pair of lungs he pronounced sound intensified his desire to take one home with him.

Leland had always had a wonderful way with children. He could calm their fears with affectionate teasing, dry their tears with a fond tweaking of a nose, always holding out the jar of hard candies he kept alongside for a small hand to dip into when the examination was over.

"Next!" he called out to one of the church ladies who was standing in the doorway ushering in the next small "patient."

Leland finished the paperwork on the last patient before he looked up to greet the newcomer. When he did so, he stared right into the eyes of the prettiest little girl he had seen that day. At the same time it was with a stab of recognition. It was uncanny. This child could have been Ava at the same age!

Tendrils of dark hair curled around a rosy face and fell in lustrous curls onto her shoulders. Long-lashed brown eyes regarded him steadily, a tiny tentative, smile tugging at the rosebud mouth.

Leland held out both hands. "Well, little lady, come in. Don't be afraid. I won't hurt you. What is your name?" he asked.

"Laurel," she replied, approaching him slowly. She didn't seem afraid but had a sort of touching dignity.

Poor little tyke, Leland thought. A long journey, now this.

He proceeded with the examination, allowing Laurel to hold the tongue depressor before he looked down her throat, let her listen to *his* chest, hear *his* heart beat, then place the stethoscope on her own while he listened.

All the while he spoke to her gently, all thoughts of the boy he had planned to take home with him slowly vanishing from Leland's mind. If God had blessed him and Ava with another little girl of their own, she couldn't have looked more like this child. The longer he talked to her, the more he gazed into her sweet little face, saw her smile, heard her laugh at his silly jokes, the more convinced Leland became that this was the child he was meant to have. And the conviction grew within him that this child would bring with her the blessing he had prayed for, to his wife, to their marriage, to their home. With her, God would restore the joy that had been missing so long.

Had he not asked God for direction? This strong inner drawing toward this little girl *must* be His sign. How else was he to know God's will but in the very human feelings he was experiencing?

He leaned forward and took both Laurel's little hands in his.

"Would you like to come home with me, Laurel, be my little girl? We have a big back yard with trees and a swing. And there's even a pond with goldfish swimming in it. I think you would like it."

Laurel looked into the strong face searching hers for an answer. Behind his glasses, kindly blue eyes twinkled. She felt the warmth reach out from him to enfold her.

"Well, Laurel, what do you say?"

"Yes." She nodded solemnly.

Leland felt his heart leap. Suddenly his glasses misted and he took out his handkerchief to wipe them. Then, clearing his throat, he said, "Come on, then, let's make it official."

Leland made short work of the red tape. Having completed all the necessary papers with his usual dispatch, he was getting ready to leave when he saw the Hansens.

He hesitated for a minute, wondering whether to speak to them or not. Although their farm was a good distance from

Meadowridge Township, he had delivered all five of their children. The last two had been difficult births for Mrs. Hansen, a case of too many, too close together and not much time to recover before the next pregnancy. He'd warned her to be careful, to let up on some of the heavier chores for a while.

"Those big fellows of yours are old enough and strong enough to take on some of the load, aren't they?" he had asked her.

She had nodded meekly, but said nothing. Her husband had been present. Maybe that was it. Was Cora Hansen afraid of her husband?

Dr. Woodward turned away without greeting them. He didn't much like Jess Hansen. Seemed an insensitive, uncaring sort.

Just then Reverend Brewster spoke and Leland turned to answer him. When he looked again, he saw Jess Hansen with a little girl following him. At the door she turned to wave at Laurel, who waved back.

Leland lifted Laurel up into the buggy, placing the small suitcase on the floor in front of her so she could put her feet on it. Then he went around, got in beside her, smiled down at her as he picked up the reins.

"Well, Laurel, we're off. We're going home."

Home! The word made Laurel feel strange, excited but at the same time a little afraid. She had not allowed herself to think "home" or say the word for months. Home meant the cozy, little rooms on the top of Mrs. Campbell's house. She had missed it so much, and Mama—Laurel felt the old sadness sweep over her and she resolutely set her jaw and looked out around her.

Dr. Leland's horse trotted along a pleasant, curving street lined with shade trees. Neat houses were set back from the road, with pretty gardens behind picket fences. Then they slowed to a halt, and the horse stopped in front of a white frame house without Dr. Woodward even saying "Whoa!"

Laurel glanced at it curiously. It had lace curtains at the dark green shuttered windows, and baskets of pink geraniums swung along the railings at the top of the deep porch. It looked like a nice house, a friendly house, Laurel thought as Dr. Woodward helped her down, took her hand and led her up the steps and into the house.

"Are you hungry, Laurel? Would you like something to eat?" he asked.

Laurel shook her head and said politely, "No, thank you."

Thinking she might be refusing out of shyness, Leland suggested, "Well, I am, and thirsty, too. I'll tell you what. We'll go into the kitchen and see if Ella, our cook, has some lemonade and maybe some cookies. Then we'll go upstairs so you can meet my wife. Come on," he said, and Leland took Laurel's hand again and led her into the sunny spotless kitchen.

A half hour later, Ella Mason, the cook, hands on her hips, raised her eyebrows and looked at Jenny Appleton, the hired girl who came three days a week to clean.

"Well, what do you think of this?"

It was more a declaration than a question, so Jenny shrugged.

"What the missus will say is what I'm wonderin'." Ella gave a shake of her head.

"Well—" Jenny ventured, but Ella went on as if talking to herself and did not notice.

Ella got out the vegetables she was preparing to scrub and shook one of the carrots to emphasize her words. "She'd agreed to a boy, you know."

"Girls aren't so messy or noisy either, for that matter," Jenny declared, thinking of her own mother's brood of six and the bedlam Jen went home to each evening.

Ella rolled out dough for a pie on the cutting board.

"She's never got over it, you see. The little girl dyin' like that." Ella shook her head. "Don't know as if she can take to another one. It would be like she was trying to replace Dorie, don't you know?"

Jenny leaned against the counter listening. She had only worked for the Woodwards this past year. But of course the whole town knew about their tragedy.

"I say, either way, it's a good thing," Ella went on. "This house has been gloomy too long. A child will make a difference, boy *or* girl."

"That's for sure." Jenny nodded. "When I first come here to work, it was so quiet it near gave me the creeps. I used to say to Ma when I'd go home in the evenin' that I didn't even mind the noise there so much after being here all day. I told her—"

But Ella wasn't interested in whatever Jenny had told her mother. A seraphic expression suddenly crossed her plump, rosy-cheeked face. "I think I'll make a custard pudding for tonight. Children like something smooth and sweet, you know." She paused, then remarked thoughtfully, "She's a pretty little thing, ain't she?"

Ella opened a cabinet, took out a big bowl, got down the basket of fresh eggs, and began cracking them one by one into it.

Jen realized the discussion was over for now. Ella was too busy with her recipe to talk.

Jenny went to the broom closet and got out the carpet sweeper. She'd just do the rugs in the hall downstairs and see if she could hear anything to report back to Ella when the doctor took the little Orphan Train girl upstairs to meet the mistress.

Jenny felt sorry for Mrs. Woodward, although she did not know her very well. She was a pretty, dark-haired lady, even if she was too thin and had such mournful eyes. She spoke in a soft voice and gave very few directions about the housework Jenny was to do, but spent most of her time in her upstairs sitting room.

One afternoon Jenny had ventured up with a note from Dr. Woodward, delivered by a hospital messenger. The note said he had an emergency and would be late coming home for dinner. The note could have gone straight to Ella, Jen found out. In fact, after she'd read it, Mrs. Woodward had folded it and asked Jenny to take it down to the kitchen.

But it was *where* Jenny had found Mrs. Woodward that had been so strange and sad. She had knocked at the sitting room door which was always closed. When there was no answer, Jenny had inched it slowly open. But Mrs. Woodward wasn't in there.

Thinking she might have one of her sick headaches—and might be lying down, Jenny tiptoed down the hall to the bedroom. But the door was ajar and she was not in there either.

Then Jenny had heard the sound of sobbing. It came from directly across the hall. Turning, Jenny could see through the half-open door leading into a spacious, airy room flooded with sunlight. It was a room that she had never been asked to clean or dust, a child's room, belonging to a little girl, from the looks of it. And there sitting on the floor by the window seat was Mrs. Woodward, in front of a big dollhouse, holding a teddy bear in her lap.

Jenny stood there frozen, the note in her hand, not knowing whether to go or stay. Just then Mrs. Woodward had turned her head and seen her. For a few seconds neither of them moved nor spoke. Then Mrs. Woodward got to her feet and came over to the door. "What is it, Jenny?" she asked quietly.

Jenny could see that her pale cheeks were wet with tears. Embarrassed, she had stuttered out about the boy from the hospital and handed Mrs. Woodward the note.

Later, back in the kitchen, Jenny related what she had seen to Ella.

"Oh, my, don't I know?" Ella clucked her tongue. "She didn't want a thing in that room touched after Dorie died. With my own ears, I've heard the doctor beg her many times, 'Ava, please,' he'd say, 'you're just making it harder on yourself,' and she'd say, so pitiful, 'Lee, I can't, it would be like losing her forever. It's all I have left.' "

Remembering that incident and the conversation with Ella afterwards, Jenny unconsciously shook her head.

Would this Orphan Train girl *really* make a difference? Or would it just make things worse?

Leland left Laurel sitting on the porch swing when he went upstairs to tell Ava what he had done. He found her still lying on her chaise in her sitting room. He told her as quietly and quickly as he could.

Ava Woodward stared at her husband with an expression of grieved betrayal.

"Oh, Lee, how could you? Bringing a little girl into this house...she could never take Dorie's place!"

"She's not intended to take Dorie's place. No one could do that. She'll make her own place here. Give her time. Give yourself time, a chance to know her," he entreated.

Ava shook her head, tears glistening in her dark eyes as she looked at him in disbelief.

"You said you were getting a boy and I agreed to that. I understood what a boy would mean to you." She clasped her thin hands together, held them to her chin in a pleading gesture. "You know how I longed to give you a son of your own." Ava closed her eyes, recalling the months, the years, her hopes had risen only to be dashed. "But this...you're asking too much of me, Leland."

"Darling, I would never knowingly do anything to hurt you." He took a step toward her, but she held up her hand to ward him off, turning her head away from him as he leaned forward to kiss her.

The silence that followed stretched interminably between them. She did not move to stop him as he went to the door, stood there for a full minute. Then she heard the door close quietly behind him as he left the room.

6

The few days after Laurel arrived at the Woodwards had been the longest Ava could remember. After her first startled reaction to the fact that, instead of a boy orphan of about ten or twelve, Leland had brought home a little girl nearly the same age as the child they had lost, Ava had maintained a cold, hurt silence.

It seemed an unspeakable breach of understanding on his part, an inexplicable lack of empathy for Leland who was usually so considerate, so kind. It had created a chasm between them, wider and more dangerous than any difficulty or difference they had ever faced in their fifteen-year marriage.

Ava had not come downstairs for breakfast since Dorie died because she could not sleep at night unless she took the sleeping draughts Leland meted out to her sparingly. Since Laurel's coming, she stayed in bed until she heard Leland leave the house to go on his house calls every morning. Then Ava shut herself up in her sitting room. She refused to allow herself to wonder what the little girl did with herself. It was, after all, Lee's responsibility, she told herself, and she assumed he had made arrangements for Jenny to look out for the child.

She and Leland had had the worst argument of their entire marriage the night he had brought the little girl here. They had both said things they knew they would regret later. But the hurtful words had been said and still hung between them tensely.

Leland had slept on the couch in his office, as he often did when Ava was unwell, and had been uncomfortably sleepless and troubled. He spent a good deal of the night praying that Ava would relent, would come around and accept Laurel, who had to be the dearest little girl in the world.

The third morning, Ava rose and stood at her door, listening to Leland speaking to someone downstairs. The child? Hearing the front door close, Ava lifted shaking hands to her throbbing temples. She had awakened with all the frightful warning signals. She knew the signs—the shooting flashes of light zigzagging before her eyes, the dizziness, the tension in her stomach, the clamminess of her palms—all signaling the onset of a sick headache.

She should have known! Getting so upset always brought on one of her migraines.

She pressed her fingers over her eyes for a minute. Dear God, what was she to do? She dearly loved her husband, had always tried to comply with his wishes. And she wanted him to be happy, wanted to live up to his expectations of her, but *this* she simply could not do!

Ava had prayed about accepting a boy. At length, she had seemed to have peace about it, even though she knew it would be difficult, at least at first. But a boy was so different in every way from a girl that there would have been no reminders of her own little daughter. A girl nearly the same age as Dorie would have been if she had lived? Well, that was simply too much to ask of her!

Ava walked over to the window overlooking the garden. Pushing the curtain aside, she looked down and saw Leland, hand in hand with the little girl, walking along the flagstone path to the back gate leading out to the stable.

Leland was going on his house calls this time of day, Ava knew. She watched as Leland bent down, one hand gently stroking the child's long, dark curls as he talked to her. Then he kissed her cheek and went through the gate. The little girl jumped on the bottom ledge, leaning over the top and waving her hand. For a few minutes the child stayed there, swinging back and forth on the open gate. Then as the sounds of Leland's horse's hoofs and buggy wheels died away, she got down, turned and started walking back through the garden.

There was something pathetic about the droop of her shoulders, the way her feet lagged, an air of loneliness about the small figure in the drab denim dress and pinafore. In spite of herself, Ava's heart was touched.

Suddenly the stabbing pain in her head made Ava sway slightly. She grabbed onto the nearby chair to steady herself, then staggering with vertigo, she stumbled over to her chaise lounge and lowered herself onto it.

If she could only sleep for a few hours, the headache might go away or at least diminish. She prayed for oblivion, to block out not only the physical pain, but the pain of her heart's distress. She prayed to be released from her feeling of guilt and failure. She prayed to be free of the sting of Leland's accusation that she was shutting out a child who needed caring parents, a home.

Laurel sat on the bottom step of the polished staircase. The house was hushed. There was not a sound anywhere. Not the rattle of pans or the noise of any activity coming from the kitchen, for this was Ella's afternoon off. No murmur of voices or of doors opening and closing, people coming and going from the doctor's office at the side of the house. Dr. Woodward kept office hours only three mornings a week. The other days he went to see sick people in their homes. Today he would be gone all afternoon, he had told Laurel when he left.

Laurel sighed. She was lonely. She was glad to be in this lovely big house with Dr. Woodward. But she missed her two friends, Kit and Toddy. Dr. Woodward had promised she could have them over to play in a few weeks.

That was a long time to wait. Laurel sighed again. But Dr. Woodward said his wife had not been well and until she felt better it would be best not to have other children here.

Laurel had only seen Mrs. Woodward briefly. She was a very pretty lady, but when Dr. Woodward took Laurel in to meet her that first evening, she looked very pale and had only murmured a few words. Then Dr. Woodward sent Laurel out to the hall, telling her to wait for him there. She had stood uncertainly just outside the sitting room door, not knowing what else to do. And that was when she heard Mrs. Woodward say, "Lee, why in the world did you bring that child here?"

Remembering, a sad little ache pressed against Laurel's chest. Mrs. Woodward did not want her. So what was going to happen to her? Would she be "placed out" somewhere else? Just thinking about it gave her that scary feeling again.

But Dr. Woodward was so nice. He seemed to like having her here, and everyone else was so kind. Ella, the cook, was jolly and Jenny, who came three times a week, was always friendly and ready to chat.

But today Jenny hadn't come and the house seemed big and empty. What could she do all afternoon? Laurel wondered. There was nothing much for a girl to play with here. Funny, but the room Dr. Woodward had said was hers that first night held lots of things a *boy* might like! There were books about Indians, a building game, and a set of toy soldiers. But Laurel would have liked something like paper dolls to cut out, or jackstraws or a book of fairy tales.

She sighed again and took out her locket, pressed the place on the back that snapped it open, and looked long and lovingly at the pictures in the two ovals. Laurel still missed her mother. But their life together at Mrs. Campbell's was getting dimmer and dimmer. Of course, she didn't want to forget, but there had been so many new experiences since then. Still, she always looked at the pictures and kissed the photos of her parents every night before going to bed.

Sometimes she lay in bed, reliving some of the things she and Mama used to do together. Certain things they did every week, like taking the rent money down to Mrs. Campbell.

Laurel remembered how Mama would carefully count out the exact amount, taking it from the tin box where she put the money her students paid for their music lessons and placing it in the envelope marked RENT. There were other envelopes marked FOOD, TITHE, CLOTHING MATERIAL, even one marked FUN. That was the one Laurel liked best, because out of that came the rare cups of ice cream they bought at the stand in the park after a trip to the Zoo, or a new piece of music for Mama to learn, then teach to her piano students. Sometimes FUN meant an excursion downtown. Taking a horse-car was always an adventure, and then those special trips to the Art Museum. There, Mama would show her the big paintings in gold frames that hung in room after room in a vast building.

"Your father was an artist, Laurel," Mama would say, her eyes very bright.

"Did he paint these?" Laurel once asked, pointing.

"No, he had to sell most of his work. Although some of the ones I thought were his best ones didn't sell. If he had lived, I believe he would have been famous," her mother told her, then added, "but I've kept them all packed away except for that one we have over the piano."

Laurel thought of that painting now. It was of a lighthouse on a cliff overlooking the ocean. The sun in the picture was very strong, casting sharp shadows on the white building and on the beach below and the sparkling blue water. It was a happy painting, one that made Laurel feel good inside when she looked at it.

"That was painted the summer we spent at Truro," Mama had told her. "You were hardly more than a baby, Laurel, but I used to take you down to the beach with me and take off your little shoes and stockings and let you put your feet in the sand. We'd sit under a big umbrella and sometimes your father would sketch us, or set up his portable easel and paint. Oh, darling, I wish you could remember!" Mama would say, looking sad.

Now, as she thought of those times, Laurel's feeling of aloneness sharpened along with an intense longing for her mother. Laurel crossed her arms and hugged herself, rocking back and forth slightly.

Time hung motionless. It would be ages before Dr. Woodward returned. Aimlessly, Laurel began to count the rungs of the stair railings on each step. Humming a little tune she recalled her mother's music students practicing over and over, she moved up slowly from step to step.

Finally, she reached the top of the stairway. Now what could she do to pass the time until Dr. Woodward came home and took her for a buggy ride as he had promised?

Laurel pulled herself to her feet, holding onto the banister. Feeling the satiny surface, she was strongly tempted to mount it and slide backwards down its smooth length. She fought the temptation for a full moment. Resisting it, she decided to go and look over the books in her room once more to see if any of them had interesting pictures. If so, she could take one outside and sit in the porch swing and look at them while she waited for Dr. Woodward to come home.

She started down the hallway toward her room when, passing a half-opened door, she halted. She had passed this room a dozen or more times before, but the door had always been closed. Now it stood open so Laurel could look inside.

Curious, Laurel moved closer and peered in. Nobody was there but it had a waiting look, as though expecting someone to come at any minute. A little girl? For surely this room was intended for a little girl, Laurel thought, inching closer.

Sun poured in through crisp, white ruffled curtains onto the flowered chintz cushions of the window seat, gilding the blond curls of a big doll seated in a small wicker chair by a low table all set with little dishes. Under the window were shelves full of toys, games, and books.

Drawn irresistibly forward, Laurel pushed open the door and stepped inside, looking around her with wide-eyed wonder.

Walking very slowly, as if in a dream, Laurel went to the middle of the room and pivoted, gazing from the scrolled white iron bed, with its ruffled coverlet, piled high with dolls and stuffed animals, to a tiny red rocking chair decorated with painted flowers in one corner next to a large, peaked-roofed dollhouse.

What a wonderful, wonderful room!

Laurel tiptoed over to the dollhouse and knelt down in front of it, gazing into the tiny rooms. There was a parlor, a bedroom, a little nursery with a canopied bassinet in which a tiny china doll nestled. There was even a kitchen, with wee little pots and pans! Laurel put out her hand to move one of the dollhouse occupants that had fallen out of a winged chair next to the fireplace, complete with brass andirons.

But just as she did, a voice from behind her ordered sharply, "Don't touch that!"

Startled, Laurel jerked around, dropping the little figure. Mrs. Woodward was standing in the doorway. Masses of dark hair tumbled wildly around her shoulders and her eyes were fiery coals.

"What are you doing in here?" she demanded furiously.

Laurel was so frightened she burst into tears.

A lavender dusk had fallen over the garden as Leland came through the gate, went up the back porch steps and into the house. There were no lamps lighted yet and Dr. Woodward set down his medical bag and stood for a few minutes, sorting through the mail left on the hall table.

Then he lifted his head in a listening attitude. From somewhere in the house, he heard the sound of soft singing—a familiar, low, sweet melody that struck a reminiscent chord deep within him. He had not heard it in a very long time. And where and when, he could not think.

He went to the bottom of the staircase and, out of long habit, started to call up that he was home. Then he thought better of it, and instead, climbed the stairway, hoping against hope that Ava might be feeling better. Their problem weighed heavily upon him. Nothing was worth this estrangement. The little girl would have to go. He must find a good home for her, a place where she would be welcomed, where she would be loved as she deserved to be loved.

When he reached the landing the sound of singing became clearer. Puzzled, he moved along the hall toward his wife's sitting room.

At the door he paused. What he saw made his heart leap. Stunned, he stood there unmoving.

The room was in shadows. Only a soft, violet light filtering through the filmy curtains illuminated Ava's profile. She was seated in her rocker, holding Laurel in her lap, gently rocking her. The child's head rested on Ava's shoulder as if it belonged there.

When Ava saw Leland's figure silhouetted in the doorframe, she put her index finger to her smiling lips warningly.

It was then he remembered the song Ava was singing. It was the lullabye with which she used to rock Dorie to sleep.

Later that night, as Leland cradled his wife in his arms, long after they had both put Laurel to bed, she wept quietly. "Oh, Lee, to think I frightened that dear little thing, scared her into tears! I'm so ashamed. I have been so selfish, Lee, so self-absorbed, so wrapped up in my own feelings I haven't thought of anyone else's. Can you ever forgive me?"

"There's nothing to forgive, my darling," he murmured, smoothing back her hair from her forehead, tangling his fingers in its silky waves. "I love you and all I ever wanted was your happiness."

"We *will* be happy again, Lee. I feel it, I know it! And I promise you this will be a home for Laurel to be happy in, too!"

7

The Fourth of July in Meadowridge was celebrated with enthusiastic fervor—parades, picnics, political speeches, patriotic pantomimes held at the town park, with a lavish fireworks display after dark.

The whole community entered into the festive occasion. Main Street was decorated with red, white and blue bunting banners, and each storefront displayed its own American flag. At Tanner's Field, where a softball game between the town's two rival teams would be played in the afternoon, the bleachers were festooned with streamers and balloons.

By eleven o'clock families carrying wicker baskets, laden with special holiday food, began to arrive at the city park looking for the ideal spot to picnic. In the white-latticed gazebo in the center, the Meadowridge Town Band, attired in their gold-braided, bright red jackets buttoned in shiny brass, were tuning up their instruments for the music they would be providing throughout the day.

Ava brushed Laurel's dark curls and then tied them with a dark blue satin ribbon in a flat bow.

"There now, turn around so I can see how you look."

Obediently Laurel swung away from the mirror, holding out her skirt for Ava's approval. She was wearing a blue and white striped chambray dress with a square white eyelet lace collar threaded with narrow red ribbon.

"Just perfect," Ava declared with satisfaction. "Perfect for the Fourth of July and for this beautiful summer day." She patted Laurel's cheek. "You'll be the prettiest little girl at the picnic."

"All ready to go?" asked Dr. Woodward, coming to the door of Laurel's bedroom. He looked at them both admiringly. "What a lucky man I am to be escorting two such lovely ladies."

"You *could* be slightly prejudiced, you know, Lee," Ava chided him playfully. "But isn't Laurel a picture?"

"I see two pictures," declared Dr. Woodward, beaming. "If there were going to be a beauty contest today, you would both win hands down."

"Will there be a contest?" asked Laurel.

Dr. Woodward chuckled. "Well, maybe not for beauty, but there'll be plenty of contests—potato sack races, best pie contests, watermelon eating contests—more contests than you can shake a stick at!"

Laurel giggled. Dr. Lee, as she had begun to call him, was always saying funny things like that. Who would shake a stick at a contest?

"Come on, let's get going," he urged. "You can already hear the band music from the park. We don't want to miss anything."

"Just wait until I put on my hat," Ava pleaded gaily, thrusting a long, pearl-headed pin into the band of white roses circling the crown of her straw hat. "There, we're ready!" she said with satisfaction, giving Laurel's hair ribbon a final flip.

Leland held out his arm to his wife, reached his other hand to Laurel, and the three of them went downstairs and out to the buggy. Laurel loved riding in the buggy, especially when all three of them rode together. That wasn't often because Dr. Lee needed it most of the time for his work. Today he had fastened the canvas top back so that she could feel the sun on her head and back as they trotted down the street on the way to the park.

Looking up she saw Dr. Lee, smiling over her head at Mrs. Woodward who smiled back at him. That gave Laurel a nice warm feeling in her tummy. Things at the Woodwards' had become very pleasant. The three of them spent many happy hours together. Ever since that awful time Mrs. Woodward had frightened her in Dorie's room, things had changed.

Dr. Lee had explained to Laurel about Dorie so that she understood.

"You see, Laurel, we lost our little girl just as you lost your parents. And now, we can all help each other. You'll be our little girl and we'll be your parents."

Laurel had nodded. But, unconsciously, she felt for the heart-shaped locket under her dress, as if to remind herself that no one could *ever* take the place of her *real* parents.

Dr. Woodward maneuvered his buggy between the other vehicles, buggies, wagons and gigs that were lined in zigzag rows, horses hitched to the rail fence that surrounded the park. Then he assisted Ava out, lifted Laurel down, and removed the covered picnic basket Ella had packed for them.

"Where would you like to settle, my dear?" he asked Ava. "I see there are still some empty tables near that cluster of oak trees."

Before she had a chance to answer him, a shrill voice called, "Ava! Ava Woodward, wait a minute!"

They all turned in time to see a plump, blonde woman, holding onto her hat with one hand, while with the other she was pulling along a tousle-headed boy. Laurel recognized him as the same obnoxious boy in her Sunday school class who thought it funny to pull her curls when he stood behind her.

When she reached them, the woman said breathlessly, "Oh, Ava, my dear, it is *so* good to see you!"

Laurel felt Ava stiffen as if to ward off an unwelcome embrace. The other woman ignored this rebuff and went right on talking. "We have *all* missed *you* so. I cannot *begin* to tell you how my heart has gone out to you all these months in your sorrow. We thought, at least...*some people* thought you would *never* get over it and—"

"Thank you, Bernice, I appreciate that. I'd like you to meet our Laurel," she said, interrupting the sticky flow of words. "Laurel, this is Mrs. Blanchard and her son, Christopher."

At this, Mrs. Blanchard lowered her voice significantly as though Laurel were deaf and said, "When I heard you and Dr. Woodward were taking in one of those waifs, Ava, I couldn't believe it! After all you've been through to take such a chance—Why, you can't tell what kind of background they come from. I've heard most of them have lived by their wits on city streets—"

"I think you're mistaken, Bernice," Ava cut in coldly. "If you'll excuse us, Doctor is beckoning us. We must go and get our table—" Ava took Laurel's hand tightly in hers and left the woman standing there with her mouth open.

Later, Laurel overheard Ava repeating the conversation to Dr. Woodward. This time her icily polite tone of voice changed. She was obviously very angry.

Dr. Woodward tried to calm her down. "Bernice Blanchard!" he scoffed. "Everyone knows what a rattle-brain she is, speaks before she thinks, likes to hear herself talk. Don't give it another thought, my dear."

"But if she'd say a thing like that to my face, what is she saying behind my back?" demanded Ava.

"What difference does it make, darling? We know the truth. Don't let it spoil things for you."

"I just don't want her spiteful remarks to make things difficult for Laurel as she's growing up in this town. Or for any of the other Orphan Train children," Ava said.

"Put it out of your mind. It isn't that important."

"I don't know, Lee. After all, Bernice is the town banker's wife. She has a lot of influence." Ava sounded doubtful.

"It's too nice a day to worry about something like that. Remember, 'This is the day the Lord hath made, let us rejoice and be glad in it'!" the doctor said, patting his wife's hand reassuringly.

Dr. Lee often quoted the Bible, Laurel had begun to notice.

Sometimes it was his way of ending a discussion, she realized, but it was a nice way. Otherwise, Mrs. Woodward went on and on, fretting about something.

But on this lovely summer day there did not seem to be anything that could disturb anyone for long. There was not a single cloud in the sky. The sun was warm, but there was a breeze gently fanning the leaves overhead. It was, as Dr. Lee kept saying, "a grand and glorious Fourth."

Ava seated herself comfortably at a picnic table, her parasol protecting her from the sun. Lee stood, surveying the holiday activities underway, nodding and returning the greetings of many who passed on their way to their own picnic spots. Of course, as the town doctor, Lee was known by nearly everybody in Meadowridge. Ava was aware of a few curious looks and unconsciously put a protective arm about the child.

Then all of a sudden Laurel, pointing toward a small child across the park leaped down off the bench, and called happily. "There's Toddy! Oh, can we ask her to have lunch with us? Toddy! Toddy, over here!" she shouted, waving her arms.

The two girls were so happy to see each other, they flung their arms around each other and jumped up and down. Ava and Dr. Woodward smilingly watched the reunion. When they found that Toddy had been left on her own by the Hales' maid, they immediately invited her to join them.

The girls chattered excitedly, so fast that their words tumbled out, overlapping the other's. Ava watched them fondly remarking to Lee, "The dear little things. How much they must have to talk about. Laurel says nothing about her life before the Orphan Train, but I'm sure there are sad memories for all the children."

"Well, they look happy enough now," Dr. Woodward commented.

"Yes, I know, but—"

Leland took Ava's hand, raised it to his lips, and kissed it. "Better not to dwell on the sad part, my dear. Laurel has a brand new life with us now. Children soon forget the past."

"I suppose you're right," Ava said, but her eyes lingered on the two little girls, their heads close together.

A few minutes later they were diverted by the arrival of the Hansen family. This would not ordinarily have attracted the Woodwards' attention except for the fact that both Toddy and Laurel scrambled to their feet and hand in hand ran toward another little girl who had come with the Hansens. Ava saw that she was taller than the other two, with smooth brown braids. To Ava's shocked surprise, however, she was still wearing the drab dress and pinafore assigned by the orphanage!

Soon, Laurel came running over to ask if Kit could eat lunch with them, too.

"Of course," Ava smiled. A minute later Laurel returned with a disappointed face, saying Mrs. Hansen needed Kit to help serve their lunch.

"Well, perhaps she can come over later for lemonade and cake," suggested Ava, wondering why the Hansen woman couldn't see that the three little orphans needed this time to be together. Mrs. Hale had already rendered an invitation through Toddy for Laurel to come watch the fireworks display from their upstairs balcony. *She* certainly understood.

Kit, a sweet, shy child did come over later, and seeing the trio so happy together encouraged Ava to do something. She decided she would speak to Mrs. Hansen herself about allowing Kit to come, offering to drive Kit home to their farm afterward.

So, when one of the Hansens' boys came over to get Kit after she had only been with the other two a half hour, Ava walked over to where the Hansens were picnicking, and introducing herself, made her plea.

But Ava's persuasion failed to work on Mrs. Hansen who shook her head.

"No, Kit has to come with the rest of us," she said firmly.

"But the children are so looking forward to it. Surely you wouldn't want to deprive Kit of a chance to be with her friends after such a long separation—" Ava protested.

But Mrs. Hansen raised her chin defensively and her mouth was set in a stubborn line. "Kit has chores to do before it gets dark, Miz Woodward. We're gettin' set to leave now" was her reply.

Ava saw that no extension of her considerable charm would work on the woman, so she sighed and turned to leave. Seeing Kit's expression, she impulsively took the child's face in both hands. Leaning down, she kissed her cheek. "There'll be another time, Kit, I promise. We'll plan to have you come visit Laurel very soon."

Later she fumed to Lee. "What a shame, disappointing Kit like that. How can people be so insensitive?"

"She's a different kind of person from you, Ava, doesn't see things the same way."

"But to treat a child like that—"

"None of the Hansen children seem abused to me, my dear, and Kit looked fine," Leland said in an attempt to placate his wife. But he kept to himself his own concern that had sprung up the day he saw that Jess Hansen was taking Kit home with him. The child looked too delicate for heavy farm chores... but then, what could they do about it?

Ava bit her lower lip in frustration. She had seen something in Kit's eyes that haunted her. No matter what, she was going to do something to help the child.

8

One afternoon in early September, Leland looked in the door of Ava's sitting room. Every surface and space was covered with all sorts of fabric in a melee of color and pattern.

Glancing up, Ava saw him and motioned him into the room.

"What's all this? A circus?" he asked in amazement.

Laurel, who was sitting in a pile of jumbled cloth, giggled as she always did at Dr. Woodward's jokes.

Ava gave him a distracted glance and held up a length of material she was examining. "No, silly, we're choosing material for Laurel's school clothes. Mrs. Danby is coming tomorrow and it's going to be a week of selecting patterns, cutting and fitting and pinning. You are going to be completely surrounded by sewing women!"

"A circus! I was right." Dr. Woodward struck his head in mock horror. "Maybe I'd better take the week off and go fishing."

"Nothing of the kind, Lee. We need your opinion on some of these outfits," Ava said, pretending to be stern. "You have excellent taste."

"Mrs. Danby doesn't think so!" he declared. "The last time she was here for a week of sewing, she glared at me every time I ventured near. I think she thought I was going to perform surgery on her precious sewing machine."

At this, Laurel rolled over in a fit of giggles.

Dr. Woodward raised his eyebrows. "At least, someone appreciates me."

"I appreciate you, too, Lee. Didn't I just say as much?" Ava said. Then holding up a colorful swatch, she asked, "What do you think of this?"

He came over and took the piece and draped it about Ava's head and shoulders, then stepped back to admire her.

"Lovely! Pink is *your* color. I've always loved you in it," he said. "The first time I ever saw you you were wearing pink."

Ava smiled at him indulgently. "Actually, it was a dusty rose dress I was wearing—and *this* is coral."

"Whatever it was, you were ravishing in it," he said in a gentle, teasing voice, and leaned over to kiss her uplifted face.

For a moment they looked at each other, then at Laurel and both of them smiled, holding out their arms to her. She scrambled over the mountain of material and was drawn into the circle of their embrace.

"I'd better get out of here and let you ladies get on with whatever it is you're doing," Dr. Woodward said and started toward the door.

Ava, preoccupied with her choices once more, was holding up the rosy material to Laurel. "This will be such a becoming color for you. We'll have Mrs. Danby make it up into a little suit with a short jacket and lace collar. Oh, it will be perfect! And you will be the prettiest little girl in the whole school!"

Hearing Ava's happy chatter, Leland paused at the doorway, turning to see his wife give Laurel an impulsive hug. It gladdened his heart to see her so happy. She was completely absorbed in readying the child's wardrobe for school. It was her nature, he knew, to throw herself into a project. Yes, whatever it was—joy or grief—Ava was apt to plunge right into it!

As he made his way slowly down the stairs, he felt the vague stirring of uneasiness. As a doctor, Leland knew the danger of that kind of intensity, the extremes of emotional highs and lows to which his wife was prone. Now Laurel had become the focus of Ava's concentrated time, attention, devotion.

But wasn't this new interest in life, this enthusiastic acceptance of Laurel exactly what he had hoped would happen? Why, then had a tiny seed of fear planted itself within him and taken uneasy root there?

Mrs. Danby, the town's best seamstress, arrived on the dot of eight o'clock the next morning and took possession of the upstairs spare room. There she and Ava made the final decisions about patterns, materials and trimmings. Soon her big sewing scissors were slashed authoritatively into the cloth with a sureness that would have unnerved anyone lacking her expertise.

Laurel stood patiently while Mrs. Danby, a tape measure around her neck and her mouth full of straight pins, knelt on the floor draping, tucking, hemming, all the while with tight-lipped murmurs and grunts and little pushes, indicating which way she wanted Laurel to turn.

The result of all this week-long activity was a complete new wardrobe for Laurel. Besides four new school dresses, there was a Sunday-best outfit and blouses, jumpers, skirts, and jackets, as well as new camisoles, petticoats, and bloomers.

On the first morning of school, Laurel was late coming down to breakfast and Dr. Woodward sent Jenny upstairs to see what was delaying her.

When Jenny walked into her room, Laurel was still in her petticoat, staring into the open armoire filled with her new clothes.

"My land, Laurel, you'll have all the other girls green with envy!" remarked Jenny in awe, thinking her own little sisters and brothers were lucky to have a couple of hand-me-downs and a new pair of sturdy boots to start school. "So what are you planning to wear?"

Laurel turned a stricken face to Jenny. "I don't *know*—"

There had never been any choice at Greystone and before that, Mama had always laid out her clothes for her to put on in the morning.

"Didn't Mrs. Woodward say what you were to wear?" Jenny asked.

Laurel shook her head.

"Well, come on then, I'll help you. You mustn't be late the first day of school now. What would your teacher say if you come in like the ten o'clock scholar in the nursery rhyme?" Jenny bustled over to the armoire, studied its contents with a slight shake of her head, then pulled out a bright blue dress trimmed with darker blue braid. She held it up for Laurel's approval. "How about this? Here, then, let me help you."

Jenny slipped it over Laurel's head, guided her arms into the sleeves, and proceeded to button the dozen small buttons in the back. When she got to the top, Laurel's chain caught and Jenny fumbled to untangle it. As she struggled unsuccessfully to free the chain or to get the button into the opening, she said, "I'd better unfasten this clasp, Laurel."

"No!" exclaimed Laurel sharply, jerking away from Jenny both hands on her neck, holding the chain.

Startled, Jenny stared at her. "Whatever is the matter? I was just—"

"I can't ever take this chain off! Not ever!" Laurel shook her head vehemently.

"I meant just until I got the top button done." Jenny explained, puzzled by Laurel's reaction. When she saw the child's eyes fill with tears, she thought, *Why she's afraid! Probably about going to school the first day.* But Laurel's next words surprised her.

"I can't take this off, Jenny, because Mama told me not to."

"But Mrs. Woodward would understand that we—"

"I don't mean *her! She's* not my *mama,*" Laurel said in a low voice. With that, she took a step closer to Jenny, pulled the chain out and held up the small, heart-shaped locket. Opening it, she held it up for Jenny to see the pictures inside. *"This* is my *real* mama, and this is my *real* father."

Jenny studied the faces of the lovely, dark-eyed young woman, the handsome, serious young man, then Laurel's small, anxious one. Her thoughts were mixed. She thought of her mistress whose whole life had changed since the coming of this little girl, and of Dr. Woodward who already adored her. What would they think if they had seen the quick, possessive way Laurel had challenged the idea that either of them were her *real* mother or father?

"I'm sorry, Jenny," Laurel said quietly. "I didn't mean to yell at you."

"All right, dearie, never mind. Turn around now, and I'll do the buttons carefully so as not to catch the chain again. We'll have to hurry now. Dr. Lee is waitin' to drive you over to school."

Jenny was in the kitchen with Ella when the doctor drove off with Laurel sitting beside him in the buggy, both of them waving to Ava who stood on the porch waving her handkerchief as they left.

Unconsciously Jenny shook her head. People were already saying the Woodwards were spoiling their "little orphan." Not that Jenny agreed. She had never seen a child spoiled by too much love or caring. What bothered her now was whether Laurel would ever be able to love them back enough.

It was a strange situation, Jenny thought to herself as she began her dusting. There was still that closed door upstairs that had belonged to the Woodward's *real* daughter, Dorie. Just as there was that locket where Laurel kept her *real* parents.

Laurel's heart was hammering as she entered Meadowridge Grammar School's fenced schoolyard, filled with boisterous children. Her hand tightened on the handle of her lunch pail, and she felt her mouth go dry when she tried to swallow. The distance from the gate over to the school building looked so far, and if she made it over there, how would she ever find the right classroom?

At the moment she was about to panic, Laurel heard someone calling her name. Turning, she was grateful to see Toddy, red-gold curls flying, running toward her across the crowded playground.

"Laurel!" Toddy came up to her smiling and breathless, holding out her hand to clasp Laurel's. "I'm so glad to see you! Let's wait here and see if Kit comes," she suggested.

At once Laurel sighed with relief. When Kit came, everything really would be all right. The three of them would be together again.

9

Christmas 1894

The Christmas program put on by the schoolchildren in the church social hall was a great success. Everyone said so, parents congratulating Miss Cady and complimenting each other on performances of their offspring. Ava, basking in the many comments on Laurel's solo of "O Holy Night," clutched Leland's arm excitedly and whispered, "Lee, we must see that Laurel has singing lessons! Her voice is surely a God-given gift."

Unaware of the plans for her future already spinning forward in Ava's mind, Laurel found Kit and Toddy and the three of them settled together in one corner to enjoy the refreshments and compare notes about the coming holiday week.

"I'm so thankful I didn't miss a line of your poem, Kit!" Toddy gave an exaggerated sigh of relief as she forked up a large bite of applesauce cake.

"You read it so well, Toddy. You made it sound much better than I thought it was when I wrote it," Kit told her. "And Laurel, you didn't seem a bit nervous doing your song."

"I *was*, though. I thought my voice sounded shaky on the first few notes," confessed Laurel, glad that it was over.

"No school for ten whole days! And if it keeps on snowing, we can go sledding!" Toddy said with a little bounce.

"I don't have a sled," Laurel said.

"Well, you'll probably get one for Christmas." Toddy nodded her head confidently. "Bob Pennifold's father...you know, he runs Pennifold's Hardware Store...and he said a lot of folks have put in orders for sleds to give their children for presents."

"Oh, well, maybe," agreed Laurel, brightening.

Kit did not say anything. She knew there would be no such things as sleds for Christmas at the Hansens' farm.

Soon people began searching for their wraps and boots as they prepared to leave. Ava called Laurel over, handed her the new white sheared rabbit fur tam and muff. The set was "an early Christmas present," Ava had told her when she had given it to her that evening.

Toddy made both girls promise they would come over the first day after Christmas to see the Hales' tree. Its tip touched the ceiling of the parlor, she told them, and was decorated with ornaments Mrs. Hale had ordered from a store in San Francisco. Just then, Helene and Mrs. Hale called to her and Toddy went off to join them. Kit left to say goodnight to Miss Cady and Laurel, tucking her hands into her muff, walked out with the Woodwards.

Coming out into the cold, starry night from the warmth of the church social hall, the air rang with cheerful voices calling out "Merry Christmas!" as people found their buggies and wagons, and gathered their children for the ride home.

Dr. Woodward helped Ava and Laurel into theirs and tucked a warm rug over their knees. Snow was still falling gently, slowly covering the rooftops of houses and lawns along the way home, muting the sound of the horse's hoofs and buggy wheels on the snow-softened road.

"Tired, darling?" Ava asked, putting her arm around Laurel's shoulder and drawing her close.

Laurel nodded, but she really wasn't as tired as she was preoccupied with her own thoughts. The Woodwards had set up their tree in the parlor on Sunday when Dr. Woodward was home and could help. He mostly supervised Laurel's and Ava's hanging of the ornaments and then finally climbed up the ladder to place the glittery star at the top.

Before they left for the Christmas program that evening Laurel noticed some brightly wrapped packages had already been placed underneath the tree. Laurel had been busy for weeks making her presents—an embroidered glove case for Ava and four finely hemmed linen handkerchiefs for Leland with his initials satin-stitched in the corner. They lay, prettily wrapped and hidden in her bottom drawer. She had been wondering how to get them under the tree without anyone seeing her. As soon as they got home the opportunity presented itself.

"Would you like a cup of cocoa, Laurel?" Ava asked her as they came into the house. "I'm going to make some. I got quite chilled on the drive home."

"No, thank you. I had the hot spiced cider after the program. I think I'll go get ready for bed," Laurel replied and she kissed Ava good night and went upstairs.

What luck! she thought. She would wait until they were both safely in the kitchen having cocoa, then she would slip downstairs and put her gifts under the tree.

Ava was still standing at the bottom of the stairs, lost in thought, when Leland came in the door after taking care of his horse. He came up behind her and put his arms around her waist, leaning his cold cheek against hers for a minute.

"Oh, Leland! Laurel is such a treasure. We are so blessed." Ava sighed happily.

"I couldn't agree more, my dear."

"And with the voice of an angel."

"She sang very nicely indeed."

"Nicely? Is that all you have to say about it?"

"Well, I'm no music critic."

"You don't have to be to recognize talent like that."

"Didn't I hear you say something about making some hot cocoa?" Leland asked mildly.

"Yes, but don't change the subject." Ava removed her hat and veil, placed them on the hall table while Leland helped her off with her fur-collared cape. "We must see that Laurel's voice is properly trained." Eyeing her reflection in the hall mirror, she patted her hair absentmindedly then turned around with a small frown. "Whom should I ask about a voice teacher for her, do you suppose? Mr. Fordyce, the music teacher at the high school?"

"I'm sure I have no idea." Leland shook his head. "There's plenty of time for that."

"No, not really, Lee. It is important to start early, I've read. See that she doesn't acquire any bad habits, doesn't strain her vocal cords, learns to breathe correctly, that sort of thing."

"Laurel's only twelve, darling," Lee protested gently.

"It's soon enough. It may even be a little late!"

"Well, that may be so, my dear."

"I'm sure I'm right about the necessity of nurturing a natural gift like hers."

"Well, nothing has to be decided tonight," Leland murmured.

"You think I'm being silly, don't you?" Ava accused.

"No, not silly, my dear. Maybe just overestimating Laurel's talent *and* her desire. Maybe Laurel won't even be interested in developing her voice. Maybe, she'd rather do something else entirely."

"But it's up to us as *parents* to guide her in what's best for her. We have a responsibility to see that Laurel appreciates her gift and does whatever is necessary to cultivate it." Ava's tone became higher, more intense. "You must not have heard all the comments I heard tonight about Laurel's singing. Everyone was so complimentary, marveling at the quality of her voice." She faced him, eyes flashing. "She *has* a gift, Leland, and I intend to see that she doesn't waste it!"

"Fine, my dear," Leland said soothingly, seeing how excited his wife was becoming. "Come along, how about the cocoa you promised?" and Leland took her hand, leading her toward the kitchen at the back of the house.

Unknown to either of them, Laurel, standing at the top of the staircase, her packages in her arms, had heard their conversation.

As their voices faded away, her hand went unconsciously to the delicate chain she always wore and she fingered the heart-shaped locket. The familiar sadness swept over her. Mama had seemed very close to her tonight, especially when she was singing.

Ever since she was a very little girl, Laurel had known all the Christmas carols. She could recall clearly sitting beside Mama at the piano while she played and sang all the lovely old songs, and Laurel had sung along with her.

Christmas was always a special time in that small apartment at the top of Mrs. Campbell's house, even though they had only a tiny tree set on the table and a few little gifts. It was special because Mama made it so. Laurel closed her eyes and she could almost see it all again—the candles' glow, the sound of the piano, Mama's beautiful smile, her graceful hands moving over the keys—

Laurel loved to sing, knew that when she sang she felt a soaring sensation, as if a part of herself left and became one with the song, with the music. She remembered Mama saying, "Why Laurel, you sound just like a little lark!"

When she sang it was always for her—for Mama.

10

The Class of 1900

Laurel stood at the hall mirror retying the bow at the collar of her pink shirtwaist when Dr. Woodward came downstairs and stopped behind her.

"Good morning, my dear, you look as fresh as a daisy," he complimented her. "All ready for the Senior Picnic, are you?"

"Yes, Papa Lee." Laurel whirled around to greet him. "I'm waiting for Dan. He'll be here in a few minutes. We'll walk over to school and meet the rest of the class. There will be hay wagons to take us out to Riverview Park for the picnic."

"That sounds like fun." Dr. Woodward smiled. "Well, I have office hours this morning, so I'd better get out there. Have a good time."

"We will, Papa, thanks," Laurel assured him, offering her soft cheek for his kiss.

Leland went out the side door, stopped in the garden to pick a rosebud from one of his wife's prized bushes to put in the lapel of his tan linen jacket, then proceeded to his small office at the back of the house.

At three months past fifty, Leland was still handsome, with well-defined features and a pleasant smile. There was more silver in his thick wavy hair now, but with his erect, lean build, he had the appearance of a much younger man.

A few minutes later, standing at his office window, he watched Laurel and Dan Brooks go out the front gate together. Fondly, his eyes followed Laurel's graceful figure and the lanky one of the tall boy at her side as they turned in the direction of Meadowridge High School.

He was pleased that Laurel was going to their class picnic with Dan. He liked the young fellow. Of all the boys whose bicycles had cluttered up the front walk since Laurel was about fifteen, or who had parked themselves on the front porch, bringing valentines or flowers, boxes of candy and Christmas gifts, Dan was Leland's favorite.

If he had had a son of his own, Leland would have wanted one like Dan. The boy was courteous, intelligent, dependable. He could carry on a decent conversation with an adult, which was more than Leland could say for half of those who had stood tongue-tied and awkwardly ill at ease in the Woodwards' hallway, waiting for Laurel to come down and rescue them.

Leland only hoped Laurel had the good sense to recognize Dan's good qualities and appreciate them. Maybe in a few years things would develop between them and become more than a friendship. Of course, they were still very young, plenty of time to think of the future.

Just then looking up at Dan, Laurel's head tilted sideways, and Leland could see her enchanting profile—the small sweet nose, the slender neck above the ruffled edge of her high-necked blouse. Just this week, in anticipation of her official entry into young womanhood via graduation, Laurel had begun pinning up her dark, wavy hair. It made her look very grown up.

Unconsciously, Leland sighed. Was it possible it had been ten years since as a seven-year-old child, Laurel had come into their home?

"Lee, still alone? No patients yet?"

Ava's voice interrupted his thoughts and Leland turned to see her face peering around the office door.

"Yes, I mean, no—I'm alone, no patients. Come in, darling," Leland invited.

Ava slipped in, closing the door quietly behind her.

Looking at her, Leland was struck, as he always was, that she seemed to grow lovelier with each passing year. Her figure was still girlishly slim, the dark hair still untouched by a single strand of gray, her skin pale and smooth, translucent as fine porcelain. Of course, since Laurel had come into their lives, they both seemed rejuvenated.

At the moment, however, a small anxious frown cast two vertical lines between Ava's dark, winged brows. Her expression alerted him that something was troubling her. A tiny twinge of concern stirred, tightening his chest. Ava tended to get upset about small, unimportant things. What was it now?

Leland went over to her, took both her hands in his, and was startled to feel they were icy.

"What is it, Ava, what's wrong?"

"Did you see Laurel?" she asked.

"Yes, right before she left. She looked charming, as usual."

"Yes, that pale pink blouse is so becoming—" Ava said with a distracted air, then rushed on. "Did you see her leave with *that* boy?"

"With Dan? Yes, of course, why?"

"*Why*? That's why I'm so upset. He's taken her to every single graduation event. *That's* what upsets me. He's totally unsuitable."

"Unsuitable?" Leland repeated in surprise. "How do you mean *unsuitable*? I think he's a capital young chap. What do you mean?"

"His *family,* Leland, *that's* what I mean."

"There's nothing wrong with the family, as far as I know. His grandmother and aunts are patients of mine. They're members of the church. They're fine ladies. I don't know what you're talking about."

"I *know* he lives with *them,* Leland, and everything looks very respectable, but—" Ava lowered her voice. "His mother lives in Chicago and his father, well, no one seems to know much about him. But the *brother,* Dan's *uncle, is Ned Morris—*" Ava broke off in dismay. "Surely, you know he runs a pool hall on the other side of town."

Leland started to laugh. Shaking his head he protested, "But, darling, what's that got to do with Dan? He lives with Mrs. Morris over on Elm Street—"

"Leland, you're purposely trying not to understand." Ava sounded exasperated. "I just don't want Laurel associating with that sort of person."

It was Leland's turn to be irritated. "Laurel isn't associating with Dan's uncle, my dear, so I don't see the problem."

Ava hesitated a moment before answering.

"The boy is obviously in love with Laurel. Doesn't *that* disturb you?"

"In love? At *their* age?" Leland scoffed. "They aren't even out of high school yet."

"They will be in a week, must I remind you, and then—"

"Ava, my dear, you're borrowing trouble. Besides, Dan told me he has applied to medical school. He's got long years of study ahead. He hasn't time to be serious about anything but getting his education. I *know* what that's like. It will be a long time before he can think about anything else."

Ava seemed somewhat appeased. "I just don't want him getting any ideas about Laurel," she went on. "You know how she is. I'm afraid he might convince her to make some kind of promise about the future—"

"Be sensible, Ava. You must be imagining things. I haven't noticed Laurel treating Dan in any special way. No more than any of the other young men who've come calling. Laurel doesn't even see as much of him as she does her girl friends, Toddy and Kit. I believe you're worrying unnecessarily. Besides, I don't think Laurel would keep anything as important as being in love from *us.*"

"I suppose you're right, Leland," Ava sighed. "You usually are!"

Leland put his arms around her, held her. "Sweetheart, you must not fret about things that may never be! Remember the Scripture, 'Sufficient unto the day,' " he said soothingly. "Now, why don't you find something better to do than worry about two youngsters who have nothing on their minds but having a wonderful day at a picnic?"

"Laurel, I love you," Dan whispered.

"Oh, Dan, I wish you wouldn't say that," Laurel protested softly.

"But, it's true. You must know it, Laurel. Why can't I say it?"

After the delicious picnic prepared by the mothers of the Junior Class and served by rising Meadowridge Seniors, most of the "honorees" had paired off and left the picnic area, to roam along the wooded paths through the park or to follow the trail down to the river.

Dan and Laurel had climbed up the hillside to the meadow overlooking the river and had settled under the shade of a gnarled, ancient oak. The afternoon seemed to stretch endlessly under a lapis lazuli sky. The hum of insects among the wildflowers in the tall grass floated on sweet-scented summer air. The sun was a drowsy warmth. For a while Dan lay on his stomach, gazing at Laurel, wondering if she had any idea what a picture she made. What was she thinking about?

Laurel leaned her head back against the tree, feeling the roughness of its bark through the thin material of her blouse and camisole.

With eyes half-closed, Laurel could see Dan, his head turned so that his clear-cut profile was outlined against the cloudless blue background of the sky. Her mind drifted aimlessly and she began to mentally rehearse the lyrics of the song she was to sing at the Honors Banquet.

It was then that Dan had raised himself to a sitting position, reached for her hand, brought it to his lips and kissed the tips of her fingers.

When he declared, "I love you, Laurel," she tried to pull her hand away, but Dan held it fast.

"Why is it wrong for me to say what I've felt all these months...for years actually. I guess it's just *this* year I realized what it's going to be like when I go away to medical school next fall and won't be able to see you every day."

Laurel met his earnest, brown eyes and felt her own heart respond to what he was saying, but at the same time she was afraid. She knew "Mother" did not like Dan and she felt torn between her two loyalties, not knowing how to explain one to the other without betraying either of them.

"What I want to know, Laurel, is do you care for me?" Dan's voice was intense, pleading. "I mean *really* care, more than just a friend, more than anyone else...enough to wait ...until I finish my training, become a doctor? I know that's a long time, an awful lot to ask. But, Laurel, I don't know how I can go off next fall, leave Meadowridge and not know that you—that you—"

"Oh, Dan, I *do* care, but I don't think you should talk like this. We're both...well, we're just getting out of high school. We have our whole lives ahead of us. Don't you think it's too early for us to make plans, or promises?"

"Don't you ever daydream about the future, Laurel? Wonder what it will be like to make our own decisions, our own choices?"

"Of course, I do—" began Laurel, then stopped short. Of course, she daydreamed but she had never shared those daydreams with anyone. Laurel had always had a "secret life" filled with dreams and plans about the future. But, mostly, she lived in the present, drifting from day to day, trying to please everyone, trying to make "Mother" and Papa Lee happy, proud of her.

Like with her music. "Mother" was always so interested in the new songs Mr. Fordyce gave her to learn, so thrilled every time Laurel was asked to perform. Ava always had Laurel sing for her Sewing Circle when it met at the Woodwards' but "Mother" never guessed how nervous it made Laurel to sing for an audience, how much it cost her to meet those expectations.

And now Dan was pressuring her, wanting her to make a commitment to him. Gently, Laurel withdrew her hand.

"Dan, it's too soon for us to make any promises. Can't you be satisfied to know I *do* care very much about you? Isn't that enough for now?"

Dan sighed heavily. "I guess it will *have* to be."

He got to his feet, walked over to the cliff, bent down and picked up some small stones and stood tossing them down into the river below. Laurel looked over at his tall figure, the shoulders drooping slightly with disappointment. Then she leaned back against the tree again and closed her eyes.

Sometimes she wished she could go away somewhere where no one expected anything of her at all. She let her mind wander back to that old fantasy, the one kept locked in her heart all these years, the story she used to tell herself at night when she was lying in bed not quite ready to go to sleep.

It was then she planned how, when she grew up and finished school, she would go back to Boston and find Mrs. Campbell's old house. She would ring the doorbell and Mrs. Campbell would come to the door. Seeing her, her old landlady would throw up her hands and say, "Why, land's sake, if it isn't Laurel Vestal, all grown up!" Then she would take Laurel upstairs to their old apartment unlock the door, and Laurel would walk inside and everything would be just the same as the last time she had seen it.

Laurel would go through it, room by room, remembering—the upright piano with the candleholders on either side of the music rack with her father's painting of the lighthouse hanging over it, her mother's rocker over by the window with the little footstool where Laurel used to sit. In the bedroom, Laurel would picture the trundle bed they pulled out from under her Mama's high poster, and in the corner the table with the lamp and the books—

Sometimes, at this point, Laurel would fall asleep. But the next night and the night after that, she would begin her journey again. The longer she was with the Woodwards, the less she had done that. But today it all came back to her as clearly and vividly as ever.

It was not that Laurel was unhappy. Her life at the Woodwards could not have been happier or more pleasant. It would have been hard to find a more loving, caring atmosphere for a child to grow up in.

But all through the years, Laurel had clung to her memories like a drowning person clutching at a straw, as if by letting go, she would drift down the stream, be swept into the rushing current, and lose something vital. Lose her other life, that life with Mama that filled her with such sweet longing and sadness.

Why could she not let it go? Was it because it had taken her so long to accept that her mama had really died? For weeks she had refused to believe it. Mama had promised she would come back—

Or couse, eventually, the reality had penetrated. Still, buried deep in her child's heart was the determination that one day she would go back and find that lost part of herself.

"Come on, Laurel. Everyone's starting back. They're loading up the wagons to go back into town!"

"Wake up, Laurel!"

Toddy's voice broke into Laurel's thoughts, and she opened her eyes, blinking into the sunshine. Toddy and Chris Blanchard were standing over her.

"We just came up from the river," Toddy said, holding up her white cotton stockings and shoes. "We went wading!" Then, pointing to the hem of her bedraggled skirt, she made a face. "Miss Klitgard will look daggers at me! So very *unladylike*, Miss Hale!" she declared, mimicking one of their teacher-chaperones for the picnic.

It was such an exact imitation they all laughed.

Joining in, Dan held out his hands to Laurel and pulled her to her feet. "Time to go!" Then, hand in hand, they walked back down the hill to the picnic area where the wagons for the ride back to town were loading.

As the three wagons, drawn by plodding farm horses and filled with young people singing at the top of their voices, lumbered into the school yard, passers-by on Elm Street smiled nostalgically, recalling their own bygone youth.

In one last exuberant burst of song, the strains of the school song echoed through the early evening air: "Forever we'll remember thee, Meadowridge High, we'll faithful be!" and ended with riotous laughter and clapping hands.

Dan jumped down from the end of the wagon and held up his arms to Laurel, who placed her hands on his shoulders. Lifting her down, he held her a moment longer than necessary. "I'll walk you home," he whispered.

"Oh, you don't need to, Dan. It's still light. Besides, don't you have to get to work?" Laurel asked, knowing Dan had a job at the pharmacy three nights a week.

"I have time," he assured her planning to skip supper in order to make it to his job by six.

"You're sure?" Laurel sounded doubtful.

"Yes," Dan told her, drawing her hand through his arm as they started out of the school yard.

Toddy and Chris, heading toward the Hale house, called and waved as they went in the other direction.

"I *can* take you to the Honors Banquet tomorrow night, can't I, Laurel?" Dan asked on the way home.

Laurel hesitated. "I don't know, Dan. Papa Lee and Mother plan to attend and I think they expect me to go with them."

He frowned. "Well, I realize parents will be there, Laurel, but our whole class will have its own table and—"

"Maybe I'd just better wait and see—" Her voice trailed off uncertainly.

Dan knew better than to persist, but his jaw tightened.

They said nothing more until they reached the Woodwards' white picket fence. Dan opened the gate for her and they went through into the back garden, fragrant now with June roses.

"About the Banquet, Laurel—" he began.

"I told you I'd have to see, Dan," Laurel reminded him gently.

Dan did not want to argue about it. Anything to do with Laurel's parents' wishes always presented a problem. He'd run into that barrier often enough before.

"I know, but I'd just like to know—"

"I understand. But if Mother and Papa Lee want me—" Laurel sighed softly. It was so hard to explain to anyone, even Dan, how easily Mother's feelings were hurt.

Just then they heard the squeak of the screen door opening and Mrs. Woodward came out onto the back porch, a slim figure in a filmy white dress. She walked to the edge of the steps, peering into the gathering lavender dusk.

"Oh, there you are, Laurel darling!" she called. "I was getting worried. It's nearly five-thirty. I thought you'd be home way before now. I was afraid there might have been an accident...those narrow country roads and those top-heavy wagons—"

Laurel moved quickly away from Dan and took a few steps forward so Ava could see her.

"No, Mother, everything's fine! Nothing happened! I'm sorry you were worried."

"Oh, well, as long as you're home safe!" Mrs. Woodward sounded relieved. "Come along, I'll run a nice tub for you. You must be tired after such a long day."

"I'll be there in just a minute. Dan's here. He walked me home."

"Hello, Mrs. Woodward." Dan stepped into Mrs. Woodward's line of vision.

"Oh, hello, Dan." There was a definite coolness in Ava's voice.

Laurel winced inwardly. Why did Mother always ignore Dan unless he made it a point to force her to see him, speak to him? He had never mentioned this to her, but it was so obvious, it hurt Laurel for him.

"Well, come along, Laurel, or your bath water will get cold." Mrs. Woodward disappeared into the house.

"I'll have to go in." Laurel turned to Dan. "It was such a nice day. Thanks for seeing me home." As she put her foot on the first step of the porch, Dan caught her hand and held it.

They stood for a long minute in the soft twilight, looking at each other. Laurel drew in her breath. She saw something in Dan's eyes that both stirred and frightened her.

Withdrawing her hand, she said breathlessly, "Good night, Dan," and ran lightly up the steps and into the house.

11

On the afternoon of the Honors Banquet, Laurel walked over to the high school for her final rehearsal of the songs she was to sing that night and at the graduation ceremony.

This last week of the school year, the building was nearly empty. A few students were sitting in the sunshine looking at the yearbook when Laurel went up the steps and inside. As she walked down the deserted corridor, she heard the sound of a trumpet solo being played haltingly. She opened the door to the Music Room and quietly took a seat at the back. The boy with the trumpet struggled on valiantly until Mr. Fordyce spoke to him.

"That's enough for today, Billy. You need some practice, young fellow. Guess we've had too much baseball weather lately, eh?" He tousled the youngster's hair affectionately. "But I expect you to know that piece by heart next week."

"Yes, sir," the boy mumbled getting to his feet. There was much scuffling and clatter as he packed his instrument in its carrying case and hurried out into what was left of the beautiful afternoon.

Then Mr. Fordyce looked over, acknowledged Laurel's presence, and beckoned her forward while he took his place at the piano. Mr. Fordyce had given Laurel private lessons for years, and she considered him a friend.

"All right now, Laurel, let's begin with scales before we go into your numbers."

Laurel adjusted the music stand, placed her music sheets on it and, when Mr. Fordyce struck the first note, she took a deep breath and began.

Less than an hour later, Mr. Fordyce stopped playing and announced, "There, that's it. I think we're through for today. You can over-rehearse, you know."

Laurel was surprised. Usually Mr. Fordyce made many corrective comments, made her go over and over her pieces. Now he stood up, gathered his music, shut the lid over the keyboard.

"Then, it sounded all right?" she asked doubtfully.

"It was fine, Laurel. You'll do splendidly, I'm sure."

Laurel hesitated, there was something in the way he spoke that vaguely troubled her. She stood by the piano uncertainly. She felt there was something he was *not* saying that was more important than what he had said.

"Mr. Fordyce?"

"Yes, Laurel,"

"Did I do something wrong?"

"No, not at all, Laurel. Everything was fine, on pitch, on key. Be sure and rest your voice for the next few hours. Drink some hot lemonade before the performance."

"There's nothing else you wanted to say to me?" she persisted.

Mr. Fordyce continued busily stacking music sheets, then he turned toward her, his face thoughtful. "I guess, I was just wondering what your plans are for after graduation."

"I'm not sure—" she said.

Mr. Fordyce opened his briefcase and began stuffing the music sheets inside. When he looked up again, his face was serious, his eyes grave as he regarded her.

"No plans, eh? What about your voice?"

"I do want to continue my lessons through the summer—" she told him, smiling tentatively. "That is, if you—"

"Laurel! I didn't mean just this summer!" He sounded irritated "You *have* a voice, you know. Don't you care about

it? I know dozens of others who would die for what you have."
He sighed heavily. "Laurel, I've taught you all I can. I can't
do any more to help you develop your voice. There's so much
you still need to know, to learn. But you can't do it here in
Meadowridge. There's no one here who has what you need."

Laurel stared at him.

Again Mr. Fordyce sounded annoyed.

"But you have to *know* that, not have me *tell* you. You have
to *want* it for yourself. Some things cannot be taught. For a
singer there has to be something inside that tells her she
has to go on, that she will *die* if she cannot learn everything
there is to learn, to seek to be the best she can be with the
talent she's been given." He stopped, shook his head. "If you
don't have that desire, Laurel, well, what more can I say?"

"But where could I go? Who could I find to teach me?"

"You'd have to go somewhere like Chicago or Boston
where there is a music conservatory, where there are
teachers who can give you what you need—" He paused
again. "Haven't you even discussed the possibility with
your parents? Surely, they could afford to send you. Your
mother has always been so supportive of your singing—"

"No. I guess we just assumed I'd go on taking lessons from
you, that I would sing in the choir, or for social occasions—"
Her voice faltered. For some reason Laurel felt apologetic,
confused, and something else she could not quite name.

"You mean singing for your friends' weddings, some-
body's funeral service, for the Ladies Aid Guild meetings?"
Mr. Fordyce's tone was sarcastic. He shook his head again.
"Forgive me, Laurel. I've seen so much wasted talent I think
I've become—" He stopped, head down, as if deep in thought.
Then he raised his head and looked straight at Laurel.

"Well, Laurel, I think, after graduation, you should sit
down with Dr. and Mrs. Woodward and discuss this seriously. In fact, if you like I'll come and talk to them. Suggest a
school or teacher."

Laurel twisted her hands nervously. "Maybe—yes, I suppose...I don't really know, Mr. Fordyce. I'll have to think about it."

"Yes, I hope you will do that." Mr. Fordyce seemed weary. Then he attempted a lighter tone, "And, Laurel, don't worry about tonight. You'll do just fine. Enjoy the next few days. High school graduation is very special. There's time enough to think of the future."

"Thank you, Mr. Fordyce," Laurel murmured and, picking up her music, left.

Outside, she felt disoriented. She started walking but not in the direction of home. Instead, she turned and headed for the town park. There she found a bench near the duck pond and sat down. She realized she was trembling.

She tried to remember everything Mr. Fordyce had said, but what kept repeating itself over and over in her head were the words, "You would have to go to Chicago or *Boston* where there is a music conservatory, teachers." Was this the sign she'd been praying for? If she could go to *Boston*, then perhaps she could trace her real parents, find out about Mama's death, where she was buried, what had happened to all their things. The hope Laurel had carried for so long, hidden in her heart, burst into new life! Maybe this was the way being opened for her.

Her singing had been so much a part of her life that she had never considered it as separate from herself, as something to be developed, cared for, polished, like a rare instrument. She had sung all her life, as a little child alongside her dear mama at the piano; after coming to Meadowridge, at school and at church. Later she had sung in the choir.

It was Mother who insisted on her having lessons with Mr. Fordyce. But what Mr. Fordyce was suggesting was something different entirely. He was talking about her studying voice seriously, devoting her life to singing.

Laurel knew that something strange and wonderful happened to her when she sang. She felt a lifting, soaring sensation that carried her far beyond the room, the people, the faces of the listening audience or congregation. It was a feeling she never experienced in any other way.

Is that what Mr. Fordyce was trying to get her to express? To speak of that inner joy she felt while she was singing? Or had he meant more than that?

Yes, Laurel was sure Mr. Fordyce was looking for something else in her answer today. He was trying to see if she had that necessary desire, testing her to see if it was strong enough to make the choice of a life of total dedication.

Laurel realized that now was the time of decision. Would it be wrong to use her voice as a means to pursuing her real desire? If the Woodwards would finance her musical education in *Boston*—

Unconsciously, Laurel fingered the locket she still wore around her neck. She thought of that long-ago promise she had made to herself that, just yesterday, at the picnic, had come back to her so vividly.

Of course, Laurel knew it was foolish to suppose anything was still there. Even Mrs. Campbell might be gone. But maybe she could find out something about her father, his family, the Vestals.

Would it be deceitful to combine studying voice, which should please Mother especially, while she pursued her long-cherished dream of solving the mystery surrounding her own background?

Laurel tried imagining the discussion with Papa Lee and Mother, Mr. Fordyce had suggested. What would they say? Would they let her go?

It was too much to think about now. There was the banquet tonight, Baccalaureate service the following day, then graduation and the Graduation Dance to look forward to— Laurel rose and started walking slowly home.

She wouldn't say anything about this yet. Not tell anyone, not even Dan. There was plenty of time. The whole summer before anything would really have to be decided.

12

The evening of graduation day, Dan walked over from Elm Street to the Woodwards' house to escort Laurel to their class party. He carried with him a small corsage of sweetheart roses for her.

Before ringing the doorbell, he adjusted his tie, ran a nervous finger around the inside of the unaccustomed high, stiff shirt collar, and straightened his new navy blue jacket.

To his dismay it was Mrs. Woodward, not Laurel, who answered the door.

"Good evening, Dan," she greeted him. "How nice you look!" She smiled but there was the usual wariness in her eyes. "Do come in. You're a little early, aren't you? Laurel is not quite ready yet, which doesn't really matter, because we have to wait for Dr. Woodward. He was called out on an emergency, but he should be along soon. He wanted to see Laurel before you left for the party."

Dan tried to swallow his disappointment. All day he had been looking forward to this evening, the chance to be alone with Laurel. The early part of the day had been chaotic, with the graduation ceremony, the long program of speeches in the hot auditorium, and afterwards family and friends crowding around. The picture-taking session had dragged on endlessly. He had hardly seen Laurel.

But tonight was different. Tonight was *their* night. As graduates, they were almost adults by most standards.

Tonight was their exclusive party. Even though it would be well chaperoned by teachers and some parents, Dan planned to manage having Laurel to himself for once—at least, that's what he had hoped.

"Come along, out to the side porch and have a glass of iced tea," invited Mrs. Woodward, leading the way across the parlor out through the glass doors onto the side porch.

Its white wicker furniture gleamed in the gathering twilight; the plump flowered cretonne cushions were crisp and new. On a round table in the center was a tray holding tall glasses and a crystal pitcher filled with amber liquid, aswim with lemon slices and mint leaves.

Everything at the Woodwards' was always so perfect, thought Dan, not shabby, mended and drab like his grandmother's house. All the rooms in the house on Elm Street, except for the parlor which was rarely used, needed paint, new wallpaper, new curtains, rugs or furniture. It was a very old house; it smelled old, looked old, felt old. His grandmother had been very young when her father had built it. She had been married from there, moved back into it after she was left a young widow with three little girls. Dan's mother was the only one of them who had married and left home; his two maiden aunts still lived there.

Dan was thinking about his mother when Mrs. Woodward's voice interposed, "I suppose your family is mighty proud of you, Dan. Being the class salutatorian is quite an honor."

"Yes, ma'am, it is," replied Dan, still standing awkwardly, holding Laurel's corsage, not knowing exactly where to sit.

Mrs. Woodward, occupied with pouring the tea, turned to hand him a glass when she saw his problem. "Would you like me to take the flowers up to Laurel, or would you rather just set them aside for now, and give them to her yourself?" she asked.

"Well—" he hesitated.

With a barely perceptible sigh she put the glass back on the tray and held out her hands for the corsage. "Here, we can just set them down over here. They're very pretty, Dan, but the color—I'm not sure with Laurel's dress—" her voice trailed off doubtfully. Then she added, "Well, I'm sure it won't matter, she'll appreciate them anyway." Mrs. Woodward shrugged slightly as though it were not important.

Dan felt his face grow hot. Why hadn't he thought to ask Laurel the color of her dress? All he'd thought of was how much she loved roses, and the pale yellow ones with a blush of coral seemed so right for her. But now he was unsure.

Dan tensed. Why had Mrs. Woodward had to say anything? Why did she have to spoil his pleasure? Make him feel uncertain? He felt a raw resentment rise up within him. But then, to be fair, she didn't know he had splurged his hard-earned money to buy them, or how long he'd stayed at the florist shop deciding which ones to get.

Mrs. Woodward picked up the filled glass again and, placing a small embroidered napkin under it, held it out to him.

Dan took it and backed up toward the chair behind him and sat down, balancing the glass carefully. He glanced cautiously in Mrs. Woodward's direction as she gracefully seated herself opposite him.

"And what are your plans now that you've graduated, Dan?" Her soft voice somehow accentuated his discomfort. He wished Laurel would come. He had never spent much time with Mrs. Woodward, and he always felt uncomfortable around the lady, even in these brief times. He cleared his throat.

"Well, I'll be working full-time for Mr. Groves at the Pharmacy for the summer, then in the fall I'll be going to college—"

"Oh, and where will that be?"

"I'll be going back to Ohio—"

"Ohio? Why is that?"

"Well, it's near my father's folks and—"

"Your father?" There was a hint of surprise in Ava's voice.

Dan's mouth felt dry. He didn't want to have to go into a long explanation about the family. It was all so complicated. All his relationships were. Even his own questions about them had never been satisfactorily answered. All he really knew was that for reasons he had never been told, his parents had lived apart since he was a little boy. His father had been in the Army and died in Cuba during the Spanish-American War. Since he was nine, Dan had lived in Meadowridge with Grandmother Morris, his aunts Sue and Vera, while his mother worked as a milliner in a big city department store.

"Yes, I'll be attending the State College and I can spend weekends with them. They have a farm, I can help out—"

Dan took a gulp of tea and felt a piece of ice lodge in the back of his throat. He worked it forward to keep from choking.

"I see," Mrs. Woodward said in a tone that implied she did not see at all.

He glanced over at her, looking cool and serene in a light flowered dress with a wide bertha collar edged in deep lace, dark hair swept back from a pale, aristocratic face.

Dan had a momentary mental picture of his mother meeting Ava Woodward. It was hard to imagine. They were so different. His mother had had a hard life, so his aunts were often fond of saying. An image of her came to Dan—the thin face, anxious eyes, her brow puckered in a perpetually worried frown. Yes, he guessed she had a lot of things to worry about, a woman struggling alone to work and support a child. And she had done that. Regularly every month a money order came to Dan's grandmother, and every fall she had sent money for his new school clothes. As Dan had "shot up like the proverbial weed," as Grandma Morris complained, the cost of his clothing went up, too. That was the reason his mother hadn't been able to afford the train fare to visit the last few years. Dan had not seen her in over a year until she had arrived for his graduation.

They had been awkward with each other after so long a time apart. They seemed to have little to say to each other. She was going to stay until the end of the week and then would be leaving again. He had felt guilty leaving her tonight. Not knowing about the long-planned graduation party, she had thought they would have a little family get-together. Even Uncle Ned was coming.

Thinking of his uncle, Dan felt self-conscious. He knew Mrs. Woodward did not approve of him, or at least of what he did. But if it weren't for Uncle Ned, many things would have been impossible for Dan. He might have even had to drop out of school at the eighth grade as so many of the fellows did to help out at home. And Uncle Ned had promised to help him with college and medical school expenses.

Just then, to Dan's immense relief, the screen door opened and Dr. Woodward came out onto the porch, saying jovially, "Well, here I am, my dear. Hello there, Dan."

Dan got to his feet as the doctor extended his hand and in doing so spilled some of his tea. Neither Dr. or Mrs. Woodward seemed to notice, and Dan quickly brushed it off his new white flannel trousers, hoping it wouldn't stain.

Desperately, he wished Laurel would hurry and come.

Upstairs, Laurel slid a filigreed silver comb, one of her graduation gifts, into her swirl of lustrous dark hair, then took a step back from the mirror to judge the effect.

"How does that look, Jenny?" she asked.

Jenny, standing alongside, waiting to help Laurel into her evening gown, nodded approvingly, "Lovely! Land sakes, Laurel, but you do look growed up, with your hair up and all."

"I'm supposed to look grown up, Jenny! I'm eighteen and finished school!" Laurel laughed, the high, sweet laugh that always reminded people of wind chimes.

"Don't seem any time since I was helping you get dressed to go to Toddy's surprise birthday party!" Jenny shook her head in disbelief.

That afternoon, as Jenny and Ella sat proudly with the Woodwards at the graduation ceremony, watching Laurel march up to receive her diploma, they had both remarked that it seemed only yesterday since Laurel was a little girl.

"Well, let's get your dress on now," Jenny suggested. "You know Dan's come, don't you?"

"Yes," Laurel said and slipped her arms into the dress Jenny was holding, then turned around so that Jenny could button the tiny satin-covered buttons down the back.

"My but this *is* a pretty dress!" Jenny nodded appreciatively as the silk voile fell in ruffled tiers over the taffeta underskirt. The delicate blue-violet material set off Laurel's coloring—her peach-bloom complexion, her dark eyes and hair. Its exquisitely embroidered bodice traced the graceful line of her shoulders, the tucked bandeau, her small waist. "You do look a picture."

Even allowing that Jenny was hopelessly prejudiced in her favor, Laurel knew the dress was flatteringly becoming. And it *was* a very grown-up dress!

"You're wearing this, aren't you?" Jenny picked up the necklace of seed pearls and tiny amethysts from the top of the dressing table.

She saw Laurel hesitate a second. Her hand went to the chain and locket she never took off before she answered.

"I suppose Mother will wonder if I don't—" she sighed, then she tucked the locket under her dress into her chemise leaving the thin chain barely visible, and turned so that Jenny could clasp the pearl necklace around her neck.

Then Jenny handed her a small beaded purse, in which was a scented handkerchief, a small brush, some extra hairpins, a slim silver container for rice powder, a tiny vial of eau de fleur cologne, and her gloves.

"Oh, Jenny, thanks!" Laurel exclaimed. "Thanks for everything and for the lovely present, too!"

Jenny had given Laurel a scrapbook with gold printed letters on the front "Schoolday Memories."

"I thought it would be a nice thing for your keepsakes," Jenny said, pleased that Laurel seemed to like it as much as several of the expensive graduation gifts the Woodwards had given her.

"Oh, it will be just right for all my mementos…like this!" Laurel dangled the small tassled dance card before putting it in her evening bag, too. "Thank you, Jenny. Good night!"

Laurel gave her a hug, then pirouetted across the room to the doorway, waved and went along the hall and down the stairway.

"Good night! Have a good time, Laurel!" Jenny called after her.

For some reason Jenny shivered. She didn't know why on such a balmy June evening! A strange, unwanted thought crossed Jenny's mind. What will happen to Laurel now? She did not like the cold, shuddery feeling that passed over her, and she quickly set about picking up some of Laurel's discarded clothes, hanging them up in her armoire, and then turning down her bed.

The walk from the Woodwards' to Meadowridge High had been all too short for Dan who had wanted to delay sharing Laurel as long as possible. As they strolled through the soft summer evening, he had been newly aware of everything about her—the sweet smell of her freshly washed hair, the delicate violet scent of her, the rustle of her gown. He had not wanted their time alone together to end.

But it did, just as they reached the school steps. Chris Blanchard, with Toddy coming from the other direction, greeted them. The girls immediately began to chatter, admiring each other's gowns and flowers and exchanging news about graduation gifts. Then the four of them went into the building together.

Japanese lanterns, strung from the ceiling rafters, shed mellow rosy-golden light, transforming the school auditorium. Lively music was playing and couples were already on the dance floor. Standing at the threshold the foursome was at once surrounded by their classmates, everyone in high spirits with a new sense of freedom since being graduated that afternoon.

"There's Kit!" exclaimed Toddy, waving her over to join them.

Kit, Laurel thought, had never looked so lovely. She had changed from the atrocious dress she had worn for graduation into an elegantly simple lace-trimmed blouse and slightly flared white skirt. White roses were tucked into the braided coil of her dark hair and her smooth, olive complexion was faintly flushed. Her smile was radiant and she seemed happier and more carefree than Laurel had ever seen her. And why not? She had given a superb valedictory speech and been awarded a scholarship to Merrivale Teachers College. It couldn't have happened to a nicer person, Laurel thought fondly.

Everyone clustered around Kit to congratulate her, and she laughed and accepted it all with a new sparkle.

Just then the band blared a fanfare. Mr. Dean, the athletic coach, was on the stage and held up his hand to quiet the hum of conversation to make an announcement.

"Ladies and Gentlemen...you noticed that *since this afternoon*, I am not addressing you as *boys and girls!*" he joked. This comment received a general laugh and a spatter of applause. He smiled and continued. "Now, you have been together as a class for four years and probably think you know each other pretty well, but, how often have you *really* talked to a member of your class who wasn't a *special* friend? Well, tonight we thought we'd give you a last chance to meet and talk to someone you might have wanted to for a long time, and were too shy, too busy or too scared to talk to before!" He held up a large box decorated in their class colors of green and gold. "In here on slips of paper are names of famous people, but separated into first name and last name. Each of you will have to find the matching part. And when you do, you and your match will have five minutes to ask questions and find out something about that person you didn't know, and vice versa!"

A buzz of comments and laughter followed this as everyone lined up to draw a slip of paper from the box.

Inwardly, Dan groaned. If this was going to be a night of party games...when all he wanted to do was to be with Laurel—

But when he found that the person who completed the name he had drawn—"Robin"—was Toddy, holding a slip of paper on which was written "Hood," his heart lifted in relief.

"Not fair!" she pretended to pout. "We know each other too well." She glanced around. "Shall we trade with someone else."

"Not on your life! There are lots of things I don't know about you and I mean to find out!" Dan teased. This was great! With Toddy he could relax, not have to search his mind for questions or make small talk with some girl who was practically a stranger. Dan had always been so busy with his after-school job and his studies that he had not had time to do much socializing. Actually, the only girls in his class he knew other than Laurel to speak to were Laurel's two best friends, Kit and Toddy.

"Well, then, come on," Toddy laughed, "and I'll tell you all the deep, dark secrets of my life." They found two chairs on the edge of the dance floor and sat down. "Now, I'll ask you the question everybody's been asking me most of the day. What are you going to do now that you've graduated, Dan?"

"But you know that, don't you? I'm going away to college in the fall, and then on to medical school. That is—"

"I think that is wonderful, Dan! Most of the boys don't think past college if that—" She sighed. "Take Chris—"

"*You* take him, Toddy!" Dan laughed. "It's *you* he wants."

"That's just it. Just what I'm talking about, Dan. We should all have plans, ambitions and dreams beyond Meadowridge."

"Doesn't Chris?"

"He's going to the same college his father did, then he'll come home and go into the family business."

"Are you sure? You may be selling Chris short, Toddy."

"Maybe. Maybe college will change him."

"It's bound to. College changes everyone."

Toddy's pretty face looked serious. "I wish—"

"What do you wish, Toddy?"

"Oh, nothing," she said, giving her head a little toss. "Now it's your turn to ask me something you don't know about me."

"Did you read the Class Prophecy?" Dan asked.

"Of course, why?"

"Well, was it true? Are you going to become a famous actress?"

For a minute Toddy looked startled, then she seemed to shudder slightly. "Oh, no!"

"But you won the Drama Prize at the Awards Banquet for playing Portia in *A Merchant of Venice.*'"

"Well, that's all it was, playing—I want to do something much more worthwhile than *that!*" she declared.

A whistle blew. "Time's up!" shouted Mr. Dean. "Did you get to know one of your classmates better?" A loud "Yeah!" came forth. "Good!" the coach beamed. "Now, we're going to have some music. Enjoy the rest of the evening!"

Chris came to claim Toddy for the first dance. Dan went in search of Laurel, only to find to his chagrin that she had already been wisked onto the dance floor.

Not wanting to dance with anyone else, Dan was forced to stand on the sidelines, watching until the set was over. When the third dance ended, he began weaving his way through the dancers over to her when another announcement was made.

"Ladies and gentlemen, the next dance is a 'Paul Jones.' Ladies make a circle and gentlemen form a circle around them, moving counterclockwise to the music. When it stops, whoever you're standing opposite is your partner for the next set."

"Come on, let's get into the circle!" said Toddy, grabbing both Laurel's and Kit's hands.

The music started and the two circles began to move. Some of the guys, trying to guess when the band was going to stop playing and wanting to be opposite a favorite partner, would either quicken or slow their pace accordingly. Laurel saw that Dan was one of those. He was trying to keep his eye on her position. But when the music finally stopped, he was standing right in front of Kit.

Amused, Laurel glanced at her friend, then caught her breath. She had never realized before how beautiful Kit was. There was both delicacy and strength in her fine features. Her luminous gray eyes lighted up and a smile trembled on her sweetly curved mouth as she held out her hand to Dan.

For a moment Kit's face was unmasked. And then Laurel saw something more, something she wasn't intended to see. Kit was in love with Dan!

13

Then summer was over. The maple trees along the street began turning gold. The Virginia creeper clinging to the sides of the house blushed crimson. In the mornings, thin frost glistened on the lawn and mist rose, blurring the sharpness of the blue line of hills surrounding Meadowridge.

Soon, like leaves scattering in the wind, everyone would be going away, each to a different destination, a whole new life—Toddy to Europe with Helene and Mrs. Hale; Kit, for her first year at Merrivale College. Chris Blanchard had already left for the University and Dan had gone off to college. Only Laurel was left behind.

Returning home one September afternoon and hearing in the distance a train whistle at the Meadowridge crossing, Laurel paused to listen. It had such a melancholy sound, as wistful as her own thoughts.

She sighed, unlatched the gate, and walked up the path and into the house. For the first time the place was depressing. The home that had always seemed so warm and welcoming now seemed somehow cold and hostile. In just a little over a week, everything had changed—ever since she had brought up the subject of going away to a Music Conservatory to continue her vocal studies.

Laurel had avoided Mr. Fordyce all summer, hoping not to run into him on the street or at church, afraid he would press her for a decision. Realizing she had been putting it off, and apprehensive of the outcome, she had gathered her courage and first broached it with Papa Lee. She had gone around to his office at the back of the house early one morning before any patients were due.

She recalled every detail of that scene now with a little shudder.

"Dismiss it from your mind" had been Dr. Woodward's first shocked reaction. "A young lady your age traveling across the country by herself? It's out of the question."

Laurel bit her tongue, ready to remind him that she had taken that same long trip years ago as a child. She had carefully rehearsed all the reasons he ought to give her permission to go, backing them up with Mr. Fordyce's supportive comments. She thought she had met every objection he might raise, but she had not been prepared for this unexpectedly abrupt refusal.

In a voice that shook she pleaded, "Will you at least think about it, Papa Lee, discuss it with Mother?"

"Discuss what with me?" a voice behind her asked, and Laurel turned to see Ava standing in the office doorway, her arms filled with purple asters she was bringing from her garden for Leland's waiting room.

The scene that followed was worse than Laurel could have imagined. Ava's reaction was immediate and volatile. Her face turned pale, her eyes dark and wild with alarm.

"But you can't possibly go so far and alone! No, I won't hear of it!" she protested. "Leland, talk to her!"

Laurel looked helplessly at Dr. Woodward. The face that had always beheld her with such indulgent love was now grave, the eyes usually twinkling with affection and fondness now seemed unfathomable.

"But, Mother, *you* were the one who wanted me to study voice in the first place. It was *you* who said I had a gift I should develop. I would never have even thought of it if you hadn't encouraged me, had Mr. Fordyce give me lessons—"
Laurel turned a bewildered gaze on Ava.

"But I never dreamed it would take you away from me—from *us!*" she said indignantly. Then changing her tactics, she added, "I still believe you have a gift and I want you to go on with your lessons, of course."

"But Mr. Fordyce says he's taught me all he can. He says I *need* further training elsewhere—at a Music Conservatory—if I'm to learn what I must learn—"

"To do what? To become a professional singer? To go on the stage?" Ava flung out her hands in a helpless gesture. "I never heard of such nonsense. What is Milton Fordyce thinking of to put such ideas into a young girl's head?"

"Papa—" Laurel began, but Dr. Woodward held up his hand warningly.

"I don't think we should discuss this further right now. I have patients coming in a few minutes and we all need to calm down," he said soothingly. "Ava, my dear, there is no use upsetting yourself. Nothing will be decided or settled right away. When we are all more composed, we can talk about this reasonably."

But they had not talked it over calmly or reasonably. They had not talked it over at all. Laurel waited for one of them to reopen the discussion, but nothing was ever said. It was as though the whole subject had never been mentioned.

Everything went on as before, and yet everything had changed subtly. Laurel felt both of them watching her, not angrily but with disappointment and bewilderment. She sensed they felt they had somehow failed to make her happy since she wanted to leave them.

In turn, she felt guilty and ashamed, knowing they must think her unappreciative, ungrateful. Ava's face became strained. A sad, anxious expression gave it a pinched look. Laurel struggled with her conscience. Her deep desire had always been to please, but something new began to assert itself. Did she not have a right to explore the person she was apart from these dear adoptive parents? And if they had not believed in her talent why had they encouraged her? It was all so dismaying and disturbing.

Dreams do not die easily, however, and Mr. Fordyce had fueled Laurel's hope. The memory of Kit's graduation speech strengthened her. "To thine own self be true." Laurel must be true to herself, she thought. She could not continue living the safe, sheltered life others wanted for her. Her own true identity demanded to be free. Whether that would be through her voice or whatever might be waiting for her in Boston, she knew she must pursue it.

She was torn between loyalty to her secret goal and loving sympathy for the Woodwards, and decided not to spoil the holidays by bringing up the subject of leaving until after the New Year.

So Laurel plunged herself into the church choir's Christmas performance of Handel's *Messiah,* so that much of her time was taken up by rehearsals. Willingly taking on Ava's Christmas list, she kept herself busy with shopping and wrapping presents. In the kitchen she helped Ella and Jenny with the holiday baking.

Sometimes she felt like a puppet, with someone else pulling the strings, making her move and get up in the morning. Too often there were purple shadows of sleeplessness under her eyes, their lids swollen by tears shed at night. What was to become of her? she daily asked herself. Was she wrong? Was leaving selfish? Desperately Laurel prayed for guidance: "Show me Thy way, Lord, that I might find favor with Thee."

Dan wrote he could not come home for Christmas; he couldn't afford the train fare. Lost in her own dilemma, the uncertainty about her future, Dan seemed very far away.

The days before Christmas seemed outwardly serene, peaceful, but within Laurel, a fire storm raged.

The performance of the *Messiah* was hailed by everyone who attended as the finest program Meadowridge Community Church choir had ever presented. Afterwards there was a reception in the festively decorated social hall. It was the custom to hang small gilt-paper cornucopias on the church Christmas tree. Inside each cornucopia was a slip of paper bearing a Scripture verse. These were considered each person's special Bible message for the coming year.

When Laurel opened hers, she read: "Be strong and of good courage; be not afraid, neither be thou dismayed; for the Lord, thy God is with thee whithersoever thou goest" (Joshua 1:9). It seemed a confirmation, and Laurel took it as such. Her conviction grew that she *must* go.

The New Year came and a week later Laurel gathered up her courage and went into Dr. Woodward's office. The sun was streaming in through the windows of the small L-shaped office, a fire going in the Franklin stove took the chill off the January morning. Its warmth accentuated the combined smells of old leather from the shelves of medical books, the Jonathan apples in the bowl he kept on his desk to reward small patients, and the spicy pine scent of the crackling wood.

At Laurel's entrance, Dr. Woodward looked up with pleasure, but that look slowly faded into alarm as she stammered out her reason for coming.

In a voice that shook slightly Laurel told him she had written the Music Conservatory in Boston for an application, and that Mr. Fordyce had given her names of a few well-known teachers she could contact and now she was determined to go.

He took a long time responding. He turned and gazed out the window for an interminable minute, his hands under his chin, his fingers pressed together forming an arch. When he looked back around at Laurel, his eyes were full of concern.

"Do you have any idea what this will do to your mother?" he asked solemnly.

Laurel felt her heart accelerate frantically. Steeling herself for the attack on her emotions that would follow, Laurel begged, "Papa Lee, I *have* to go. Please don't make it any harder than it's going to be!"

But it had been hard, the hardest thing Laurel had ever done in her life. The last thing she had ever wanted to do was hurt these two dear people.

When all possible arguments against her going failed, the Woodwards retreated into injured silence. Laurel hardened her heart self-protectively, knowing if she did not she would be trapped by pity. Even if she came back, she had to go now. Didn't they see that?

The night before her departure, while packing in her bedroom, she heard Ava's muffled sobs. Overcome with compassion, she almost ran down the hall to her adoptive mother's room. She wished there were some way to comfort her. But she knew the only comfort Ava would accept would be compliance. Knowing she could not give that, Laurel put her face in her hands and wept.

She had meant to bring only happiness to these two who had given her so much. Instead, she was causing them grief and distress.

Morning came at last. A gray, wet mist cloaked the barren trees outside her bedroom window. Her train departed at seven. She knew Ava would not come down to say goodbye, or see her off. Laurel dressed and carried her suitcase and small valise downstairs. She stood in the front hall, straining to hear some movement upstairs that might indicate that either Ava or Dr. Woodward were up, that perhaps they might relent and give her their blessing before she left.

Laurel stood in front of the hall mirror, as she had so many other happier times, to put on her hat. As she did, she saw an envelope propped against the vase. In Dr. Woodward's bold scribble was her name. She picked it up and opened it. Inside were five crisp twenty-dollar bills and two fifty-dollar bills. But there was no note.

Laurel pressed her lips together tightly. The night before, he had kissed her cheek and said "Good night, my dear" as usual. At least there had been no last-minute request that she change her mind. Ava had nursed a migraine in her room all day. It was no more than Laurel expected.

Her heart was heavy with all that was unspoken between them.

A minute later she saw Jenny's reflection in the mirror behind her as she came from the kitchen and stood in the archway of the dining room.

Slowly Laurel turned around. Jenny sniffed and wiped her eyes with a balled handkerchief. Laurel felt a rush of affection for Jenny, who had been her confidante, her comforter, her exhorter, her friend. Spontaneously the hired girl opened her arms and Laurel went into them. She could feel Jenny's shoulders shaking with suppressed sobs.

"I'll be back. Don't cry!" Laurel whispered, patting her.

"Your cab's out front." Jenny sniffled, pushing Laurel away gently. Her plump chin was trembling as she looked at her with red-rimmed eyes and in spite of her brimming tears, nodded approvingly. "I must say, you do look very smart and grown up, Laurel."

Laurel walked over to the foot of the stairway and stood there a minute, looking up. Should she go back upstairs, knock at Mother's door, say all the things that were in her heart to say? She glanced over at Jenny who met the look with a sorrowful shake of her head.

Laurel sighed. Jenny was right. It would just make things worse. She picked up her coat, put it on, straightened the brim of her hat. Walking resolutely to the front door, she blew Jenny a kiss, picked up her bags, and went out into the mist-veiled morning.

She closed the door behind her and its click took on symbolic significance. She knew she was leaving something precious and yet something from which she had to flee, or it might cripple her forever.

At the station, Laurel waited impatiently. Now that she had come this far, she wanted no further delay. She was tense with apprehension, the nervous anticipation of all that lay ahead.

The platform was deserted. Laurel saw no one she knew. No other passengers from Meadowridge seemed to be boarding the early train. Except for the clerk in the office, no one was around.

Finally the train rounded the bend and came to a stop with the screech of steel brakes on the rails, steam hissing from its engine. No one else boarded, and only mailbags were exchanged from one of the boxcars farther down the line.

The whistle blew shrilly. Heart pounding, Laurel moved toward the train. At the entrance to the coach, she turned to take a last look around. She remembered the first time she had seen the rolling Meadowridge hills when she had stepped off the Orphan Train onto this same platform years before. When would she see it all again?

"All aboard, miss," the conductor said, coming up beside her and offering his hand to assist her up the high steps into the train.

Entering the car, she saw it was nearly empty except for a few sleeping passengers. She found an unoccupied seat and put her valise in the rack above, then sat down on the scratchy red upholstery. She was taking off her hat when she heard the chug of the engine and felt the train begin to move. As it lurched forward, Laurel pressed her face against the window, looking back to watch until the yellow station house was out of sight.

14

Boston! She was here at last! Laurel thought to herself peering eagerly out the window of the hired hack. She had followed Mr. Fordyce's instructions to take one from the train station and go straight to the rooming house near the Music Conservatory.

Until now Boston had been only a name in a history book. A name associated with the Boston Tea Party and the poem she had memorized in school about Paul Revere's ride to Lexington to warn of the British coming. Now, here she was in the heart of the great historic city called "the Hub of the Universe" and "the Cradle of Liberty."

As she looked first to the right and then to the left, she was filled with excitement. The city was alive with people and activities, a long distance from Meadowridge's sleepy, small-town atmosphere. It bustled with noise and movement. Here things happened, here anything seemed possible.

Of course, she could not remember much about Boston from the days she had lived here with her mother as a little girl. Children are only aware of their immediate surroundings, and Laurel's memories of that time were centered on her life with Mama in the cozy upstairs flat of Mrs. Campbell's house.

The streets were winding and rather narrow, lined with tall brick buildings of imposing architecture. The heart of the city was a jumble of businesses, banks and churches. Trolleys sped right down the middle of the street, vying for space with wagons loaded with produce and elegant buggies. And right in the center was a huge park where people strolled and children played.

Laurel had given the cab driver the address of the rooming house run by a distant relative of a former college classmate of Mr. Fordyce.

"I'm sure it's not luxurious, but it's clean, comfortable, and conveniently near the Conservatory," he had told her. "The rates are very reasonable and that's important since there are always unforeseen expenses once you're a student, and everything adds up."

Everything he had told her about the boardinghouse was true. What Mr. Fordyce hadn't told Laurel, she soon found out for herself. Mrs. Sombey, the landlady, was insatiably curious. Laurel felt she was being interviewed for a position instead of renting a room, and only managed to escape by saying she had to go right over to the Music Conservatory. Eager to begin her adventure, she covered the few short blocks quickly.

Laurel's heart sounded like a percussion instrument to her as she stood looking up at the Music Conservatory building. Her first instinct was to turn and run. How dare she think herself ready to brave such a prestigious institution, present herself as a candidate for admission as a student here?

Well, she had come this far and she was not going to turn back now. She reminded herself of all that her decision had cost her emotionally, to say nothing of the Woodwards. Fortifying herself with her own version of the Scripture verse that speaks of setting one's "hand to the plow," Laurel started up the stone steps and opened the door into the entrance lobby.

Once inside, a cacophony of sounds greeted her ears. Assorted music floated through the transoms of a dozen practice rooms, merging into an unplanned symphony. Woodwinds, violins, cellos, piano and French horns, all blended in an exciting, if not perfectly harmonic, whole. From somewhere she heard a soprano vocalizing the scales and echoing down the hall came an a cappella chorus of male and female voices.

Proceeding timidly, Laurel followed a sign with an arrow directing her to the Administration Office. In a burst of laughter a group of chattering young people, carrying portfolios and music sheets, came rushing down the main steps. Laurel moved against the wall to let them go by, thinking soon she would be one of them. A thrill of nervous excitement rippled through Laurel. She *was* actually here! Here, where others like herself had come to take that step into serious musical training.

Mr. Fordyce's oft-repeated admonition to all his students rang in her ears as clearly as the sound of a flute being practiced in one of the rooms: "A career in music is one of the most difficult professions in which to achieve success. It takes more than talent and interest. To attain even a minimum, one must be absolutely dedicated, be convinced that music is the most important thing in life."

Laurel felt something tighten within her. Was that *her* feeling about music? To be truthful, she knew it was only means to an end. But she would honestly try not to waste this opportunity. If she were accepted, she would do her best. That she could promise.

An hour later Laurel's initial excitement had drained away. She held in her hand a sheaf of forms that must be completed before she could apply for her first interview for admission to the Conservatory. Telling herself she was just tired from the long train trip and that things would look brighter once she was settled, she went back to the rooming house and unpacked. At least, she was here in Boston, her plans underway. It would all work out, Laurel assured herself. But a week later she encountered a more discouraging setback.

At the Music Conservatory, Laurel was shocked to find that she would have to audition before she could qualify for admission, and the audition list was long. Perhaps she should have applied long before leaving Meadowridge to insure a place on the list for next fall's classes. After applying for an audition, she would be given a date and time to appear before a board of the faculty. Then it was a matter of waiting to find out if she was accepted as a student.

Laurel's heart sank. She had never imagined it would be so difficult. She was sure even Mr. Fordyce was not aware it would take this long. In the meantime, what was she to do?

As Laurel left the Admissions Office, she encountered another young woman checking the bulletin board on which the audition list was posted.

"I know just how you feel," the girl said. "I applied the first time last spring. If you have a coach—preferably, one of the teachers here—your chances are better."

"A coach?"

"Yes, someone to keep you on your mark so that when you do get to audition, you're at peak."

"But, I don't know anyone—" Laurel began, feeling even more discouraged. "How does one find a coach?"

"Well, I was lucky that my violin teacher is a recognized coach. Do you live in Boston?"

"I just came. I mean, I've only been here a short time."

The girl frowned. "You mean you don't know anyone locally who could help you?"

Laurel shook her head.

"Then I'd advise you to check at the office. They should have a list of teachers willing to coach." The girl made a wry face. "It's expensive though. They charge by the hour and they want their money first. You know how it is with musicians, always broke! But it's worth it...at least, I *hope* it's worth it."

With that, the girl picked up her violin case, wished her luck, and left. Laurel stared at the long list of names and scheduled audition dates. It was discouraging but not hopeless, Laurel told herself.

Following the advice the other student had given her, Laurel checked at the office for a list of coaches. Everything the girl had said was confirmed. The list of available coaches was much shorter than the list of hopeful applicants for auditions, the hourly price of lessons daunting.

Downhearted, Laurel left the cavernous hall outside the administration office, pushed open the door to go out of the building, and found it was raining very hard outside.

One thing she had learned since arriving in Boston midwinter was that the weather was as uncertain as her future now looked. Luckily she had taken an umbrella with her when she started out that morning.

Buttoning the top of her coat, she shifted her music portfolio more securely under one arm, then opened her umbrella and, using it as a shield against the driving rain, she started down the steps.

Preoccupied with her new set of problems and trying to hold the umbrella steady against the gusty wind, Laurel did not see the figure hurrying up the Conservatory steps heading directly toward her until their two umbrellas collided with a jarring thrust, halting them both.

"Oh, sorry!" a male voice said just as Laurel exclaimed, "Excuse me!"

As she righted her umbrella, Laurel saw a tall, young man in a caped coat, also carrying a portfolio. For a moment they inspected each other. Then he lowered his umbrella to tip his hat. At that moment the wind whipped the hat out of his hand and sent it whirling down the steps, depositing it in a puddle at the bottom of the steps.

"Oh, my!" cried Laurel in dismay.

But the young man only laughed. As he started after it, he called back over his shoulder, "No problem!"

Laurel hurried to the bottom of the steps, where he was retrieving the hat, shaking the water from its brim.

"I'm dreadfully sorry. I wasn't looking where I was going!" Laurel apologized. "Is it ruined?"

"No harm done," he assured her. "It will dry out." He replaced the top hat at a rakish angle and grinned. "Beastly day, isn't it?"

What an attractive man! Hatless, his thick hair had sprung into a tangle of dark curls, Laurel observed. His eyes, too, were dark and crinkled in the corners, as if he found much to laugh about. How wonderful to take life as it came, she thought, the mishaps as well as the lucky moments.

"Well, I must be off, or I'll be late!" he said and went bounding up the steps and into the building.

Laurel stood there a minute longer, staring after him. His easy laughter reminded her of Toddy, who had always helped her see the bright side. She suddenly missed her old friends more than ever. Both Toddy and Kit had always been there for her when things went wrong. And things seemed to be going very wrong for her right now.

Sighing, she moved on in the direction of her boarding-house. Maybe she should have reported to the Conservatory the minute she arrived, found out about the possible delay of enrolling as a student. But there was something Laurel had wanted to do first.

Finding Mrs. Campbell's house had been a priority. Mama had made Laurel memorize her address in the unlikely event she should ever get lost, and Laurel had never forgotten it. But when she got there, she discovered that the whole row of old frame houses on the street she remembered had been destroyed by fire several years before, and a warehouse had been erected in their place.

The neighborhood itself looked run-down, not at all as she remembered it. Of course, she had only been a child then, and it was possible that nostalgia had distorted the facts.

Although this was a disappointing setback, her hoped-for source of information gone, Laurel was still determined to pursue her search for her real family.

All this had meant countless, time-consuming hours, and long, usually fruitless excursions. The days of February, spent in the musty archives of the courthouse slipped away. Here, Laurel had pored over old records, checking out hunches and hints that led nowhere.

Finally one day in the County Records office, much to her joy, Laurel found the marriage license issued to Lillian

Maynard of Back Bay, and Paul Vestal. Shortly afterward she also found her father's death recorded, though no place of burial was given. And Laurel made the rounds of several cemeteries, looking for his grave, all to no avail.

But the most traumatic trip of all was the one she took out to Greystone Orphanage. She went by trolley, having to transfer twice, then walked up a long steep hill. Her heart was pounding, not so much from the climb, but from remembered apprehension, reliving that awful morning when she and her mama had come there together. It was the last time she had ever seen her mother.

The large stone building stood like a fortress, the chain-link fence surrounding it every bit as prison like and forbidding as she remembered. She had thought she could go in, make some inquiries, and see if she could gain any more information that might help her in her search. But the emotions that assailed her were too overwhelming. Laurel had turned around, practically run back down the hill and caught the next trolley that came along. The experience was too shattering to repeat, and she had never gone back.

Now Laurel suspected she had wasted valuable time that might have been better spent establishing herself as a student at the Music Conservatory. Her name had been placed on a long list of applicants, but her audition date was still weeks away. And she had learned that, in addition to giving a successful audition, one was required to supply three professional recommendations. Even with all that, there was no guarantee of acceptance.

Laurel's spirits were at a new low when she wrote to Mr. Fordyce, explaining her dilemma and asking him not to mention this latest delay to her parents. So far she received no reply.

But what could he do, after all? She had no other professional connections. Where had she sung except at church and school? And no one in the big city of Boston had ever heard of Meadowridge!

15

March blew into Boston like the proverbial lion, blustery days of cold rain which more often than not turned into sleet, coating streets and sidewalks with hazardous ice.

On one particular morning, the wind off the river was knife sharp as Laurel cut across the Common, her head bent, her umbrella slanted against the stinging rain. She had gone to the Conservatory to check the auditions list, in case her name had moved any further up. Of course, it had not. Neither had she heard from Mr. Fordyce yet. Perhaps she should see about getting a coach. That, of course, meant spending money. She had been holding onto her cash reserve, but now she wondered if she should not make that investment. Oh, there was so very much to think about, to decide.

Laurel had never dreamed living on her own in the city would be so expensive. The money Dr. Woodward gave her before she left Meadowridge seemed more than adequate, but everything cost so much more here than she had imagined. She knew she would have to find work soon or—or what? Laurel did not even want to contemplate what might happen when her money ran out.

The thought of returning to her small room at the boardinghouse on this dreary day was too depressing. There she would have nothing to think about but her troubles.

Besides, she was suddenly very hungry, so she headed for the small restaurant on the corner where she could get some lunch.

Pushing open the door of the restaurant, Laurel immediately felt its warmth enfold her. The delicious fragrance of freshly baked bread and the aroma of newly brewed coffee tickled her nostrils with their promise of satisfaction. A bowl of the thick vegetable soup made here daily and a slice of the crusty bread would revive her energy and her spirits.

She gave the pretty, dark-eyed waitress her order, then looked out the window. Laurel always chose a table by the wall near a window if it was available because she liked looking out on the busy street. It made her feel less lonely to watch other people, make up stories about them, where they were going, where they had been.

This was a game she had begun playing since she had moved here. After living in Meadowridge where she knew almost everyone and everyone knew her, it was a strange sensation to be alone in a city the size of Boston, where no one ever called you by name. Homesickness was a battle Laurel fought daily. Although she had only been here a few weeks, they had been the longest weeks of her life.

That's why she liked this cheerful little place with its friendly atmosphere. It was still early for the usual lunch crowd. Laurel enjoyed seeing the easy camaraderie between the staff and the customers, even though she was too shy to be a part of it.

As she sat there staring at passers-by, Laurel wondered what she could do to earn some money to stretch her small amount of cash beyond her rent and bare necessities. The first and most natural thought was to give piano lessons to children. But, in a city filled with aspiring musicians all in need of extra money to pay for their tuition and extra coaching, would there be an excess of them offering music lessons?

Refusing to be defeated before she even tried, Laurel decided she would place an ad in the newspaper. She would state her willingness to give lessons at pupils' own homes, both piano and voice.

All at once, the irony of her situation struck her. How similar to her mother's! Here in this same place, Boston, Lillian Vestal, too, had been forced to find work as a music teacher in order to support herself and her small child.

Laurel's memories of her mother were priceless, kept locked in her heart all these years like precious jewels. Now, she felt free to take them out, handling them delicately, examining, marveling and appreciating the magical childhood she had been given, even in the direst of circumstances.

She cherished the memory of being held in loving arms, of the pretty face above her framed in a cloud of dark hair, of the low, sweet voice singing her to sleep. At Greystone those memories had devastated her and yet, at the same time, sustained her. Then she had pretended their separation was only temporary, that soon they would be reunited. Even after she went on the "Orphan Train" to Meadowridge and was adopted by the Woodwards, her "real" mother had remained a phantom presence in Laurel's life.

Thinking about her, Laurel looked out the restaurant window into the rain-swept street, trying to bring that face into clear focus. But it was another one that superimposed itself on the vague image. It was Ava Woodward's face Laurel saw. Her face as she had last seen it—drawn, white, with alarming purple shadows ringing her eyes. The memory struck her conscience. She could hardly bear to think of Ava or of Dr. Lee. But if she had broken their hearts, her heart was breaking, too.

"Here we are, miss," announced the waitress in a cheerful tone.

Laurel turned away from the window as the steaming bowl of soup was set before her, and Ava's reproachful image disappeared.

Laurel ate, gradually feeling revived and more hopeful. Surely things must get better.

"Will there by anything else, miss?" the waitress asked. "For dessert today, we've got a lovely caramel custard and there's apple cobbler just out of the oven."

Laurel's mouth watered at the suggestion, but until she had a job she had to be careful, so she shook her head regretfully.

"No thanks, this will be plenty," she said, visions of Ella's delectable pies and cakes flashing tauntingly through her mind.

Just at that moment the door of the restaurant burst open and, with a gust of wind and rain, a young man dashed inside, closing his umbrella with a flourish as well as a great showering of water onto nearby patrons.

"Oh, sorry! I do beg your pardon!" he said in a deep, rich voice, bestowing an absolutely irresistible smile upon his victims.

His entrance in so small a place could not go unnoticed and Laurel, with the other customers, turned her head to look at the arrival. To her amazement, it was the same young man she had collided with on the steps of the Conservatory a few weeks before.

Mr. Pasquini, the restaurant owner, came hurrying forward, greeting him with the enthusiasm one reserved for a long-lost relative or visiting celebrity.

"Welcome, welcome! How went the tour?"

"Bravissimo!" replied the young man, divesting himself of his coat and hanging it on the wooden cloak-tree near the door. "It was better than we expected. Sold out crowds every night. But I missed your wonderful pasta...and no one can make bread like Maria!" He kissed the tips of his fingers in an extravagant gesture of praise.

"Well, come along, sit, sit! First some minestrone, yes? Then, some linguini, maybe?"

The young man rubbed his hands together in evident anticipation.

"Fine, fine!" Smiling, he looked around, and quite suddenly he met Laurel's gaze.

Aware that she had been staring, fascinated, she flushed and averted her eyes, looking down into her empty soup bowl. For some reason her heart was giving quick little leaps.

Her first impression of the young man was reaffirmed. He was extremely handsome. This time she noticed his teeth—very white against olive skin. Possibly he was of Italian descent, he seemed so at home here. There were quite a few Italian people living in the vicinity of her boardinghouse and the Music Conservatory.

Mr. Pasquini had mentioned a "tour." Did that mean the young man was a professional musician returning from a successful road tour? That day they had bumped into each other so unceremoniously on the steps of the Conservatory, Laurel had assumed he was a student. Although her curiosity about him was piqued, she had learned nothing more.

Having finished her lunch, she could not continue to occupy a table without ordering something more. Since it was near noon, the restaurant was beginning to fill up as all the "regulars" were arriving.

Reluctantly Laurel put on her coat and, taking her check, went up to the cash register to pay. There she noticed Mr. Pasquini hovering at the table of the young man, engaging him in lively conversation. Laurel got her change and with no further reason to linger, went out again into the stormy March day.

It seemed an odd sort of coincidence to see that young man again, Laurel thought, as she struggled to raise her umbrella. In this big city she rarely saw anyone twice. It was a city of strangers where she, too, was a stranger.

Her decision to advertise for piano pupils in the newspaper now settled, she knew she must get a newspaper to see how such ads were worded and how much it would cost. There was a newsstand on the corner about a block from where she lived. Braving the wind, she decided to walk to save carfare and by the time she reached the newsstand the hem of her coat and dress were quite soaked and she could feel the damp seeping in through her thin leather shoes.

Miserable and shivering, she hurried along the slick sidewalks, being splashed by the horses and carriages that went by the busy thoroughfare. For some reason she thought of her father who had been run over and killed on just such a stormy day in this very same city. Her father was still such a shadowy figure in her life. Laurel had no real memory of him, although she was two when he died. All she had was the picture in the locket.

When she had first come to Boston, Laurel had made the rounds of galleries and art dealers' shops, hoping that by chance, she might someday find one of her father's paintings.

But after she learned Mrs. Campbell's house had been razed by fire, she assumed they had probably all burned in the attic where they were stored.

Chilled to the bone, Laurel reached the boardinghouse and mounted the narrow stairway to her second-floor room. Longingly she thought of Ella's cozy kitchen where she had come in from school on many a rainy day to find hot chocolate or spicy tea waiting, and homemade cookies, still warm from the oven.

Quickly she got out of her wet things and curled up at the end of the bed, spreading the newspaper out in front of her. As she turned over the rain-dampened pages, going toward the classified section, something caught her eye, an item in the society news.

"Mrs. Bennett Maynard will be the hostess of a soiree next Tuesday evening to benefit the Symphony—"

The name seemed to leap at Laurel from the page. She noted the address—in the most exclusive residential section of the city. The brief article gave only the most discreet information: "Symphony supporters, only those holding season tickets, are invited to call between the hours of four and six. The Symphony's Music Director will speak on the selection of next year's program and possible guest artists to be featured in future performances."

Could *this* Mrs. Maynard be her grandmother?

Laurel determined that the next day she would take the trolley out to that part of town and look for the house matching the address given. Maybe, at last she would see the place that belonged to her mother's family, the house where Lillian Maynard had grown up and left to marry Paul Vestal.

Laurel was pretty well convinced now that her young parents had eloped. Why else the estrangement? A girl from Boston's Back Bay, with breeding and background, marry a penniless artist? Why, such an alliance would have been considered unthinkable in an earlier day. Yet the young couple was so madly in love, Laurel romanticized, that perhaps they knew there was no other way to be together. And in running away they had irrevocably broken all their ties. Yes, she would go and see. Maybe even tomorrow, Laurel decided.

But the next morning she awakened with a sore throat and fever and the next two weeks she was laid up with a heavy cold and laryngitis. When she finally made it shakily out of bed and went over to the Conservatory, she found to her despair that she had missed her scheduled audition date.

16

Laurel's disappointment over the missed audition was combined with unexpected relief. Maybe she really wasn't ready. It would be far worse to try and fail. After all, she could not be blamed for having a bad cold. But, if, unprepared and uncoached, she was rejected, that would be her fault.

What she had heard about the auditions was confusing. She did not know how the decision was made. Did the board base a student's acceptance on the difficulty of the piece or on the clarity of vocalization, on poise and stage presence or on one's presentation with integrity to the composer? Laurel had no idea.

Perhaps missing her audition was all for the best. Before the next auditions were scheduled, she would have time to find a coach to help her. But a coach cost money. That meant she must find a way to supplement her income.

Ever since her arrival in Boston, Laurel had received a small check from Dr. Woodward at the first of each month. Because of the circumstances under which she had left Meadowridge, however, she felt guilty using his money and so far she had resisted cashing any of the checks. But unless she found some way of earning some soon, she would be forced to do so.

To Laurel's delight the ad she had placed in the newspaper brought immediate response from many of Boston's socially active mothers. With their children industriously occupied at the piano at home, these ladies were free to be about their visiting or shopping or having tea with friends, a very convenient arrangement.

Laurel's first pleasure in receiving so many responses to her ad was soon diminished somewhat when she realized that teaching music in her pupils' homes meant hours of her time spent on trolleys, trams and on foot to reach the various addresses.

Neither had she imagined teaching to be so tedious. Listening over and over to clumsy little fingers stumbling over scales, or distorting such simple tunes as "Welcome, Sweet Springtime" sometimes made her feel like screaming. But her determination to be independent was more important than the boredom and weariness. It was a price she was more than willing to pay. Saving money for a coach meant practicing many small economies.

Her first resolution was that of eating only one full meal a day. It took some ingenuity for her to smuggle fruit and crackers, concealed in her music bag, past her eagle-eyed landlady, and make tea on a small spirit-burner bought in a second-hand store. For her one meal Laurel continued to frequent the restaurant on the corner, a few blocks from her rooming house.

After a short spring Laurel discovered Boston's summers were as extreme as its winters. Hot and humid days were followed by breathless nights when the air barely stirred the curtains of her bedroom windows. To make matters worse, several of her pupils canceled their lessons to vacation with their families at second homes on the coast of Maine or Cape Cod, where Boston's affluent spent their summers.

The unaccustomed heat and the prospect of the loss of extra income upon which she had come to rely were depressing, and Laurel struggled not to succumb to feelings of loneliness and self-doubt. She had to keep reminding herself of her main purpose in coming east.

With less traveling and teaching to take up her day, Laurel had more time to think about contacting Mrs. Bennett Maynard whom she had come to believe was her grandmother. She often took out that newspaper article and reread it. If this *really* was her Mama's mother, how did she go about approaching her? Since the woman must be advancing in years by now, it wouldn't do to show up on her doorstep, announcing herself. The encounter must be arranged with careful thought and tact.

One Saturday, Laurel decided to go out to the address given and see for herself what might have been her mother's childhood home. She took a trolley to the end of the line, then at the direction of the conductor, walked another few blocks. She strolled along quiet streets, lined with impressive homes set well back from the boulevard over which arched tall, shady elms.

Laurel walked slowly, looking for the house number in the clipping she held in her hand. Then, all at once she saw it! Displayed discreetly on a polished brass plaque set among climbing ivy in the post of a brick wall was the house number she was looking for.

Number 1573 was a stately pink brick of Federal architecture, its many windows covered with black louvered shutters. Curved double steps with ornamental black iron railings led up to a paneled front door flanked by tubs of espaliered trees.

There was no sign of life, not on the street itself, nor in the house. No movement at all behind those shuttered windows. Did Mama's family go to Maine or Martha's Vineyard, in the summer?

For a long time, Laurel stood looking at the house, then slowly turned and retraced her steps. She was hardly conscious when she left the luxurious serenity of that part of town inhabited by the city's wealthy and pretigious citizens and boarded the trolley to return to the workaday life of the rest of the population of Boston.

Laurel got off at her usual stop, still distracted by her pilgrimage, walked over two blocks to the little restaurant where she took her evening meal. Entering, she was glad to see her favorite small table in the corner vacant. Seating herself, she picked up the menu, looking at it without actually reading it.

Her thoughts were filled with the significance of her afternoon excursion. The grandeur of those mansions, guarded by ornamental iron fences or well-trimmed boxwood hedges, their manicured terraces and shuttered windows had cast a strange spell on Laurel. She tried to imagine the beautiful girl of her locket, with her laughing eyes and flowing dark hair, her dainty figure and exquisite clothes, who had lived in one of them and who had become her mother.

Now she began to see Mrs. Campbell's flat in all its shabbiness through the eyes of one once accustomed to luxury and comfort. She saw the shiny black of her mother's one coat with its worn fur collar and cuffs. The rare treats of cake or fruit to celebrate small occasions must have been eked out of a meager income. Yet Laurel had never heard her mother complain—not even when her living conditions brought about the illness that caused her death!

Laurel's thoughts were interrupted by a rich, male voice. "I recommend the lasagna tonight."

Laurel started and looked up at the waiter. She fumbled with the menu as she recognized him as no other than the young man with whom she had collided on one of her first times at the Conservatory. The very same one whom she had seen later right here in this restaurant.

Surprised speechless, Laurel simply stared at him. His smile widened and he said, "To answer your question. Yes, I am a student at the Conservatory, and I work here part-time to support myself *and* my voice coach!"

Laurel felt her face flame with embarrassment.

"Oh, well, I—" she stammered. "I'm sorry, I didn't—"

"Don't apologize, please! We all—at least most of us—have to work while we attend the Conservatory. It goes with the territory, as they say. Surely there is no such thing as an artist of any kind who doesn't have to struggle, is there? If so, I haven't heard of one, much less met one." His dark eyes sparkled with amusement. "Now, what about you? I mean, what would you like for dinner?"

Flustered, Laurel looked down at the menu, none of the selections making sense. It was usually her pocketbook that dictated her order anyway.

"May I make a suggestion?" he continued. "I've personally sampled the minestrone soup and found it to be, as usual, delicious. But then, perhaps, it's too warm an evening for soup. Maybe something lighter. The lasagna is delicious and, with a fresh green salad, perfect." He paused. "Even though we both know we have encountered each other before, may I introduce myself formally?" He gave a small bow. "I'm Gene Michela."

It would have seemed rude not to do the same. "I'm Laurel Vestal."

"Am I correct in assuming you are also a student at the Conservatory?"

"Well, not exactly. At least, not yet. That is, I haven't been accepted. I missed my audition and—I found out I should have a coach— So I've been teaching, giving piano lessons. I had ten pupils but now most of them are away for the summer and I—" Suddenly she halted, blushing. Why on earth was she talking so much, telling all this to a—a *waiter?*

But he was regarding her sympathetically, nodding with understanding.

"Oh, dear!" Laurel exclaimed. "I don't know what I'm saying, I mean, I don't know what I want to eat—" she broke off. Laurel closed the menu and handed it back to him.

"I'm sorry. I didn't mean to rush you. Would you like some time to decide? And while you're deciding may I bring you a glass of vino, perhaps?"

Laurel shook her head vigorously.

"No? Then a refreshing glass of lemonade instead?" His smile was disarming.

"Yes, that would be lovely," Laurel murmured, still blushing, wondering why she was making such a fool of herself.

She comforted herself with the thought that she did not have to come here again—that is, unless she wanted to eat! Actually there was no other eating establishment close by where she could get such delicious, inexpensive food. Oh, dear! Then why had she chattered on like that? Was it because she seldom had a chance to talk to adults, only the children she taught? She tried to avoid her garrulous and inquisitive landlady except when the rent money was due, and she had not really made any acquaintances among the other roomers who all seemed much older and not especially friendly. This Gene was very nice. Besides, he was a student at the Conservatory, which gave them something in common. No, it wasn't as if he were a total stranger.

By the time Gene was back, Laurel had managed to recover some of her composure.

"I've consulted with Mario, the chef—" He wisked a tall frosty glass off the tray and set it in front of her with a flourish— "and he has suggested the perfect selection for a summer evening—a combination plate of prosciutto, chilled asparagus, fresh tomatoes, cucumbers, cheese, bread. May I bring it out for you?"

Dazzled by all this attention, Laurel could only nod again, hoping that the price of a "chef's choice" would not make it necessary to eat crackers and oranges in her room for the rest of the week. She watched him as he waited on other diners. He handled each one with the same affability as he had with her.

The attractively presented plate proved tasty and delightful as well as filling. As Laurel was finishing, Gene appeared with a chilled dish of pistachio ice cream, garnished with a thin chocolate wafer.

"Compliments of the chef!" He set it down on a small round lace paper doily.

Laurel started to protest. But Gene, glancing over his shoulder, laid his forefinger against his mouth. Laurel followed the direction of his glance and saw Mr. Pasquini standing at the cash register, nodding and smiling at them.

There was nothing for Laurel to do but eat the ice cream with relish. However, it left her with a dilemma. Did she leave a tip? From their brief conversation Gene must know she was on as slim a budget as he. Would he be insulted if she tipped him, after all his tactful kindness in serving her? Or would he naturally expect one? And what amount? While she struggled with this, Gene reappeared with her check on a small tray, then stood behind her chair as she rose, thanked him, and moved over to the cash register.

He waited at a discreet distance while she paid, then escorted her to the restaurant door, which he opened for her with a little bow. "It was a pleasure serving you, Miss Vestal. I hope we meet again."

It was not until Laurel was back on the sidewalk and had counted her change, that she realized neither the lemonade nor the pistachio ice cream was included on her bill.

Laurel was halfway down the block when she heard her name called.

"Miss Vestal! Miss Vestal, wait, please!"

She turned to see Gene Michela sprinting after her. Had she forgotten something? she wondered, stopping and turning around.

He reached her, flushed and panting. "Miss Vestal, beg pardon, if this seems too personal but—but do you attend church?"

Startled, she nodded, then quickly amended. "Yes, I do, but I haven't since coming to Boston. I mean, I don't belong to one—"

Gene shook his head vigorously and held up a protesting hand.

"What I meant was—" and he held out a small card. "I'm singing at a wedding at this church next Saturday afternoon. It would be perfectly all right if you slipped in the side door and sat at the back." He smiled shyly. "I would like for you to be there...if you have no other plans."

Laurel looked down at the card he had handed her and read the scribbled name of the church, not knowing whether to laugh at this bizarre invitation. But Gene seemed so eager, so anxious, so appealing that her heart melted.

"Well, I'll try—" she began rather hesitantly.

"Oh, yes, *do* try." He smiled. "I'll sing as if you were there anyway!" Then with a wave of his hand, he backed away a few steps. "I've got to get back to the restaurant. I've diners waiting for dessert. Goodbye, Miss Vestal!" And he turned and ran back down the street.

What an astonishing young man, Laurel thought, amused. In spite of herself, in the days that followed, she found her thoughts turning more and more to Gene Michela. He certainly was impetuous and unconventional. Handsome, too, and terribly charming. Too good-looking, too assured, too charming?

Whatever conclusion she drew from this impulsive act, on the following Saturday, a little before three, Laurel found herself entering the side door of an imposing stone building.

The church, one of the oldest in Boston, was tall and stately, set back from the street, surrounded by an iron fence. It was completely different from the small, white frame Community church in Meadowridge, and yet there was something strangely familiar about it, Laurel thought as she opened the door at the side entrance and slipped inside.

The interior was dim and quiet, for it was a good forty-five minutes before the scheduled ceremony. Down the long aisle to the front of the church, about ten pews on either side were bowed with white satin ribbon, obviously reserved for the wedding guests.

Laurel felt a bit like an intruder, but finding a seat in the rear, shielded by one of the stone pillars, she sat down. She occupied herself by gazing around at the arched stained-glass windows. Sunlight slanted through, giving the colors only a pale radiance. Each window depicted a symbolic event in Jesus' ministry—the Feeding of the Multitude, the Healing of Jairus's Little Daughter, the Good Shepherd and—Laurel drew in her breath as her glance moved to the next window—Jesus with the Little Children.

From out of her past a pale memory struggled to break through. She had seen that window before. Could *this* be the same church she had attended with her mother?

Laurel felt excitement tremble through her.

Here in Boston everything seemed like a giant link connecting her to her past, to her childhood. Maybe everything was leading her back to her roots, to her family, to her identity.

The deep tones of the organ reverberated through the empty church and with a start, Laurel realized that the organist had arrived and was testing his chords for the wedding music.

It seemed strange to Laurel to be attending the wedding of strangers. Yet a few minutes before the bride entered, when Laurel heard Gene's rich tenor voice filling the whole building with its glorious sound, she knew it had been worth overcoming her timidity to come.

Listening to Gene sing, the beautiful words of "O Perfect Love," Laurel felt little prickles along her scalp and down her spine. Truly *his* was a God-given gift and she thrilled to its splendor. There was more to that young man than she had thought. Much more! One could not sing with such a voice and not be aware of its Creator.

Tears welled up in Laurel's eyes. Coming into this church, seeing the window, hearing Gene's voice had been an emotional experience. Before the wedding ceremony was over, Laurel rose and left quietly. She was too deeply moved to chance meeting anyone, especially Gene Michela.

In spite of herself, Gene was much in her thoughts over the next few days. But she carefully avoided Pasquini's Restaurant for a few days, not wanting to appear to be encouraging special attention from Mr. Pasquini's part-time waiter!

Still most of her thoughts that spring were centered on Mrs. Maynard. Week after week Laurel was drawn back to the street where the Maynard mansion stood. She would sit on one of the benches in the shady park across from it, staring at its impressive facade. If this *was* her mother's family home and Mrs. Bennett Maynard *was* her grandmother, would she not have wondered all these years what had happened to her own daughter? Surely, if Laurel presented herself, wouldn't she be happy to see her granddaughter at last? Or did she still harbor the old resentments? Had she cut off her emotions concerning the daughter as completely as she had cut off communication with her?

April passed into May, May into June, and each time Laurel took the long trolley ride, there was no sign of any activity around the house. Apparently the occupants were away.

During her "visits" Laurel pondered how she would go about contacting Mrs. Maynard upon her return to Boston in the fall. She had no desire to shock her. No, first she would send flowers and a note, saying she had reason to believe they were related and asking if she might call.

Of course, there was no way of knowing what Mrs. Maynard's response would be. What if, after the flowers and note, there was no answer? If not, Laurel decided, she would follow up with another note and, armed with a copy of her parents' marriage certificate, and her birth certificate would simply go to the house and ask to see Mrs. Maynard. Of course, it was very possible the woman would refuse to see her.

Then what would Laurel do? She could only guess that the old woman's curiosity would be aroused. Certainly Laurel's resemblance to her mother would not go unnoticed or overlooked. Then she would show her the pictures in the heart-shaped locket. After that, surely there could be no mistaking who she was.

Still, Laurel knew she should prepare herself not to get that far. Could she be satisfied that at least she *had* found her parents' graves, proof that they were married, that she was their daughter and their rightful heir?

The rest of the story, the lost fragments of her early life and background she had pieced together. Her parents—the wealthy debutante and the struggling artist—had fallen in love and risked everything to be together. How they had met was still a mystery. But Laurel knew that until her father's death, her mother had been happy with her choice. Why, after Paul Vestal's death, the young widow had never been reconciled with her family, Laurel did not know. Surely there had been no reason why their daughter had lived on the edge of poverty when the Maynards were perfectly capable of providing for her. The cold hard truth might be they had never forgiven Lillian for what she did.

As Laurel sat contemplating the austere, shuttered house across the street, she asked herself if it were possible, after all these years, for the needless bridge of bitterness to be crossed? And what did *she* herself actually want from all this? She searched her heart honestly. She wanted nothing. Nothing, more than the Maynards' acknowledgment that she existed.

With summer coming, Laurel had more immediate worries. Her pupils' long vacation would deplete her small savings and soon it would be time to register at the Conservatory to audition for acceptance as a student for the coming year. Even with all her scrimping, Laurel had not been able to return Dr. Woodward's checks.

Knowing that the new schedules for classes, auditions, and list of coaches would be posted before the opening of school, Laurel went to the Conservatory one sultry day in June.

In the Administration Office she spent a great deal of time filling out forms. She hesitated a long time over the question: "Who will be responsible for your tuition, to be paid before the start of each semester?" Laurel did not want to write in Dr. Woodward's name and yet, if she wrote her own, the next questions "What is your employer's name. The source of your income?" would have to be answered honestly.

Would she have to wait another six months before applying to become a student, when she was assured of having enough money to pay for it? And what about finding and paying a coach?

Laurel sighed and shoved all the papers into the portfolio in which she carried her music, and decided to think everything over before completing her application. Explaining briefly to the woman behind the reception desk that she would be back later, Laurel started out of the office. As she did so, she bumped into someone just entering. Her portfolio fell from her grasp onto the floor, sending her music sheets flying every which way. As she stooped to retrieve them, so did the newcomer and, in their combined attempt to gather up the papers, their two heads banged together.

For a moment Laurel was stunned. Dizzily she looked up and saw the other person holding his forehead, a pained expression on his face. As they stared at each other, his look of discomfort changed to one of amused recognition and with mock indignation he demanded, "Miss Vestal! Don't you ever look where you're going?"

"Oh, my goodness! Mr. Michela!" she exclaimed.

In her confusion Laurel bent down again in an attempt to pick up the scattered music and so did Gene. They bumped heads a second time. This time they both collapsed into fits of helpless laughter. As their laughter rose, surrounding them in a sensation of idiotic delight, their eyes met and a remarkable thing happened.

Why, it's like something straight out of a romantic novel, Laurel mused.

Of all the people in Boston, of all the possible students at the Music Conservatory, of all the days of all the weeks of the summer, why had her path crossed so often and so unexpectedly with that of this charming young man?

As this question flashed through Laurel's mind, all her girlish dreams of falling in love came into focus. She had imagined how it would be to meet the right person, had hoped that person was Dan, had mourned when it was over between them, had nurtured a secret hope that someday, in some strange new place, she would meet someone else. Now he was here. And it was not a dream!

17

It seemed natural for them to leave the administration office together, walk through the lobby and out the front door of the building into the blinding sunlight.

"It's really good to see you again, Miss Vestal," Gene said, "or should I say *bump* into you again?"

"I'm not always so clumsy, believe it or not!" Laurel laughed as she paused at the stone balustrade and set down her portfolio so she could tighten the ties. Without raising her eyes from the task, she said shyly, "I heard you sing."

"*Did* you?" Gene sounded pleased. "I so hoped you would."

"You *are* very good, you know." Laurel continued checking the ribbons of her portfolio to see if it was closed securely. "You really have to sing, don't you?"

"It's my life!" he replied.

"It shows," she said seriously, at last looking up at him.

Gene's dark eyes sparkled with enthusiasm as he suggested they sit down on the steps in the sunshine. Suddenly they seemed to have so much to say to each other, about music, about themselves. Gene told Laurel he had just returned from a month's tour with a choral group.

"It gave me a taste of what a concert singer's life would be like. On the road two weeks at a time, trying to sleep sitting up on a day coach, staying at run-down hotels, terrible food!" He laughed. "For an Italian boy the latter has to be the worst of all! Speaking of food, I'm hungry. How about you?"

It was past noon, and Laurel realized she had had nothing since breakfast.

"Come on." Gene stood up and held out his hand to her. "Let's go get a hot dog."

At the concession stand a ruddy-faced man in a limp chef's cap and apron, took their order. He forked sizzling weiners into long buns, then slathered them with mustard.

"My treat!" Gene held up his hand warningly when Laurel opened her purse. "Not that the menu is very elegant, but just wait until I have my debut at La Scala! Then we'll really celebrate!"

Buoyed by his playful optimism—that he would actually one day perform at the famous Italian opera house and she would be with him on that occasion—Laurel held their hot dogs while Gene bought two bottles of soda. Then they found a bench and sat down to eat.

As they continued to chat, Gene mentioned names of composers and famous singers as if they were close friends. Laurel found all this fascinating even though, by comparison, her own knowledge was very limited.

After they finished eating, they walked along the flower-bordered path down to the lake. Gene took off his jacket and spread it on the grass for Laurel to sit on. They went on talking as though they had known each other forever, yet in their conversation was the excitement of discovery.

The afternoon was slipping away when suddenly Gene scrambled to his feet.

"Laurel, I'm sorry, but I didn't realize it was getting so late. I can't take you home, or I won't make it to work on time!" he exclaimed. "It's not such a great job, but I need the money."

"Then maybe I'll see you later at the restaurant."

"Oh, this is a second job—just temporary. I'm, filling in for the regular who's sick." He seemed embarrassed. "I could make up something that would impress you, but the truth is I'm a night watchman at a warehouse."

"Oh, Gene, you don't have to try to impress *me!*"

"Of course you're right. My father always says all work is noble as long as it's honest."

"I believe that, too," she declared, although it was the first time she had thought much about the nobility of all work.

"But I did intend to take you home." Gene frowned. "I don't even know where you live. And I don't know how to get in touch with you—to see you again!"

"I can give you directions. You take the Number 10 trolley and—"

"Sorry, Laurel, but I don't have time to listen." Gene was already moving away, walking backwards as he spoke, "Could you meet me instead? Here? Tomorrow afternoon?"

"Yes!" she called. "Tomorrow afternoon! Right here." She nodded her head frantically as Gene, with a final wave of his hand, turned and made a run for it.

Laurel pressed both her hands to her mouth, giggling. How wild this was! And yet how happy she felt! She had not been this happy in weeks and weeks. She picked up her music portfolio and strolled in the other direction to the trolley stop.

She was still smiling to herself when she got off at her street and turned slowly toward the rooming house. Yes, this had been her happiest day since coming to Boston.

The next afternoon Gene was in the park waiting for her when Laurel arrived. Her heart gave a funny little flip-flop when she saw him pacing impatiently up and down. When he saw her coming, he broke into a big smile and rushed up to her, both hands extended.

"Laurel! I'm so glad to see you! I was afraid you might not come. To tell you the truth, I thought I'd dreamed the whole thing! The crazy way we kept bumping into each other— literally!" He threw back his head and laughed, a rich, full laugh. "And then last night, I kept kicking myself that I hadn't ditched the stupid job and seen you right to your doorstep. I thought maybe you'd think I was...I don't know...rude, irresponsible or something, and change your mind about meeting me."

Laurel shook her head. "Of course not! I told you I understood. Really!"

"Sure?"

"Positive." She laughed at his incredulity. "I wouldn't have come if I hadn't wanted to, if I thought you were...well, any of those things."

"Truthfully?"

"Yes, truthfully." She smiled. "Why don't you believe me?"

"I do." He squeezed her hands he was still holding. "Let's always promise to tell each other the truth, no matter what," he said earnestly.

Solemnly Laurel nodded, thinking how strange it was that it *didn't* seem strange at all for Gene to assume that there would be an "always" for them.

The rest of the afternoon flew by again. They never seemed to run out of things to talk about, to share and laugh about together. Gene had a wonderful sense of humor and was a raconteur. Everything that had ever happened to him seemed, in the telling, to be humorous, exciting, or an unexpected adventure. Laurel could not remember ever enjoying being with anyone so much.

By the end of the second day they had spent together, Laurel knew a great deal more about Gene. He had grown up in a small New England coastal town, part of a large, close Italian family with grandparents, many uncles and aunts and cousins. Although most of his relatives were fishermen, they were proud and supportive of Gene's pursuit of a singing career. Gene had won a scholarship to the Conservatory and had come to Boston right out of high school. But in spite of his paid tuition, he still had to work at odd jobs to support himself, pay for his coach, his rent. The Pasquinis, old family friends, were also kind, feeding him and giving him a job at the restaurant.

"Do you have a coach, Laurel?" he asked.

"No, not yet. I suppose I'll have to get one." She hesitated. "I—I really haven't done much about preparing for my audition either. Actually, hearing all you've done, all you've sacrificed to continue at the Conservatory makes me wonder about my own—well, my seriousness of purpose."

Gene looked puzzled. "I don't know if I understand what you mean—"

To her surprise, Laurel found herself confiding the roundabout way she had come to Boston. Her story just seemed to pour out, and before she knew it, she had told Gene the real reason for her move.

"I never really thought seriously about studying voice. But when my high school music teacher brought it up, it seemed like a good excuse to do what I'd been secretly planning all these years."

"And have you found out about your real family yet?" Gene asked.

Laurel told him what she knew.

"It's my grandmother, or the person I believe is probably my grandmother, that I still have yet to see." To be putting all this into words made Laurel realize she had never told anyone else in the world. And yet it seemed the most natural thing in the world for her to be telling Gene.

"I'm a little afraid, I think," she added.

"Would you like me to go with you when the time comes?"

Laurel felt the sweet surprise of his concern, the sincerity of his offer as if he were already a part of her life, and it touched her deeply.

As the days went by, they saw each other nearly every day, spending the afternoons together in the park. Within a short time Laurel realized being with Gene was the high point of her day—what she looked forward to each morning when she woke up, what she thought about the last thing before going to sleep at night. She was happier than she had ever been, happier than she had ever imagined possible.

Gene was everything Laurel wasn't—outgoing, optimistic, enthusiastic. His personality complemented hers in every way. Gene's drive and ambition, his willingness to work hard to achieve his goals influenced Laurel to make a decision. Feeling she should cut her old ties of dependency to the Woodwards, she determined to get a job that would give her a *regular* income, not accept any more of Dr. Lee's checks. Only when she could afford it herself would she find a voice coach and apply to the Conservatory. It was the only fair thing to do, the only right choice.

Often when they talked together, sharing their thoughts, the deep things of their hearts, Gene would say, "Everything happens for a purpose, Laurel, nothing by chance! Like our meeting the way we did. There's a reason for it all. God has a plan for each of our lives. Nothing is an accident, although it may seem like one. I've always believed that. He gave me my voice so that I could not only make my living, but so I could contribute something to other people's lives, too. I'm never happier than when I'm singing. That's how I know I'm fulfilling His purpose for me."

Although not completely convinced herself, something that happened shortly after she made her decision to look for a job made Laurel a believer. Taking what she thought was a shortcut back from the park to her rooming house one afternoon, she passed a Music Store with a sign in the window HELP WANTED, PIANIST.

On impulse, Laurel entered the store and found they needed someone to play the sheet music they sold to customers. When she sat down and sight read several pieces for the owner, Mr. Jacobsen, he hired her on the spot.

She could not wait to tell Gene the good news the next day. After congratulating her heartily, he told her he had some news of his own.

"Actually both good news and bad news."

"What do you mean?"

"Don't look so worried. The good news is I have a new job, a singing job! Just in the chorus, but at least I'll be singing. Gilbert and Sullivan. *The Pirates of Penzance.*"

"But that's wonderful, Gene!"

"Wait till you hear the rest." He held up his hand. "The bad news is that it's at a summer theater at the Cape."

"Cape Cod?"

"Yes, I'll be away for the rest of the summer—two weeks rehearsal, two weeks for the run of the show, maybe a chance to try out for the next one."

Laurel felt her heart sink.

"I hate the idea of being away from you," Gene said. "But, I can hardly turn down a chance like this."

"Of course, you can't," Laurel replied. "Anyway, it's only for a few weeks."

"That's right. The time will pass quickly."

"Yes, it will," Laurel agreed, not believing a word of it.

"I have to be there first thing Monday, so I'll leave Sunday on the morning train. But we've got today and Friday," Gene reminded her. "We'll go to the outdoor concert at Greenwood Gate Park on Saturday. We'll take a picnic supper and have a glorious last evening together. How does that sound?"

"Perfect." Laurel, already dreading the long separation, tried to sound happy.

Saturday afternoon Laurel dressed as carefully as if she were going to a ball. She chose one of the outfits Mrs. Danby had made for her the summer before and ironed it carefully. A short Spanish-style jacket of crisp, yellow cotton edged with trapunto embroidery, worn over a lawn blouse with delicate yellow featherstitching on the collar and cuffs, and a flared skirt belted with a wide green cumberbund. With it she would wear a basket-weave straw picture hat.

To avoid the probing curiosity of her landlady, Mrs. Sombey, Laurel tried to slip down the stairs to wait for Gene outside. There he might also escape running the gamut of the ill-concealed envy and criticism of the other roomers who gathered in the parlor whenever there was the slightest chance of anyone having a "gentleman caller."

She was unsuccessful. As if on cue, Mrs. Sombey appeared in the lower hall just as Laurel was coming down. Her ferretlike face creased in a saccharine smile as she remarked with exaggerated sweetness, "Oh, my, Miss Vestal, how nice you look. I expect you're going out again with your young man? I *do* like to see my young ladies enjoy themselves," she purred. "And what a lovely ensemble! It looks very—shall we say, 'tray sheek'? Cost a pretty penny, I'd imagine," she simpered. "Or did you make it yourself, you clever little thing?"

When Laurel had first taken a room at Mrs. Sombey's, she had managed to say as little as possible about herself except that she planned to attend the Conservatory. But every month when she went to pay her rent, she was subjected to what she came to think of as an "inquisition." She was sure Mrs. Sombey investigated her mail, certain that she examined the postmark and return address on every letter.

Laurel had thought of moving, but this place was clean, quiet and convenient to the Conservatory, and since Mrs. Sombey only rented to women, Laurel had felt comfortably secure staying there. Except for the annoyance of Mrs. Sombey's insatiable curiosity, Laurel had been reasonably content.

It was just since Gene had come into her life that the landlady's interest in her comings and goings had begun to irritate Laurel.

Still it was not in her to be rude, so trying not to be as abrupt as she felt inclined, Laurel murmured a thank-you and proceeded to the front door. Before she reached it, quick as a cat, Mrs. Sombey was there, parting the curtains on the glass partition and peeking out.

"Well, here comes your fellow now, Miss Vestal. And he's...yes, well, I do declare, he's carrying a hamper. Does that mean you're going on a picnic? Well, my, my, how very—"

Laurel gritted her teeth, and not waiting for more, slipped out and hurried down the steps to meet Gene just as he came up to the house.

As usual, Laurel caught her breath at her first sight of him—the dark, windblown hair, eyes dancing with anticipation, smile lighting up his whole face.

When he saw Laurel, he stopped and put one hand on his breast.

"What a vision you are!" He said dramatically. "I should have brought you flowers!"

"Flowers?"

"Yes, of course! Flowers are the accepted gifts of courtship, aren't they? Instead, I brought you food!" Gene held up the basket. "Thanks to Mrs. Pasquini, who packed us a lunch you won't believe. I kept telling her there would only be two of us, but Benigna, who is a realist as well as a romantic, assured me that music stimulates the appetite."

"Come on." Laurel slipped her hand through his arm. "Let's be on our way before Mrs. Sombey thinks of some excuse to come out here and interrogate you!"

At the park, they roamed over the acres of rolling hills dotted with lovely old trees above the semicircular amphitheater where the orchestra would assemble later for the program. After a few minor debates as to the ideal spot, they agreed upon one. Gene opened the large wicker basket, took out a small rug and spread it out on the grass, tossing two pillows upon it. Next came a blue checkered tablecloth, plates, napkins and silverware. Then Gene began setting out a platter of thinly sliced ham, squares of cheese, small containers of black olives, cherry tomatoes, pasta salad, sliced cucumbers.

Laurel's eyes widened.

"My goodness, you were right. That's quite a lot of food!" she exclaimed, thinking of the limited diet she had been living on for the past weeks.

Gene was busy slicing a twisted loaf of crusty bread on a small wooden cutting board. "Well, you don't have to eat if you're not hungry," he teased.

"Oh, I'll force myself!" Laurel retorted, dipping a tiny tomato into a fluted bowl of dilled mayonnaise and popping it daintily into her mouth. She was getting better at the kind of bantering repartee Gene delighted in.

There was a container of chilled lemonade and another of strong Italian coffee to have with an array of fresh fruit as well as lemon tarts.

They ate with relish, talking and laughing, completely relaxed and happy in each other's company. Laurel tried not to think that the next day Gene would be going away for weeks. Every time the thought threatened to spoil things, she determinedly pushed it to the back of her mind. There would be time enough to miss him when he was gone. Now, it was enough to enjoy him.

"What will you have for dessert, madam?" Gene held up a bunch of glistening purple grapes in one hand, a perfectly rounded blushed peach in the palm of his other.

"Oh, I don't know—I'm so full but—why don't we share a peach?"

"No sooner said than done," Gene said, deftly cutting it through, removing the stone, and handing half the fruit to Laurel.

"Oh, it's so juicy!" she said, as she bit into the luscious slice. The juice ran down her chin and she tried to capture it with her tongue.

Whipping out his immaculate white handkerchief, Gene leaned forward and gently wiped her mouth and chin. He was so close Laurel could see the spiky thick eyelashes shadowing his brown eyes.

Then Gene said huskily, "Oh, Laurel, I can't remember what my life was like before I met you. Now I can't imagine it without you!"

She caught her breath. "I know. I feel the same way," she whispered, knowing it was true.

Then his firm, cool mouth was upon hers in a tender, lingering kiss.

As the kiss ended, Gene murmured, "I hear bells ringing, music playing—"

"I do, too," sighed Laurel. "It must be some kind of spell."

"It's called being in love," Gene said softly and kissed her again. Then he chuckled. "Truthfully, I think it's the orchestra tuning up their instruments. The concert will begin as soon as it's dark. We'll want to go down closer," he told her, getting to his feet.

Gathering up the remnants of their picnic, they repacked the hamper, picked up their pillows and blanket, and moved down the hillside.

The sky had turned a hyacinth blue and a faint evening star had appeared by the time they were settled. Soon the snowy-haired conductor marched on stage to the podium, rapped his baton and the first haunting strains of Vivaldi's *Four Seasons* rose into the evening air.

Gene was humming the melody from the finale as he and Laurel walked through the park and toward the trolley stop at the close of the concert. It had been a glorious evening and now Laurel felt melancholy, knowing it was coming to an end, that tomorrow Gene would be gone.

They were quiet on the ride back to the rooming house, holding hands, gazing into each other's eyes with longing as the awareness of the parting deepened. When they got off, they walked the last block very slowly, until they could delay the inevitable no longer.

At the corner, Gene drew Laurel away from the circle of light shining from the lamppost into the shadows and took her into his arms. His cheek rested against hers, his lips moved along her temple, and she heard him murmur her name.

She closed her eyes and felt him kiss her eyelids, the top of her nose. Then he kissed her mouth and it was sweet and thrilling beyond anything she had ever imagined.

"Oh, Laurel, I love you so," Gene whispered, then sighed, "but I have nothing to offer you. I'm as poor as the proverbial church mouse. Even with my scholarship, and taking any odd job I can find, I barely make enough to pay board and room, to say nothing of my coach. It isn't fair when I have no idea how or when—"

Laurel placed her fingers on his lips, shutting off the flow of words. Then she put her arms around his neck, bringing his head down against her cheek, wanting to comfort and reassure him. Most of her life Laurel had been sheltered, cherished, protected. Now she was experiencing a new emotion—a desire to give. A strange new tenderness filled her heart so full she could hardly speak.

"It doesn't matter. I'm poor, too, Gene. But we'll both make it. We'll help each other. I feel it, I *know* it. It will take time, but we're young, and we have all the time in the world!"

18

The week after Gene left for Cape Cod seemed endless. On her half-day off, Laurel took the trolley out to the secluded neighborhood where the Maynards lived. To her surprise she saw a gardener clipping the thick boxwood hedge and a man on a ladder washing the outside of the downstairs windows. Preparations were obviously underway for the return of the owners.

The sight of all this activity both excited and unnerved Laurel. After a sleepless night, she decided it was now or never. If she was ever to find out if Mrs. Maynard was her grandmother, she should not delay any longer.

Laurel had learned from Ava, whose garden was her hobby and delight, about the legendary language of flowers. Together, they had enjoyed making up arrangements to convey secret messages as was the custom in old-fashioned times. So when Laurel went to the florist shop to order the flowers she wanted to send Mrs. Maynard along with her note, she recalled some of those meanings. Whether or not the lady would understand their significance did not matter. It gave Laurel a feeling of reaching out in a special way.

After much deliberation she chose a mixture of gladioli and white peonies, softened with maidenhair fern, symbolizing strength, sincerity and discretion. Laurel placed the note she had labored over composing to be delivered with the box of flowers.

> Dear Mrs. Maynard,
>
> I am writing because I have reason to believe we are related. I am the daughter of Lillian Maynard and Paul Vestal, born in this city September 1884. If you would be so gracious as to receive me, I would like very much to call upon you so that we may discuss this possibility further.
>
> Sincerely,
> Laurel Elaine Vestal

She used the double name on her birth certificate, which, she had been told, was given her in honor of her two grandmothers, though Laurel was not sure which of the two was Mrs. Maynard's name.

Underneath her signature, she had put the address of Mrs. Sombey's rooming house.

A week dragged by and every day Laurel hurried home from work hopefully. But no message came from Mrs. Maynard. She did, however, have one or two letters from Gene, all hastily written, telling of the thrills of rehearsals, the stimulation of being with other singers, and assuring her of his love. These she read over and over.

By the end of the week, Laurel resolved that she would not be put off nor would she wait any longer. There had been enough time for Mrs. Maynard to recover from any shock the note had given her and to consider the possibility that the writer *could* be her granddaughter. Now Laurel was determined to appear in person, and unless she was refused admission, she would confront her with the fact of her existence.

As she dressed for this momentous meeting, to bolster her courage, Laurel kept repeating to herself a Scripture verse she had memorized: "Ye shall know the truth, and the truth shall make you free."

It was as important for her as it was for Mrs. Maynard to at last confront the past, acknowledge it, face the truth then—Well, however Mrs. Maynard chose to react, she, *Laurel*, would be free, no longer haunted by the possibility that her mother had never told her parents of her baby's birth. Maybe the estrangement had been too bitter, the parting too harsh, the pain too deep. Laurel remembered asking her mother once about the grandmothers for whom she was named and if she would ever meet them. Now she recalled the reply. "Someday... when all is forgiven."

Forgiven? Did Mama mean that she must forgive her parents, or that she needed *their* forgiveness?

At last, dressed in a dove-gray linen suit, a dainty white blouse, and wearing a polished straw hat ringed with white daisies, Laurel was ready. For a minute she stood thoughtfully, fingering the chain of her gold locket. Then she carefully pulled on white cotton gloves, picked up her handbag containing the copies of her parents' marriage certificate and her birth certificate, and went downstairs and out of the house. She walked resolutely to the corner of the street where she took the trolley out to the quiet neighborhood, to one household whose serenity she was about to shatter.

The butler answering the door was tall, his demeanor haughty. He held out a small silver tray for a calling card which Laurel could not supply.

"I have no card," she replied with what she hoped was suitable poise. Inwardly she was trembling. "But I think Mrs. Maynard will see me."

The man looked coldly suspicious. "Then whom shall I say is calling?"

"Miss Laurel Vestal."

"One moment, miss." He started to close the door, but Laurel slipped inside before he could leave her standing on the porch.

He gave her a withering look, turned sharply on his heel, and disappeared down the hall. Laurel clenched her hands together nervously. She strained her ears and thought she heard the murmur of voices coming from beyond the closed door at the end of the hallway.

Left alone, she looked around her. The foyer was oval in shape with recessed alcoves in which were placed marble busts. The parquet floor was partially covered by a runner of dark red carpeting extending from the doorway and up a broad staircase with wide polished banisters, leading to the second floor. At the curve of the balcony was a tall window with stained-glass panels through which a milky sun shed pale light into the otherwise shadowy interior.

It seemed an age since she had been left there, stiffly waiting, until the door at the end of the hall clicked, and she saw the figure of the butler returning. His expression had settled into what seemed to be permanent disdain.

"Although this is *not* Mrs. Maynard's regular 'At Home' day, she *will* see you," he addressed her in an icy tone. "Come this way, please."

Laurel followed, though the impulse to flee was strong. She fortified herself by remembering why she had come and why it was necessary to see it through.

At the end of the hall, the butler opened a door and announced, "Miss Vestal, madam," then stepped back for Laurel to pass into the room.

Her first impression was of overpowering ostentation—thick Oriental carpets, heavy carved furniture, gold-framed portraits on paneled walls. Then she saw that there were three people instead of the one she expected.

As she advanced a few steps, a man got to his feet and moved slowly behind the chair of one of the women. All of them were regarding her with curiosity and something else. Obviously she was an unwelcome intrusion, her ill-timed appearance interrupting a pleasant summer afternoon.

But at least *one* of them *should* have been warned of her coming. Laurel looked from one lady to the other. Which one was Mrs. Maynard? Which one was, possibly, her grandmother?

Her hands tightened on the tortoise-shell rim of her handbag. It somehow gave her strength, knowing that inside was the proof that she belonged here as much as any of them—or at least, that she had the right to come. "Ye shall know the truth and the truth shall make you free" flashed through her mind again, giving her added courage.

"Mrs. Maynard?" She spoke in a low, steady voice.

There was silence. The man made a slight impatient movement, as if shifting from one foot to the other. There was a moment's hesitation before one of the women spoke, "*I* am Mrs. Maynard."

Immediately Laurel focused her attention on the speaker.

Mrs. Maynard was thin, everything about her finely honed—the aristocratic nose, the unrelenting line of her mouth, the erect posture, the proud way she held her head, all bespeaking self-discipline and a certain inflexibility. She was a splendid-looking woman, who might have once been beautiful, Laurel thought, with her features, her beautifully coiffed iron-gray hair.

But as they regarded her, Laurel wondered what secrets were hidden behind those pale-blue eyes.

Then Mrs. Maynard spoke again. "This is my cousin, Mrs. Farraday, and her son, Ormand."

Only the man acknowledged the introduction with a nod. Mrs. Farraday merely stared at Laurel with wide-eyed annoyance.

"You wished to see me?" Mrs. Maynard's voice was cool with a distinct Boston accent.

"I am Laurel Vestal, Mrs. Maynard. You may recall I wrote to you a few weeks ago, asking if I might call?"

It was an effort for Laurel to keep her voice from shaking. She sensed she was on dangerous ground and that Mrs. Maynard was not going to make it easy for her. Nor did Laurel want to embarass her in front of the two who were eyeing her visitor with undisguised suspicion.

When Mrs. Maynard did not reply, Laurel had to push further. "You *did* receive my note, did you not?"

Mrs. Maynard inclined her head slightly, but did not speak.

Laurel could sense the hostility mounting in the room and she rushed on hurriedly, before her courage failed altogether. "I have been waiting for an answer. When I did not hear from you, I decided to come in person."

There was a sharp intake of breath from the other woman, who straightened up in the tapestried armchair in which she was sitting. "The very idea!"

Laurel froze momentarily. No doubt she had committed some terrible social blunder. In this echelon of society, if someone did not reply to one's request to call perhaps it meant they did not wish to receive that person. But it was too late to worry about that now. She had come for some kind of answer, and she would stay until she got it. Unconsciously Laurel squared her slender shoulders.

Mrs. Maynard laid a restraining hand on her cousin's arm. "Gertrude, please, I'll handle this." Then waving one ringed hand toward a straight chair near the door, she asked, "Would you care to sit down, Miss Vestal?"

Still standing, Laurel suggested, "Perhaps I could come back at a more convenient time?"

At this suggestion, Laurel thought she saw a flicker of relief in the otherwise rigidly composed expression. Mrs. Maynard rose from her chair. "Yes, perhaps that would be best. We are due at a meeting of the Symphony Society very shortly and as Chairwoman I cannot be late."

"Would you care to give me another day and time?" Laurel persisted, unwilling to let this opportunity pass without some definite commitment.

Mrs. Farraday made a clucking sound to indicate her irritation.

Ignoring her, Mrs. Maynard moved toward the door, extending one arm toward Laurel as though ushering her out. "I will send word when that can be arranged."

Having come this far, Laurel was not to be put off. As the older woman's hand rested on the doorknob, Laurel drew out the envelope containing the extra copies of her parents' marriage certificate and her birth certificate and handed it to her. "In the meantime, Mrs. Maynard, perhaps you would find these interesting."

The thin, controlled mouth seemed to quiver slightly, and there was a second's pause before she held out her hand to take the envelope.

When the drawing room closed behind her, Laurel heard Mrs. Farraday declare, "The nerve of the girl!"

And in an entirely different context, Laurel agreed. It had taken nerve—all the nerve she could muster.

Outside again and in the warm summer afternoon, Laurel realized she had been holding her breath. She let out a long sigh. After the dimness of the shuttered interior of the Maynards' house, the bright sunshine was dizzying. She leaned against the brick wall for a moment to gain her equilibrium.

Well, it was done! She had carried out her part. The rest was up to Mrs. Maynard.

19

Laurel was thrilled to see a letter from Gene waiting for her on the hall table of the rooming house when she returned. She had never needed something to lift her spirits more. Gene's letters always did that. He wrote easily almost as if he were talking to her. From his descriptions of some of the people in the operetta cast, funny incidents that happened in rehearsals or even during the performances, Laurel could get a picture of backstage life.

She ran upstairs to her room, tore open the envelope, and devoured every word. But this letter was different from most of the others she had received from him. It was short and contained an unexpected message.

"I am making a quick trip to Boston. Since the theater is 'dark' Sunday and Monday, I'll leave right after the performance on Saturday night and be there some time Sunday. I have a surprise for you. I can't wait to show you."

Anticipating Gene's coming brightened what proved to be a depressing week for Laurel. Mrs. Maynard's promise to get in touch with her and arrange another meeting had not been kept. As each day passed without word, Laurel's disappointment turned into a kind of indifferent resentment. Their brief encounter had not endeared Mrs. Maynard to Laurel.

Maybe it was her own fault. Her expectations had been high. Laurel had imagined that once her grandmother saw her, recognized the unmistakable resemblance to her own daughter, there would be a joyous reunion. But it had been anything but joyous.

In spite of her initial cool reception by Mrs. Maynard, however, Laurel persisted in her desire to be acknowledged for who she was. Now it was much more than a validation of her identity; it had become a vindication of her parents' cause. Mrs. Maynard should take the responsibility for the unhappiness she had caused her daughter, for the way that courageous young woman had been forced to live—and die. She should face up to the fact that, because of her own arrogance and unforgiveness, her granddaughter had been placed in an orphanage to be reared by strangers.

Though in her heart Laurel knew these were less than ideal motives, she held to them stubbornly.

The night before Gene's arrival, Laurel was restless. He had been away for so long—nearly three weeks now. What if he had found someone else among the pretty actresses and singers in the cast? If not, there were always the summer people, many of whom entertained at lavish parties in their homes during the run of the play. Gene was so attractive, so talented. He was sure to be showered with flattering attention. The more she thought of it and of the mysterious note announcing his visit, the more Laurel imagined the worst. This, combined with the depressing circumstances of her heritage, sent her into an unaccustomed decline and she paced the floor, sleepless.

Toward morning, her gaze fell on the little slip of paper on which she had copied the Scripture verse she had memorized before her encounter with Mrs. Maynard: "Ye shall know the truth and the truth shall set you free." Well, she would soon know the truth about Gene, too, and about the love he had declared in his letters. Breathing a hopeful prayer, she fell into a deep sleep and awakened refreshed.

Rising hurriedly, she put on a pink linen that was one of Gene's favorites, then posted herself at her bedroom window to watch for him. While she waited she patted her hair distractedly, gave the bow on her sash an extra fluff, and fiddled with the frilled ruffle outlining her bodice.

He had mentioned a "surprise" in his letter. Just what kind of surprise? But she shook off the persistent dark thoughts. If she truly loved Gene, she would just have to trust him until he had a chance to speak for himself.

Spotting him coming down the street, Laurel flew down the stairs, slid the lock noiselessly back, and slipped out the front door. She was waiting for him at the top of the porch steps when he came through the gate, a square, brown paper-wrapped parcel under his arm.

One foot on the first step, he looked up at her, and her heart melted. He was regarding her with eyes filled with love, as if she were the only woman in the world. His mouth, parted in a smile, was as sensitive and sweet as she remembered.

"Hello, Laurel," he greeted her softly as she came down the steps toward him. "I've missed you, more than I can tell you, more than I thought possible."

Such a wave of relief swept over her that she was giddy. "I've missed you, too, Gene," she confessed breathlessly.

"Then no one stole you away from me while I was away?"

The question was posed with such guilelessness that Laurel had to look deep into his eyes to be sure she had not asked it herself! Overcome by the irony of his question, Laurel began to laugh and soon Gene was joining her in a hearty duet, laughing uproariously.

"I see someone peeking through the curtains of an upstairs window," he said at last, when the last ripple of merriment had subsided. "Come on! Or I'll give Mrs. Sombey the first shock of the day by kissing you right here in broad daylight!" He grabbed her hand.

"Better not!" Laurel protested in mock alarm. "Or I'll be thrown out bag and baggage!" Then, in her best imitation of her landlady's voice, she said, "I run a respectable establishment, I'll have you know!"

And suddenly Laurel thought of Toddy. How like something her old friend would have said! Yet the laughter and the jesting had come spontaneously, bursting into bloom in the fertile soil of Gene's love, his approval. She felt so free!

"Let's walk over to the park where we can find some privacy and you can welcome me back properly," he suggested with a mischievous gleam in his eye.

After Gene's first suggestion had been carried out as promptly and satisfactorily as both had hoped, Gene put the package in Laurel's lap.

"Go ahead, open it," he directed, watching her eagerly.

"What is it, Gene? You shouldn't really be spending your money on presents for me." Laurel's fingers tugged at the knotted string.

"Stop fussing," he ordered "Open it!"

She laughed and pulled at a knot. Impatient, Gene whipped out his pocket knife and cut the string. "There!" he said and Laurel tore away the paper.

For a minute she simply stared. Then she turned to Gene. She opened her mouth as if to say something, but no words came. Looking down at the contents of the package, she slowly put both hands on either side of the narrow wood frame and lifted the little painting from the box.

The canvas was small, perhaps twelve by fourteen inches, the style Impressionistic. It might have even been a preliminary study for a larger, more detailed painting to be done later. This was done on the spot in daylight, without special attention to props or artificial lighting.

The subject was two figures—a woman and a sunbonneted child on the beach. The woman's face was shadowed by a wide-brimmed straw hat and the parasol she was holding; one graceful arm was extended to help the little girl make a mound in the sand. It was simple and heartfelt and absolutely delightful.

As Laurel gazed at it, a dozen emotions assailed her, prompted by the vaguest memories. In the lower right-hand corner were the tiny initials PV/86.

"Turn it over, Laurel," Gene said softly.

On the back, written with casual brush strokes, were the words—"August 1886, Lil and Baby L. at C.C."

Eyes brimming with tears, Laurel looked at Gene. "Where did you find this?" she asked in a barely audible voice.

Gene's face was animated as he replied, "In a little art gallery at Martha's Vineyard. I was just wandering around one afternoon when we didn't have a rehearsal. Actually, I was looking for some kind of little gift to bring you when I spotted this in the window."

"Oh, Gene, I'm sure this is one of my father's paintings!" Laurel exclaimed. "Do you suppose there are more?"

"I intend to go back and take a good look," Gene said seriously. "The new owner has stacks of unframed canvases in the storage shed behind the shop that he hasn't had time to sort through. He says this is one of the finest examples of Impressionist paintings he's seen."

"The style is very like the painting that hung over our piano when I was a little girl. The same sky and sand and feeling of lightness and a certain...serenity, I guess you'd call it." Laurel sighed, returning the painting to the box. "When I asked Mama why Papa painted so many seascapes, she told me that every summer a group of their artist friends would rent a house at the beach and take turns living there. It was something they looked forward to all year—a break from the humdrum routine of the rest of the year."

"Then we may be on to something. When I told this fellow, Ed Williams, that I knew the daughter of the artist, he told me he would get in touch with you when he had had a chance to evaluate all the paintings. He seemed to think your father's work may be quite valuable."

"Gene, how can I ever thank you?" Laurel asked as she began rewrapping the canvas.

"Seeing you so happy is all the thanks I need." Gene took the package from her and retied the strings tightly. "In fact," he said, giving her a long look, "I want to spend the rest of my life making you happy."

Laurel held her breath, not daring to speak. It was a moment of knowing for them, a moment of decision, of choice and commitment.

"I love you, Laurel. I think I knew it from the first day. Do you...would you...can we be—" he faltered.

"Yes, yes, yes!" Laurel answered every question in a breathless rush. "I want that too. But how—"

"We'll work it out, my darling—" Gene drew Laurel close, kissing her with a new tenderness. When it ended, they searched each other's eyes as if in confirmation of the sweet promises they had just made.

Gene jumped to his feet, tossed his hat up in the air and caught it by its brim as it came sailing down again. "I'm the happiest guy in Boston!" He grinned.

"Oh, Gene!" Laurel sighed happily.

"I'm also the hungriest! Come on, let's go get some breakfast!" He took her by the hand, tucking the wrapped picture under his arm and together they left the park.

Late that afternoon Laurel went to the train station to see him off again.

"No more of these partings," Gene told her. "I have enough money now to last me through the next semester at the Conservatory. I'm not going to take any more jobs that mean going out of town or on tour. That is unless—"

He halted, took both her hands and held them tightly.

"I want us to be married, Laurel, as soon as possible. I don't know how we'd manage or how—"

Caught up in his declaration, Laurel ventured, "I have my job and Mr. Jacobsen talked about giving me a raise."

Gene frowned. "But your own plans to start in at the Conservatory—"

She took a deep breath, casting about for words to express what was only now becoming clear to her. "Gene, I realize that I don't have the same urgent desire as you to pursue a career in music. That drive, that belief that my voice is my priority is just…missing. I love music, I enjoy playing and singing, but I don't think it could be the focus of my whole life. Not the way it must be to succeed. I just don't think I want it that much—" She paused, hoping he would understand. "Or maybe it's just that I've found I want something else more."

Just then the train whistle blew and the conductor was announcing, "All aboard!"

Pulling Laurel to him for a final kiss, Gene shouted above the noise of hissing steam and grind of gears. "I must go darling! See you in two weeks!" And he was gone, swinging up the steps and disappearing through the door of the car.

20

Two days later, Laurel propped the painting against the mirror of the bureau, then stood back to study it. She felt a deep thrill and pride knowing that Paul Vestal, the father she could not remember, was the artist.

She had recognized it as his right away. But she had not been prepared for her emotional response. Laurel ran her fingers lightly over the canvas, feeling the rough brush strokes. Looking at it, she could almost recall the warmth of the sand under the small bare feet of the chubby baby her father had captured in the painting. Strangely, she seemed to be experiencing again what could only be the vaguest kind of memory imprinted somewhere in the innermost part of her brain—the salty scent of the sea breeze bending the tall dune grass behind the figure of her mother, the clarity of the light, the cloudless blue of the windswept sky, the sun-washed roof of the weathered shingled cottage in the distance.

The fact that this painting now belonged to her, and that there might be more to come, sent a thrill shivering through Laurel.

The amazing coincidence of how Gene had found it made Laurel's head spin. She ticked off all the unrelated events that had brought this painting into her possession—What if she had not bumped into Gene on the steps of the Conservatory? What if she had never gone to Pasquini's to eat? What if they had not again collided in the administration office that day? What if? It could go on and on. Gene had not come into her life by chance, Laurel was sure of that now.

She thought of him now—back on the Cape—and the power of their love cast out all fear. He would be appearing in the next presentation of the summer light-opera series, with time to check again with the gallery owner to see if there were any more of Paul Vestal's paintings available. After the run of the second operetta, Gene planned to go to New Bedford for a short visit with his parents before returning to Boston. He was earning good money, and Laurel was proud he had been selected from the chorus of *The Pirates of Penzance* for the other show. She missed him, of course, but their time would come. Meanwhile, she was content to wait for him.

All this came back to Laurel as she stood looking at the painting. It all flowed together somehow—her coming to Boston to trace her heritage, her early plans for the Conservatory. Then she had met Gene and everything had changed. Her world circled around Gene now, everything else seemed less important. Finding a way to be together was all that mattered.

The next day when Laurel came in from work, Mrs. Sombey, twittering with excitement, was waiting for her in the downstairs hall.

"This came for you today, Miss Vestal," she said, her curiously light eyes protruding with greedy interest. "A handsome carriage drove up and stopped right out front and a driver in a fine, dark blue coat come right up to the door and asked if this was where Miss Laurel Vestal lived! When I said it was, he handed me this." Mrs. Sombey's hand was quivering as she handed Laurel a creamy vellum envelope with a red wax seal.

The handwriting on the envelope was in a fine Spencerian script, and Laurel knew instinctively it was from Mrs.

Maynard. Not about to open it in front of Mrs. Sombey, Laurel simply thanked her and started up the steps.

Mrs. Sombey's face crumpled with disappointment. Abandoning her usual put-on airs of prissy refinement, she blurted out, "Ain't you going to see who it's from?"

"Of course," Laurel replied over her shoulder, continuing to mount the stairway. She felt no obligation to satisfy her landlady's curiosity.

Ripping open the envelope, she noted the formal salutation:

> My dear Miss Vestal,
>   I have cleared my social calendar and will be at home Monday next from 3 to 5 in the afternoon if you would care to call. I shall send my carriage and driver if your reply is affirmative.
>
>   Cordially,
>   Elaine Maynard

Elaine! So *she* was the Elaine Laurel had been named for! She folded the note and replaced it in the envelope. Now that the long-awaited invitation had come, strangely enough it did not give her the satisfaction she had expected.

That evening she penned a reply as brief and impersonal as Mrs. Maynard's had been. She agreed to the meeting, but declined the offer of the carriage, stating simply that she would arrive on her own between three and four.

Coincidentally, the next day's mail brought a letter from Ava, the first Laurel had received from her since leaving Meadowridge.

> My darling girl,
>   This letter should have been written months ago, but I was too preoccupied with my own sorrow. My main and inexcusably late reason for writing now is to assure you of my love and to ask your forgiveness if my actions caused you any needless guilt.

It has taken me a long time to face myself and to come to terms with the unhappiness I have caused those I hold most dear in the world.

For ten years you have given me enormous joy and never a moment's distress. You filled our home and my heart with more happiness than I ever thought I would know again. For this I am truly grateful.

Lee brought you home from the Orphan Train that day with the hope that you might take the place of our little daughter who died. Let me say you did not do that. Instead, you created your own special place and we could not love you more if you had been born to us.

Lee showed me the check you returned with your sweet note, saying you had been dependent on us long enough, and since you had left home without our approval, you did not feel it was right to continue accepting support.

How can I put this so you will understand? I was wrong not to let you go with a glad heart, allow you your freedom and your chance to be independent. It is your Papa Lee's and my pleasure to help you financially or any other way we can while you pursue your voice studies. We *are* your family and we want to support you wherever you are, whatever you choose to do.

I regret that my own sorrow at parting with you kept me from giving you my full blessing. I was like the Chinese princess in one of your favorite stories that I used to read to you, do you remember? She clipped the wings of her beloved songbird so he could not fly away and leave her. What happened, I'm sure you remember. The bird stopped singing! It is *I* who forgot!

So, now as you read this, I hope you realize that I, who love you so dearly, release you from the bonds I tied around you. Love should make us strong, capable and free to do whatever God's gifts enable us to do.

Be free, my darling, to be whatever you can be, desire to be, want to be. I believe, whatever makes you happy

will bring happiness to others. I pray God's special
blessing on you now and always.

Your loving mother,
Ava Woodward

Laurel read the letter over two or three times, savoring
each sentence, almost memorizing each word. Her heart
swelled with love and tenderness for the one who had written it. For this to have arrived the day before she was to meet
with Elaine Maynard seemed remarkable. It gave Laurel
the inner confidence she needed to face whatever the next
day held for her. Regardless of her grandmother's attitude,
whether she accepted Laurel or denied her did not seem
quite as important, quite as necessary to her now.

Again Laurel dressed with exquisite care for her interview with Elaine Maynard. A navy blue silk with embroidered collars and cuffs, a matching straw sailor hat with
crisp grosgrain ribbons, white gloves and dark blue
handbag.

Her appearance and departure in the early afternoon
caused more inquisitive glances and raised eyebrows on the
part of Mrs. Sombey, who did everything but ask Laurel
why she had not left for work that morning and where she
was going now and if she could afford to lose a day's pay.

"When you wasn't down at the usual time, I almost come
up to see if you was sick, Miss Vestal," the landlady said, her
eyes traveling impertinently up and down Laurel, taking in
every detail of her costume. "I know you always leave
promptly at eight to catch the eight-fifteen trolley so you
won't be late for work, so I couldn't help wonderin'—" Her
voice trailed off, begging an answer.

Laurel smiled complacently and shook her head. "No, I'm
quite well, thank you, Mrs. Sombey," she replied calmly and
went out the door.

Her landlady would have been even more curious if she
had seen that just around the corner, Laurel hailed a hack-

ney cab and rode out to the Maynard residence in extravagant style.

It was precisely two minutes before three when Laurel mounted the steps and lifted the polished knocker of the front door. She turned and looked down the street at all the other fine houses lining this sedate enclave of the wealthy. There was a subdued splendor in the atmosphere, an understated but clearly defined exclusivity about the Square, setting it apart from the workaday world Laurel knew.

Standing there, waiting for the door to be opened, Laurel could not help wondering how different her own life would have been if Lillian Maynard had not been banished by falling in love with—"the wrong man."

"Good afternoon, miss," came a quiet voice from behind her, and Laurel recognized the same aloof butler of her last visit. This time he did not regard her coolly or skeptically, but stepped back immediately and opened the door wider.

At least she was expected, she thought, stepping inside.

"Mrs. Maynard will receive you in the parlor, if you will come this way."

The butler's manner was pointedly different, she observed, not condescending, but deferential. He opened the double door leading into a smaller room than the one into which she had been shown the last time. It was beautifully if less formally furnished, with a more intimate atmosphere, enhanced by the afternoon sunlight shining in. There was a piano in one corner, graceful chairs covered in needlepoint, bookcases flanking the fireplace, a hearth now hidden by a Japanese fan-screen.

"Good afternoon, Miss Vestal." Mrs. Maynard's thin, high voice greeted Laurel from where she sat in one of the high-backed chairs. She did not rise to offer her hand or in any way to make a gesture of welcome. She merely waved toward the oppposite chair. "Do be seated."

Laurel tensed. All the confidence she had built up began to evaporate under Elaine Maynard's ice-blue gaze.

Mrs. Maynard seemed to be waiting for Laurel to speak first. Laurel, acting on some inner reserve, waited for Mrs. Maynard to open the meeting she had called.

Silence stretched between them. Mrs. Maynard's eyebrows lifted slightly. Then she spoke. "Well, Miss Vestal, I understand from your note you have some reason to believe we are related."

"Yes, Mrs. Maynard. I assume you have had time to look at the papers I left with you. They are copies of a marriage certificate and birth certificate — proof that my mother was Lillian Maynard and that *I* am your granddaughter." Laurel's voice was surprisingly steady.

Mrs. Maynard waved a dismissive hand. "My dear young lady, certainly you must know papers can be forged! That is not proof of anything! What do you hope to gain by such a claim?"

Laurel was shocked. She thought she had prepared herself for any of several possible reactions from Mrs. Maynard, but not this cynical sarcasm.

"I have the originals—" she protested. She started to open her handbag, then remembered she had left them locked in her bureau drawer. She stared at Mrs. Maynard incredulously.

"Did you really think I would accept this? Someone walking in here off the street making all sorts of assertions? Do you take me for some kind of gullible, sentimental fool? Naturally, I would seek legal advice. I have my lawyer checking your shoddy copies. He was very skeptical of the whole matter, but promised to pursue it. But I *am* curious — what *did* you hope to gain by coming here and making this — this announcement?"

Laurel's slowly rising indignation at these insinuating accusations was suddenly overcome by a curious calm. She stood up.

"I did not come here for any reason other than to satisfy my own conviction that you are my grandmother, my mother, Lillian Maynard's mother. I thought you would be glad, yes, *happy* to meet me! Perhaps, you never knew you even had a grandchild. Did you not ever wonder? Did you not care what had happened to your daughter after she left this house? After you drove her out?" Laurel's voice rose in spite of her effort to maintain her composure. "I look around me at this place, with all its luxury, all its obvious wealth—and I think of the shabby little flat where my darling mama and I lived, where she struggled to support us both by giving music lessons! And I wonder if you ever gave us a thought all those years! Did you know she died in the charity ward of a State Tuberculosis hospital? That I was put in an orphanage? And later on, an Orphan Train, to be adopted by strangers?"

At Laurel's words Mrs. Maynard visibly paled. Her mouth twitched and her bony hands gripped the chair arms until the knuckles were white and the huge sapphire ring flashed fiery lights.

"Orphanage?" she repeated.

"For two years I lived at Greystone Orphanage."

"Greystone?" The woman's jaw dropped slightly.

"Yes, Greystone...only a few miles from here, Mrs. Maynard." Laurel drew herself up, breathing hard, thinking of the cold stone buildings, the yards of bare floored corridors, the high curtainless windows.

"Mama never said a word against you or my grandfather, never explained why you had become estranged from her. I suppose she thought I was too young. Perhaps if she had lived, she might have told me the truth—that you could not find it in your cold hearts to accept the young man she loved. Could not accept the fact that their love was so strong she had to choose between him and her parents." Laurel's voice trembled and she shook her head. "I'm sorry for you, no, I *pity* you! You missed so much. You missed knowing a beautiful young man, a talented artist, who may still become famous! Worse still, you lost your only daughter—"

"Enough!" Mrs. Maynard put one shaky, blue-veined hand up, shielding her face. Her voice, sharp and keen as a knife, cut through the breathless words.

Laurel's whole body quivered with the strong emotions coursing through her. "Don't worry. I'm going now, Mrs. Maynard. If I upset you, I apologize, but I'm not sorry I came or that I told you the truth. Because it *is* the truth—all of it. You asked me what I hoped to gain by coming. Actually nothing. I don't need anything you have, Mrs. Maynard. I have the tenderest memories of my real parents who loved each other and me dearly. I have loving adoptive parents, and I'm engaged to marry a wonderful young man. I don't need you. I don't want anything from you. Good day, Mrs. Maynard."

Still trembling, Laurel cast a pitying look at the old woman who was leaning to one side of the massive chair, her face covered with both ringed hands. Laurel moved toward the door. Her hand was on the knob when the imperious voice rang out once more.

"Wait! Stop!" A pause, then, "Please, Miss Vestal—Laurel, come back."

Struck by the change in the tone, the hint of a plea in the request, Laurel dropped her hand and, turning slowly around, faced Mrs. Maynard. The older woman's face looked deathly pale, almost gray, the eyes haunted.

"You are right. Lillian *was* my daughter. All these years I've tried to forget that—forget her, but—the minute you walked in that day, I knew it was impossible. You look so much like her—But it was a great shock. A terrible shock." Her hand shook as she put it up to her forehead where a vein in her temple pulsed. "I must admit my cousins, who were visiting that day, as you may recall, tried to convince me you were some sort of an impostor, a fortune hunter, urged me to have my lawyer check you out." She paused and toyed with the double strand of amethysts and pearls about her neck. "Of course, I followed their suggestion because...well because I hoped it was not true." She closed her eyes wearily. "You see, you must understand—it's been so long ago—"

Laurel did not reply, but listened.

"Lillian was our only child, born late in our marriage. My husband—my late husband Bennett—adored her. She was literally the 'apple of his eye.' A beautiful, happy child, a great joy to us—She was so gifted, so bright—Bennett took her everywhere with him....We dressed her like a doll in French-made clothes...she was...exquisite—" Mrs. Maynard's voice broke.

After a moment she began to speak again.

"That's why it was so hard to accept...what happened. She was only eighteen...her whole life ahead of her—We were planning her debut, a magnificent ball, to introduce her to Boston society. It was all arranged when she told us she was in love—" Mrs. Maynard's voice grew strained, husky. "Bennett flew into a rage, demanded to know how she had met this fellow. We had given her every advantage—piano lessons, voice and art lessons...it was there she met...Paul Vestal." The name was uttered with contempt. "When Bennett discovered he was her art teacher, penniless, with no background, no prospects, he decided he could not let her throw her life away. He forbade Lillian to see him—immediately made plans to take her away to Europe, hoping the distance between them would make her forget him, cool the romance. Of course, in retrospect, it was the worst thing he could have done. Lillian was sweet-natured but also strong-willed. And the result was on the eve of our sailing date, she ran away—eloped."

The room was still, absolutely quiet. Laurel waited for Mrs. Maynard to continue.

"Bennett never got over it. It broke his heart, hastened his death, of that I'm positive. And he never forgave her. He died only a year and a half later. He had forbidden me to answer the letter she wrote us after she was married, forbade me to contact her in any way." Mrs. Maynard sighed heavily. "I obeyed. What else could I do? I had always obeyed him. We had been married nearly thirty years, and that is how I was brought up to believe, that a wife obeys her husband."

Laurel said nothing and eventually Mrs. Maynard went on.

"Bennett suffered through a long agonizing illness. He lingered for months and I was with him almost every minute. When the doctors told me the end was near, I thought about Lillian, wanted to get in touch with her, bring her home to say goodbye to her father. But Bennett was adamant. When I suggested trying to find her, he got very upset, said we had no daughter. And he made me promise I would not ever attempt to contact her—even after his death."

Hearing this sequence of events, all the missing pieces she had wondered about for so long, Laurel was overcome. As she saw tears fill Mrs. Maynard's eyes and roll down the wrinkled cheeks, her heart wrenched. All this unnecessary suffering and sorrow. What a terrible, twisted thing so-called love could become.

"When last week my lawyer came to me, authenticating all the same things you said...that my daughter had died in a tuberculosis sanatorium, that there was a child—" Mrs. Maynard bit her trembling lip, dabbed her eyes with a dainty, lace-trimmed handkerchief. "But it was just now when you—you mentioned Greystone Orphanage that something inside me—to think I've been on the Fund-raising Board of Greystone Orphanage for years—and not to know my own grandchild was there, only a few miles away all the time—"

At this, Mrs. Maynard bowed her head and put both hands up to her face. Under the lacy shawl the old woman's shoulders shook convulsively.

All at once, Laurel was moved by compassion and in another minute she was on her knees on the floor in front of Elaine Maynard, her arms around her.

21

It was still light when early that evening, to Mrs. Sombey's complete astonishment, an elegant landau, glistening black with red-rimmed wheels drawn by a handsome dapple gray horse halted in front of her rooming house. The rig was driven by a haughty-nosed driver in gray broadcloth coat, black high hat, gloves and high shiny black boots. From her post behind her stiff, lace curtains she watched in open-mouthed amazement as he climbed nimbly down, opened the carriage door, and assisted one of her boarders out. When she saw it was Laurel to whom he bowed slightly and tipped his hat, she could hardly contain herself. So mesmerized was she by this unusual occurrence that Laurel was up the porch steps and coming in the front door before Mrs. Sombey had a chance to do more than back up a few steps to save herself a bump on the nose as Laurel opened it.

"Oh, Mrs. Sombey, I'm glad you're here," Laurel exclaimed.

Something was up, that was for sure, the landlady told herself, seeing the girl's flushed cheeks. Hastily she assumed nonchalance, flopping her feather duster, pretending she had been dusting the hall table all along. But Mrs. Sombey would never have guessed the explanation Laurel was about to give her.

"I'm moving out. I have just come to get my things."

"Moving out?" Mrs. Sombey repeated, nonplussed. "Just like that? Without giving any notice?" She drew herself up huffily. "I'm sure I had no idea you wasn't satisfied with your lodgings, miss. You certainly never gave the slightest indication—"

"Oh, it's not that, Mrs. Sombey. My room has been...well, fine...that is, until now. You see I'm going to stay with my grandmother on Wembley Square."

Laurel had no way of knowing what the name of that prestigious residential section meant to someone like Mrs. Sombey.

"Wembley Square?" she repeated through stiff lips. "Your *grandmother!* Well, indeed, Miss Vestal, you never said nothing about having relatives in Boston before. I thought you was— I mean, you being from the Midwest and all, I naturally assumed—" the landlady was, for perhaps the first time in her adult life, at a loss for words.

"I know. But it's really too complicated to explain, Mrs. Sombey." Laurel smiled apologetically and then breezed by her and ran up the steps. "I'll just pack up my things now. My grandmother's driver is waiting for me," she called back over her shoulder.

Indignant at being taken so off guard by all these unexpected events, Muriel Sombey vented her furious frustation by hurrying to the foot of the stairway and, losing her pseudogentility, shrilled up after Laurel's departing figure. "There'll be no refund for the rest of the month, Miss Vestal, you understand? If I'da known you was leaving, I could have rented that room twice over for what you've been payin.'"

At the landing Laurel stopped and leaned over the banister, saying sweetly, "Of course, Mrs. Sombey. I understand. I did not expect any refund."

Laurel was not sure what awakened her—muted sounds from somewhere deep in the house, the snip-snap of a gardener's clippers in the garden just below the bedroom window. Or maybe it was the quietness itself, accustomed as she was to waking to the sound of delivery-cart wheels on the cobblestone street outside Mrs. Sombey's boardinghouse, the shouts of the drivers on the delivery wagons, the voices of the other roomers standing in line outside the hall bathroom, the repeated slam of the front door as they left the house on the way to work.

Laurel had noticed many times before the sedate pace of life on Wembley Square. Even the horseless carriages seemed to run noiselessly, while pedestrians moved with a purposeful dignity. The whole neighborhood exuded an aura of quiet charm and permanence.

In contrast, Laurel lay in bed in a kind of daze, thinking how quickly everything had changed since the previous afternoon. Three hours after her arrival at the Maynard residence, she had been on her way to her rooming house to pack up all her belongings and move in here with her grandmother!

"Grandmother," Laurel whispered the word, feeling its taste on her lips as she said it. Mama's mother.

Her eyes roamed the room, sweeping up through the lacy crocheted canopy of the dark mahogany four-poster to the little desk between the two windows, the small white marble fireplace. Mama's girlhood room, where *she* had slept—in this very bed—played with her dolls, studied her lessons, dreamed her romantic dreams! Here, in this spot!

After all the years of imagining, the reality was almost overwhelming. Laurel sighed and stretched, then snuggled once more into the lavender-fragrant sheets, the satin-covered feather quilt.

When she had returned with her belongings last evening, Laurel had found Mrs. Maynard looked very tired. They had a quiet supper together before the fire in the small parlor—delicious, delicate food, well-prepared and tastefully served. But neither of them had eaten very much. At length

Mrs. Maynard had regretfully admitted, "If you will excuse me, my dear, I really think I must retire. This has been quite an emotionally exhausting day for me. I'm no longer young nor very resilient, I suppose."

"Of course, Grandmother, I understand."

Mrs. Maynard rose and passed by the place where Laurel was sitting. Laying her hand, as light and dry as a winter leaf, against Laurel's cheek she said, "At least I can look forward to many such evenings with you in days ahead, and tonight sleep peacefully, knowing my grandchild is under the same roof." She sighed and seemed about to say something else, but did not. Then she drew from her pocket an envelope, yellowed with age, worn around the edges.

"I think you should read this, Laurel," she said. "I've kept it all these years, wept over it, if the truth be known, and wished with all my heart that I had acted upon my real feelings at the time. Maybe reading it will help you understand—Well, I'll leave that to you, my dear."

Her grandmother left the room in a lingering scent of violets. Laurel held the envelope, looking at the familiar handwriting. Even before she opened it, she knew who had written it. Carefully she took it out and, by the light from the fireplace, read the letter.

She had taken it upstairs to the bedroom and read it again before going to sleep. It was lying on the table beside the bed where she had put it, and now Laurel reached for it again.

With the early autumn sunlight streaming through the windows, Laurel read the words her mother had penned so many years ago, feeling her own young, in-love heart respond with special understanding.

> Dearest Mother and Father,
>
> By the time you read this, Paul and I will be a long way from Boston. We were married by a justice of the peace at the Court House a few days ago. It was not the

church wedding I'd always dreamed of having, with my beloved and loving parents in attendance. But since you have made it clear that you would never accept Paul as the man I love and have chosen to be my husband, we felt we had no other alternative.

As you must know, I would rather have had your approval and blessing, but since you withheld it and declared it would never be forthcoming, I had to make the hardest decision of my life. It breaks my heart to have to choose between my parents and Paul, and I still feel it did *not* have to be thus.

I thank you from the bottom of my heart for my happy childhood and home and all the loving care, the many advantages and privileges you showered upon me. Whatever you may think now, I am not ungrateful.

I love you both dearly and never wanted to hurt you in any way. I hope there will come a time when you will forgive me and know that you have not really lost a daughter but now also have a wonderful, gentle, kind, talented young man, willing and anxious to be a son to you both. Always,

Your loving Lillian

Laurel was still holding the fragile, thin sheets of paper when a soft tap came on the bedroom door, and a maid in a ruffled cap and apron peered in.

"Morning, miss. Just came in to light the fire and warm up the room before you got up, then to tell you your grandmother would like you to join her for breakfast."

Laurel sat up smiling and motioned the young woman regarding her so curiously to come in. She guessed the household staff was all agog over the news of the sudden, unexpected appearance of a Maynard granddaughter.

One of the first notes Laurel wrote, seated at her Mama's little desk in her former bedroom, was to Gene.

"You are simply not going to believe all that has happened to me since you left," she wrote. "You will first wonder at my change of address, I know, so I must tell you the wonderful thing that has happened."

Laurel's pen skimmed over the stationery as she told Gene all that had taken place since they parted. "I can't wait until you meet her! She's very grand, so be prepared! Most of all, I want *her* to meet *you*."

If Laurel's letters about her new life with Mrs. Maynard were exuberantly enthusiastic, they only reflected her own euphoria. One day followed the other in a kind of sunlit splendor. Mrs. Maynard had so much to show Laurel—keepsakes, photos, the portrait that had been painted of Lillian as a child and had once hung over the fireplace in Mr. Maynard's study, even her baby clothes that had been kept in a locked trunk. They spent many happy hours together, poring over these and albums and scrapbooks of Lillian's school days.

"You can see why it was such a blow to us, can't you, my dear?" Mrs. Maynard would ask Laurel over and over. "To lose her was like losing a part of ourselves."

Laurel longed to ask why it was necessary, why they had never given her father a chance, never even met him. But the harmony existing between her grandmother and herself was so comforting, so sweet, Laurel was loath to break it. There would be time for some of those hard questions later, after they were better acquainted. Just now they were moving slowly, cautiously into this new relationship.

Afternoons were spent in any number of pleasant ways—a carriage drive in the afternoon, or shopping in some of the lovely, exclusive stores where Mrs. Maynard was immediately recognized or stopping for tea at one of the luxurious hotels where they were always greeted by the maitre d' and ushered to Mrs. Maynard's special table overlooking the park, now brilliant with autumn colors. Here they were served by solemn, uniformed waiters an elaborate medley of dainty sandwiches, hothouse strawberries dipped in chocolate, truffles or glazed fruit flan or iced petit fours, with fragrant oolong tea.

Sometimes in the evenings, at Mrs. Maynard's request, Laurel would play the piano for her.

"You have Lillian's musical talent, that's evident," Mrs. Maynard sighed. "You must go ahead with your plans to attend the Conservatory. Of course, I will take care of all your fees, arrange for a coach—"

Laurel began to feel like Cinderella. What would Gene think of all these offers? Would her grandmother's generosity extend to him? He was actually the one with the *real* talent. She had mentioned him often, but her grandmother had not seemed interested in pursuing the discussion. In fact, she seemed to have forgotten all about Laurel's engagement. There was so much else to talk about and enjoy together. Her grandmother liked to play chess and taught Laurel the intricacies of the game. With their time so pleasantly occupied Laurel did not notice how quickly it was passing until one day she received a short note from Gene, saying he would be back at the end of the week.

"And where did you meet this young man?" Mrs. Maynard asked, a slight frown puckering her thin, high-arched brows.

"At the Conservatory, Grandmother," Laurel replied, deliberately omitting an account of the unorthodox manner in which she and Gene had really met. Somehow Laurel did not think Elaine Maynard would approve of so casual an introduction. Neither did she tell about their further meeting at Pasquini's Restaurant where Gene waited on tables.

On this afternoon when Gene was expected, Laurel and her grandmother were in the small parlor, awaiting his imminent arrival. Mrs. Maynard was seated in her favorite wing-back chair, her hands busy with needlepoint while her eyes keenly observed her granddaughter. Laurel was too excited to sit down. Everyting about her fluttered—the ruffles on her skirt, the tendrils of waves escaping from her coiled hair, the handkerchief she carried as she moved back and forth from door to window.

"Do light somewhere, child. You are as nervous as a butterfly," complained Mrs. Maynard.

"I'm sorry, Grandmother. It's just that I'm so anxious for Gene to come, for the two of you to meet." Laurel turned a radiant face on her. "Oh, I know you'll be impressed. He's so handsome, so charming, has such a wonderful personality. And, oh, Grandmother, you should hear him sing!" Laurel sighed rhapsodically.

"Is he planning a professional career?" was Elaine's next question.

"Oh, that's inevitable! He has a glorious tenor voice. He's already been on tour twice—only in the chorus, up till now. But a career has to be built slowly. This summer at the Cape theater he was in *The Pirates of Penzance.*"

Mrs. Maynard pursed her lips "Very few ever actually make it, you realize, don't you, Laurel? Only the very best, and that after years of training and study, and certainly a year or two in Europe—"

"Oh, I have no doubt Gene will make it. He is determined and certainly has the talent."

"But does he have the means to finance such a long period of training, a family willing to support him until he is at a point where he can demand...shall we say...a living from his voice?"

Laurel hesitated. Should she tell Mrs. Maynard that she knew very little about Gene's family, only that they were hard-working Italian fishermen, that Gene had to work at menial jobs to support himself, that they had already discussed the future of his career and her part in helping him attain his goals?

Even as she considered how much to confide of their plans, the sound of the knocker echoed through the downstairs. A bold, confident knock. Laurel smiled, thinking that neither fancy facades, shiny brass knockers, nor formidable butlers would ever intimidate Gene. She started over to the parlor door, ready to rush into the hall.

"Thomas will show your guest in, Laurel," her grandmother said sharply.

Laurel halted, surprised by the reprimand in Mrs. Maynard's voice.

A minute later there he was, right behind the solemn Thomas. Laurel's heart spun at the sight of him. He looked marvelous, his skin still attractively bronzed from days on the beach. Nor could her grandmother fault his attire. He was dressed for the occasion in a light beige twill suit, crisp striped shirt with snowy stiff collar, a waffle-straw hat tucked under one arm.

Laurel swelled with pride as she reached for his hand and drew him into the parlor. Then, turning to Mrs. Maynard she introduced him.

"Grandmother, I'd like you to meet Gene Michela. Gene, my grandmother, Mrs. Maynard."

Elaine held out her hand and Gene walked over and bowed over it as he spoke in his clear, rich voice. "A pleasure, Mrs. Maynard."

"Mr. Michela." Elaine was politely formal. "Please be seated. Laurel tells me you have spent the last several weeks at the Cape."

It was only then that Laurel was conscious of the chill in the room. It was as if someone had opened a door and a winter wind had swept through. Somehow Mrs. Maynard had deftly taken control of the conversation and begun to conduct what amounted to an interrogation. The situation took Laurel unawares at first, but once she had grasped what was happening, she grew tense with anxiety.

Thomas brought the tea service in on a round silver tray and set it down on a low table in front of Mrs. Maynard. Alerted that Gene was under some kind of scrutiny, Laurel watched with mounting apprehension as he took one of the dainty napkins, flicked it open, placed it on his knee, asked for lemon instead of cream, accepted one of the tiny triangles of watercress sandwiches, answered all Mrs. Maynared's probing questions with ease and never with his mouth full. Laurel was ashamed of herself for fretting. Under any other circumstances, it would never have occurred to Laurel to worry about the kind of impression Gene was making. He was always the perfect gentleman, had impeccable manners. Still, it was her grandmother's unrelenting observation that made Laurel uneasy, and she couldn't help the image that came to mind—that of the spider spinning her fatal web.

Then quite unexpectedly Laurel heard her grandmother say as though puzzled.

"Michela? Is that an Italian name or perhaps Portuguese? I understand there is quite a large Portuguese population in the coastal communities. Where did you say you were from originally? New Bedford?"

Laurel snapped to attention. She felt a strange sense of déjù vu. Of time turning backward. Weren't those the same words her grandmother had quoted Bennett Maynard as having said in the confrontation with her mother so long ago? A confrontation that had probably taken place in this very room!

"Paul *Vestal?* What kind of name is *Vestal?* Polish? Hungarian? Is he from one of those Balkan countries always in revolution? How long has he been in this country? A year or two? You mean he's an *immigrant?* Lillian, your ancestors came here on the Mayflower! Men of quality, old families, men of the cloth, lawyers, teachers—you have a long and illustrious lineage. And you want to marry this man with no background, some *foreigner?*"

She imagined the same icy tone she was hearing now in Mrs. Maynard's voice, and felt a blaze of anger ignite within her. How insulting Mrs. Maynard was being in her cool, civilized "drawing room" manner! Laurel glanced over at Gene to see if he was feeling it, reacting to it. But he looked perfectly relaxed, listening to Mrs. Maynard with polite attentiveness. Of course, he was too sensitive not to feel the sting, but too gracious to show any emotion. He was behaving as a perfect guest. It was her grandmother who was taking advantage of her position as hostess. Hostess? The Grand Inquisitor, rather! Gene was not on trial here, Laurel thought indignantly.

Or was he? Quickly Laurel remembered an enigmatic conversation she and her grandmother had had over tea one afternoon. Mrs. Maynard had remarked casually that soon she wanted to introduce Laurel to some young people of her acquaintance, daughters and sons of some friends in "our set."

So that was the game? She was trying to prove Gene unsuitable. No wonder she had ignored Laurel's mention of her engagement.

Laurel felt a chilling reality, as if a smothering cloak, were dropping over her head, almost heard the clang of a trap bolting, locking her in, shutting Gene out. It was history repeating itself. Lillian and the unsuitable "foreigner" Paul Vestal all over again. But this time it was Laurel and Gene Mrs. Maynard was trying to break up.

Laurel felt her smile freeze on her lips as she sat there holding the delicate handle of her teacup balanced on her lap. Her eyes moved from Gene to her grandmother, back and forth, like watching a tennis volley. She was pleased to see that Gene was holding his own, replying to all Mrs. Maynard's outrageous questions with complete poise.

Her heart warmed and melted. What a true gentleman he was! Never mind he was probably not measuring up to all her grandmother's invisible criteria, possibly missing the mark of her prerequisite targets for approval and acceptance. What did that matter? Her mother had been brave enough to withstand such pressure, to follow her own heart, to find happiness with the good man she had loved and married. Laurel remembered Mama saying once that to have known even a short time of perfect happiness was worth the sorrow she had known afterwards.

Apparently her grandmother was only looking for shallow externals. In Gene, Laurel had found more than a pedigree or even a handsome face and courtly manners. In him, she had found inner goodness, gallantry, lasting values.

Then Gene was on his feet. "I must be on my way now, Mrs. Maynard. Thank you for allowing me to visit Laurel here, and for the honor of meeting her grandmother."

Laurel rose with him. Setting down her cup, she said, "I'll walk you to the door. Excuse us, Grandmother." She slipped her hand through Gene's arm and together they went out of the parlor and into the hall.

"Gene," she whispered, "I want you to meet me tomorrow at our old place in the park. We must talk, make plans. It is impossible here."

He squeezed her hand, his eyes darkening with understanding. "Yes, of course. I'm working tonight at the restaurant and a private party tomorrow night, but shall we say two tomorrow afternoon?"

"I'll be there."

Laurel did not return to the parlor but went upstairs to her bedroom. She closed the door, went over to the window, and watched Gene's departing figure on his way to catch the trolley.

"I love you!" She blew a kiss, then turned and resolutely got out her suitcase and began packing.

22

Gene was waiting for Laurel when she arrived in the park, flushed and breathless from hurrying. He caught both her hands and raised them to his lips. Then, putting his arm around her waist he led her over to a bench where they sat down.

"What is it, darling? What's troubling you?" he asked, all tender concern.

In as few words as possible, Laurel explained her feelings. "It's almost eerie, Gene. It's starting all over again, just like it was with Mama—at least, the way I imagine it was with Mama. My grandmother doesn't even realize what she's doing." She paused, looking worried. "I don't want to hurt her, but of course I can't stay." She hesitated, not wanting to tell Gene it was specifically Mrs. Maynard's attitude toward him that had brought about her decision. "I don't want to go back to Mrs. Sombey's, so I must find another place to live."

Gene was silent for a minute, his brows furrowed as if in deep thought. Then he said slowly, "This is too important a decision to make impulsively, Laurel. You've waited too long to find your mother's family to walk out."

"But—"

"Wait, let me finish." Gene held up his hand to stem her protest. "Granted, your grandmother is old and set in her ways. She's used to managing things, servants, other people's lives. Your leaving won't change her, Laurel, except in ways you don't want to be responsible for. I could see you mean a great deal to her. After so many years of denial, having you, her own granddaughter in her home...can't you see? It's given her a new lease on life. Of course, she's full of plans for you. Just think what her life must have been like all these years before you came. Think—" he lifted her chin with his thumb and forefinger and searched her face— "Think what they will be like if you leave her now."

"But, Gene, she wants me to become something I'm not! At least Mama was raised to be a socialite. I wasn't." She smiled ruefully. "And I used to think Mother—my *adoptive* mother—was possessive!"

Gene laughed. "See?"

"But what shall I do?"

"I think you should be patient with her—gentle and understanding the way you always are. Give your grandmother time to get to know you. Gradually she will loosen the tight grip she has on this newfound happiness. Right now, she's afraid it will slip out of her hands, and that would be like losing her daughter all over again." When Laurel began to weep quietly, he held her close. "Don't worry, I'll help you darling. Together we can win your grandmother over. I'm sure she doesn't want to make the same terrible mistake *twice*."

"Yes, I suppose you're right, Gene—in fact, I *know,* you are." She sniffled and he whipped out a huge white handkerchief to mop her tears.

He took Laurel's hand, smoothing out the fingers, one by one.

"It may be a few weeks before everything can be worked out...and I didn't want to say anything about it until I was sure. But there's a very good chance that I'm going to be hired by the Conservatory as one of their coaches on a good salary plus, of course, coaching fees. If that happens, we could get married right away." He looked at her hopefully. "Unless you've changed your mind?"

"Of course I haven't changed my mind. But can we really afford it? To get married, I mean? We discussed it before and never thought we could. This wouldn't mean your giving up your singing career, would it? I wouldn't want to do anything to delay your dreams coming true."

"Laurel, don't you know by now? You *are* my dream come true! You *inspire* me, make me want even more to succeed, in my career. Actually, this would provide me with more time on my own to practice, study languages, like German and French for example, in which so many operas are written. But the main thing is, we would be together." He raised her hand and kissed it. "Besides that, I have some very good news for you from Ed Williams, the owner of the art gallery at the Cape."

Laurel was all eager attention.

"I didn't know this before, but he has a gallery here in Boston. He has a partner who is actually an expert, a real art expert and critic. It seems his partner came up to look over this cache of paintings I told you about, your father's among them." Gene paused significantly. "Well, this other gentleman, Karl Sandour is his name, became very excited when he saw Paul Vestal's paintings. There are quite a few—most of them beach scenes—very light, vivid colors, local scenes, families and children, all in very natural, appealing settings. Williams's partner, this Mr. Sandour, wants to have what they call a retrospective of American Impressionists and particularly of your father's Cape Cod pictures."

"Oh, how wonderful, Gene! But—" her sunny smile faded—"I wish it could have happened while he was living."

"Yes, well I'm sure he would be happy to know the daughter he painted so often will be receiving the benefits."

"What do you mean?"

"Williams and Sandour want you to see all the paintings, decide which ones you want for yourself, then give them permission to put the others on exhibition and for sale. They will take care of all the expense of cleaning the canvases, framing them, the cost of brochures, advertising, everything, and of course they will take a percentage of all sales." Gene paused again and said quite carefully. "But from what they tell me, Laurel, even with that, you should be a very wealthy young lady."

Laurel stared back at Gene. It was taking a long time for all he had said to sink in. For so long she had hoped to trace her parents, find her identity, claim her true heritage. But she had never expected anything like this. Emotion swept over her, she felt her eyes fill with tears, her mouth tremble as she tried to speak. With a look of complete understanding, Gene took her in his arms and held her, while she put her head on his shoulders and wept.

"But I don't understand, Laurel. Why must you go?" Elaine Maynard's expression was a mixture of bewilderment and distress. "I've tried to make you comfortable here, assured you of my intention to support you at the Conservatory, provide you with anything you need—"

"I know, Grandmother, and I appreciate all you've done, all you want to do for me. But I have other plans now. Gene Michela and I are going to be married. He has been offered a position now at the Conservatory and will be well able to support me. I want to share this with my adoptive parents, have Gene meet them. We'll be married there in Meadowridge in November and then come back to live in Boston."

Mrs. Maynard shook her head as if not comprehending. "But, Laurel, I had it all planned, I intended—*wanted* you to make your home here with me until such time as you met some suitable young man. I planned to give you a reception to introduce you to people of our class, our kind—" Her words faded away as if she realized she was saying all the wrong things.

"Grandmother, it's not that I'm ungrateful. I know you have the best intentions in the world, but your plans are not my plans. We don't see alike, don't value the same things." Laurel spoke with quiet dignity. "I have found the person I love, the one with whom I want to spend the rest of my life. Gene Michela is everything I want, everything I've always hoped for, or need. When you get to know him better, you'll see I'm right. In fact—" Laurel leaned forward, looking intently into her grandmother's eyes. "I wanted to find my roots to satisfy my own longing to belong. Gene taught me to look for ways to give back what I already *have*. Both of us want you to be part of our life."

That sincere request seemed to touch a chord in a heart that had protected itself for years from feeling pain, regret, love. The long-suppressed vulnerability gave way. Speechless, Elaine Maynard held up her arms to her granddaughter. A minute later the fragile old woman was held in the young one's strong arms. Tears of forgiveness and reconciliation mingled on cheeks pressed close. Love withheld, love given, love renewed encompassed in a healing embrace.

Though outwardly reconciled to the inevitability of Laurel's leaving, as the time grew near for Laurel's departure for Meadowridge to prepare for her November wedding, Elaine Maynard's resistance to the idea stiffened. Laurel knew she had to somehow break through the wall her grandmother was building to shut out acceptance of Gene.

One Saturday evening in early October, she approached her. "Would you like to attend church with me tomorrow, Grandmother? Gene has been hired as soloist, and you've never heard him sing. I wish you'd come with me."

A shadow seemed to cross Mrs. Maynard's face and she turned away, visibly distressed.

"Is something wrong, Grandmother?" Laurel asked anxiously.

"It's just that—well, I haven't been...for a long time." She sighed. "Your grandfather was so bitter after...Lillian...we stopped going. Then when he was so ill and died, I felt God had—" her voice broke. Then, straightening her thin, elegant shoulders, she lifted her chin. "Yes, Laurel, perhaps that's what I *should* do, go back to church."

Sunday morning, looking regal in a gray, fur-trimmed coat and a feathered toque, accompanied by her granddaughter, Elaine Maynard took her place in the pew identified by a small brass plaque engraved with the MAYNARD family name.

It was a magnificent church, she thought, contemplating the stained-glass windows and, at the opening chords of the magnificent organ, she reminded herself that she and Bennett had contributed generously to its purchase. But when she heard the rich fullness of the tenor voice raised in worshipful praise, she knew *that* was the true contribution, the real gift.

She felt tremors coursing through her as the words of the first hymn resounded into the rafters: "All creatures of our God and King, lift up your voice and with us sing, Alleluia! Alleluia!" But it was when Gene sang the stirring lyrics of "It Is Well with My Soul" that Elaine was most deeply touched. Unexpectedly, the woman who had always prided herself on never publicly displaying emotion was moved to tears as the words reached the innermost places of her heart.

Believing no one was aware, she was surprised and comforted as Laurel's hand pressed hers. Looking at her granddaughter, she smiled. *How blessed I am,* Elaine thought. *Thank You, Lord, for bringing her into my life—and the young man she loves. Forgive an old woman her past sins.* With a sigh of thankfulness, Elaine briefly closed her eyes, listening to the words of the hymn repeating them in her own heart: *Yes, it is well with my soul—*

23

Meadowridge was riotous with changing color—gold and russet and bronze—when Laurel returned just before Thanksgiving to await her wedding day.

Ava had insisted on commissioning Mrs. Danby to make the wedding gown and it hung now, a splendor of ivory lace and taffeta, in the closet of Laurel's old room. In fact, every moment since her homecoming had been filled brimful with preparations for the ceremony that would take place in the Community Church the week after Thanksgiving, not to mention plans for that most New England of all holidays. Ella had been cooking for days, eager to make a good impression on "Mr. Gene," and Jenny had come back to lend a hand with fall cleaning and polishing until the house fairly sparkled.

On Thanksgiving morning, when Gene was scheduled to arrive, Laurel insisted on going to the station by herself to meet him. A glance from Dr. Woodward stilled Ava's suggestion that they all go down in their newly acquired motor car to welcome Gene to Meadowridge, and Laurel set out on foot alone.

The yellow frame Meadowbridge train station was a nostalgic symbol to Laurel. Imprinted on her memory forever was the day she and the other orphans, shepherded by Mrs. Scott, were paraded out on the platform. Laurel remembered that shivery sensation inside, in spite of the fact that she was holding Toddy's hand on one side, Kit's on the other. Seeing it now, ten years later, brought all those feelings rushing back. Still, she knew she had been one of the lucky ones.

She thought also of the morning she had left Meadowridge to go to Boston, not sure she would ever come back. The empty heartsickness she had felt that misty morning gripped her as the slant-roofed station building came in sight.

But today there was not the slightest tinge of sadness in Laurel. Her step was as light as her heart, her pulses racing with excitement. Her anticipation mounted as she heard the train whistle in the distance. Clasping her hands tightly together, she moved to the edge of the platform peering down the tracks for the first sign of the engine rounding the bend. In her head she could hear the conductor's voice. "Meadowridge! Next stop, Meadowridge!"

And then she saw him, swinging down from the train's high step minutes after it had screeched to a stop, steam hissing, the grinding noise of steel against steel.

"Gene! Gene!" she called, waving her hand. She caught her breath as he came toward her, seeing his dark eyes sparkling and the smile that always made her heart turn over. Then she was swung up in his arms and she heard him whisper her name. Foolish tears gathered in her eyes as he set her back down on her feet.

"Let me look at you! These have been the longest weeks of my life!"

They said all the little, inconsequential things lovers say to each other, then Laurel gathered her wits about her enough to give directions to the baggage clerk to have Gene's luggage sent up to Meadowridge Inn where Dr. Woodward had made reservations for him.

"The house isn't far, so I thought we'd walk. I want to show you everything," she said almost shyly, hardly able to believe that he was really here with her in Meadowridge.

"It looks like I thought it would, only more so—" Gene remarked on the way. "Like everyone's dream 'hometown.'"

"Well, yes, maybe it does!"

As they strolled, hand in hand, Laurel realized she was seeing things with the long familiarity of childhood and Gene with fresh eyes. He marveled at the size of the elms, the willows on the sloping banks of the river when they crossed the arched stone bridge leading up to Main Street. The sun was out strongly now brightening the paint on all the houses along the way. Shining through the fretwork of gabled dormers, it cast lacy shadows on the clapboard. Autumn had been mild here, and most of the gardens still boasted flowers. Heavy-headed dahlias in various shades of orange, purple, yellow and white nodded in the brisk breeze.

Then finally they turned onto a winding lane with tall, arching trees and Laurel pointed to a white frame house with dark green shutters at the end.

"There it is." She smiled up at him. "Come on."

As they approached Gene saw a bunch of colorful Indian corn tied with wide yellow satin ribbon hanging on the front door that a minute later was flung open by a slender, dark-haired woman. Behind her stood a handsome, gray-haired man.

Laurel and Gene came up the porch steps together.

"Gene! How wonderful to meet you at last!" Ava said warmly and Dr. Woodward shook Gene's hand, saying, "Welcome...son."

Laurel felt tears again and her throat felt thick with emotion as she looked at these two she loved so dearly, then at the man she had chosen. A gladness surged up in her and a heartfelt prayer.

"Thank You, God, for all my blessings." The words of her favorite Psalm rushed into her mind, its beautiful words echoing in the fullness of her happiness: "Trust in the Lord, wait on him and he will bring it to pass. Trust him and he will give thee the secret desires of thy heart."

Dinner was served promptly at four. Jenny had come to help and could not seem to stop smiling as she served them. Every time she happened to catch Laurel's eye, which was often, she gave her a solemn wink.

Everything was perfect, Laurel thought, glancing to see if Gene appreciated Ava's artistry in arranging the table with its centerpiece of fruit and flowers—purple asters, marigolds combined with golden pears, and flame Tokay grapes. Her best Devonshire lace and linen cloth and napkins had been brought out, polished silver and glistening crystal, the good china that as a child Laurel had always admired—its design of the East Indian symbol of the Tree of Life in burnt orange and blue.

The food was a triumph of Ava and Ella's combined efforts. Ella herself brought in the turkey—golden brown, smelling deliciously, surrounded by tiny crabapples and parsley—then set it before Dr. Woodward with an air of deserved pride. This was followed by bowls mounded with snowy-white, light-as-air mashed potatoes, squash and creamed peas and pearl onions. Gravy boats were passed as well as numerous cut-glass containers of condiments— watermelon, pickles, peach chutney, quince jelly, and of course cranberry-orange relish. Two carafes of sweet apple cider were set at each end of the table to be poured into delicate, thin-stemmed goblets.

"Let us give thanks," Dr. Woodward said, bowing his head, holding out his hands to Laurel on his left and Gene on his right as was their custom. Ava completed the circle.

"Most gracious Father," he began. "We are more aware than ever of Your unmerited favor, the many blessings You have lavishly given us. We thank You especially for our daughter, Laurel, and for the fine young man who will be her husband and our son. We thank You for the blessings of health, food and shelter, love of family and friends, and unwarranted bounty. We ask to be led by You in all things and be worthy to be called Your children. We ask this in the precious name of Your Son, Jesus Christ. Amen."

In a blur of happiness Laurel ate, not being entirely aware of what she tasted, filled as she was with a warmth and contentment that seemed to take up all the space within her, leaving very little for food. She looked at each of the people at the table, smilingly, silently loving them with a complete acceptance and gratitude.

Ava suggested they wait until later to have a choice of pie—pumpkin, apple or pecan—since everyone claimed they could not eat another bite just then. So taking their coffee the four of them went into the parlor.

It was getting dark outside with the quick falling darkness of an early winter day. The curtains were drawn, lamps lighted, and Dr. Woodward put a match to the fire that had been laid earlier. The kindling caught immediately with little snapping sounds, sending up spurts of bright flame. Soon a nicely burning fire glowed brightly in the hearth, reflecting on the brass fender and andirons in the shadowy room.

"Why don't you play for us, dear?" Ava suggested and Laurel took her place at the piano.

For a few minutes her fingers roamed the keyboard as if trying to find exactly the right melody for this special time. As she began to play a piece she knew was one of Dr. Woodward's favorites, her eyes circled the familiar room—the firelight burnishing the frames of the paintings, the polished furniture, the prisms of the candlesticks on the mantlepiece. Memories came flooding back—the first time she had seen this room, had discovered the piano, lifted its lid and let her fingers grope for the keys to play the simple little tune her mama had taught her years and years ago, guiding her tiny hands.

She played on, moving from one song to the other, an almost forgotten medley of music that the Woodwards most enjoyed. As her fingers moved across the keys, her mind wandered back and forth, in and out, everything coming together, past and present. All the varied experiences of her life, all the things that had happened began to take shape, form, fit into a whole.

As she played on, unconsciously a thrilling rightness of this moment she was sharing with the three people she loved most in the world swept over Laurel. All at once Laurel knew the joy of homecoming.

She had been on a lifelong journey to find her "real family," her "real home," and now she realized with a heart filled with understanding that her Heavenly Father had done "abundantly above all that we ask." He had given her more than one family and one home.

Sitting at the piano, in the comforting warmth of this familiar room, with the family He had provided for her, Laurel realized at last that she was no longer an orphan, but a lost child who had finally come home.

SINS OF THE FATHERS

Recent Titles by Sally Spencer from Severn House

THE BUTCHER BEYOND

THE DARK LADY

DEAD ON CUE

DEATH OF A CAVE DWELLER

DEATH OF AN INNOCENT

A DEATH LEFT HANGING

DYING IN THE DARK

THE ENEMY WITHIN

GOLDEN MILE TO MURDER

A LONG TIME DEAD

MURDER AT SWANN'S LAKE

THE PARADISE JOB

THE RED HERRING

THE SALTON KILLINGS

STONE KILLER

THE WITCH MAKER

SINS OF THE
FATHERS

Sally Spencer

This first world edition published in Great Britain 2006 by
SEVERN HOUSE PUBLISHERS LTD of
9–15 High Street, Sutton, Surrey SM1 1DF.
This first world edition published in the USA 2006 by
SEVERN HOUSE PUBLISHERS INC of
595 Madison Avenue, New York, N.Y. 10022.

British Library Cataloguing in Publication Data

Spencer, Sally
    Sins of the fathers
    1. Woodend, Charlie (Fictitious character) - Fiction
    2. Police - England - Fiction
    3. Detective and mystery stories
    I. Title
    823.9'14 [F]

    ISBN-13: 978-0-7278-6395-9 (cased)
    ISBN-10: 0-7278-6395-9   (cased)
    ISBN-13: 978-0-7278-9181-2 (paper)
    ISBN-13: 0-7278-9182-0   (paper)

All Severn House titles are printed on acid-free paper.

Typeset by Palimpsest Book Production Ltd.,
Grangemouth, Stirlingshire, Scotland.
Printed and bound in Great Britain by
MPG Books Ltd., Bodmin, Cornwall.

Prologue

The English Lake District – January 1962

From the moment the shivers had taken hold of him, Jeremy Tully had been convinced that he was dying.

Now, several hours later – if it *was* hours, rather than minutes or days, both of which seemed equally possible – the shivering had almost stopped.

Tully took no consolation from this fact. He knew enough about hypothermia to understand that rather than indicating that his condition was improving, it was a sign it was getting much worse. What had happened was that his body – independent of his mind – had decided, in a desperate attempt to preserve its glucose, to partly shut itself down.

But the attempt wouldn't work.

Nothing would work.

He was dying. That was the end of it – the end of him.

There were three of them on the ledge – Tully himself, Bradley Pine and Alec Hawtrey.

Of the trio, Alec was easily in the worst shape. He was the oldest member of the party – the least physically fit from the beginning – and when he had fallen and broken his leg, it had only served to stack the odds even further against him.

Every time the other two had attempted to move the injured man, he had screamed with agony.

But it was now a long time since Alec had even had the strength to express his pain.

So he would probably go first.

Then, Tully thought, it would be his turn.

But Bradley would not follow them down the route to oblivion. He wouldn't die – however intense the blizzard grew,

1

however long it took the rescue party to find them – because he was a survivor.

More than that – Bradley Pine was a planner, who always thought three steps ahead. So that while his *body* might be trapped on this mountainside, his mind was already back in Whitebridge, making its next move.

The snow no longer seemed to be lashing them quite as fiercely as it had been. Perhaps the blizzard had finally decided to let up, Tully thought. Perhaps he would live through the experience after all.

He uncurled a little from the foetal position that his battling body had instinctively taken. His muscles did not want to cooperate, but he forced them to, because he had to see for himself if it were really true that the weather was getting better – that there was finally some faint glimmer of hope.

What he *did* see, through the swirling snow, was that Pine had shifted position, so that now he was bent over Alec Hawtrey.

What he *did* see was the large sheath knife in Pine's hand.

He wanted to shout out to Pine that he should put the knife away. Wanted to tell him that Alec was probably past the point of conscious suffering, and it would be no act of kindness to rob him of what dignity he had left by killing him now – that he should just be allowed to die of natural causes.

But the words would not come – not as a shout, not even as a whisper.

And perhaps, he thought, with a mind half-turned to ice, it wouldn't have mattered even if the words had come. Because perhaps what he was witnessing wasn't a *mercy* killing at all.

Whitebridge Evening Courier – 6th April 1965

The sudden death of Seth Johnson, Member of Parliament for the Whitebridge Constituency since 1945, has created turmoil in both the leading political parties.

Labour has been losing ground for a number of years, and, in the considered opinion of many political observers, has only maintained the slim majority it now holds because of Seth Johnson's personal prestige. The Labour candidate selected to fight for Johnson's seat in the coming by-election will, therefore, have an uphill struggle.

The Conservative Party is currently deciding between two strong candidates.

The first, Henry Marlowe, has been Chief Constable of Central Lancashire for the last three years, and was Deputy Chief Constable before that.

The second, Bradley Pine, is a local businessman, whose company (Hawtrey-Pine Holdings) is one of Whitebridge's most successful manufacturing firms. Many of our readers will remember the tragedy which occurred three years ago, when, despite Bradley Pine's heroic efforts to save him, Alec Hawtrey lost his life in a mountaineering accident.

The election promises to be one of the liveliest in quite some time, and you may rest assured that the Courier will be covering it in the greatest possible detail, every step of the way.

One

Henry Marlowe stood at the very back of the Sleaburn Village Hall, watching the man on the small stage as he addressed an audience which had dragged itself out on a densely foggy evening, just for the privilege of hearing him speak.

Bradley Pine looked good, Marlowe thought reluctantly. Better than good. He looked sharp. He looked caring. He looked like a man who was confident of winning the coming by-election.

And the bastard probably *would* win!

'For nearly twenty years, this constituency has been in the hands of a party which hates individual freedom and individual responsibility with a passion,' Pine was telling his eager listeners. 'A party which wants to reward the scrounger for his idleness – and will do it at your expense. Well, my friends, it's time to draw a line in the sand – time to show them, with this election, that we won't stand for it!'

The audience applauded enthusiastically.

'It should have been me standing on that platform,' Marlowe said softly to himself.

He deserved it, he thought. Nobody had worked harder to win the selection committee's approval than he had. *Nobody* had bought more drinks, slapped more backs or done more favours. And it had all been for nothing!

Now this jumped-up little creep had been handed the mantle that he – the upholder of law and order throughout the county – had been denied.

It didn't seem right.

It didn't seem fair.

And Marlowe found himself wondering if – even at this late stage in the proceedings – there was anything he could do to seize back what was properly his.

* * *

4

Bradley Pine opened the door of the village hall and stepped out into the chill night air. He supposed that instead of making such a rapid exit, he could always have stayed longer – shaking a few more hands, making a few more personal promises. But, on the whole, he felt that would have been running an unnecessary risk – because the more time the glittering star spends among his acolytes, the greater the danger that some of the glitter will begin to flake off.

The fog had thickened while he'd been making his speech, and his car – which was conveniently parked in the country lane behind the hall – was no more than a vague shape. Even so, he could not fail to notice, as he drew closer to it, that a man was standing beside the vehicle.

'Who's that?' he asked.

'It's me,' said a voice that he recognized instantly as belonging to Henry Marlowe.

'I saw you standing at the back of the hall, Henry,' Pine said. 'It was very good of you to put in an appearance.'

'I didn't have much choice, did I?' Marlowe growled. 'I couldn't have people saying I was a sore loser.'

'No, of course you couldn't,' Pine agreed. 'Especially since such an assumption on their part would have been so patently unfair.'

'What's that supposed to mean?' Marlowe demanded. 'Is it meant to be some sort of joke?'

'Certainly not,' Pine assured him.

'Then what's your point?'

Pine sighed. 'I suppose I was just giving you the opportunity to show that you could accept defeat gracefully.'

'You could have supported my nomination, you know,' Marlowe said, showing no desire to do anything of the kind. 'You could have dropped your own candidature and given *me* your backing.'

'I seriously thought about doing just that,' Pine said, with the kind of sincerity that only a politician can ever truly manage.

'Did you? Well, you didn't show much sign of it!'

'But, ultimately, I had to base my decision on what I thought would be best for the Party, Henry. I knew I could win the seat, you see, and I very much doubted that you could.'

'In the current political climate, we could have put up a

5

turnip as our candidate and it would still have romped home,' Marlowe said.

'Perhaps you're right,' Pine conceded.

'You know I'm right.'

'But you still shouldn't look on this as a rout, Henry. You should see it more as a postponement.'

'Should I?'

'Of course. It won't be long before you're selected for another constituency. And think what an advantage it will be for you to have a friend in Westminster, speeding the process along.'

'Throwing me crumbs from his table would be closer to the truth,' Marlowe said bitterly.

'That's a little harsh,' Pine said. 'Listen, Henry, I'm very grateful for what you've done for me—'

'And so you bloody-well should be!'

'—but even gratitude must eventually have its limitations. You can rely on my help in the future, there's no question about that – but you can't keep drawing on debts from the past, as if they were some kind of bottomless well.'

'I could destroy you, you know!' Marlowe said.

'Not without destroying yourself,' Pine countered.

'So what?' Marlowe asked defiantly. 'It might almost be worth it!'

'You know that's not true,' Pine told him. He glanced down at his watch, though given the combination of night-time darkness and swirling fog, he knew he would be unable to read it. 'I'm afraid I really do have to go now, Henry. I'm due at St Mary's Church.'

'Oh, so you've suddenly found your religion again, have you?' Marlowe asked aggressively.

'I never lost it,' Pine said mildly. 'It's simply been in moth balls all these years – and now I'm taking it out for an airing.'

'You're a cynical bastard,' Marlowe said.

'And you are perhaps not quite cynical enough, Henry,' Pine responded, opening the door of his Cortina and climbing in. 'You see things far too much in terms of black and white. The politician's art is to be able to distinguish the various shades of grey, and it's an art you'll have to learn if you're ever to start climbing the political ladder yourself.'

He turned the ignition key and, despite the dampness in the atmosphere, the Cortina fired first time.

Henry Marlowe stood and watched as the vehicle's tail lights were swallowed up by the fog.

If ever a man was asking to get himself topped, he thought, that man was Bradley Pine.

The three people – two men and a woman – who were sitting in the corner of the public bar of the Drum and Monkey that night were regulars, not only of that particular boozer but of that particular table.

The older of the two men, Chief Inspector Charlie Woodend, was in his early fifties. He was what people in Whitebridge would call 'a big bugger', which meant that even violent drunks would think twice before taking a poke at him. He was wearing a hairy sports jacket and a pair of cavalry twill trousers, both items selected at random that morning from a wardrobe containing half a dozen similar jackets and several pairs of trousers which were almost identical.

The younger man, Constable Colin Beresford, was in his early twenties. He was wearing a blue suit which looked like it should have been reserved for Sundays. Occasionally, he would take a surreptitious glance at his watch, for while he felt honoured to be sitting in the company of the others, he was also conscious of the fact that it had been quite some time since he'd last checked on the state of his poor, demented mother.

The woman, Detective Sergeant Monika Paniatowski, was around thirty, and a blonde. She was smartly – though not expensively – dressed in a two-piece check suit, the skirt of which was short enough to reveal that she had rather sensational legs. Her largish nose suggested that she might be Central European in origin – and the nose did not lie. She could not have been called a beautiful woman, but to label her as merely 'attractive' would not have done her justice, either.

The barman, who had been watching them – and waiting for a signal which would indicate they required two more pints of best bitter and one vodka without ice – turned to the landlord, who was polishing beer glasses.

'Have you noticed that though there's not been a major crime for weeks, "the usual suspects" are in here again tonight,' he said jokingly.

The landlord placed the pint mug which he had been shining down on the counter.

'You've got it arse-over-backwards, haven't you, lad?' he asked. 'Since they're the bobbies, they'd have to be "the usual *suspectors*".'

The barman chuckled. 'Which would make Cloggin-it Charlie the *Chief Suspector*, I suppose,' he said. 'Chief Suspector Woodend! I rather like the sound of that.'

'I think we've gone quite far enough with that particular line of whimsy,' the landlord cautioned.

'It's only a joke!' the barman protested.

'It's always a mistake to take the piss out of the customers,' the landlord told him gravely. 'They're our bread an' butter, in case you need remindin'.'

'I know that, but—'

'An' Mr Woodend alone spends enough in here to keep us in puddings an' all.'

It was Father Taylor who greeted Bradley Pine at the door of St Mary's. He was a young priest, who had been in the parish for less than three years, and thus presented a marked contrast to Father Kenyon, who had served this particular flock for so long that there were now very few of the communicants of the church under the age of forty who had not been personally baptized by him.

'Welcome, Mr Pine!' the young priest said, full of enthusiasm. 'It's good to see you.'

'It's good to be here, Father,' Pine replied.

He was speaking no more than the truth. Though he might have glibly told Henry Marlowe that he had put his religion in moth balls, that had never really been the case, and recently he had found it a great source of comfort and a great source of strength.

'Are you here for a moment of quiet prayer?' Father Taylor asked. 'If so, I'll leave you to it.'

'No, I . . .' Pine began. 'I'd rather like to make my confession. I know it's not the normal time, but . . .'

Father Taylor laughed. 'This is a church, not an office with fixed opening hours,' he said. 'If you wish to confess your sins, I'm more than willing to hear them at any time.'

'That's . . .er . . .very kind of you, Father, but Father Kenyon

8

is my usual confessor,' Pine said awkwardly.

'So he is,' Father Taylor agreed. 'But we in the priesthood are all God's instruments. Each and every one of us serves as no more than a telephone line to the Almighty.'

Pine frowned. He knew the young priest meant well – and it couldn't have been easy, coming into a parish in which the other priest was already an established figure – but he was not sure he was quite comfortable with the casual, modern way that Father Taylor talked about his religion.

'If you don't mind, Father, I'd prefer to make my confession to Father Kenyon,' he said.

A look of disappointment flickered across Father Taylor's features, and then was gone.

'Of course I don't mind,' he told Pine. 'Father Kenyon's in the vestry. I'll go and fetch him.'

Pine watched the young priest cross the church. He supposed he could have confessed to him rather than to Father Kenyon – they *were* both God's instruments, as the priest had pointed out – but he had a feeling that Father Taylor was perhaps a little too unyielding for his taste.

Father Kenyon, on the other hand, was almost as much of a politician as he was himself. Father Kenyon would give him the absolution he needed, even though the old priest would probably have a pretty shrewd idea of where he was going when he had made his confession – and even what he would do once he got there!

There was some truth in what the landlord of the Drum and Monkey had said earlier about Charlie Woodend's drinking habits. The chief inspector liked pubs, especially his local. He claimed that best bitter was nature's way of lubricating the brain, and given his success rate in clearing up cases, there were very few people – at least, few below the rank of chief superintendent – who were prepared to dispute it. That night, however, Woodend hadn't gathered his team together to discuss an investigation. Instead, he planned to make an announcement about what was potentially a very delicate situation. And now – having been in the pub for over two hours, and with four pints under his belt – he supposed he'd better get on with it.

He cleared his throat, looked from Monika Paniatowski to Colin Beresford and back again.

9

'Inspector Rutter was given his final clearance from the police shrink the day before yesterday,' he said. 'Which means that he'll be reportin' for duty again tomorrow mornin'.'

There was an awkward pause.

Then Constable Beresford said, 'Well, sir, I must admit that certainly *is* good news.'

Good news? Woodend repeated silently.

It all depended on who you were – and how you looked at it.

It was good news for Bob Rutter, certainly – he'd been saying for some time that he'd finally got over the nervous breakdown he'd suffered as a result of his wife's murder, and was eager to climb back into the saddle.

It was good news as far Woodend himself was concerned, too. He'd worked with Rutter since his days down in Scotland Yard, and had come not only to trust him absolutely, but almost to regard him as the son he'd never had.

But what about Monika – Bob Rutter's one-time lover, his co-conspirator in the adulterous affair carried on behind Rutter's blind wife's back? She'd been wracked with guilt when Maria was murdered, even though the affair was long over by then. How would she feel about having to work closely with Rutter again?

Not that any of these considerations were on young Beresford's mind at that moment, Woodend realized. He was much more concerned about the effect that Rutter's return would have on *him*.

The landlord leaned out over the bar counter. 'Phone call for you, Mr Woodend,' he called out.

Woodend rose to his feet and walked over to the bar.

'Do you think there'll still be a place for me on the team when Inspector Rutter gets back, Sarge?' Beresford asked Paniatowski, the moment the chief inspector had gone.

Paniatowski took a sip of her vodka. 'You know, Beresford, the question you should really be asking yourself is not whether you'll be *allowed* to stay on the team, but whether you *want* to.'

'Why wouldn't I want to?'

'Because, if you do stay, you'll be working directly under the man who's at the very top of Mr Marlowe's Shit List. And some of that shit is bound to stick to you eventually.'

10

'Maybe you're right, but it doesn't seem to bother you too much,' Beresford pointed out.

'It bothers me a great deal,' Paniatowski corrected him. 'I'd like to be the first female chief inspector in the county, but I'll never get promotion as long as I'm Cloggin-it Charlie's bagman.'

'So why don't you put in for a transfer?'

'I've given that possibility serious consideration,' Paniatowski admitted. 'But in the end, I just can't bring myself to do it.'

'Why not?'

Why not indeed, Paniatowski wondered.

Because, she supposed, she owed Woodend.

Because a couple of times when she'd been in danger of drowning in a sea of her own neuroses, he had kept her afloat.

Because there was a bond between them that . . . that she didn't even want to start trying to analyse.

'He's very good at what he does,' she said, knowing full well she was copping out of really answering the question – and not giving a damn. 'I'm learning a lot from him – more than I think I could learn from any other senior officer on the Force.'

'I think *I* could learn a lot from both of you,' Beresford said seriously. 'And if that means joining the Shit List myself, it's a price that I'm more than willing to pay.'

Woodend returned from the bar, looking thoughtful.

'What's happened?' Paniatowski asked.

'It seems there's been somethin' of a blip in the normally smooth an' democratic process of electin' ourselves an MP,' Woodend told her.

'Sorry, sir, I'm not sure I quite understand what you're getting at?' Beresford said.

'He means one of the candidates has been murdered,' Paniatowski translated. 'Which one is it, sir?'

'Off-hand, I'd have to say it was the one who'd *really* pissed somebody off,' Woodend replied.

11

Two

There was very little traffic moving on the dual carriageway which ran between Whitebridge and Accrington that night, and the few drivers who had chosen to brave the thick fog did so with all the hesitation and timidity of an old lady negotiating an icy puddle.

'I can remember when this road was first opened, in the early fifties,' Woodend said, peering through the windscreen of his battered Wolseley into the swirling confusion. 'The local press made such a noise about it that you'd have thought it was the newest wonder of the world, beside which the Great Pyramid at Giza and the Coliseum in Rome shrank to mere insignificance.' He paused for a moment. 'Do either of you remember all the fuss?'

'No, I can't say that I do, sir,' Beresford replied – truthfully – from the back seat. 'I was only a little kid, back then.'

'And I'm not *that* much older than the constable,' Paniatowski said, from the front passenger seat.

'Babies!' Woodend said, in mock disgust. 'I'm workin' with babies. I'm more like a nanny to you than a boss.'

'And a very good nanny you are, sir,' said Paniatowski, who actually *did* remember the opening of the dual carriageway quite well, but had learned from previous experience that when Woodend was in the mood to blow off steam about 'the modern world', as he somewhat disparagingly called it, the easiest thing was just to let him get on with it.

'At long last, accordin' to the *Evenin' Courier*, two of the great mill towns of Lancashire had a connectin' road that was worthy of them,' Woodend continued. 'Aye, an' where do you think they found the space from to make this modern wonder?'

'They pulled down houses and despoiled the countryside,' Paniatowski said, deadpan.

'They pulled down houses an' despoiled the countryside!'

12

Woodend agreed. 'Bloody good houses, some of them. Houses that had stood for two hundred years, an' would have stood for *another* two hundred if they'd been left alone. New houses went, an' all – houses that had only just gone up. An' I don't even want to talk about the huge bleedin' gash they tore through the fields and meadows!'

'Well, that's progress for you, sir,' said Beresford, who had not been with the team long enough to have learned any better.

'Progress!' Woodend repeated, derisively. 'The road hadn't been opened for more than a few months before them same newspapers were complainin' that traffic was movin' along it at a snail's pace, an' sayin' that what Central Lancs really needed was a new dual carriageway to take some of the pressure off the old dual carriageway. An' what's the next step after that? A new-new dual carriageway to take the pressure off the old-new dual carriageway?'

He stopped speaking, not because he had run out of things to say on the subject but because of the flashing orange lights which had suddenly – and somewhat eerily – appeared out of the fog.

'We've arrived, an' to prove it, we're here,' Woodend told his team.

The lay-by was long enough to accommodate half a dozen parked lorries, but there was only one there at that moment – a twelve-wheeler with the name 'Holden Brothers Transport, Carlisle' painted on its side in large blue letters. Most of the rest of the available space was taken up by several police patrol cars, an ambulance and a Land Rover.

'I see Dr Shastri's already here,' Woodend said approvingly as he parked behind the doctor's Land Rover. He turned his head to address the constable in the back of the car. 'Have you met our esteemed an' intrepid police surgeon yet, Beresford?'

'Can't say I have, sir.'

'Then you've a real treat in store for you, lad. You're bound to fall in love with her – she could bring a statue out in a sweat – but however tempted you might feel to go romancin' her, I'd appreciate it if you'd curb the urge.'

'I beg your pardon, sir?'

'She's the best police surgeon that we've had in a very long while, so I don't want her fallin' for a handsome young bobby, getting' hitched to him, an' leavin' the job.'

Beresford felt himself starting to blush. Sergeant Paniatowski seemed to appreciate when Mr Woodend was joking and when he wasn't, the constable thought, but so far it was not a skill he had entirely mastered himself.

A uniformed inspector walked over to the Wolseley. 'I've secured the site, sir,' he said.

Woodend winced.

Secured the site!

Why was it that so many bobbies now felt the need to talk like that, he wondered. At what point had good straight-forward policing become tangled up in jargon?

'Who found the stiff?' he asked aloud.

'The driver of that lorry. He pulled in because the fog was getting thicker. He noticed the body straight away, but thought it was just a tramp lying there at first. It was only when he got right on top of it that he could see there'd been foul play.'

'An' where is he now?'

'I got one of the lads to drive him into town. I thought he could use a good hot cup of tea.'

Now that *was* good policin', Woodend thought – an' not a hint of jargon in sight.

'Right, well, I suppose we'd better go an' look at the corpse,' he said.

Emergency spotlights had been set up in a rough circle around the dead man, and kneeling next to the body was a woman wearing a heavy sheepskin jacket over a colourful silk sari.

'How's it goin', Doc?' Woodend asked.

Dr Shastri looked up from her grisly work, and favoured him with one of her more radiant smiles.

'My dear Mr Woodend,' she said warmly. 'What a great pleasure it is to see you.'

'The feelin's mutual,' Woodend told her. 'What can you tell me about the body?'

Dr Shastri clicked her tongue disapprovingly.

'Always so eager to get down to business, with not even a hint of polite chit-chat first,' she said. 'You are completely bereft of social skills, aren't you, you poor fellow?'

14

Woodend grinned. 'Completely,' he agreed. 'Now what about my stiff, Doc?'

'He was killed by a blow to the back of the head.'

'How hard was it?'

'Very violent indeed. If you wish to replicate the effect for yourself, I suggest you get a packet of crisps – any flavour will do – place it on a flat surface, and bring the palm of your hand down on it, as hard as you can.'

Woodend grimaced. 'So whoever delivered the blow almost certainly meant to kill him?'

'Undoubtedly. Especially in the light of the injuries the killer inflicted on his victim *after* he had delivered it.'

'An' what might they have been?'

Dr Shastri straightened up, and moved away from the body.

'See for yourself, my dear Chief Inspector,' she invited

The corpse had been placed on to a large plastic sheet. It was dressed in an expensive blue lounge suit, and since it was lying on its front, the wound to the back of the head was clearly visible.

The killer must have used *massive* force to stove in his skull like that, Woodend thought, letting his eyes travel slowly from the wound itself to the shoulders of the jacket, which were stained bright red.

'He was not killed here,' Dr Shastri said conversationally, 'so although pieces of his brain will have been spattered everywhere, I have very little hope of being able to recover any of them.'

Behind him, Woodend heard Beresford gulping for air.

'Easy, lad,' he said over his shoulder. 'Think of it as no more than a piece of dead meat.'

He turned his attention back on the corpse. There had been real anger – real *hatred* – behind the attack, he thought.

'Where are the injuries which were inflicted after he was dead?' he asked Dr Shastri.

'Ah, I must turn him over in order for you to see the results of the *post-mortem* attack,' the doctor said, crouching down again. 'It might be wiser for you to leave now, Constable.'

'I'll be all right,' Beresford said, unconvincingly.

'Very well, that is your choice,' Shastri said, and expertly rolled the corpse over on to the other end of the plastic sheet.

It was the victim's mouth that Woodend noticed first – or

rather, the place where the mouth had been. All that remained now was a mush of bone, muscle and flesh.

'Jesus!' Woodend said.

'I think I have managed to find most of the teeth,' Dr Shastri informed him. 'Not that I expect them to tell us anything that we don't already know. I should have thought it would be fairly obvious to anyone what had happened to him.'

'Aye, you don't need a medical degree to see he's been given a right good hammerin',' Woodend agreed.

'But it is the other wound which truly fascinates me,' Dr Shastri continued. 'I do not think I have ever come across an attack quite like that before.'

'The other wound?' Woodend asked.

Dr Shastri laughed. 'Tear your eyes away from his face for a moment and examine his mid-section,' she suggested.

The chief inspector shifted his gaze downwards. Pine's jacket was open and largely undamaged, but his shirt had been slashed by the same cut which had ripped through the flesh and muscle it had been covering.

The incision had opened up the dead man from just below his sternum right down to his pelvis, and exposed most of his stomach and a great deal of his intestines, thereby turning what had once been an ingenious biological machine into no more than a pile of bloody offal.

'It must have been very messy work to carry out,' Dr Shastri said, clinically. 'To tear through someone else's stomach in this way, you need a fairly strong stomach yourself.'

Yes, that was exactly what you would need, Woodend thought, as behind him, he heard the sound of Constable Beresford throwing up.

Three

Woodend stood in the reception room outside the chief constable's office, waiting for the green light (set into the door-frame) to flash and buzz, as a signal that he was now permitted to enter the inner sanctum.

He was anticipating a long wait, since this was the style of the man he had been summoned to see. Henry Marlowe measured his own importance by the fact that he *could* keep his subordinates waiting, and Woodend had no doubt that even once he was inside the office itself, the chief constable would prolong the wait by pretending to study whatever documents – however irrelevant to the matter in hand – that he happened to have on his desk at that particular moment.

The chief inspector looked out of the window. The fog which had plagued Whitebridge the previous day had almost completely lifted, and the late spring sun was making its first appearance in nearly a week. Birds were swooping and diving in the air over the police car park, and squirrels were busy scuttling around the bases of the nearby trees.

Life was renewing itself everywhere, Woodend thought fancifully, though – thanks to a person or persons as yet unknown – Bradley Pine would most definitely not be taking part in that particular process.

The green light buzzed.

It was probably a technical fault, Woodend thought, glancing down at his watch and noting that he had been standing there for no more than a couple of minutes. Or perhaps it was human error – a case of Marlowe pressing the button accidentally. Whichever it was, the chief constable couldn't be willing to see him already. But since the light undoubtedly *had* flashed – and his was not to reason why – he knocked on the door, then turned the handle and stepped inside.

Marlowe looked up from his paperwork immediately –

17

another first! – and said, 'I'd like a progress report on the investigation into Bradley Pine's murder, Chief Inspector.'

Woodend scratched his ear. 'There hasn't *been* any progress to speak of,' he admitted. 'The patrol cars have been alerted to look out for Pine's vehicle, but since the body wasn't discovered until most people were gettin' ready for bed, there wasn't much more we could do.'

This was the point at which the bollocking should come, Woodend thought. This was the point at which Marlowe should tell him that any halfway decent chief inspector would already have had the murderer under lock and key.

But that didn't happen. Instead, Marlowe said, 'Being the first senior officer at the scene of the crime does not automatically give you the right to be put in charge of the investigation, you know.'

'I appreciate that, sir,' Woodend replied.

'However, after having given the matter due consideration, I *have* decided to assign the case to you,' Marlowe continued, 'though naturally, taking into account both the prominence of the victim and the particularly gruesome manner of his death, there will be some conditions attached.'

'What sort of conditions?' Woodend wondered.

'I want this murder cleared up as soon as possible.'

'Which means?'

'Within the week.'

'I can't promise that,' Woodend told the chief constable. 'Conductin' a murder investigation's isn't like runnin' a bus company, where you know the route you goin' to have to cover, an' you can draw up some kind of timetable for how long it should take you.'

'Well, of course I realize that, but—'

'In fact, it's much more like gardenin'.'

'Gardening!' Marlowe exclaimed. 'How could it possibly be like gardening?'

'Because you can do all kinds of things to encourage the seeds to begin sproutin', but until they actually do, you can't even think of beginnin' to think of harvestin' them.'

The chief constable shook his head – slowly, and almost despairingly. 'There are times when you don't sound at all like an officer working in a modern police force,' he said.

'There are times when I don't *feel* much like one, either,'

18

Woodend admitted. 'Listen, sir, you've often enough made it quite plain that you don't have a lot of confidence in my ability to lead an enquiry—'

'And you've often enough given me ample grounds for that belief—'

'—so why don't you simply assign the case to somebody you *do* have confidence in?'

Marlowe swallowed hard.

'It's true that there have been times when your approach has made me seriously doubt your competence,' he said, 'but there have also been times – especially in dealing with crimes of a bizarre nature – when you seem to have been able to solve cases which have quite baffled most of your colleagues.'

It was not a wise move to grin at his boss's obvious discomfort, but Woodend did it anyway.

'Thank you, sir,' he said. 'That means a lot to me – especially comin' from you.'

'I don't know *why* you should have been so successful in those cases,' Marlowe continued, hurriedly. 'Perhaps, after all, it was no more than a matter of luck.'

'Aye, that might explain it,' Woodend agreed.

'Or perhaps, when the crime *is* bizarre, your brain is better attuned to the insane mind behind it than those of more *professional* officers.'

'So it's a case of set a nutter to catch a nutter, is it?' Woodend asked innocently.

'I wouldn't have put it quite in those terms, Chief Inspector,' Marlowe said frostily, 'but you will concur with me that Bradley Pine's murderer is a dangerous lunatic, won't you?'

'Murderers are pretty much dangerous by definition,' Woodend agreed, 'an' slittin' open another man's stomach is not somethin' I'd normally associate with a well-balanced feller.'

'Precisely!' Marlowe said. 'So, in this particular investigation, there'll be no real need to delve very deeply into the victim's background, will there?'

'I'm sorry, sir,' Woodend said, 'I think I must have missed a step in the logic of that argument.'

Marlowe sighed. 'Bradley Pine was killed by a madman, so it is certainly worth looking closely at any madmen who he might have had dealings with in the past,' he explained.

'On the other hand, it would be a complete waste of time to dwell too much on the dealings he had with people who were perfectly sane.'

'It doesn't work like that,' Woodend said.

'What do you mean?'

'There was real rage behind the attack on Bradley Pine, an' maybe that rage had taken the killer to the point of madness. But the *cause* of the rage may have been perfectly understandable an' perfectly sane.'

'You're splitting hairs,' Marlowe said dismissively.

'People sometimes kill simply because they've been taken beyond the point of endurance,' Woodend argued. 'An' what's got them to that stage is often somethin' that happened a long time ago.'

'You will not waste time and resources looking too closely into Bradley Pine's background,' Marlowe said firmly. 'That is a direct order, and though I will not personally be here to see that it is enforced—'

His mouth snapped shut like a steel trap, as if he'd suddenly realized he'd said too much.

'What was that, sir?' Woodend asked.

'I will not be supervising you directly in this investigation, but whoever assumes that responsibility will be working to the remit that I have given him,' Marlowe said, attempting to blur his previous statement.

'You'll be replacin' Bradley Pine as Conservative candidate, won't you?' Woodend asked.

'The idea has been mooted,' Marlowe admitted, 'but that is really no concern of yours, Chief Inspector. *Your* task is to track down the brutal and insane killer who may well yet turn out to have had no connection with Bradley Pine at all, but merely selected him because he was in the wrong place at the wrong time.'

Woodend said nothing. If Marlowe was prepared to accept that particular theory as a possibility, he thought, then persuading him that the moon was made of green cheese should be a doddle.

'And speaking of Pine's movements, I might be able to point you in the right direction, there,' Marlowe continued.

'Oh aye?'

'Indeed. I attended a meeting that Bradley addressed

yesterday evening, and at the end of it he came up to me for advice.'

'What kind of advice?'

'Nothing that could possibly have any relevance to the case. He wanted to know how I thought his speech had gone down, and wondered if I could make any suggestions to improve his performance in the future.' Marlowe paused. 'I think he was beginning to realize he was completely out of his depth, you know. I think he was starting to regret accepting the nomination at all, when there was another – clearly more able – candidate available.'

'An' that candidate would be?' Woodend asked.

'That candidate would be *me!*' Marlowe said, not quite sure whether or not he should take offence.

'Of course it would, sir,' Woodend said.

'But that's neither here nor there,' Marlowe ploughed on. 'The important point is that he happened to say to me that when he left the village hall he intended to drive straight to St Mary's Church. Bradley was a Roman Catholic, you know, though you shouldn't hold that against him.'

'I won't,' Woodend said, wisely concealing what would have been his second broad grin of the meeting. 'Us Buddhists tend to be very tolerant of other religions, sir.'

'Are you a *Buddhist* now?' Marlowe asked.

'I am,' Woodend lied.

Marlowe shook his head. 'Extraordinary – though not really all that surprising,' he said.

The chief constable glanced involuntarily at the telephone, then at his watch, then at the telephone again.

He was on tenterhooks, Woodend thought. He knew he was almost certain to be contacted by the Conservative Party Selection Committee, but he wouldn't really be at ease until the call had actually been made.

'Can I go, sir?' the chief inspector asked.

'Yes, yes, by all means,' Marlowe said impatiently, as if the murder case were now no more than an annoying distraction.

Woodend turned and walked to the door. He was already turning the handle when he heard Marlowe say, 'You will remember what I told you, won't you, Chief Inspector?'

'I'm sorry, sir?'

'You are not – under any circumstances – to carry out a detailed check on Bradley Pine's background.'

'Oh yes, I'll remember that,' Woodend assured him.

'Good, because if you don't . . .'

'You've no worries on that score, sir. Us Buddhists have memories like elephants. It's part of the trainin'.'

Woodend stepped out in the reception room and closed Marlowe's door behind him.

I'll remember it, all right, he thought, *but that's a long way from sayin' I'll pay any attention to it.*

Four

Whenever the chief constable was holding one of his press briefings – and how he *loved* to hold his press briefings – he would describe the room in which Woodend was now standing as 'The Incident Room'. Once the briefing was in full flow – and his normally high opinion of himself was inflated even further – he would go so far as to talk about it as 'The Nerve Centre of Our Investigation, Located in the Very Heart of Police Headquarters'.

It wasn't a description that DCI Woodend found it easy to subscribe to. The nerve centre of any investigation that he took part in was, as far as he was concerned, in his head.

Beside, whilst he was willing to admit that he had – in common with most other Northern men from a working class background – an almost complete ignorance of the subject of human biology (that sort of thing was best left to the women, who made a sort of hobby out of it) he was pretty sure that the heart did not reside in a person's feet, whereas the 'Incident Room' was quite clearly in the basement.

In fact, the Incident Room *was* the basement. Or rather, the basement *became* the Incident Room whenever a major crime had been committed, but otherwise served as a repository for junk which didn't seem to particularly belong anywhere else.

The junk which had built up since the last major case had been cleared away overnight. Now the basement contained a dozen desks, set out in a horseshoe pattern so that the detective constables manning them could see both each other and the large blackboard which had been erected at the broad end of the horseshoe.

Woodend studied the young DCs for a moment.

Every one of them was talking energetically on the phone, and taking copious notes as he went.

Yesterday, they had all been based in small stations dotted

throughout Central Lancashire, the chief inspector thought, and the caseloads they had been handling involved such crimes as burglary, car theft, wilful damage and arson. Now they had been trawled into headquarters, and suddenly found themselves in the middle of a real murder inquiry. All of which meant that they were as excited as little children who'd discovered, on Christmas morning, that Santa had brought them *exactly* the toys that they'd wished for.

Woodend nodded to Detective Sergeant Dix – a grey-haired veteran who was supervising the initial phases of the operation – then positioned himself by the blackboard.

He cleared his throat. 'For the benefit of those of you who don't already know me, I'm Chief Inspector Charlie Woodend, an' I've been put in charge of this investigation,' he said.

The detective constables looked up from their tasks with interest. They all *did* know him – if only by reputation.

'Finish the calls you're makin', then listen up to what I've got to tell you,' Woodend told them.

The detective constables galloped through their calls and replaced the receivers.

'Let's get one thing out of the way immediately,' Woodend said. 'There is absolutely nothin' glamorous about a murder investigation. It's hard work, an' it's frustratin' work, but if we all pull together, we just might get a result.' He paused to light a cigarette. 'At the moment, you've got only one task in front of you, which is to find out where Bradley Pine went last night an' what happened to his green Cortina once he'd been killed. Is that clear so far?'

The detective constables nodded enthusiastically.

Kids! the chief inspector thought, with a mixture of concern, affection – and envy.

'It's not actually *necessary*, in operational terms, for you to be told the precise details of the murder,' he continued. 'Strictly speakin', all you need to know in order to do your jobs is that, as the result of actions by a person or persons unknown, Bradley Pine is dead. But I've always believed that if you're part of a team you should be kept informed – as much as is practicable – about what's goin' on. That's why I've asked Sergeant Dix to tell you exactly what happened to Pine last night, even though that same information is still bein' withheld from the press.'

24

The constables looked pleased – as well they might.

'But before you're briefed, let me give you one word of warnin',' Woodend said. 'When you go off duty tonight, there'll be loads of people – wives, girlfriends an' mates – who'll be itchin' to be filled in on the gory details. An' there'll be a great temptation to tell them, because everybody likes to be the centre of attention an' interest – everybody likes to reveal secrets. But it's a temptation you must resist. Is *that* clear?'

The detective constables nodded earnestly, as if to say that *of course* the secret was safe with them.

'Good!' Woodend said. 'Because if word *does* get out – an' I find it came from any of you – I'll get the offender's balls between a couple of Accrington bricks an' crush them to a pulp.'

The young constables – for whom a surging in their loins was still a recent enough experience for it not to have lost its novelty value – grimaced.

Woodend paused again to allow time for their scrotal sacs to return to their normal positions.

'Your team leader will be Detective Inspector Rutter,' he continued. 'At the moment, he's travellin' up from London, but he managed to ring me while he was changin' trains at Crewe, an' I've filled him in on most of the details.' He turned to the grey-haired sergeant. 'You've worked with Bob Rutter before, haven't you, Sergeant Dix?'

Dix nodded. 'I have, sir. He's a good man.'

'He's a *very* good man – one of the best – an' he has my full confidence,' Woodend said.

But was that entirely true any more, he wondered. Could Bob Rutter handle so much stress on his first day back on the job?

Well, there was only one way to find out.

'If you study the way DI Rutter works, you should learn a lot from him,' he continued. 'But one more word of warnin' – mess with him, an' what he'll do to you in return will make bein' fed through a meat grinder seem like a holiday by the seaside.'

He'd done all he could to smooth Rutter's passage back into the job, he thought.

Now it was up to Bob.

*   *   *

25

The man stepping down from the train which had just pulled in at the main platform of Whitebridge Railway Station was in his early thirties, carrying a suitcase, and dressed in a smart blue suit.

He looked – to anyone giving him a casual glance – like a successful businessman. A closer examination, however, revealed quite a different story. The lines etched into his face told a tale of worry and strain – possibly even of despair – and any observer would have been forced to conclude that if he *was* a businessman, he had not been so successful recently.

There were other signs that all was not well. He seemed ill at ease, and instead of heading briskly for the exit – as any businessman with a tight schedule would – he remained on the platform, looking back longingly at the train from which he had just disembarked.

The truth was that Bob Rutter was far from sure it had been a good idea to return to Whitebridge at all – and now was fighting the very strong urge to get back on the train and let it take him where it would.

The train guard was walking along the platform, checking that all the doors had been properly closed. Satisfied that they had been, he returned to the guards' van, blew his whistle, and climbed aboard.

Rutter watched the train pull out of the station, then picked up his suitcase and walked towards the exit.

The station occupied an elevated position above the town, and once clear of the ticket gate, a panoramic view of Whitebridge opened up before Bob Rutter.

There were the cathedral and the bus station; there the old cotton mills, many of which had now been converted into other more-or-less viable businesses; there the canal, along which large barges had once carried the spun cotton cloth to the seaport of Liverpool.

He remembered the first time he had come to Whitebridge, three years earlier. Then, he had been following in the wake of his boss, who had transferred from Scotland Yard – who had been *ejected* from Scotland Yard – and was about to take up a new posting in the Central Lancs CID. Then, he'd had a wife who was just learning to cope with blindness and motherhood. Then, he had yet to meet Monika Paniatowski and embark on an affair with her which he bitterly regretted – but could not quite bring himself to wish undone.

Was it *only* three years? Bob Rutter asked himself.

It felt like a hundred.

He felt a hundred.

He walked over to the taxi rank.

'Where to?' the cabbie asked.

Where to, indeed, Rutter wondered.

He had in his pocket the key to the house that he and Maria had lived in – the house in which she had been murdered. The murderer had set a fire to cover his grisly crime, but the insurance company had informed Rutter, by letter, that all the damage had been repaired, and the house was once again perfectly habitable. So he could always go there, if he wished.

'Where to?' the cabbie repeated, with a slight edge of impatience entering his voice.

'Whitebridge Police Headquarters,' Rutter said.

Five

Constable Beresford and DS Paniatowski were already in the office when Woodend arrived, and from the evidence of the poisonous cloud of cigarette smoke which hovered above them, it was clear they'd been there for some time.

'So how have you two been keepin' yourself amused while I've been addressin' the troops?' Woodend asked, taking his customary seat and lighting up a cigarette of his own to add to the general fug.

'We've been researching into Bradley Pine's background,' Paniatowski told him.

Woodend chuckled. 'Our Mr Marlowe won't like that, Monika. He won't like it one bit.'

'He won't?'

'Definitely not. He's given me specific instructions that we're not to delve too deeply into Pine's past.'

'Why would he have done that?' Paniatowski asked.

'I'm assumin' it's because he doesn't want us diggin' up anythin' with even the whiff of scandal attached to it.'

'But why should that matter, now that Bradley Pine's dead?' Beresford wondered.

'Because while *he's* dead, there are other people – possibly includin' our esteemed chief constable – who might also be involved in the scandals, an' are still very much alive,' Woodend explained.

'What scandals are you talking about, sir?' Beresford asked.

'I've no idea,' Woodend admitted.

'Then how can you be sure there are any scandals?'

'Because it's in the nature of the beast.'

'I don't understand,' Beresford confessed.

'Then listen carefully, lad, an' you just might. You can vote for who you like at the local elections, but all the important decisions about the town are made over drinks in the bar of the Golf an' Country Club. The fact is that Whitebridge is controlled by a group of fellers who've never even thought of standin' for election – because they've never seen the need.'

'I still don't see it,' Beresford admitted.

Woodend shook his head, half-pityingly. 'Ah, to be young an' innocent again,' he said. 'The Whitebridge Establishment runs this town like a well-oiled machine, an' what keeps the oil flowin' is favours an' mutual back-scratchin'. So Mr A will do somethin' for Mr B, and Mr B will do somethin' for Mr C, et cetera, et cetera. Of course, none of this comes free, an' eventually the favours will have to be paid for. But the payment won't necessarily be made to the person who granted you the favour in the first place. You see what I mean?'

'I'd be happier if you'd spell it out a bit more,' Beresford said.

'Let's say Mr W wants a favour from Mr A. Now Mr A doesn't owe him a thing, but Mr N does – an' Mr A owes Mr N. So Mr W gets Mr N to put the pressure on Mr A.'

'But that's nothing short of municipal corruption!' Beresford said, outraged. 'That's *illegal*!'

'Maybe it would be, if it was all carried out as crudely as I've just described it,' Woodend agreed. 'But it isn't. I doubt money ever changes hands. I doubt anythin's ever put down in writin'. A wink an' nod is all they need. An' sometimes not even that – because they share the same values, an' they understand each other perfectly. So even if you could pin down the details of some of their deals – an' that would take a lot of effort, an' a lot of luck – the best you're goin' to end up with is somethin' that's a bit morally questionable.'

'That's better than nothing,' Beresford said.

'Is it?' Woodend asked. 'Who to? Them buggers up at the Golf Club don't care what people like *you* think of them. All they need is the approval of their mates – an' they get that readily enough, because all their mates are wallowin' around in the same trough of shit that they are.'

'But then—'

'But then, occasionally, your opinion *does* matter, like when they're runnin' for Parliament. So what I think Marlowe is worried about is that I might find a skeleton in Pine's cupboard which is busily engaged in scratchin' the back of a skeleton in his.' Woodend turned to Paniatowski. 'Wouldn't you agree about that, Monika?'

'Yes, I would,' Paniatowski said cautiously. 'But surely Mr Marlowe must know that whatever instructions he gives you, you'll go your own way – just like you always do.'

'He does know that,' Woodend agreed. 'But he's gamblin' on the fact that what he's said will cause me to rein myself in just a *little* bit.'

'Why run even that risk?' Paniatowski wondered. 'Why not put one of his normal lapdogs in charge of the investigation?'

'Ah, that's because he's badly in need of a result on this one,' Woodend said.

Paniatowski nodded sagely. 'Yes, I can see that,' she said.

'Can you see it, Beresford?' Woodend asked.

'I think so,' the constable said.

'Then explain it to me.'

'Mr Marlowe will be running his campaign on the basis that if he was a good chief constable, he'll make a good MP.'

'But?'

'But he won't look as if he's been much of a chief constable at all if he can't come up with Bradley Pine's killer.'

'Exactly. You're only as good as your last arrest, an' the last arrest Marlowe has to have before polling day is the arrest of Bradley Pine's killer. So that's why I'm on the case, because – as much as he hates to admit it – he thinks I'm the man most likely to get him his result.'

'But if you don't – and he loses the election because of it – he's going to hold you personally responsible!' Beresford said.

'Which would be totally unreasonable, but perfectly in character,' Woodend agreed.

'And if he loses the election because of something you've uncovered about him, it'll be even worse,' Beresford said, with growing horror.

Paniatowski smiled. 'Now do you understand why I said you should think twice before trying to join this team?' she asked the constable.

There were no fields in the Greenfields area of Whitebridge. No fields, no trees, no municipal gardens – no signs whatever of the natural world.

In the old days, when the mills had all been working at full steam, the inhabitants of Greenfields had been spinners and tacklers. They had been poor, but they had also been honest and hardworking. They kept their two-up-two-down terraced houses freshly painted and scrupulously clean, and even though each house was separated from its neighbour in the next street by no more than two small back yards and a narrow alley, the residents had some justification for regarding their homes as little palaces.

All that had changed since the mills began to close down. The mill workers had sought fresh occupations and left the area, and the houses had been taken over by folk whose main concern was to avoid work of *any* kind.

The bobbies who had to walk the Greenfields beat all hated it. The crime they came across there was petty but often very unpleasant, and was perpetrated by people who were both vicious and unimaginative. It was a slum. It was a dump. The current residents would rather spend their money on boozing and betting than on feeding and clothing their children.

It was certainly not an area in which anyone would expect to find a two-year-old Ford Cortina, but that was exactly what the motor patrol found at ten forty-seven that morning.

The fug in Woodend's office was getting thicker by the minute, and Beresford, who hadn't been smoking for anything like as long as the others, was starting to find it hard to take.

'So tell me what we know about Bradley Pine, Monika,' Woodend said, before adding to the pollution by lighting up yet another Capstan Full Strength cigarette.

'We know that he was what you call a self-made man,' Monika Paniatowski replied.

'Interestin' label,' Woodend said. 'A self-made man. What exactly does that mean?'

'What it says. He was brought up in Holy Trinity Orphanage over in Brinsleydale.'

'It's a Catholic orphanage, isn't it?'

'I should think so, with a name like that. Anyway, when he left the orphanage, at the age of fifteen, he went to work as an apprentice in Hawtrey's Mattresses—'

'Which is now Hawtrey an' Pine Holdings?'

'Correct.'

'So how did a penniless orphan eventually get to be a partner in the business?'

'Through being clever and inventive.'

'How so?'

'He came up with an idea which is now widely used in the production of interior sprung mattresses, and for which he holds the patent. It didn't exactly make him a multimillionaire, but it did give him sufficient cash to buy his way into the company.'

'An' this would have been when, exactly?'

'About fifteen years ago.'

The chief inspector did a quick mental calculation. 'So Pine would have been in his early-to-middle twenties at the time?'

'That's right.'

Woodend whistled softly. 'I see what you mean about him bein' self-made. I seem to remember readin' somewhere that the other half of the company – Hawtrey – is dead now. Is that right?'

'Yes, it is. But you're wrong to assume that Pine owned half the company. Alec Hawtrey held on to just enough of the stock to make sure he remained the majority shareholder.'

'Remind me what happened to Hawtrey,' Woodend said.

'He died in a mountaineering accident up in the Lakes, a couple of years ago.'

'How old was he when this happened?'

'In his mid-fifties.'

Woodend sniffed. 'Seems a bit long in the tooth to be buggerin' about climbin' mountains,' he said. 'So what happened to Alec Hawtrey's shares after he died?'

'They went to his widow, Thelma.'

'So she's the one who's actually in charge?'

Paniatowski shook her head. 'She makes slightly more money out of the company than Pine did, but she doesn't take any active part in running it.'

'An' the business is healthy, is it?'

'More than healthy. It's fighting fit. It posted record profits last year, and had to take on a lot of extra staff in order to meet demand.'

'You've done very well to come up with so much on the feller in such a short time, Monika,' Woodend said approvingly.

'Thank you, but I can't really claim much personal credit for it,' Paniatowski told him. 'I got most of the material out of his political manifesto.'

'So now let's get on to the really big questions,' Woodend suggested, taking a deep drag of his cigarette. 'What was the motive behind Bradley Pine's murder, and – perhaps even more importantly, in terms of openin' up the investigation – why did the killer mutilate him once he was dead?'

The other two looked him blankly for a moment.

Then Paniatowski said, 'I've no idea. I've never come across a case of murder and mutilation before. Have you, sir?'

'Only once,' Woodend told her. 'It was while I was at the Yard. The victim had been beaten to death, then his killers had cut off his genitals an' stuffed them in his mouth.'

Beresford shuddered, and put his hand protectively – and instinctively – over his lap.

'Did you ever find out the reason for the castration?' Monika Paniatowski asked.

'I did. It turned out that the dead man had raped the sister of the two fellers who murdered him. I can't say I was entirely surprised by the result. I suspected it might be somethin' like that right from the start, because what they'd done made a twisted kind of sense, you see. But this is a different matter altogether. Whoever killed Pine smashed in his mouth an' slit open his stomach. What kind of message was that meant to send?'

'Smashing in his mouth could have signified that he talked too much,' Paniatowski said.

'An' slittin' open his stomach signified that he *ate* too much?' Woodend asked.

'Probably not,' Paniatowski agreed.

'I suppose that sex could have been involved,' Beresford suggested, tentatively.

'In what way?'

'Well, I'm not entirely sure,' admitted Beresford, who was still a virgin, but would have died rather than admit it to the other two. 'Maybe he treated a woman very badly, and this was her revenge.'

'Fair point,' Woodend agreed. 'What have we found out about his love life so far, Monika?'

'Not a lot,' Paniatowski admitted. 'There hasn't been time.

But we do know that he wasn't married, nor ever had been – which is quite unusual for a man in his late thirties.'

'Aye, it is,' Woodend said. 'Is there any indication that he might have been inclined the other way?'

'There's no record of him ever having been arrested for loitering outside public lavatories, if that's what you mean,' Paniatowski said.

'Not that that rules out the possibility of his bein' homo-sexual,' Woodend said. 'Still, there's no point in just sittin' here an' speculatin', is there? It's time we got diggin'.'

'Into his past or his present?' Paniatowski asked.

Woodend grinned. 'He doesn't have a "present",' he said. 'He's bloody-well dead.'

'Into his recent past, or into his more distant past?' Monika Paniatowski amended.

'Into both.'

'In spite of what Mr Marlowe said to you?'

'Aye, we can't let a dickhead like him get in the way of us doin' our job properly, now can we? So how shall we divide it up?' Woodend thought for a moment. 'Beresford, you can go up to the mattress factory an' see what you can find out about Pine's rise to fame an' fortune.'

'You want me to go on my own, sir?' the constable asked, sounding somewhat alarmed.

'Why not on your own? Do you want me there beside you, holdin' your hand?'

'No, but—'

'It's about time you learned that there's a lot more to bein' a detective than just wearin' your best suit to work. Don't worry, lad, you can do it. I've got confidence in you.'

Beresford either blushed with embarrassment or glowed with pleasure – and very possibly both.

'Thank you, sir,' he said.

Woodend turned to Paniatowski. 'You're still a Catholic, aren't you, Monika?'

'Not exactly,' the sergeant said, with some show of reluc-tance.

'But you do know more about the mysteries of the faith than either me or Beresford?'

'I suppose so.'

'Then you get to go to St Mary's, which is where, accordin'

34

to our beloved chief constable, Pine was headin' when he left the village hall meetin'. See if he arrived at the church as he expected to, an' if he *did* arrive, how long he stayed an' who he talked to.'

'And what will you be doing, sir?' Paniatowski asked.

'Me? I shall be descendin' into the Heart of Darkness.'

'I'm sorry, sir?' Beresford said.

'He'll be going where no man with honest working class credentials would ever normally dream of showing his face,' supplied Paniatowski, who was well tuned in to Woodend's mind.

'I still don't get it,' Beresford admitted.

'First, I shall be poppin' into the morgue – which *isn't* the Heart of Darkness – to have a quick word with Dr Shastri,' Woodend explained. 'Then I'll take myself over to the Whitebridge Golf an' Country Club – which is.'

'Where they'll kill the fatted calf, and welcome you with open arms, like a long-lost brother,' Paniatowski said.

'I somehow doubt that,' Woodend replied. 'But since I *am* a police officer engaged in a murder inquiry, they won't be able to actually bar the door to me, either – however much they'd like to.'

Six

St Mary's Roman Catholic Church had stood at the crest of Woodstock Hill for over five hundred years.

In its early days, when Whitebridge was no more than a small village in which a collection of downtrodden peasants scratched out a meagre existence, the gothic spire and sturdy square tower must have been a truly formidable sight. Even in the modern Whitebridge – a city that had recently begun to experiment with high-rise buildings – it was still the most impressive structure around, eclipsing the Anglican cathedral which the Protestant ecclesiastical planners had foolishly decided to construct on the flat ground in the town centre.

The edifice's history was chequered, as most history is. Though it was originally built as a Catholic church, there had been a period – a little over three centuries, in fact – when it had fallen into the hands of King Henry VIII's breakaway movement, the adherents of which had smashed the statues and stripped away all other signs of Papistry. But the world turns – as it inevitably will – and in the mid-nineteenth century, Catholic cotton money had been used to purchase the church and re-consecrate it into the old faith.

Monika Paniatowski could have left her bright red MGA right in front of the church – there were parking restrictions in force there, but what did that matter when you were the law? – yet instead she chose to park at the bottom of the hill, even though that meant subjecting herself to a long, steep climb.

The reasoning behind her decision was simple. Her sporty car was one of the most distinctive vehicles in Whitebridge, so people seeing it parked outside the church might be forgiven for assuming she had gone inside to pray.

And that was an assumption she really did not want *anyone* to make.

Ever!

That was an assumption it was worth climbing the highest and most gruelling *mountain* to avoid.

As she toiled up the steep gradient, Monika found herself thinking about her past in general, and her mother in particular – and with these thoughts came an involuntary physical reaction which made her feel as though her bowels were slowly turning to water.

Her mother had been a devout Roman Catholic. It had been Agnieszka Paniatowski's faith that had sustained her during those long, terrible, years while she and her daughter had crisscrossed war-torn Europe as refugees on the run. Never once – despite all the hardship they had endured, despite all the horrors they had seen – had that faith of Agnieszka's wavered.

And neither had her little daughter's. Even as a small child, Monika had understood that she was both a Pole and Roman Catholic – and that the two things were so intertwined that she could no more separate the one from other than she could separate her mind from her body, or her heart from her soul.

It was only later, in the supposed safety of this English mill town where they had come to live, that she had finally lost her faith – and even then she had not so much *lost* it as had it *torn from her* by what was said from the other side of the confessional grill.

Monika is thirteen years old. Her body is beginning to fill out, and the boys at school have started to notice her.

And not just the boys.

Not just at school.

She is sitting in the confessional of St Mary's Church. Her *church. On the other side of the grille sits* her *priest.*

'Bless me, Father, for I have sinned,' she says. 'It has been a week since my last confession.'

For a moment, she can say no more, but when she does *speak again, the words spill out of her and feel like they will never stop. She tells how her stepfather came to her room, late at night and smelling of drink, and put his hand on her shoulder. She describes how that hand – that big, beefy, demanding, hand – burrowed its way under the blankets and found its way to her young breasts. With tears streaming down her face, she recounts what happened next – how he climbed*

37

into her bed, how he forced her legs apart, how he . . . how he . . .

'Do you think perhaps you led him on, my child?' the priest, Father O'Brien, asks.

She is not even sure she knows what that means.

'Led him on?' she repeats.

'Man is but an imperfect being, prone to temptation,' the priest intones. 'Did you tempt him, Monika? Did you cause him to think that his attentions would be welcomed?'

'No. I didn't. I swear I didn't.'

'But did you, deep within yourself, want him to do it to you, my child?' the priest persists.

She feels like yelling at the top of her voice that of course she didn't want him to do all those terrible things to her.

She wants to scream out that the priest must be a bloody fool for even thinking to ask that.

But she is in a confessional, talking to a holy man who represents Mother Church, and all she says is, 'No, Father, I didn't want him to do it.'

There is a long silence from the other side of the grill, then the priest says, 'But did you enjoy it, my child?'

Enjoy it! Did she enjoy it? Can't he even begin to imagine how soiled she felt when it was all over?

'No, Father,' she says, almost in a whisper. 'I didn't enjoy it all.'

'Then you have done nothing wrong, my child, and there will be no penance to pay. You may continue with your confession.'

'Is that it?' she asks herself. 'I've done nothing wrong? And that's the end of the matter?'

She leaves the confessional with her faith sorely tested – but still intact. And then, a week later, as she is walking past the Catholic Club, she looks through the window and sees Father O'Brien and her stepfather drinking pints of Guinness together.

And, fool that she is, she takes comfort from that!

She actually believes that the priest is telling her stepfather that he must stop molesting her.

But later that night she wakes up to find the familiar hands making their familiar demands of her body, and knows that nothing has changed – that, despite the priest talking to her stepfather, no change has even been suggested.

She has been to her last confession. She has lost her belief in the priesthood, and with it, her belief in God.

Monika had reached the level of the church. She was finding it hard to breathe, though it was her memories, rather than the steep climb, which were the source of her difficulties.

She studied the main doorway, with its vaulted Gothic arch and its stone statue of the Madonna and Child.

She did not want to walk through the heavy oak door – did not want to hear it slam closed behind her, like a baited trap.

This is stupid! she told herself angrily.

She wasn't a frightened little girl any more. She was a police officer. *Other* people were frightened of *her*. And since she had a job to do, she'd better start bloody-well doing it.

Her breathing was more regular now. She took a resolute step forward, turned the handle, and pushed the door open. Then, after only the slightest of hesitations, she stepped through the gap and allowed the church to swallow her up.

Woodend hated the morgue. Not because it was full of dead people – that was, after all, why it was there – but because of the chemicals.

For days after he had made a visit to it, he was convinced that he stank of formaldehyde. It wasn't a rational conviction – he accepted that, just as he accepted the fact that when he met Dr Shastri outside her grisly kingdom, he could detect no odour of death clinging to her. Yet still he would scrub and scrub at his flesh, and still the all-pervading smell would not go away.

He could almost taste the chemicals that morning – swooping down on him through the air like kamikaze swallows, mingling with the acrid smoke from his Capstan Full Strength and being drawn into his lungs – but, as usual, the delightful Dr Shastri seemed blissfully unaware of them.

'I have cut up our little friend in accordance with your wishes, Oh Master,' the doctor said, bowing like the pantomime genie in *Aladdin*. 'Even so, I am afraid that I'm unable to tell you much more than I told you last night. The blow to his head was inflicted with considerable force, as is fairly obvious from the extent of the injuries sustained. Death would have been almost instantaneous.'

'Do you think that a woman could have delivered the blow?' Woodend asked.

'A strong woman, most certainly,' Dr Shastri replied. 'A very angry woman, quite possibly. What would have caused a woman more problems would have been moving the body. Dead weight, for that is what he had become: our little friend would have been quite heavy.'

'An' you're certain he *was* moved?'

'Oh, yes. Wherever it was that he was killed, it was certainly not in the lay-by.'

'Any idea what weapon was used?' Woodend asked.

'The proverbial blunt instrument,' Dr Shastri told him.

'No more than that?'

'I found tiny slivers of metal in the wound, but certainly no single piece large enough for me to be able to tell you with any confidence that they came from a set of eighteenth century candlesticks which can be found only in Doomlock Manor, the home of the mad and dangerous Lord Homicide.'

Woodend grinned. 'What can you tell me about the post-mortem injuries?' he asked.

'Again, not much more than you have seen for yourself. His mouth was smashed in, his stomach was slashed open.'

'But was the mutilation to the stomach done with any kind of medical precision?'

'Now why would you ask that?' Dr Shastri wondered. 'Could it be that you have already decided, Chief Inspector, to "fit up" one of my esteemed colleagues for the murder?'

'As a matter of fact, I was thinkin' of pinnin' the whole business on you,' Woodend said.

'A good choice,' Dr Shastri told him. 'I would certainly be a more colourful and interesting defendant than most of the drab, sad men you usually bring to trial. But in answer to your question, I would have to reply that this particular murderer was not in any way precise. I would almost say that our little friend was butchered, but that would be being unfair to butchers, many of whom know more about anatomy than half the surgeons currently operating in our great hospitals.'

'Now that *is* a cheerful thought,' Woodend said. 'Why did he make such a bloody mess of the mutilation? Was it simply because he had no idea what he was doing?'

'Perhaps,' Doctor Shastri said cautiously. 'But it is equally possible that the killer *wanted* to make a bloody mess.'

'Why would he have wanted to do that?'

'I am no psychologist, but it seems to me that the attack which ended the victim's life – and the mutilation which followed it – were both spurred on by very deep emotion. The aim of mutilation, I think, was to humiliate Bradley Pine – even in death.'

'Why?'

'I don't know,' the doctor confessed.

'But you could make a guess?'

'Perhaps. Did you know that when the British pulled out of India, and my poor country was partitioned, I was living there myself?'

'No, I didn't,' Woodend admitted.

'The sectarian violence which broke out, once your soldiers and policemen had withdrawn, was terrible to behold. Moslems massacred Hindus, and Hindus massacred Moslems. No one was spared – not the old, not the young, not the crippled and infirm. And in some cases, the massacres were followed by mutilation of the corpses. I saw some of those mutilated bodies. The outrages committed on them were not a perfect match with what was done to Mr Pine, but I sensed the same kind of rage at work.'

'So our killer was a very angry man?'

'Our killer, I believe, felt an anger such as you and I have never experienced – and hopefully never will.'

Seven

Her mind and emotions firmly back in the present – though still deeply scarred by the events of the past – Monika Paniatowski took up a strategic position next to the font and – even though she knew that Father O'Brien was long dead – found herself scanning the church for signs of the old enemy.

Not a member of the clergy in sight, she noted. In fact, the only people in the church at that particular moment were several old ladies – and one old man – who were knelt stiffly in prayer in the pews in front of the high altar.

She felt the urge to smoke – partly to calm her nerves, partly as an act of defiance – but then she remembered something that Charlie Woodend had told her early on in their working relationship.

'Whatever you do, don't go rubbin' up potential witnesses the wrong way, Monika,' Woodend had said.

'Never?'

'Never!' Woodend had confirmed sternly. Then he'd chuckled, and continued. *'Unless, of course, you think you can squeeze some advantage out of makin' them lose their rag.'*

But there was no advantage to be gained from rubbing up the priests of this church the wrong way.

At least, not yet!

She found herself wondering how Woodend would have reacted if he'd been the priest sitting on the other side of that confessional grill of her childhood.

Would he have sat back, and done nothing to save her?

Would he have gone out and drunk a few friendly pints of Guinness with her abuser?

Of course he wouldn't. He'd have been more likely to take the man round the back of the church for a few quiet words, and when they returned, the abuser would have both a black eye and a pronounced limp.

Yes, that was how Charlie Woodend would have handled it if he'd been that priest. But then, Charlie would never have contemplated becoming a priest in the first place.

She heard a set of heavy footsteps approaching from her left, and turning, saw that a youngish priest – certainly not more than thirty or thirty-one years old – was walking towards her.

He smiled warmly. 'I am Father Taylor,' he said. 'And who might you be, my child?'

'I'm far too old to be your child,' Monika said, thinking, even as she spoke, that she was certainly *sounding* childish.

'I didn't mean to offend you,' the priest told her, his smile still firmly in place.

'And, as regards your question, I *might* be any number of people,' Monika continued, trying to sound more adult – trying to sound more *sophisticated*. 'But, as it happens, I'm a detective sergeant from Whitebridge CID.'

The priest did not even look at the warrant card she was holding out to him, nor did he seem the least put off by her deliberate rudeness.

'What's your name?' he asked gently.

'It's on the card.'

'I'm sure it is, but I haven't got my reading glasses with me.'

'I'm Sergeant Paniatowski.'

'Do you have a Christian name?'

'Not being a Christian, I'd have to say that I don't. But I do have a *first* name.'

Why was she acting like this, she asked herself. Father O'Brien had been an ugly old man with bad teeth, a squint and a wart on the end of his nose. Father Taylor had fine white teeth, and the nose and eyes of a Hollywood leading man. They had nothing in common – except, of course, that once you'd learned to detest one priest, it was very easy to learn to detest all of them.

'So what's this *first* name of yours?' Father Taylor asked.

'It's "Sergeant"!' Paniatowski said, still refusing to soften to this man of the distrusted cloth.

The young priest laughed easily. 'Now that is an unusual name, whether you're a Christian *or* a heathen,' he said. 'So let me see if I've got this straight – you're Sergeant Sergeant Paniatowski, are you?'

43

Paniatowski laughed too, despite herself. 'No, not really,' she said. 'I'm Monika.'

'And my Christian name is Fred,' the priest told her. 'You may call me Father Fred, if you wish.'

'How about if we forget the "Father" business and I simply call you Fred?' Paniatowski asked.

'That would be fine,' the priest conceded. 'Though most Catholics do normally put a "Father" in front of it.'

'I've already told you I'm not a Catholic,' Paniatowski said.

The priest laughed again. 'Of course you are,' he insisted. 'I spotted you as belonging to the True Faith the moment you walked through the door. And I'm never wrong.'

'You are this time,' Paniatowski insisted.

The priest slowly shook his head from side to side. 'You may deny it – you may not even know it to be true – but you're tied to Mother Church by bonds of faith as strong as steel.'

'I'm investigating a murder,' Paniatowski said.

The smile drained from Father Taylor's face, and was replaced by a troubled expression.

'Ah yes, poor Mr Pine,' he said. 'But I've already told the other policemen everything I know.'

'*What* other policemen?'

'The ones your Inspector Rutter sent to talk to me, after I'd phoned the police station and told him Mr Pine had been here last night.'

Oh God, with everything that had been going on, she'd almost forgotten that Bob was back, Paniatowski thought.

But he *was* back, and she'd have to see him later – however much she might dread the prospect.

'Is something wrong?' Father Taylor asked.

'No. Why should there be?'

'You've suddenly gone rather pale.'

'Maybe that's because I don't like churches,' Paniatowski said aggressively. 'Would you mind going over the same ground with me that you probably went over with them?' she continued, a little less harshly.

'Not in the slightest,' Father Taylor replied. 'I want to do everything I can to help.'

'Did you notice anything odd about Mr Pine last night?'

'We're all odd in our own ways. It's the way God made us.

44

But I certainly wouldn't say that Bradley Pine was any more than his "normal" odd – which is to say, just about as odd as you or I.'

'How well did you know him?'

'Not well at all, I'm afraid.'

'Because he's not a regular church-goer? Because he didn't start putting in appearances at this church until he'd clinched the Conservative nomination and worked out he'd need the Catholic vote?'

'I wonder if you can really be as cynical as you seem?' Father Taylor asked, looking pained. 'I pray that you aren't.'

'You still haven't answered my question, *Fred*,' Monika Paniatowski said flatly.

'You're right, of course. The answer that you're looking for is that I didn't know him well because he chose not to know *me* well.'

'I understand every word in that last sentence, but put them all together and I'm still not sure you've actually told me anything I wanted to know,' Paniatowski said.

'Then I'll explain it in another way, which hopefully you'll find clearer,' Father Taylor said. 'Most of our parishioners have one particular priest with whom they feel especially comfortable, and Mr Pine felt especially comfortable with Father Kenyon.'

'Why is that? Don't you have much pull with the older parishioners? Are you here mainly to attract the younger set?'

Father Taylor laughed good-naturedly again.

'It's nothing like as simple as that, Monika,' he said. 'As you can plainly see for yourself, I'm a priest, not a pop star. Some of the older parishioners prefer to talk to me, and some of the younger ones are much happier with Father Kenyon. I like to think that each makes his or her own choice, although, of course, we are *all* guided by God.'

'So how long would you say Bradley Pine was here?' Paniatowski asked briskly.

'I wasn't keeping a record, but I would guess it was a little more than half an hour.'

'That's an awful lot of praying,' Paniatowski said.

'Do you think so?' Father Taylor asked, with just a hint of reproach in his voice. 'It seems to me that since we're all such miserable sinners, we can never have too much prayer.'

45

'After he'd prayed, did he go to confess his sins?' asked Paniatowski, who was starting to feel uneasy – and was not quite sure why.

'Yes, he did.'

'To Father Kenyon?'

'To God. Although Father Kenyon was certainly there in the confessional with both of them.'

'Do you know where I'll find Father Kenyon at the moment?' Paniatowski asked.

'I saw him go into the vestry about five minutes ago.'

'And do you think it will be all right if I disturbed him?'

'I don't see why not. I think he only went in there for a smoke. He's a terrible slave to the weed.'

'I think I could use a cigarette myself,' Paniatowski told him.

'I've no doubt you could. It's always a strain.'

'What is? A murder investigation?'

'I wouldn't know about that. But I *do* know it's a strain setting your feet on the right path again.'

'The only path I'm looking for is the one that leads to the vestry,' Paniatowski said tartly. 'Which way is it?'

'Straight through that door,' Father Taylor said, pointing.

'I'll see you again, Fred,' Monika said.

'Yes, I rather think you will,' Father Taylor agreed.

Paniatowski was halfway between the priest and the vestry door when she heard Father Taylor call out, 'Oh, Monika, one more thing.'

She stopped, and turned around. 'Yes?'

'I just want you to know that when you *do* return to the Church, I won't take offence if it's Father Kenyon whom you choose to welcome you back.'

Eight

The green Ford Cortina, which had belonged to the late Bradley Pine, was parked in the alleyway which ran between the backs of the houses in Gladstone Street and the backs of those on Palmerston Row.

The car, like its late owner, had been put through some very unpleasant and disfiguring experiences. It no longer had its windscreen wipers or indicator lights, and was resting wheel-less on piles of old bricks. The boot had been forced open, and whatever it might once have contained had been removed. And a quick glance under the bonnet revealed to Bob Rutter that the car no longer had an engine.

'Round here, they'll nick *anything* that's not actually nailed down,' Sergeant Dix said in disgust. 'In fact, even if it *is* nailed down, these buggers will find some way to prise it up.'

'Do you think this could be the spot where Pine was killed?' Rutter wondered.

'I doubt it,' Dix replied.

'Why?'

'Well, for a start, what reason would he have had for even *being* here in the first place?' the sergeant said.

Then he chuckled to himself.

'What's so funny?' Rutter asked.

'I was just thinking – a posh gentleman like Mr Pine wouldn't be seen *dead* in a place like this.'

Dix had a point, Rutter thought. Policemen came to Greenfields. Debt collectors came to Greenfields. But anybody who didn't actually *have to* visit it steered well clear of the area.

Besides, it was over two miles to the lay-by where Pine's body had been found, and it seemed improbable that the killer would have taken him from here to there, and then driven the car back to the scene of the crime. It was much more likely that abandoning the car in the alleyway was no more than the last in the chain of events which began with the actual murder.

The vandals who had wrecked most of the car had kindly left the door handles in place, so Rutter was able to open the back door and look inside.

'Do you think that's blood?' he asked, pointing to a brownish, half-moon shaped stain on the back seat.

'Certainly looks like it to me,' Dix said.

Rutter glanced up, first at the back bedroom windows in Gladstone Terrace and then at the ones in Palmerston Row. As his gaze fell on several of the windows, the curtains twitched.

He was being watched from nearly every one of those bedroom windows, he thought.

'What do you think are the chances that, even though there was a thick fog last night, a few of the people who are watching us now also saw the killer abandon the Cortina?' he asked Dix.

'Very high,' Dix told him. 'It's almost a racing certainty. A decent car like this one couldn't go a hundred yards through this area without being spotted. And once it *had* been spotted, it would be tracked. It was probably being dismantled within a minute or two of the killer abandoning it.'

'So we'd better organize a house-to-house,' Rutter said.

'I suppose we might as well,' Dix agreed. 'But it won't do us any good at all, sir.'

'No?'

'Definitely not. As far as this lot are concerned, seeing something is one thing, but telling *us* about it is quite another.'

'Even though they'll know that it's a murder investigation that we're working on?'

The sergeant shrugged. 'If it's not one of their own who's been topped, they couldn't care less about it. There was a young social worker raped in this very alley, not more than a few weeks ago. It was broad daylight when it happened, and the poor girl was screaming blue murder throughout the entire attack. Yet when we started asking questions, there was nobody from Greenfields who was willing to admit they'd heard or seen a bloody thing.'

Father Kenyon was the sort of priest who was much beloved by the makers of sentimental black-and-white Hollywood movies based around the life of New York parish churches.

He was in his early sixties, and had silver hair, a roundish red face and a kindly smile. True, his clothes smelled strongly of cheap cigarettes, and the hint of whisky on his breath suggested he had already taken at least one drink that morning, but these were both permissible weakness in a man who had voluntarily signed away his right to other pleasures of the flesh.

'I'd like to ask you a few questions about Bradley Pine, Father Kenyon,' Paniatowski said.

The priest nodded sagely. 'I can well imagine that you would, and I'll answer them as honestly as I feel I'm able to.'

'As you *feel you're able to*?' Paniatowski repeated. 'And what exactly does that mean?'

'You must understand that there are certain matters of which I have knowledge that I must keep to myself.'

Even if that does mean a mother will never learn her daughter has been molested by her husband, Paniatowski thought savagely.

But aloud, all she said was, 'How long had Mr Pine been coming to this church?'

'I've known him for over twenty years. He contacted me when he first arrived in Whitebridge, just as Father Swales, the director of Holy Trinity Orphanage had asked him to.' Father Kenyon paused. 'You did know that he was an orphan, didn't you?'

'Yes, I did.'

The old priest sighed. 'It is a terrible thing to lose a parent, but from what Father Swales told me, the death of his father was something of a merciful release for Bradley.'

'Why? Was his father a bad man?'

'We should not judge lest we ourselves be judged,' the priest said, with a note of caution creeping into his voice, 'but, by all accounts, the boy led a miserable life. His father was both a drunkard and a very violent man. Though Bradley never talked about it to me himself, I have seen the cigarette burn scars on his arms with my own eyes.'

Paniatowski felt a wave of sympathy for the dead man sweep over her, then found herself brushing it angrily aside.

'Yes, well, a lot of us had fairly difficult childhoods,' she said. 'Did Bradley Pine attend Mass regularly in the last few weeks of his life?'

'Yes, he did.'

'And before that?'

'Not to attend Mass is, as you are probably only too well aware yourself, a mortal sin.'

'Which he was guilty of?'

'Next question,' Father Kenyon said.

'You heard his confession last night?'

'Yes, I did.'

'Did you talk to him outside the confines of the confessional?'

'Yes.'

'And when you talked to him *outside* the confessional, did he seem worried or disturbed about anything in particular?'

'I can't answer that.'

'But surely, if it wasn't under the seal of—'

'Let me ask *you* a question,' the priest interrupted.

'All right,' Paniatowski agreed.

'Are you able to divorce what goes on in your interview rooms from what goes on outside them?'

'I think so.'

'And *I* think you are almost certainly deluding yourself, my child. What you encounter in that interview room must be much like what I often encounter in the confessional.'

'And what is that?'

'People who are so unsure of themselves – or so terrified – that the mask they normally wear slips off, and the disguise with which they seek to clothe themselves is quite stripped away. We have penetrated their secret selves. We have seen them naked.'

'I'm not sure I—'

'And later, when we meet them again – outside the confessional or outside the interview room – we may hear them say the same words as other people hear them say, but we will interpret them differently. Because we understand them better – because we have been given the *key* to them.'

'Perhaps you're right about that,' Monika Paniatowski conceded. 'But so what?'

The priest laughed. 'It doesn't bother you. And why should it? You're a police officer, and those you question have no choice in the matter. But my parishioners do have a choice. They come to me because they trust me. They *give* me the key, rather than my having to seize it from them. And that means that though I may physically leave the confessional, there is a sense in which I will always take it with me.'

'I'm not asking any of these questions just to satisfy my own idle curiosity, you know,' Paniatowski said, experiencing a rising frustration. 'I'm doing it because I'm trying to catch a murderer.'

'Yes, I quite understand that.'

'Some people would consider that a worthwhile aim.'

'*Most* people would. And they would be quite right to. It undoubtedly *is* a worthwhile aim.'

'Then why won't you help us to achieve it?'

'Because I am restrained from doing so. And those restraints go far beyond the single issue of catching your murderer. Even if, by speaking out, I could save other lives—'

'Are other lives in danger in this case?'

'Not as far as I know. But if they were, I would still maintain my silence, because nothing can justify breaking the seal of the confessional.'

'Not even the needless suffering of a young child?'

'Not even that.'

'But would you go drinking with the man who had made her suffer – the man who continued to make her suffer?' Paniatowski demanded angrily.

The priest looked suddenly troubled. 'I'm sorry, but I'm afraid I have no idea what you're talking about,' he admitted.

Paniatowski took a deep breath. 'No, of course you don't,' she said. 'Did Bradley Pine say where he was intending to go after he left the church last night – or don't you feel able to tell me *that*, either?'

'I can see no reason why I wouldn't be able to reveal that particular piece of information if I had it,' the priest replied. 'But I don't. Bradley didn't tell me where he was going.'

A lorry had arrived to transport the battered and violated Ford Cortina to the police garage, where it would be given a detailed forensic examination, but Dr Shastri – who arrived just before the car was about to be loaded – had insisted that nothing should be moved until she had made a thorough search of the area.

'If it were women in charge of removing the car, I would

have no qualms about letting them go ahead,' she told Bob Rutter, 'but men are, by their very nature, such clumsy creatures, don't you find?'

'Yes, I do,' Rutter agreed.

They *were* clumsy, he thought to himself – in oh-so-many ways.

Dr Shastri gave the area around the battered car a brief inspection.

'Well, on with the show,' she said, in a tone not unlike that of a music hall compère.

It would have been generous to describe the floor of the alley as merely unsavoury – the council felt no strong urge to do anything about improving the environment of tenants who rarely paid either their rent or their rates – but the filth and squalor did not seem to deter Dr Shastri in the slightest. She produced a rubber mat from the back of her Land Rover, and was soon kneeling down on it and examining the grimy cobblestones.

A few minutes had ticked by – and she had shifted the mat around several times – before she looked and said, 'The murderous attack did not take place here, my dear Inspector.'

'You're sure of that?' Rutter asked.

'Absolutely positive. It is true that if Mr Pine had been killed on this spot, the local rats would have removed much of the evidence – a piece of the human brain is to them what a fine pork roast would be to you or I – but there would still have been bloodstains left behind.'

'There would have been a lot of blood, wouldn't there?'

'A veritable fountain of it. And however diligently the killer had tried to clean it up, he would inevitably have left some traces.'

'Would you mind taking a look inside the car?' Rutter asked.

Dr Shastri smiled. 'Of course not,' she said. 'I am willing to do anything at all which will contribute – even in a small way – to making my second-favourite police officer happy.'

She opened the car door, and examined the stain Rutter had spotted on the back seat.

'Now that *is* blood,' she said. 'And if it is not our little friend's blood, I would be most surprised.'

'Shouldn't there be more of it?' Rutter asked.

'Not once the heart had ceased to pump. What we have here is mere seepage.'

'And you're as sure that he *was* mutilated in the lay-by as you are that he *wasn't* killed here?'

'Indeed.'

'I wonder why the murderer waited until he reached the lay-by before he finished off the job,' Rutter mused. 'Do you think it was because it would have been too messy to have done it earlier?'

'Perhaps,' Dr Shastri said, cautiously.

'You're not convinced that's the case at all, are you?' Rutter asked. 'You've got a theory of your own.'

'I have,' Dr Shastri admitted. 'But as I have already pointed out to your superior, the admirable Chief Inspector Woodend, I am more of a plumber than a brain doctor, and my theory may well not be worth a bag of acorns.'

'I'd like to hear it, anyway.'

'Even though you run the risk – if you take it seriously – of being sent off on a wild goose hunt?'

'Yes.'

'Very well, on your own head be it. I believe that, initially, the murderer thought that whatever torment was driving him to distraction would be assuaged by simply *killing* his victim. But by the time he had reached the lay-by, he had realized that was not enough to bring him the relief he needed, and he would have to do more. That is, I believe, when he decided to inflict the final humiliation by mutilating the corpse.'

'Let me see if I've got this straight,' Rutter said. 'You think that the idea of mutilation didn't occur to him until he reached the lay-by?'

'Essentially. Although, I suppose, it is possible that the urge came over him while he was still en route to it.'

'So the reason he made the decision to go there *wasn't* simply because he needed somewhere quiet where he could finish his work?'

'That seems unlikely, don't you think? The lay-by was not *so* secluded, even in a thick fog. The lorry which drove on to it *after* the mutilation had been concluded could just as easily have arrived whilst it was still in progress. If what the killer had wanted was total privacy to carry out his grisly task, he would surely have driven the body out on to the moors.'

'So if that wasn't the reason he took the body to the lay-by, what *did* make him choose that particular spot?'

Dr Shastri smiled again. 'That is a very interesting question,' she said. 'An intriguing, infuriating question. And one that, as a simple doctor, I am happy to leave in your much more capable hands.'

Nine

Elizabeth Driver was sitting in the First Class carriage of the local train from Manchester to Whitebridge. Her eyes were taking in the countryside through which the train was passing, but her mind was fixed very firmly on what was awaiting her at the end of the journey.

As the chief crime reporter for a salacious national newspaper which sold copies by the million – but which very few people would actually *admit* to reading – she was a true queen of her dubious profession. But being a queen could have its drawbacks. To stay at the top required a very delicate balancing act, and she only had to make one little slip – one tiny mistake – to come toppling down. On her good days, she told herself this was no problem, that she could go on for ever. On her bad days, she wondered how much longer she could continue to cap the last sensational story that she'd filed with one which was even more outrageous.

The story she was on her way to cover was a good case in point. For most reporters, the murder of a parliamentary candidate would provide them with all the copy they needed. They had only to report the facts to keep their editors satisfied. But when you were Elizabeth Driver, your editor and readers wanted – and expected – much more.

The death of Bradley Pine held out the promise of more. Driver's source in the Whitebridge Police had hinted that there were macabre aspects to the killing which had not yet been released to the press.

But that was all her source had done.

Bloody hint!

It was all he *could* do. He was far too low on the totem pole to give her any of the juicy details she needed if she were to keep ahead of her rivals.

She had a serious problem with the Whitebridge Police, she

admitted – and that problem was called Charlie Woodend. Their relationship had got off to a bad start when he had still been with Scotland Yard, investigating the Westbury Manor Murder – and it had pretty much gone downhill since then.

She had tried to mend fences – God alone knew how hard she had tried. She'd done her best to charm him, and he'd been distinctly unimpressed. She'd promised to write him up favourably in her articles, and he'd told her where she could stuff it. She'd even said she'd have sex with him – had offered him, on a plate, the body that half the hacks in Fleet Street fell asleep in their lonely beds lusting over – and been rebuffed.

The low point had come when Woodend had realized that it was she who had told Maria Rutter – a few days before her murder – that her husband Bob had had an affair with Monika Paniatowski.

There was no climbing out of that particular hole, she thought. Woodend would never – ever – forgive her for what she had done. But Bob Rutter, if handled right, just might. And while that wasn't as good as having Woodend himself on her side, it was *almost* as good.

The Whitebridge Golf and Country Club had been closely modelled on the mock-Gothic palaces that many rich men with no taste had built for themselves towards the end of the nineteenth century. It was located on the north side of the city, far away from the dark satanic mills which had financed its construction. It was a pleasant enough place, Woodend admitted, if you happened to like manicured lawns and flower beds laid out with almost military precision, but for him it came nowhere near matching the savage grandeur of the moors.

There were only a few club members in the bar when he arrived and they looked at him with suspicion, for while there *were* chief inspectors in the Central Lancs Constabulary who they – at a push – would have regarded as *almost* their social equals, Woodend was definitely not among that number.

Woodend walked across the room to the bar counter. The blank-faced steward, standing behind it, watched his progress carefully, yet somehow managed to appear as if he were looking right through him.

'A pint of best bitter, when you've got the time, lad,' the chief inspector said.

The steward blinked. So apparently, while Woodend might be invisible, he was not quite inaudible.

'I'm terribly sorry, sir, but we're not allowed, by law, to serve non-members,' the steward said.

'Fair enough,' Woodend replied. 'I'm all for obeyin' the law myself, which is why – if I was you – I wouldn't go out on my bike after dark again without first checkin' my lights very carefully.'

To his left someone chuckled, then a voice said, 'That sounds like a threat to me.'

Woodend turned. The man who had addressed him was in his fifties, and was wearing a blue blazer with the club's badge on its pocket.

'A threat?' Woodend repeated. 'You've got it all wrong, sir. What you've just heard me offer was advice – kindly meant, an' purely in the interest of road safety.'

The man chuckled again, and held out his hand. 'Tom Carey, the club secretary. And you're Chief Inspector Woodend, aren't you?'

'That's right,' Woodend agreed, taking the hand.

'Henry Marlowe phoned me earlier, and said I should be expecting you,' Carey said.

'Aye, he would have done,' Woodend said. 'Normally, he'd move heaven an' earth to stop me pokin' my nose around in places like this, but since he really needs a result on the Pine case, he's had to compromise.'

'Compromise?'

'Aye. He's givin' me a bit of rope, but he's also put a few of his minders in place to make sure I don't tug on it too hard. You've been nominated as his minder here.'

Carey smiled. 'I can see you know our Henry quite well,' he said. He turned to the barman. 'A gin and tonic for me, and a pint of bitter for Mr Woodend, Donald. Put it on my account.'

The two men took their drinks over to a table.

'So how can we help you, Mr Woodend?' Carey asked.

'I'm tryin' to build up a picture of what Bradley Pine was like,' Woodend told him.

'Is *that* how the Central Lancs Police conduct their investigations?' Carey asked, sounding more curious than censorious. 'I thought that these days it was all fingerprints and blood samples. Very scientific and modern, of course – but perhaps a little boring.'

'There are fellers on the Force who rely on forensics to do their job for them,' Woodend admitted, taking an exploratory sip of his pint and quickly deciding that the golf club's beer had more than earned its fine reputation. 'But that isn't the way I work.'

'So what *do* you do?'

'I try to get inside people's heads.'

'And, at the moment, you want to get inside Bradley Pine's?'

'That's correct.'

'Well, maybe I can help you there,' Carey told him. 'Bradley was a pillar of the community, who constantly strived to improve the conditions of those less fortunate than himself.' He winked. 'That's what it says in his political manifesto, anyway.'

'But what would *you* say?' Woodend wondered.

'I'd have say that I quite admired him, but never really knew him,' Carey replied, after a moment's thought. 'I admired him because he came from nothing, and made no bones about it. He was an orphan, you know.'

'Aye, I had heard,' Woodend agreed.

'Some of the less socially secure members of this club try their damnedest to hide their origins. They spend small fortunes searching their family trees for some trace of nobility, and even have family crests commissioned. Bradley never did anything like that. Ask him about his family, and he'd admit quite openly that his father was a drunkard who had no one to blame for his early death but himself. And it must say something for the man, don't you think, that despite his refusal to put on any airs and graces, he still managed to get himself elected to the committee?'

'If he was on the committee, then you, as club secretary, must have worked quite closely with him.'

'I did.'

'An' yet you say you never really knew him?'

'None of the members really knew Bradley. He was friendly with all, but a *close* friend of no one. He didn't seem to need the assurances of support that most people do. I suppose that might have something to do with being brought up in an orphanage – you have to learn to rely on yourself alone.'

'Can you think of anybody who might have held a grudge against him?' Woodend asked.

'You'd have to be a saint for there to be nobody who held a grudge against you,' Carey said.

'An' even then, there'd be some bugger who'd find a way to pick holes in you,' Woodend agreed. 'But I'd still like an answer to my question.'

'I'm sure there were people who resented the fact that Bradley was on the committee and they weren't,' Carey said. 'I'm sure there are those who think they would have made a better parliamentary candidate. But I certainly can't think of anyone who disliked him enough to kill him.'

'Business rivals?' Woodend prodded. 'Jealous husbands?'

The question seemed to amuse Carey. 'When you're the undisputed king of the interior sprung mattresses in central Lancashire, you *have* no business rivals,' he said.

'It was a two-part question,' Woodend reminded him.

'So it was,' Carey agreed. 'Bradley's been a member of this club since soon after he registered his patent. Back then, there probably were a few jealous husbands around. After all, Bradley was young, unattached and rather good looking, so naturally there were rumours that his relationships with some of the other members' wives were perhaps a little too close.'

'Were they *just* rumours?' Woodend asked.

'Since he was not actually caught *in flagrante*, we'll never actually know for sure, but I have to say that it wouldn't surprise me if there'd been a little fire to go with all the smoke.'

'You've been talkin' in the past tense,' Woodend said. 'Haven't there been any recent rumours?'

'No. In fact, there have been none at all for a good few years now.'

'Why? Did he suddenly lose all interest in sex?'

'No, I wouldn't quite say that.'

'Then what *would* you say?'

Carey hesitated for a second, then said, 'I'm not entirely sure I should say anything at all.'

'The man's dead,' Woodend pointed out.

'Yes,' Carey agreed, 'but *she* isn't.'

'She?'

'This is all pure speculation,' Carey said cautiously.

'I'll bear that in mind,' Woodend promised.

'I think he fell in love.'

'Who with?'

'I really have no idea.'

'Come on, Mr Carey,' Woodend urged.

'I mean it, Chief Inspector. I have no idea.'

'Then how do you know that he fell in love *at all*?'

'I was in love once,' Carey said. 'It was a long time ago, but I still recognize the signs.'

'What signs?'

'The look in his eyes, sometimes. The far-away expression on his face, as if he'd suddenly started thinking about the best thing that had ever happened to him. The fact that he no longer seemed anything like as interested in other women as he had once done. It's not something you can put your finger on, but then love's like that, isn't it?'

'But you have no idea who this woman – if she exists – is?'

'None at all.'

'So she could be the wife of one of your members?'

'Given that Bradley seemed to have virtually no social life outside the confines of this club, I'd be very much surprised if the woman in question *wasn't* a member's wife.'

'There's a pretty good motive for murder, then,' Woodend said.

'I don't think so,' Carey countered.

'Why not?'

'But if she is a member's wife, then the member himself certainly doesn't know about it.'

'How can you be so sure of that?'

'I've already said that it's not hard to spot a man who's suddenly fallen deeply in love, haven't I?' Carey said.

'Yes.'

'But doing that is rocket science compared to spotting a man who suspects he's been cuckolded. That's as easy as falling off a log.'

Ten

Though a little of the skill and ball control of a professional football match may have been lacking from the lunch-time match that was being played on the cinder pitch behind Hawtrey and Pine Holdings, the players themselves more than made up for it with their ferocity and enthusiasm – and Constable Beresford, a large mug of tea in his hand, had been watching the game with pleasure for over ten minutes when it suddenly occurred to him that he wasn't actually there to enjoy himself.

He forced his gaze away from the pitch, and on to the old man in the flat cap and boiler suit who was standing next to him and had told him earlier that his name was Harry Ramsbotham.

'I'm surprised they're playing a game at all on a day like this, Harry,' Beresford said, conversationally.

'Are you now?' the old man replied. 'An' why might that be?'

'Well, when all's said and done, your boss has just been brutally murdered, hasn't he?'

'That's true enough.'

'And I would have thought they might have abandoned the game as a sign of respect.'

'Mr Pine wasn't that kind of boss,' Harry Ramsbotham said.

'Wasn't *what* kind of boss? Are you saying you all hated him? That you're all glad he's dead?'

The old man shook his head. 'You young lads,' he said, almost despairingly. 'Everythin's got to be either one extreme or the other with you, hasn't it? No, we didn't hate Mr Pine—'

'Well, then—'

'—but he wasn't like family to us, either. He was the boss. He paid reasonably fair wages, we put in a reasonably fair day's work for them. By an' large, we had no real complaints

61

about him, an' he had no real complaints about us. But nobody's goin' to break into floods of tears now that he's gone.'

'I see,' Beresford said.

'Of course, it was different in the old days,' Harry Ramsbotham continued, wistfully. 'When old Mr Hawtrey died – that's Mr *Samuel* Hawtrey, I'm talkin' about, Mr Alec's dad – they closed down the factory for the day of the funeral, an' every man-jack who worked here went to it. An' there was a funeral tea afterwards, with enough booze flowin' for all his workers to drink to his memory. But like I say, them days are gone forever.'

'I expect you're right,' Beresford agreed.

'I *am* right. Old Mr Hawtrey knew the first name of everybody who worked for him. Even Mr Alec knew most of them. But the only people whose names Mr Pine knew were the managers.' Harry Ramsbotham paused for a moment. 'No, that's not quite fair,' he continued. 'He did know the names of most of the lads he'd worked with while he was makin' his own way up the ladder to the top.'

There was the sound of cheering from around the cinder pitch, and Beresford turned to see what was happening. A young apprentice had just artfully dribbled the ball around two of his older, slower opponents and was now facing an open goal mouth.

'Take your time, lad!' Ramsbotham called out. 'Don't just kick it! *Think* about it.'

The apprentice paused for a moment, perhaps as a result of the old man's advice, then slammed his foot into the ball with tremendous force. The goalkeeper made a desperate dive, but it was a wasted effort and the ball flew into the back of the net.

'He's good enough to turn professional, that lad,' Ramsbotham told Beresford.

'Did Alec Hawtrey own the whole business before Bradley Pine became a partner?' Beresford asked.

'He most certainly did. Mr Samuel left it to him in his will – lock, stock an' barrel.'

'So how *did* Bradley Pine become a partner?'

'Bought his way in, with the money he'd made from that invention of his, didn't he? He always was a clever chap.'

'Yes, I know that,' Beresford said. 'What I don't understand is why Alec Hawtrey would *want* to sell part of his family business.'

'He didn't want to. He needed the money.'

'Why was that?'

'Ah, thereby hangs a tale,' Harry Ramsbotham. 'An' not just a tale – but a lesson to us all.'

'Go on,' Beresford said, encouragingly.

'You'd have thought Mr Alec had the perfect life. He was happily married – at least, as far as anybody knew – an' he had two lovely children, one son an' one daughter. Then one of the lasses in the typin' pool caught his eye, an' he lost all reason.'

'That can happen,' Beresford said sagely.

Harry Ramsbotham laughed. 'How would you know?' he asked. 'You're nowt but a lad.'

Beresford blushed. 'I'm sorry, I didn't mean to—'

'No, I'm sorry,' the old man said kindly. 'You can't help bein' young, an' I shouldn't take the mickey out of you for it. Now where was I?'

'He lost all reason.'

'He did. He was a man in his thirties, an' she was a slip of a girl who hadn't even reached her majority, but it made no difference to him. He started knockin' around openly with her, as if he didn't care who saw them. Well, it was only a matter of time before his wife found out, an' once she did, she started divorce proceedin's on the ground of adultery. An' this was fifteen or sixteen years ago, mind, when it was a much more serious matter than it is now.'

'Was it really *so* different then?' Beresford asked.

'Bloody right it was different. There wasn't all that much of this here promiscuity around in them days – which is not to say that everybody back then behaved like little angels.'

'No?'

'Definitely not! A lot of fellers *did* have their bit of fluff on side, an' most of the people who knew about it chose to look the other way. But if you got caught out, that was another matter entirely. If you got caught out, you were in deep trouble an' nobody decent wanted anythin' to do with you.'

'So Alec Hawtrey's sin was letting himself get caught.'

'Exactly. Couldn't have put it better myself. An' when the divorce case got to court, the judge told Mr Alec that as a leadin' light in the community, he should have been settin' a much better example for the rest of us to follow. So it didn't really come as a surprise to anybody when, in announcin' the settlement, he gave Mrs Hawtrey half the factory. It was his way of punishin' Mr Alec for behavin' so disgracefully, you see.'

'So am I to assume that Mrs Hawtrey still owns half the factory?'

'You can assume what you like, lad, but you'd be wrong on both counts.'

'I beg your pardon?'

'First of all, she wasn't Mrs Hawtrey any more. She'd got divorced an' gone back to her maiden name.'

'Yes, but—'

'An' secondly, she didn't want anythin' more to do with the factory – or even with the town. She accepted on a big wodge of cash in return for her shares, an' she moved. But in order to raise that big wodge of cash, Mr Alec had had to saddle himself with a huge debt, you see.'

'Yes, he must have done.'

'Well, despite that, the company did manage to struggle on a few more years, but in the end the debt got so cripplin' that he had no choice but to take on a partner who could put some more money into the business. An' the partner he chose was Bradley Pine.'

'What happened to the young girl from the typing pool, the one who Mr Hawtrey had been having an affair with?' Beresford asked.

The old man grinned. 'What are you expectin' me to say, lad?' he asked. 'That she couldn't live with the shame of bein' a home-wrecker, so she drowned herself in the river?'

'Well, no,' replied Beresford.

And it was quite true that he hadn't been expecting it. In fact, he couldn't really conceive of a time in which women *would* have acted like that.

'She didn't drown herself,' the old man said. 'She married him. She became the second Mrs Hawtrey. And now she's his widow.'

There was another roar from the cinder pitch as the young apprentice scored again.

'He could have a great future, that lad,' Harry Ramsbotham

64

told Beresford. 'But then you could say that of most of us – until we put a foot wrong.'

Elizabeth Driver strode into the most expensive hairdresser's salon Whitebridge could offer with the air of someone who knows quite well that she's slumming it, but really has no choice in the matter.

'I want you to dye my hair,' she told the young assistant, who was already unnerved by her imperious manner. 'I want it blonde.'

'Any particular shade?'

'Well, of course I want a particular shade!' Elizabeth Driver snapped. 'Get me the colour card, and I'll show you.'

The assistant presented her with the card, and Driver immediately pointed to a colour. 'That's the one.'

'But that seems to be your natural colour anyway,' the assistant said, parting her hair and examining her roots.

'Oh really? And I never even realized it,' Elizabeth Driver said with heavy sarcasm.

'The thing is, Madam, if you let the dye grow out, you'll get your own colour back naturally,' the assistant explained.

'That's something else I hadn't realized,' Driver said. 'Do you want my business or not?'

'Yes, but—'

'But what?'

'Before I can dye your hair, I'll have to bleach it.'

'Naturally.'

'And that could damage your hair.'

'I'll risk it,' Driver said.

'But if you'll just let nature take its course—'

'That would be fine if I'd got the time – but I haven't!' Elizabeth Driver snapped.

'Could I . . . could I ask what all the hurry is, Madam?' the assistant asked bravely.

Elizabeth Driver sighed. 'I'm doing it for the same reason that any woman changes her appearance in a hurry,' she said. 'And even a dim mind like yours should be able to guess what that is.'

'You want to impress a man,' the assistant said.

'That's right,' Elizabeth Driver agreed. 'I'm doing it because I want to impress a man.'

Eleven

Woodend and Paniatowski arrived at the door of the Drum and Monkey at exactly the same time. They hadn't arranged for that to happen, but neither was it a surprise to either of them that it had.

This was how they meshed when they were working on a murder case together. Each of them anticipated the other's actions. Each had at least a glimmering of what the other was thinking. It was as if they developed some special kind of telepathy which would continue to transmit for the whole course of the investigation, and whilst they were not quite sure how it worked – or even *why* it worked – they were always extremely grateful when it did.

'The whole problem with this case, as far as I can see, is that I've not been able to get a proper handle on it yet,' the chief inspector told his sergeant as they sat down at their table. 'An' to be fair to myself, I don't think that's entirely my fault.'

'Then whose fault is it?'

'Bradley Pine has to take some of the blame. He seems to have been a bit of a secretive bugger even *before* he turned politician.'

'In what way?'

'In all sorts of ways. For example, the secretary of the golf club, who's a sharp feller called Carey, is convinced that Pine's been carryin' on an affair for years, an' yet nobody can put a name to the woman he's involved with. An' as you know your-self, it's almost impossible to . . .'

He stopped speaking, horrified that he'd allowed himself to wander blindly into this particular emotional mine field.

'As I know myself, it's almost impossible to keep an affair hidden, however hard you try?' Paniatowski supplied.

'Yes,' Woodend agreed. 'Sorry.'

'There's no need to apologize,' Paniatowski told him. 'We

can't keep on pretending that the past never happened, especially now Bob's back at work as a walking, talking reminder that it did.'

Woodend nodded. 'Shall we get back on to the subject of Bradley Pine?'

'I think it would be a good idea if we did.'

'It's the very fact that he was so secretive himself that's makin' his murderer into such a shadowy figure. We know so little about Pine as a person that we can't even begin to guess who could have hated him enough to not only kill him, but also to mutilate him.'

'Or why the killer, once he'd done the deed, would have wanted to move his body,' Paniatowski said.

'Well, exactly!' Woodend agreed. 'He was runnin' a terrific risk takin' the corpse to the lay-by – but why take him to a lay-by *at all*? Why *do* killers move the bodies of their victims?'

'Sometimes they do it to hide them.'

'But in this case, the killer did just the opposite. He dumped the corpse in a spot where it was bound to be discovered – an' sooner rather than later.'

'Sometimes killers leave their victims in a specific place as a way of sending a message – a warning – to other people.'

'Like leavin' thieves hangin' on the gibbet for days on end? Or killin' a member of a rival gang, an' then dumpin' his body in front of that gang's headquarters?'

'Yes, that kind of thing.'

'But if the killer was sendin' a message here, who the bloody hell was he sendin' it to? Lorry drivers? Speedin' motorists? There has to be another reason why that lay-by has a special significance. But what sort of special significance could a bloody lay-by *possibly* have?'

The bar door opened, and Bob Rutter walked in. Though they were expecting him, it still somehow took them by surprise that he had actually arrived, and for a moment both Woodend and Paniatowski froze.

Then Woodend pulled himself together, stood up, and held out his hand to Rutter.

'It's good to have you back with us, Bob,' he said.

'It's good to *be* back, sir,' Bob Rutter told him, taking the proffered hand and shaking it.

Oh my God, he looks so thin, Monika Paniatowski thought. *He looks so* haunted.

But what had she been expecting, she asked herself. Had she thought he would waltz in as if he hadn't got a care in the world – as if all the terrible things which had happened to him were now no more than a distant memory?

She noticed that Rutter was looking down at her. 'I'm glad you're back, too, Bob,' she said.

But was she?

Was she *really*?

Wouldn't Bob's return do no more than open old wounds? Might she not find – despite knowing how pointless it was – that she was still very much in love with him?

Rutter sat down, and the landlord brought an unordered – but much appreciated – pint across to the table.

With one hand Rutter grasped the drink as if it were a lifebelt, while with the other he searched in his jacket pocket for change.

The landlord shook his head. 'I won't take your money, Mr Rutter,' he said. 'This one's on the house.'

'So how did your first mornin' back go, Bob?' Woodend asked, when the landlord had returned to the bar. 'Do you think you're gettin' anywhere?'

He had been aiming to sound as normal as possible – without any evidence of the awkwardness and lack of ease he was actually feeling – and listening to his own voice he decided he'd *almost* achieved that.

Rutter shrugged. 'It's been pretty much like the start of most of our investigations, sir,' he said. 'We haven't got anything like enough information yet to know where to find the leads we need, so we just have to look everywhere we can possibly think of.'

'Is Pine's car likely to tell us anything?' Woodend wondered, noting that his voice was still sounding somewhat strained.

'I doubt it,' Rutter replied. 'The thugs who stripped it down in the alley are likely to have destroyed any forensic evidence there might have been.'

The phone at the bar rang, and the three people at the table jumped as if they'd heard a shot.

The landlord picked up the phone and listened for a second, then called out, 'It's for you, Sergeant Paniatowski.'

'Who is it?'

'She wants to know who's calling,' the landlord said into the telephone receiver.

Rutter picked up his pint and drained half of it in a single gulp.

None of them were finding this easy, Woodend thought.

'The feller on the phone says he's a colleague of yours, Sergeant,' the landlord shouted, across the bar. 'He says it's been quite a while since you've spoken to one another.'

Monika Paniatowski rose to her feet slowly, as if her legs had suddenly turned to lead.

'Could you transfer the call through to the phone in the corridor for me?' she asked.

'I suppose so,' the landlord replied. 'But wouldn't you be much more comfortable taking it in here?'

'The corridor!' Paniatowski said firmly.

The landlord shrugged. 'If that's what you want, Sergeant, it's no problem at all.'

Jesus, what was going on now, Woodend wondered, as he watched his sergeant walk heavily over to the door, like a condemned woman on the way to her execution.

He became aware that Rutter had been talking to him, but had no idea what he'd been saying.

'I'm sorry, lad, but could you just run that by me again?' he asked the inspector.

'As I said, I don't think the car itself will turn out to be of much use to the investigation,' Rutter told him, 'but I think that, in leaving it where he did, the killer may have given more away than he ever intended to.'

'Go on,' Woodend said, doing his best to take his mind off Paniatowski and re-focus it on the investigation.

'He abandoned the Cortina there because Greenfields was close to home – not too close, but close enough.'

'What do you mean by that?'

'It was close enough for him to make the journey home on foot without running too much of a risk of being spotted by anyone else. But it was not *so* close to his base that if we carry out blanket interviewing in the area around Greenfields, we'll be bound to end up talking to him.'

Woodend scratched his head, then took a sip of his pint. 'You just might be on to something there,' he admitted.

* * *

69

The phone call – coming in those awkward moments after Bob Rutter's arrival – should have felt like a godsend, Paniatowski thought, as she closed the corridor door firmly behind her. It should have seemed like the emotional equivalent of being untied from the railway tracks just before the express train arrived.

But it hadn't.

Instead, it had filled her with dread.

And though she didn't quite know why a call from Chief Inspector Baxter – for who else could it be? – should have done that, she was convinced that she would soon find out.

She lifted the phone off its cradle, and heard a click as the landlord hung up the one in the bar.

'Monika Paniatowski,' she said.

'It's me,' Baxter replied.

'I wasn't expecting you to call,' Paniatowski told him, thinking – even as she spoke the words – that it seemed an inadequate response to a man who was, after all, her lover.

'Can we meet?' Baxter asked.

'When?'

'If you don't mind, I'd rather like it to be some time within the next day or so.'

She needed time to get over seeing Bob Rutter again, Paniatowski thought – and a couple of days just wasn't enough.

'Actually I do mind,' she said. 'As things are here at the moment, it might be rather difficult to arrange.'

'Oh?'

'You see, we're in the first twenty-four hours of a new murder inquiry – and you know from your own experience what that's like.'

'So are you saying that you can't spare me even half an hour of your valuable time?'

Damn him! Why was he being so persistent?

'Half an hour?' Monika asked, stalling. 'Yes, I suppose I could spare that. But it wouldn't *be* half an hour, would it?'

'Wouldn't it?'

'Of course it wouldn't. You're not living just around the corner from me, you know. It's a couple of hours drive up to Dunethorpe – and a couple of hours drive back.'

'If that's the only problem you can see, I could come across to Whitebridge,' Baxter suggested.

Paniatowski glanced into the mirror over the phone. The last time she'd looked at herself – which couldn't have been more than an hour earlier – she'd thought she was presentable enough, but now she was a complete wreck.

'You know what I'm like when I'm all wrapped in a case,' she said. 'I'm just not fit to know. So I really would rather leave meeting you until we've got a result on this one.'

'Maybe you would,' Baxter agreed. 'But I wouldn't.'

'Well, we can't always have what we want in this life,' Paniatowski said, trying her best to sound light-hearted.

'Ain't that the truth,' Baxter agreed grimly. 'We can't always have it, although sometimes – for a little while at least – we can talk ourselves into believing that we've got it.'

'You've lost me,' Paniatowski admitted.

'I never had you. That was the whole problem,' Baxter countered. 'Listen, Monika, I didn't want to do this over the phone, but—'

'Do *what* over the phone?'

'I've met a woman.'

'Really? I've met *dozens* of women since the last time we spoke. Dozens of men, too.'

'You know what I mean.'

'Yes,' Monika admitted. 'I rather think I do. I expect she's very pretty, is she?'

'She's pleasant enough, but she's nothing compared to you in the looks department. Hasn't got any of your brains, either. But at least I know where I am with her.'

'I see,' Paniatowski said flatly.

'You've no reason to sound like you think you've been badly done by,' Baxter said, with just a hint of aggression starting to appear in his voice. 'You're the one who's always insisted that there should be no firm commitment given – from either of us.'

'That's true,' Paniatowski admitted. She paused for a second. 'So is this goodbye then?'

'I wouldn't put it in quite those terms,' Baxter said. 'We still like each other, don't we?'

'Yes, I suppose we do.'

'So there's no reason why we still can't meet up now and again for a drink, is there?'

'No reason at all,' Paniatowski agreed. 'But we won't, will we?'

71

For several seconds, Baxter was silent, then he said, 'No, I don't really think we will.'

'So we might as well just say our goodbyes to each other now, and have done with it.'

'Goodbye, Monika,' Baxter said – and she thought she could hear a slight catch in his throat.

'Goodbye,' Monika replied. 'And thanks for trying so hard.'

'To do what?'

'To make things between us work.'

She was crying as she hung up the phone, but she was not entirely sure why. She had never loved Baxter, and though she had enjoyed the sex life they had shared, she'd known the earth to move much more with other men.

So why the tears, she wondered.

She supposed it could be for no other reason than that she was suddenly feeling very, very alone.

'So you think the killer is almost certainly a Whitebridge man?' Woodend asked Rutter.

'Yes. Or if he's not, he's at least *living* in Whitebridge at the moment.'

Woodend took a drag on his cigarette, and then nodded.

'I think I'd agree with you on that,' he said. 'If I wanted to kill somebody who lived in another town, I certainly wouldn't wait till there was a thick fog before I drove over there to do it.'

'The question is, how *far* would he be prepared to walk before he reached his safe haven,' Rutter said. 'Half a mile? A mile? I suppose it would depend on how strong his nerve was and what calculations he'd made about the risks . . . about the risks . . .'

Rutter stopped speaking, and gazed with horror in the direction of the corridor.

Woodend turned his own head, and immediately understood his inspector's reaction.

Monika Paniatowski was standing framed in the doorway between the bar and the corridor. It was obvious from the expression she'd forced on to her face that she was trying to appear to be her normal self – but she looked totally destroyed.

Twelve

The three men leaning against the factory wall had all been enthusiastic players in the cinder pitch football match earlier in the lunch break, but now they seemed content to merely look on while others grabbed the glory.

Well, that wasn't really very surprising, was it, Beresford asked himself. When you were getting on in years – and these men, he guessed, must be somewhere in their late thirties – you simply didn't have the stamina any more.

One of the men had a shock of red curly hair. The second was completely bald, and his pink head gleamed in the early afternoon sun. The third had a duck-tail quiff which was held in place by an impressive amount of grease, and made him look a little like Elvis Presley might have done if Elvis had been wearing a boiler suit, smoking a Woodbine, and working in a mattress factory.

Separately, the trio would probably have passed largely unnoticed and unremarked, but standing together as they were, they looked like some kind of a comedy act – the Three Stooges of Whitebridge, or Hawtrey-Pine Holdings's answer to the Marx Brothers.

Beresford ambled over to them in the casual way he thought a detective, totally at ease with the situation, probably would.

'Mind if I join you?' he asked.

'Why, are we comin' apart?' said the ginger-haired man, then laughed loudly, as if he'd cracked the most original joke in the world.

Charlie Woodend would have come back with a clever line instantly, Beresford told himself, but all he could think to say was, 'No, I just thought you might be willing to answer a few questions for me.'

'What kind of questions?' the ginger man asked. 'What's the capital of Russia? I can tell you that. It's Moscow! What's the longest river in the world? Easy! It's the Nile. Who really runs Hawtrey-Pine Holdings? Another absolute doddle! The Vatican!'

'The Vatican?' Beresford repeated.

'Ignore him,' the bald man said wearily. 'That's the only thing to do when he starts ridin' that particular hobby horse.'

'Hobby horse, is it?' the ginger man asked, aggrieved. 'Well, just look at the facts, will you? Mr Hawtrey was a Roman Catholic, Mr Pine was a Roman Catholic. Mr *Tully* was a Roman Catholic.'

'Leave off,' the bald man said. 'This is *supposed* to be our break. We're *supposed* to be havin' a good time.'

'An' I'm just *supposed* to stand here an' listen to you hintin' that I'm some kind of nutter, am I?' the ginger man asked. 'Well, you don't need to take my word for anythin', because the facts speak for themselves. You can go right through the payroll an' find the same thing – anybody with a cushy job belongs to the Church of Rome. It's a wonder to me that the Pope's not got a job here.'

'Maybe he has,' said the Elvis impersonator, in what was probably an attempt to defuse the situation by making a joke of it. 'Perhaps the only reason we don't see him ourselves is because he works the night shift.'

'Was Mr Pine a good boss?' Beresford asked, doing his best to steer the conversation towards something more fruitful.

'He was all right – as bosses go,' the Elvis impersonator said.

'An' as bosses go, he went,' the ginger man said, chuckling.

The bald man shook his head, rebukingly. 'Let's have a little decorum, shall we?' he suggested. 'The poor bugger's not even cold yet.'

'Which is more than you can say for the state Mr Hawtrey was in, when they took him off that mountainside,' the ginger man said, still laughing.

'Now that's *not* right,' the bald man said sternly. 'Mr Hawtrey was a bloody good bloke, an' even if you've no respect for Mr Pine, you could at least show a little towards him.'

'Don't get all high an' mighty with me,' the ginger man said. 'It wasn't me what killed Hawtrey – it was Pine.'

'Pine *killed* Hawtrey?' Beresford asked, shocked.

'You'll be givin' the lad the wrong impression if you're not careful,' the bald man said hastily.

'That I won't,' the ginger man countered, totally unrepentant. 'Pine didn't stick a knife in him, or blow his head off with a shotgun – or do anythin' at all like that – but he still killed him, right enough.'

'What he means to say, is that he thinks Mr Pine should never have persuaded Mr Hawtrey to go on that mountain climb with him an' Mr Tully,' the bald man explained to Beresford. He glared at the ginger man. 'Isn't that right?'

'More or less,' the ginger man agreed, reluctantly. 'Pine an' Tully were in their thirties – fit young men who could handle it when things went wrong. But Mr Hawtrey was the wrong side of fifty – an' he couldn't.'

'You can't go puttin' all the blame on Mr Pine's shoulders,' the Elvis impersonator said. 'From what I heard, there was originally supposed to be just the two of them on the climb – Pine an' Tully – an' the only reason that Mr Hawtrey ended up accompanying them was because he invited *himself* along.'

'Why would he have done that?' the ginger man demanded.

'You *know* why he did it. It was because he wanted to impress his wife!'

'So now you're sayin' *Thelma* wanted him to climb that mountain?'

'Course I'm not. Why should she want him to? It's not a woman's thing, is it? But he thought that by goin' on the climb with them, he could prove to her that he could keep up with men who were much closer to her age than he was himself.'

'I still think it was all Pine's fault,' the ginger man said.

'You would,' the Elvis impersonator responded. 'But sooner or later you'll have to face the fact that the way Mr Pine tried to keep Mr Hawtrey alive on the mountain makes him nothing less than a bloody hero.'

'If he *did* try to keep him alive,' the ginger man said. 'We've only Pine's own word for it.'

'As a matter of fact, you couldn't be wronger about that,' the Elvis impersonator said. 'Mr Pine said very little about what went on up that mountain. Nearly everythin' we do know about it came from Mr Tully.'

'Well, he would stick up for Pine, wouldn't he? He's another bloody Catholic.'

'An' I suppose the committee of inquiry – which decided that Pine did more than could have been expected of any man – was made up of Catholics as well, was it?' the mock Elvis asked.

'Wouldn't surprise me at all,' the ginger man said. 'Anyway, I wouldn't put a lot of faith in anythin' Tully said, if I was you. He was a bloody wreck when they brought him down.'

'So would you have been, if you'd damn near died of exposure,' the bald man said. 'But you are right about one thing – he was never the same man again.'

'Didn't even seem to know where he was, half the time,' the Elvis impersonator agreed. 'Makin' a clean break was the best thing he could have done, if you want my opinion.'

'Making a clean break?' Beresford repeated.

'A few months after it all happened, he resigned from the company,' the bald man explained. 'He said he wanted to leave the past behind him and make a new start.'

'So he left Whitebridge, did he?'

'Left Whitebridge?' the ginger man repeated. 'He did a bit more than that. He left the country! In fact, he left the bloody continent! He's livin' somewhere in Australia now.'

A large-scale map of Whitebridge had been pinned to the frame of the blackboard in the basement, and Rutter studied it for a moment before turning to address his team of fresh-faced detective constables.

'Some of you – especially the ones who've never been involved in a murder inquiry before – may be starting to think that we're getting nowhere,' he said. 'But if that *is* what you're thinking, you're wrong. Police work is largely a matter of elimination. The more places we can rule out, the fewer there are left where the murder could have taken place.'

He paused, to let his words sink in.

What the hell was the matter with Monika, he found himself wondering in the space the silence had granted him.

She hadn't looked exactly great when he arrived at the Drum and Monkey – and given what they'd been through together, he hadn't expected her to – but after that phone call, she looked like *death*.

A constable at the far end of the horseshoe coughed, and

76

Rutter remembered where he was, and what he was supposed to be doing.

'I've marked three spots on the map,' he said, tracing them out with his finger. 'Here in the middle of town is Point A, St Mary's Church. A bit further out is Point B, Greenfield. And right up there, at the edge of the map, is Point C, the lay-by. But we still have to find Point D – the place where Pine was killed. What I want to know from you is where you think we should be looking for that point – and where you think we *shouldn't*.'

'It's unlikely he was killed anywhere outside the city boundaries,' one of DCs suggested.

'Is it? Why?'

'He left the church at around nine o'clock, and his body was discovered a little after ten. He wouldn't have *time* to drive far, especially in a thick fog like there was last night.'

'Good point,' Rutter agreed. 'Where else?'

'He couldn't have been attacked anywhere very public,' another DC chipped in.

'Why not?'

'If he had have been, somebody would have come across the bloodstains by now.'

Rutter nodded. 'Sound thinking. So what have we just ruled out?'

'The streets. The bus station. The railway station. Pub car parks. Anywhere a lot of people go.'

'So what does that leave us with?' Rutter said.

'The murderer could have killed him somewhere indoors,' a third detective constable speculated. 'Maybe he got Pine to visit his house on some pretext or other, and did it there.'

'We'll ignore that possibility for the moment,' Rutter said.

'But, sir—' the DC protested.

'And the *reason* we'll ignore it is not because it's a bad idea. It isn't. But if that *is* what actually happened, then the only way we're going to find the place is if somebody rings us up and tells us where to look. So what we have to do is concentrate on *other* places where it might have happened. That means gardens, public parks, abandoned buildings and pieces of waste ground, all within the city boundaries. Agreed?'

The DCs nodded.

'When you joined the CID you probably thought your days

of pounding the pavements were over,' Rutter said. He smiled. 'Well, lads, I hate to break this to you, but you couldn't have been more wrong. By the time this investigation's over, your feet will have swelled to twice their normal size, and you'll think back to your days on the beat as a kind of golden age.' He paused for a moment. 'But when we catch our killer – and we *will* catch him – the buzz you'll get out of it will be like nothing you've ever known before.'

Beresford found Woodend sitting at the team's table in the Drum and Monkey. The chief inspector still had a half-full beer glass in front of him, but seemed to have no interest in draining it.

'Where are the others, sir?' Beresford asked.

'The others?' Woodend repeated, as if his mind had been somewhere else entirely. 'What others?'

'Inspector Rutter and Sergeant Paniatowski, sir.'

'The Inspector's gone back to work with the team "at the heart of the investigation".'

'Sorry?'

'He's in the HQ basement.'

'And the sergeant?'

'I . . . er . . . sent Monika home. She was lookin' tired, so I told her to go an' grab a couple of hours kip.'

Tired? Beresford thought.

The dynamic Sergeant Paniatowski? Tired?

At this early stage of the inquiry?

'So did you spend a profitable mornin' at Hawtrey and Pine's?' Woodend asked.

'I'm not sure I'd exactly say that it was profitable, sir,' Beresford admitted. 'But I did everything that you told me to do.'

'Includin' gettin' Bradley Pine's office sealed up until I have the time to take a look at it?'

'Yes. And I also went to listen to what the men working at Hawtrey-Pine Holdings had to say.'

'An' what *did* the men have to say?'

Beresford outlined what Harry Ramsbotham had told him about the break-up of Hawtrey's marriage, and Pine's injection of cash into the company. Then he recounted his conversation with the Three Stooges.

'So at least one of those fellers blames Bradley Pine for Alec Hawtrey's death, does he?' Woodend asked, when the constable had finished.

'Yes, sir, but I wouldn't pay too much attention to his views, because he's also halfway to thinking that there's a Roman Catholic conspiracy to take over the world,' Beresford pointed out.

'Still, if he thinks that what happened on the mountainside was Pine's fault, there's others who might think it as well,' Woodend mused.

'Others?'

'We know that whoever killed Pine had a burnin' hatred for him.'

'Yes?'

'An' if I was a widow who blamed him for my husband's death, I think that's just the kind of hatred that I might have.'

'You think that Mrs Thelma Hawtrey might have killed him?' Beresford asked.

'I think anybody an' everybody *could* have killed him,' Woodend replied. 'An' it would certainly be jumpin' the gun to assume that Mrs Hawtrey was our prime suspect. On the other hand, it's only human nature to blame other people for your own deep loss – an' who would Mrs Hawtrey be more likely to blame than Bradley Pine?'

'But when you think about the way that Pine was killed—' Beresford protested.

'It was a powerful blow that did for him, but the Doc said a woman could have found the strength to inflict it, if she'd been angry enough.'

'But the mutilation! Surely a woman wouldn't have had the stomach to do that?'

'Ever heard the sayin' "The female of the species is more deadly than the male"?' Woodend asked. 'Anyway, she didn't have to do it herself, did she? Maybe she's got a brother who did it for her. Or a cousin. Maybe she even hired an outside "hit-man". Though I must admit that if *I've* no idea about how to find a contract killer in Central Lancashire, I don't imagine that *she* does, either.'

'Are we going to question her, sir?' Beresford asked.

Woodend laughed. '*Now* who's the one who's eager to pin it on the poor woman?' he asked.

'I didn't mean . . . I never intended to suggest . . .' Beresford mumbled.

'We'll get round to talkin' to Mrs Hawtrey eventually,' Woodend said. 'But first we'll go an' look at where our Mr Pine worked an' played.'

Thirteen

Henry Marlowe stood at the top of the steps outside the main entrance to Police Headquarters. He was wearing his full dress uniform, which, it always seemed to him, succeeded in making him seem both noble and grave.

He looked down at the pack of journalists who had gathered at the foot of the steps. There were around a dozen of them with notebooks in their hands, and though a couple of these worked for local papers, most were from the nationals.

Which was excellent!

And what was even more gratifying was that there were a couple of camera crews in evidence.

Marlowe recollected how furious he'd been with Bradley Pine when Pine had snatched the nomination from right under his nose – and had to force himself not to smile at the memory.

Rather than the defeat he'd taken it to be then, it had all been for the best, he told himself. He could quite see that now.

Because he'd never have got press coverage like this if he'd won the nomination the first time around, whereas Bradley Pine's murder had focussed press attention on the campaign – and given it just about as good a launch pad as any prospective MP could ever hope for.

Marlowe held up his hands – palms outwards – to call for silence from the hacks.

'I find myself in a very difficult position,' he said. 'Whilst, on the one hand, I am both delighted and honoured to announce that I am standing as candidate for this constituency, I am, on the other, mortified that such an announcement should ever have been made necessary. The tragic and brutal murder of Bradley Pine has robbed this community of a talented, caring man who would have striven ceaselessly to improve the conditions of those who had voted for him, and the least I can do is to promise that I, too—'

'Have you resigned from your post?' asked a female voice from the middle of the press pack.

'—if elected, will put the needs of my constituents above all other considerations.'

'Have you resigned?' the woman repeated.

And now several of the other journalists were starting to ask the same question.

'Not, I have not resigned,' Marlowe said, giving into the inevitable. 'I have taken leave of absence, though, if I am elected to parliament, I will, of course, immediately—'

'Should you be wearing that uniform if you're on leave of absence?' the woman interrupted.

'Strictly speaking, I should perhaps have taken it off before I addressed you,' Marlowe conceded, 'but it seemed to me that you would wish to be briefed as soon as possible, and—'

'Given the seriousness of the crime, wouldn't you have served the community better by staying on in your post and leading the investigation yourself?' the woman asked.

The cameras, which had been directed at Marlowe up until this point, had now swung round and were pointed at the reporter.

Who *was* the bloody woman? Marlowe wondered.

She looked like one he'd had some dealings with before, a real chancer called Elizabeth Driver – but Driver had jet black hair, and this woman was a dazzling blonde.

'The senior officer I have left in charge of the case is perfectly capable of conducting an investigation without any guidance from me,' Marlowe said – though even as he was speaking the words he realized they didn't quite seem to be conveying the message he'd intended them to.

'So are you saying a chief constable isn't really necessary at all?' the woman asked, with a kind of naïve innocence.

It *was* Elizabeth Driver, Marlowe realized. Dark or blonde, the poisonous little bitch was back!

'I'm not sure I understand the question, Miss Driver,' he said, stalling for time.

The cameras swung back to Elizabeth Driver, as if they had decided to turn what should have been a coronation into nothing more than a vulgar tennis match.

'If a very important investigation like this one doesn't need a chief constable to guide it, then surely that's even truer of the less significant ones?' Elizabeth Driver amplified. 'In other words, Mr Marlowe, what's the *point* of having a chief constable at all?'

The cameras swung back to a visibly sweating Marlowe.

'My officers can conduct the investigation without my assistance because they are effective,' he said. 'And the reason they're effective is because that's what I *trained* them to be.'

'So if they don't catch the murderer in this case, it will actually be your fault?'

There was more to this politics business than at first met the eye, Marlowe thought. When you were a chief constable, everybody listened to what you had to say in respectful silence. When you became a politician, it seemed you were fair game for anyone who fancied taking a shot at you.

'This is a pointless discussion, Miss Driver, since the murderer *will* be caught,' he said.

'Can you guarantee that?' Elizabeth Driver asked.

'Any crime reporter worth his or *her* own salt surely knows that there's no such thing as a guarantee in a criminal investigation,' Marlowe said, in a tone which he hoped would be withering enough to finally shut the woman up.

'I'm sorry,' Elizabeth Driver said, looking deeply perplexed for the benefit of the camera. 'I thought that I'd just heard you say quite clearly that the murderer *will* be caught.'

'Well, of course, I sincerely believe that he will be,' Marlowe said, feeling as if he were drowning.

'So are you willing to stake your own reputation on the murderer being arrested?' Elizabeth Driver asked.

'Yes, I will stake my reputation on it,' Marlowe promised.

After all, he thought, what else *could* he have said?

Bradley Pine's office in Hawtrey-Pine Holdings had been so neat and efficient that it could have come straight from the Ideal Office Exhibition.

Woodend and Beresford had found no personal photographs there. Nor had there been any magazines – except those relating to the mattress trade. And the two policemen had failed entirely to discover any little notes that Pine might have written to himself about social engagements.

In short, there had been absolutely nothing of the man's personality about the room at all.

His home was providing no clues, either.

It was a modest detached residence in a street of modest detached residences. Pine could easily have afforded a much larger house, but since he seemed to make so little use of the space he already had, why would he have bothered?

The chief inspector and the constable tramped from room to room, looking for insights into the man who had inspired so much hatred that his murderer had not been content to merely end his life, but had violated his corpse as well.

The kitchen had all the pots, pans and electrical equipment necessary to produce a banquet, but the fridge contained no more than a pint of milk and a couple of bottles of white wine.

The living room had perfectly co-ordinated soft furnishings, but they gave off the distinct impression of having been chosen by an interior designer, rather than by the man who would have to live with them.

The bedroom was almost spartan in aspect, and the bedding had been tucked under the mattress with neat hospital corners.

As the two men returned to the hallway at the end of their search, they were both feeling vaguely let down.

Woodend picked up the mail which had been lying on the door mat when they arrived. There was an electricity bill, a couple of circulars, and an invitation to address a Rotary Club lunch, none of which told him anything about the late Bradley Pine.

But that did not necessarily mean that Pine *never* received personal letters, the chief inspector thought.

'When we get back to headquarters, remind me to get somebody to contact the Post Office,' he said.

'The Post Office?' Beresford repeated.

'Aye, I want any mail that Pine receives in the future to end up on my desk,' Woodend explained. He glanced up and down the neutral hallway again. 'So what do you make of all this, Constable?'

'I don't know, sir,' Beresford admitted. 'Mr Pine was either a very secretive man, or a very lonely one.'

'Or both,' Woodend said.

Perhaps it all sprung out of being an orphan. Perhaps the

main lesson that you learned there was never to get attached to other people – or even to personal possessions – because you knew that they could be taken away from you at any moment. Perhaps you came to believe that the only way to survive the experience was to avoid anything at all which could make you vulnerable.

But then what do I know? the chief inspector asked himself.

How could a man who had been brought up in the bosom of a close, loving family even begin to conceive of what it was like to grow up in an institution, as Bradley Pine had?

'Sooner or later, I'm goin' to have to visit this orphanage,' he told Beresford, 'but today I think we'll just settle for a visit to the Widow Hawtrey.'

When Monika Paniatowski had left the Drum and Monkey, she'd gone straight back to her flat.

Once inside the place which she sometimes saw as her refuge – and sometimes as her isolation cell – she made sure the door was locked securely behind her, and drew all the curtains. Then – and without even bothering to undress – she threw herself on to the bed.

She had been planning to go to sleep – partly because she was feeling exhausted, and partly because she hoped that sleep would offer her at least a temporary escape for all that haunted her. But the deep, forgetful oblivion that she craved for eluded her, and instead she found herself wrapped up in a disturbing and troublesome dream.

Fate had come calling on her.

He was tall and thin, and dressed in a monk's habit. He stood at the top of a long staircase which was surrounded by a swirling mist. And she stood at the bottom, looking up at him.

Fate crooked his finger, to indicate she should join him, and though she didn't want to, she knew that she had no choice in the matter.

She put her foot on the first step, and she was a small child again, fatherless, and travelling across war-torn Europe with her mother.

She advanced to the second step, which she found herself sharing with the stepfather who had abused her and the priest who had refused to listen to her cries for help.

Bob Rutter and his blind wife were waiting for her on the third step – and though she knew she should pass straight by them, she found herself stopping to give Bob a passionate kiss.

She pulled away, and advanced to the fourth step, but somehow Bob and Maria had got there before her. Maria was lying down, the wound in her head gushing bright red blood. Bob looked first at his dead wife with compassion, then at his ex-lover with contempt.

Monika rushed on to the next step, where poor DCI Baxter was waiting for her. But she didn't want him. She needed him – but she didn't want him.

'Look at me,' Fate boomed out from above her.

She raised her eyes reluctantly. She was close enough to see his face now – but there was no face to see, only a deep, black nothingness where a head should have been.

'I have been playing games with you,' Fate told her. 'You exist to be the butt of my sick jokes. You have no other purpose.'

'I know that,' she said. 'I think I've always known that.'

'Another step, Monika!' Fate ordered. 'Take another step!'

'I don't want to!'

'Take another step!'

She lifted her leg to mount the next stair, but it wasn't there. The whole staircase had suddenly disappeared, and she was falling . . . falling . . . falling . . .

When she awoke, she was bathed in sweat and her whole body was trembling. With shaky hands she reached for the packet of cigarettes on her bedside table and lit one up.

She thought about her dream. It was comforting – in a way – to believe that everything was predetermined, and that, however miserable you were, there was nothing you could do about it.

It was comforting – but was it true?

There was a part of her which still believed that we make our own choices – and that most of the choices she had made had been disastrously wrong.

Worse yet, she had a growing conviction that she had *known* they were wrong when she'd made them, and had chosen them precisely *because* they were wrong.

It was almost as if she wished to punish herself – as if

something inside her had decided she was unworthy of happiness.

She felt a gaping void in her life – and wondered if she would ever be able to find anything to fill it.

Fourteen

The brass plaque screwed into the gatepost had two fir trees etched on it, and the words 'The Firs' were engraved underneath. There was no number – though the house had obviously originally been designated one – but then neither was there a number on the gateposts of any of the other houses that looked out on to Lawrence Street, Bankside.

Numbers, the owners of these houses seemed to be saying by this sin of omission, were intended for much meaner dwellings than these – terraces clinging desperately to steep hillsides; semi-detacheds which were owned by bank clerks, junior school teachers and others of that ilk. In Bankside, where every house was double-fronted and detached, it would have been the height of vulgarity to give a home a number.

Woodend and Beresford walked up the drive, and when Woodend rang the bell, they heard an elaborate chime reverberate down the hallway on the other side of the front door.

The door was opened by a woman who was in her mid thirties. Had she lived in one of those houses which had numbers, she would probably have been wearing an apron at that time of day, but the owner of The Firs – and, from her manner, that was obviously what she was – was dressed in a smart suit.

'Can I help you?' she asked, in an accent which wasn't *quite* posh, but could have been with just a little more work.

She was a good looking woman as she was now, Woodend thought, his glance taking in her green eyes, pert nose and generous mouth. But when she was in her late teens and early twenties she must have been a *real* stunner – the sort of woman who turns every head in the street and causes drivers to crash into lamp posts.

He held out his warrant card for her to see.

'Mrs Hawtrey?' he asked.

'Yes.'

'We'd like to ask you a few questions, if you don't mind.'

'Is this about poor Bradley Pine?'

'That's right.'

The woman nodded. 'Of course, it would be, wouldn't it? I suppose that after what happened to him, I should have been expecting a call from you, but somehow the idea never did occur to me. Still, I'd be glad to help in any way I can. Won't you come inside?'

The lounge of The Firs was as large as the ground floor and back yard of a terraced house combined. The furnishings were opulent, the fabrics lush, and Beresford – who had had fewer opportunities than Woodend to see how the affluent lived – was most impressed.

Mrs Hawtrey directed the two policemen to a leather sofa, offered them a drink – which Woodend politely refused for both of them – and then sat down in an armchair opposite.

'Having offered you my help, I'm not sure there's much I can tell you that would be of any use to your investigation,' she said. 'In all honesty, I'd have to say that Bradley Pine was no more to me than a business partner.' She paused. 'Actually, it's not strictly accurate to say that he was even that.'

'No?' Woodend said, quizzically.

'No,' Mrs Hawtrey replied. 'I'm entitled to slightly more than half the profits of Hawtrey-Pine Holdings – and my very sharp accountant makes damn sure that I get them – but, other than that, I have virtually nothing to do with the business at all.'

'*Virtually* nothing?' Woodend repeated. 'That's not quite the same as saying *absolutely* nothing, is it?'

'No, I suppose it isn't. But any contact I *do* have with the company is largely of a ceremonial nature.' Mrs Hawtrey laughed lightly. 'I'm a bit like the Queen, in that way.'

'A bit like the Queen? You mean that it's your job to declare things open?' Woodend guessed.

'Exactly, Chief Inspector! The company had a new work-shop built last year – it needed it to meet increased demand for our mattresses – and I was asked to cut the ribbon at the grand opening. Which I dutifully did. Naturally, Bradley Pine, as the managing director, was there too.'

'But other than on occasions like that, you didn't see him at all?'

'No, I can't say that I did.'

'Not even socially?'

'I suppose it depends what you mean by *socially*. We have a number of friends and acquaintances in common, so we did sometimes run into each other at parties and weddings – and when that happened, we'd obviously exchange a few words.'

'What kind of words?'

'Superficial chit-chat, I suppose you'd call it. "How are you doing, Thelma?"; "I'm fine, Bradley. How are you? And, more to the point, where's my profits cheque, ha, ha, ha?" You know – the sort of things that people say to each other when they haven't really got much in common.'

'So, all in all, you wouldn't say that you regarded him as a friend?' Woodend asked.

'Not really, no. He was Alec's friend – had been even before they went into business together – and after Alec died, well . . .'

She let her answer trail off.

'So if Mr Pine had any enemies who'd be more than happy to see him dead, you wouldn't know about them?'

'I'm afraid not.'

Woodend leant forward slightly. 'Can I be frank with you, Mrs Hawtrey?' he asked.

'Of course.'

'It might be a little painful.'

'Go on,' Thelma Hawtrey said, though now there was a hint of caution in her voice.

'I was wonderin' if your husband's death changed your attitude to Mr Pine in any way.'

'What's my attitude to Bradley got to do with his murder?' Thelma Hawtrey asked sharply.

'Probably nothin' at all,' Woodend lied. 'But I'm tryin' to build up a picture of Bradley Pine in my mind, you see, an' it would help me to know how other people – all kinds of other people, includin' yourself – felt about him.'

Thelma Hawtrey considered the matter for some moments.

'If what you're asking me is if I blamed Bradley for Alec's death, then I suppose that, at first, I did,' she admitted.

'But not any more?'

Thelma Hawtrey shook her head. 'No, not any more, Chief Inspector. I've come to accept that Alec was up on that mountainside because that was where he wanted to be. And – by

90

all the accounts I've been given of that terrible, terrible day
– Bradley did do everything he possibly could have, in the
circumstances, to save Alec's life.'

'So you've no hard feelings towards him at all?'

'Occasionally I do catch myself thinking that Bradley could
have done more to try and persuade Alec not to go on the
climb, but then I tell myself that I'm not being fair.'

'Do you really?' Woodend asked, sounding unconvinced.

Thelma Hawtrey gave him a look which would have turned
a lesser man into a pile of smouldering cinders.

'Yes, I do,' she said emphatically. 'Because if Bradley's to
blame, then I'm . . . I'm *doubly* to blame.'

'You mustn't let yourself get upset, Mrs Hawtrey,' Beresford
said, sympathetically.

But the warning had come too late, and tears were already
beginning to stream down Thelma Hawtrey's face.

'I . . . I could have talked him out of making the climb just
as easily as Bradley Pine could,' she said, between sobs.

'Mrs Hawtrey . . .' Beresford said imploringly.

'I could have talked him out of it *more* easily. I . . . I . . .
wasn't just his friend, as Bradley was, you see. I was his *wife*.
And . . . and he was only doing it because of me.'

'Because of you?' Woodend asked.

'Alec was . . . he was older than me, and sometimes that
bothered him a little. He went climbing to prove to me that
he was still as strong and vigorous as when we married. But
he didn't *have* to prove it. It didn't bother me that he'd become
middle-aged. I loved him just the way he was.'

'Can we go now, sir?' Beresford asked urgently.

'Yes,' Woodend replied. 'I think we better had.'

'Well, apart from reducing poor Mrs Hawtrey to a flood of
tears, we didn't achieve much in there, did we, sir?' Beresford
asked – with just a hint of reproach in his voice – when he
and Woodend were out on Lawrence Road again.

'So that's what you think, is it?' Woodend asked, inserting
his key into the door lock of the Wolseley. 'That we didn't
achieve much?'

'Do you think we *did*?' Beresford asked, shocked.

Woodend got into the car, and reached across to open the
front passenger door.

'Mrs Hawtrey was remarkably frank an' open with us, wouldn't you say?' he asked, as Beresford climbed into the passenger seat.

'Yes, sir, I would,' the constable replied, closing his door. 'It must have taken real guts to admit that there are times when she blames herself for her husband's death.'

'That could be it. Or perhaps, by doin' that, she was just tryin' to shift the spotlight,' Woodend said.

'I'm sorry, sir?'

'Maybe she decided that her claim that she bore Bradley Pine no ill will for what had happened simply wouldn't stand up to much more examination, so she started cryin' as a way of switchin' the focus on to herself.'

'She did seem genuinely upset,' Beresford pointed out.

'So would I, if I thought the police were gettin' dangerously close to suspectin' me of murder,' Woodend countered.

'I think you're wrong, sir,' Beresford said.

'An' I'm convinced I'm right,' Woodend said firmly, turning the key in the ignition. 'I'm about to pull off, lad, an' when I do, I want you to turn your head quickly and take a look at Mrs Hawtrey's upstairs windows.'

'Why would I do that?' Beresford wondered.

'Because I'm tellin' you to.'

Woodend slid the Wolseley into gear, and pulled away from the kerb. Beresford turned quickly, as he'd been instructed.

'Well?' Woodend said, as they left The Firs behind them.

'I saw the bedroom curtains twitch,' Beresford admitted.

'Did you, now?' Woodend asked. 'So, far from lyin' on her bed wracked in sobs – as you might have expected her to be – the Widow Hawtrey was, in fact, watchin' to make sure that we were really leavin'.'

'I don't see that proves anything,' Beresford said stubbornly.

Woodend sighed. 'When you've been in this game as long as I have, lad, you develop an instinct for knowin' when the person you're questionin' is either lyin' or tryin' to hide somethin' from you. An' Mrs Hawtrey – for all her tears – was doin' both.'

Fifteen

Bob Rutter was the first member of the team to arrive at the Drum and Monkey for the early evening drink which had become a firmly established tradition during investigations, but Woodend and Beresford were not far behind him.

'Where's Monika?' Rutter asked, looking over Woodend's shoulder. 'Will she be coming later?'

'No,' the chief inspector replied. 'I don't think she will.'

Rutter looked troubled. 'Any reason for that?'

'No *particular* reason, no. She's ... er ... well, I suppose she's feelin' a bit off-colour.'

'She looked more than *a bit* off-colour earlier,' Rutter said. 'Do you have any idea why—'

'Leave it, lad,' Woodend interrupted – in a tone which made it clear that it was not so much a suggestion as an order.

'I'm sorry, I didn't mean to—'

'I said *leave it*!'

The chief inspector picked up his freshly-pulled pint and took a healthy swig, though he did not look as if he were enjoying it much.

'If you'd been tap-dancin' on the table when we walked in, I'd have assumed you'd found the spot where Bradley Pine was killed,' he said to Rutter. 'But since you weren't, I'm assumin' you haven't.'

'And you assume right,' Rutter agreed. 'Are *you* getting anywhere from your end, sir?'

'I think I've got a suspect,' Woodend told him, 'though Constable Beresford here is convinced that I'm way off the mark.'

'Thelma Hawtrey?' Rutter guessed.

'Thelma Hawtrey,' Woodend agreed.

He glanced down at his watch, then up at the television which was mounted high on the wall – and only normally switched on when a major football match was being played.

'The local news is just startin',' he called across to the land-lord. 'Would you mind if we watched it?'

'Not at all, Mr Woodend.'

The television warmed up just in time to catch the start of the interview that the chief constable had given to the press earlier in the day.

'You have to admit, he does look good in that dress uniform,' Rutter said grudgingly.

'A tailor's dummy would look good in it,' Woodend replied sourly. 'An', come to think of it, a tailor's dummy would prob-ably make a much better chief constable.'

Marlowe launched himself confidently into his prepared statement, but seemed to be instantly nonplussed by the off-screen female voice demanding to know if he'd resigned.

'It's a grand thing, is a free press,' Woodend said.

Marlowe was doing his best to cut the woman off, but was meeting with little success, and after a few more words had been exchanged, the camera swung round on to her.

'Good God!' Rutter exclaimed. 'That's Elizabeth Driver!'

'I'm surprised that *you're* surprised,' Woodend told him. 'This kind of case is meat an' drink to our Liz.'

'*Yes, I will stake my reputation on it,*' Marlowe was saying, on screen.

Woodend shook his head.

'Silly, silly man,' he said, though he did not look entirely distressed at having heard Marlowe make such a gaffe.

The chief constable disappeared from the screen, and was replaced by a weather man promising a fine few days ahead.

'I wish I'd been there,' Woodend said. 'It was entertainin' enough on the telly, but it must have been real fun in the flesh.'

Beresford drained his pint and stood up. 'Would it be all right if I went now, sir?' he asked.

'Aye, get yourself home, lad,' Woodend told him. 'I'll see you first thing in the mornin'.'

The chief inspector watched the constable leave the bar, then turned to Rutter and said, 'Given that it's a well-known fact the quickest way to promotion is to stay up drinkin' with your boss until the early hours of the mornin', you're prob-ably wonderin' why an ambitious bobby like young Beresford hasn't availed himself of the opportunity when it was offered to him.'

94

Rutter nodded, but said nothing.

'It puzzled me for a while, an' all,' Woodend continued. 'I was on the point of askin' him about it directly, but then somethin' inside me – a vague uneasy feelin' – made me pull back at the last minute. So instead, I made a few discreet inquiries among the neighbours, an' discovered that his mam was sufferin' from Alzheimer's disease. Well, then everythin' fell into place, didn't it? The reason he's so keen to get home is that though the neighbours are more than willin' to keep an eye on her when he's not there, he feels obliged to spend as much time with her as he possibly can.'

'Is that right?' Rutter asked abstractly, as if his mind were not really on the subject in hand.

'It is right,' Woodend confirmed. 'It's quite refreshin', in this day an' age, to come across a young man who's prepared to put his family obligations above his career, don't you think?'

'Hmm,' Rutter replied.

'You haven't heard a single word I've just said, have you, Bob?' Woodend asked.

'What was that, sir?'

'I thought not! What's botherin' you? Is it somethin' to do with the investigation?'

'Not really,' Rutter admitted. 'Did you notice that Elizabeth Driver has dyed her hair?'

'I couldn't very well have missed it. Although, strictly speakin', it's more of a case of her goin' back to her natural colour than of her dyin' it. If you remember, she was blonde the first time we crossed swords with her, when she was tryin' to bugger up our investigation in the Westbury Manor murder.'

'Don't you think she looks a bit like Monika now?' Rutter asked, and once again, it was clear he hadn't been listening.

'I can't say I noticed the resemblance myself,' Woodend confessed, 'but then *I* wasn't really lookin' for it.'

'I think she does,' Rutter mused. 'In fact, I think she looks a *lot* like Monika.'

It was already dark when Monika Paniatowski reached St Mary's Church, and she found herself wondering if she hadn't – perhaps unconsciously – been waiting for just this cover of darkness before she made her move.

'You can analyse yourself too much,' she thought. 'You can analyse yourself to the point of madness.'

She checked over her shoulder to see if anyone was watching her, then pushed the door open and entered the church.

Once inside, confronted by the vastness of the holy cavern, she was suddenly unsure what to do next.

Perhaps she should just stay where she was, at the back of the church, and wait for something – anything – to happen. But was anything *likely* to happen?

Perhaps she should go and sit down in one of the pews. But what would be the point of that? It wasn't as if she was there to *pray*!

'Hello,' said a soft, welcoming voice.

She turned. 'Hello, Fred,' she said.

'What can we do for you this time?' Father Taylor asked. 'Do you want to interrogate us about poor Mr Pine again?'

She hadn't been thinking about the investigation at all, and so the question knocked her completely off-balance.

'No, I . . . I . . .' she began uncertainly. 'I'm off-duty.'

'Ah, so it's not Sergeant Paniatowski I'm speaking to at the moment, but only Monika,' the priest said. 'Am I right?'

'Yes, I suppose you are.'

'And why is Monika here? Has she, perhaps, dropped in for no more than a nice friendly chat?'

'A friendly chat would be nice, Father Fred,' Paniatowski heard herself admitting.

'Here? Or would you be more comfortable in the vestry?'

'I think I'd be more comfortable in the vestry.'

'Then the vestry it shall be.'

They sat facing each other on two rickety chairs, in a room where the walls were draped with choirboys' cassocks which smelled vaguely of adolescent uncertainty.

'What's the secret of happiness?' Paniatowski asked.

Father Taylor smiled. 'I know just what you're expecting me to say,' he told her.

'Do you?'

'You're expecting me to say that the key to true happiness is the love of God.'

'And isn't it – at least as far as you're concerned?'

'Of course it is. In the long term. Looking at the big picture.

But we're only human, Monika, and even though we know that God loves us as we should try to love Him, we still have our own little crises to deal with. And as much as we know that they are of no real significance at all, they can still hurt – they can still cause us to behave badly.'

'Tell me about your crises,' Paniatowski said.

Father Taylor smiled again. 'Is this some kind of test that you're putting me through?' he asked.

'I don't honestly know,' Paniatowski admitted. 'Does it matter if it is?'

'Not really.' The priest cupped both his hands tightly around his left knee. 'I sometimes find it hard to love other people as I know God loves them,' he said. 'Unworthy as I am, in my own self, I still find myself sitting in judgement on them. And though God has forgiven them, I'm not sure that I'll ever be able to do the same. Do you understand that?'

Oh yes, she understood that all right. Understood that she would never forgive her stepfather and the priest who went drinking with him – and that Bob Rutter would never forgive *her*.

'But these feelings do eventually pass,' Father Taylor continued. 'Over time, I come to understand that I have no right to judge, and eventually I find myself seeing these fellow sinners of mine just a little as they must appear in the light of God's all-forgiving eyes.'

'Is there anything else you sometimes have a crisis about?' Paniatowski asked.

'I have just confessed to you the depths of my own unworthiness. Isn't that enough for you?'

'No, it isn't,' Paniatowski said. 'I don't know why it shouldn't be, but it just isn't.'

The priest released his grip on his left knee, and cupped his right one just as tightly.

'Very well,' he said, 'I'll tell you more. Though I believe that my role in life has been chosen for me by God, and though I am usually grateful beyond words that He has selected me, there are times when I'm angry about it, too – when I feel not so much picked *out* as picked *on*.'

'I . . . I don't think I've ever heard a priest talk like this before,' Paniatowski said.

'And perhaps you should not be hearing one talk like it now,' Father Taylor replied.

'*When* do you feel angry in that way?' Paniatowski asked, urgently.

'I really do think I've said enough.'

'Please! Tell me!'

The priest shrugged, helplessly.

'A young couple came to see me the other day,' he said. 'The wife had just given birth to a baby boy, and they wanted to arrange a christening. They brought their daughter with them – a beautiful little girl of four. She was holding on to her father's hand, and at one point, I saw her looking up at him. And what a look it was – so full of trust, so full of love. And I knew at that moment – though, at a deeper level I must *always* have known it – that I was doomed never to have a child look at *me* in quite that way.'

And neither will I, Paniatowski thought bitterly. I can never have children – this defective body of mine makes that impossible – so I won't experience it, either.

'There's another look I miss,' the priest said, guiltily. 'The look that a woman like you might give to a man like me, if we were entirely different people in an entirely different place.' He paused for a moment. 'You seem shocked by what I've just said, Monika.'

'No, I—'

'What did you think? That a priest was above such thoughts and yearnings? Did you imagine that the holy oil with which we are anointed was some kind of magic potion which took away our sex drives completely?'

'No, I—'

'It doesn't work like that. If sacrifice involves no pain, then it is no real sacrifice at all. And if we have no weaknesses of our own to battle against, how will we ever understand the struggles against weakness that must be endured by those whom God has put into our care?'

Paniatowski stood up.

'Are you leaving?' Father Taylor asked. 'Have I scandalized you – or merely bored you?'

'No, I'm . . . I haven't . . . it's not either of those things. I'm nervous. That's all. And when I'm nervous, I need to smoke. So that's what I'm doing. I'm going outside for a smoke.'

'You may smoke in here, if you wish, Monika. As you already know, Father Kenyon does.'

'No, I'll . . . I'd prefer to smoke in the open air.'

'And will you be coming back when you've finished your cigarette, Monika?'

'I'm not sure.'

Father Taylor shook his head. 'Which means "no",' he said. 'I think that's the right decision for you to make. I don't think you *should* come back tonight. But you will come back another time, won't you?'

'Yes . . . No . . . I think so, but I'm not making any promises.'

'It doesn't have to be me who you come and see,' Father Taylor said. 'Perhaps it *shouldn't* be me. Come and see Father Kenyon. Or see a priest in another parish, if you'd feel more at ease with that. But please don't stop now, having begun the journey back.'

'There is no journey back!' Paniatowski protested. 'As I told you earlier, I just dropped in for a friendly chat.'

'If you prefer to think of the steps you take as "friendly chats", then there can be no harm in that,' Father Taylor told her. 'But keep on having these chats, Monika, I beg you.'

'I don't need your religion,' Paniatowski said fiercely.

'You're wrong about that,' Father Taylor said, with absolute conviction. 'I see a lot of very unhappy people in my role as parish priest, Monika – but I have to tell you, in all honesty, that you're more in need of spiritual comfort than any of them.'

Sixteen

It was seven thirty-five in the morning, and Henry Marlowe sat in the hospitality suite of the BBC's Manchester studios, preparing himself for a radio interview. He was not alone. Bill Hawes, his constituency agent, was by his side, as he intended to be – especially after the fiasco on police headquarters' steps the previous afternoon – for every waking minute of every day until the election was over.

'Now remember, Henry, old chap, this is *national* radio you're going on,' Hawes cautioned.

'I know that,' Marlowe said, with some irritation.

'The Party bosses in London will be listening to your performance with keen interest,' Hawes pressed on, 'and how well you do may affect whether you're welcomed to Westminster as a cabinet minister in the making or as mere cannon fodder for the voting lobbies.'

'If I ever *do* arrive in Westminster,' Marlowe said bitterly. 'If I'm ever *elected*.'

'You'll be elected,' Hawes said.

His tone was confident and reassuring, but Marlowe took no comfort from that. He was perfectly well aware that Bill Hawes was a professional fixer – a political manipulator – and sounding confident was what he did, whether his candidate of the moment was an easy shoo-in for the seat or didn't have a cat in hell's chance of winning it.

'I don't want to be wrong-footed like I was yesterday,' Marlowe said.

'And you won't be,' Hawes promised. 'I've already thrashed out the ground rules with the man who'll be interviewing you, and he's given me his word that there'll be no mention of the fact that you've left your post in the middle of an important murder inquiry.'

'There shouldn't have been any mention of it at the press

conference, either,' Marlowe said, making it sound as if it had all been Hawes' fault.

'But even though you should skirt around the question of the murder investigation, you should still pay tribute to Bradley Pine as your predecessor,' Hawes advised.

'Should I?' Marlowe asked peevishly. 'Why?'

'Because it would seem mean-spirited of you not to.'

Marlowe sighed heavily. 'All right, I'll talk about what a hero Bradley was, and how he—'

'Not that, for Christ's sake!' Hawes said, in a panic. 'Whatever you do, don't talk about what happened on that bloody mountain!'

'But if I'm supposed to be paying tribute to him—'

'Find another way to do it. *Any* other way. Talk about his commitment to the Boy Scouts or old people's homes. Tell lies, if you have to – we can always find some way to gloss over them afterwards – but whatever else you do, don't so much as *mention* Alec Hawtrey's death.'

'Can I ask why?' Marlowe asked, with a show of petulance.

It was Hawes turn to sigh. 'I should have thought it was bloody obvious,' he said.

'Well, it isn't to me,' Marlowe counted. 'Alec Hawtrey was cremated, remember. Nobody can prove anything one way or the other now.'

'Nobody *has* to prove anything,' Hawes said, talking slowly and carefully, as if addressing a particularly slow learner. 'Even a hint of what happened could sink you. Besides, the people involved in the *cover-up* haven't been cremated, have they? They're still around, with their memories fully intact. And we know exactly who they are, don't we, Henry?'

Marlowe shuddered. 'Yes,' he agreed, 'We know who they are.'

When Joan Woodend had been in the early stages of recovering from her heart attack, she'd commented on the irony of the fact that she – who'd always scrupulously eaten her greens – should have been struck down with such an affliction, whilst Charlie – who had lived on a diet of cigarettes, beer and fried food for as long as she'd known him – should still be glowing with health.

101

Joan being Joan, of course, she hadn't actually used a fancy word like 'irony'.

What she'd said was that it was 'bloody funny, and she didn't mean funny ha-ha', that she was the one who was lying in the hospital bed.

And Woodend himself had been forced to agree with her.

What had happened to his wife had shaken the chief inspector to the core, but had made absolutely no difference at all to the way he led his own life, and at about the time that Henry Marlowe was being questioned on the radio by a suitably deferential interviewer, he himself was tucking into a subsidized fry-up in the Whitebridge police canteen.

The other two people at the table had chosen not to join him in playing Russian Roulette with their arteries. Beresford – who had cooked his mother's breakfast before he left home, and then sat there watching her, to make sure she ate it – had settled for a poached egg on toast. Paniatowski had said she only wanted an orange juice – and didn't seem to even have the stomach for that.

Woodend mopped his egg yolk with a piece of fried bread, and popped it into his mouth.

'Here's the plan for this mornin',' he told Beresford. 'Monika an' me will be piecin' together everythin' we can about Thelma Hawtrey's friends an' relations, an' what I want you to do, lad, is to approach the same question – but from a different angle.'

'What angle would that be, sir?' the constable asked.

'Take yourself off to Hawtrey an' Pine Holdings again. I want to know how Thelma behaved when she paid her occasional visits to the factory. Was she on more or less friendly terms with Pine, as she claims – or did she look at him like she wanted him dead?'

'I still think you're wrong about her, sir,' Beresford said.

'I know you do,' Woodend agreed. 'But I'm beginnin' to suspect that's probably because you fancy her.'

'Fancy her!' Beresford repeated, shocked.

'There's no shame in it,' Woodend told him. 'None of us are immune to the call of the flesh.'

'But she's an *old woman*!' Beresford said, clearly horrified.

'My guess is that she's somewhere in her mid-thirties,' Woodend pointed out.

'Yes,' Beresford agreed. 'That's what I said.'

Woodend cut up his remaining bacon rind into bite-sized pieces, speared one, and aimed it at his mouth.

'If *she's* old, what does that make me?' he asked.

'It's different for you, sir,' Beresford said.

'Is it? How?'

'You're a man.'

'Aye, an' apparently a very *ancient* one.'

'I didn't mean to suggest—' Beresford began.

'Go an' do your job, lad,' Woodend interrupted him. 'An' if they've carted me off to the mortuary by the time you get back, you can always hand your report in to Sergeant Paniatowski, can't you?'

Father Taylor entered the parishioner's side of the confessional, sat down heavily, and turned his head towards the grille.

'Bless me, Father, for I have sinned,' he said. 'It is three days since my last confession.'

'Which is not an excessive amount of time,' said Father Kenyon mildly, from the other side of the grille.

'I have been guilty of impure thoughts and impure feelings.'

'Go on.'

'A woman came to the church— '

'That would be Sergeant Paniatowski, would it?'

'Yes, it was her. I saw at once that she was a lost soul. I wanted to lead her back to the light.'

'That is why God has put us here on this earth. That is why we serve Him as His priests.'

'But somehow that no longer seems important to me. I want to *know* her – in all senses of the word – and what she chooses to believe – or chooses not to believe – doesn't matter to me.'

'You must *make* it matter to you,' Father Kenyon said sternly. 'It is your duty.'

'I know that, and I have been trying, Father. I can't tell you how much I've tried. But I have failed.'

'Then you must try even harder. You say you have sinned, and I agree with you. But do you repent those sins?'

103

'I . . . I want to.'

'We both know that is not good enough,' Father Kenyon said heavily.

'Yes,' Father Taylor agreed. 'We both know that.'

Seventeen

It wasn't so much that there was one law for the rich and another for the poor, Bob Rutter thought, as that the poor let things happen *to* them, whereas the rich *made* the things happen.

The origin of this socio-political flight of fancy of his was a small patch of land in one of the more affluent suburbs of Whitebridge, beside which he was now standing. Once, the land had housed a tumbledown cottage, surrounded by countryside. But as Whitebridge had expanded in response to the newly emerging middle class's hunger for quality double-fronted houses, the countryside had been gobbled up, until finally it was no more.

The developers had tried to buy the cottage, but when the cranky old man who lived in it had refused to sell, they'd had no choice but to build around it. True, they'd done the best they could, contriving to construct in such a way that it was only through their back windows that the nearest new residents would catch sight of the bucolic slum, but the cottage had still been generally regarded as something of a blot on the newly urbanized landscape.

Then the old man had died and left the cottage to a nephew, who immediately put it on the market. Several construction companies made a bid for it, and, in a less affluent part of town, one of them would undoubtedly have succeeded in buying it. But the residents here had no wish to see a new building replace the old one, and – since they were the sort of people who *made* things happen – they had clubbed together and put in a bid of their own.

And this was the result – a green area with trees, bushes and a few flower beds, which was too small to be called a park, but just about large enough to bear the name of 'gardens' without seeming too ridiculous.

The residents had been so proud of their initiative that they had put up a plaque to commemorate it.

Lower Bankside Gardens
Purchased by the Residents' Association
for the benefit of all

Whilst he approved of their decision to buy the land, Rutter found the plaque rather smug and self-congratulatory, and there was one small – and admittedly unworthy – part of him which was half-hoping that this was the spot on which Bradley Pine met his end.

But it was not to be. The grass was undisturbed, the spring flowers bloomed unbowed – and there was no dark staining of the earth to suggest that it was here that Pine's blood had drained away.

He had all but completed his search when he heard an angry voice say, 'This is private property, you know!'

Rutter turned. He was being addressed by an old man with a red face and a huge, white, walrus moustache.

'Can't you read?' the man demanded.

Rutter looked down at the plaque again. 'It says "for the benefit of all",' he pointed out.

'Yes, but that doesn't mean *you*!' the man said. 'It means the residents. This is an *exclusive* estate, you know.'

'So I believe,' Rutter replied. 'But, you see, sir, I'm a police officer, and we can go where we like – within reason, of course.'

'Got a warrant card?' the old man asked, still not quite willing to allow his outrage to go into retreat.

Rutter produced his card, and held it out.

'Inspector, eh?' the old man said. He held out his hand. 'I'm Binsley Morrisson.'

Rutter took the hand. 'Pleased to meet you, sir.'

'Sorry to have got the wrong idea,' Morrisson said. 'Should have been able to tell from the way that you're dressed that you weren't part of the usual riff-raff that drifts in here and acts like it owns the place.'

Morrisson looked around him, and seemed somewhat disappointed to discover that there were no shady characters around at that moment who could prove his point.

'I wanted to put a wall right around the entire estate, you know,' he continued.

'Did you indeed?'

'I most certainly did. But the Residents' Association wanted nothing at all to do with the idea. Came up with some damn silly excuse about it contravening the planning regulations.'

'As a matter of fact, it probably—' Rutter began.

'So I've been forced to take on the responsibility for the security of the area myself,' Morrisson said. He reached into his pocket, and pulled out a leather notebook. 'It's all in here, you know.'

'*What's* all in there?' Rutter wondered.

'My notes. Every time I see a suspicious character wandering around, I jot down his description. Used to take those descriptions straight to the local police station, but I could see the desk sergeant wasn't really interested. I'm sorry to have to say this about one of your lesser colleagues, Inspector, but the man seems to have no initiative at all.'

Rutter was finding it hard to keep his face straight.

'Maybe all these people you're worried about had a perfectly legitimate reason for being in the area,' he suggested.

'Like what?'

'Well, for example, they could have been tradesmen – plumbers or electricians.'

'Some of them did have bags that could have contained tools,' Morrisson admitted.

'Well, there you are then.'

'Burglars need tools, don't they? And crooks don't dress up in striped jerseys, and carry sacks on their backs labelled "Swag". They pretend to be perfectly ordinary chaps. I'd have thought, *as a policeman*, you'd have known that.'

'Burglary's not really one of my specialities,' said Rutter, who was now finding it almost impossible to keep his grin in check.

'And that's precisely the problem,' Morrisson said triumphantly, as if Rutter had proved his case for him. 'The police simply don't know what's going on. But I do, and when things do go seriously wrong – as they're bound to do – that sergeant down at the local station will suddenly be very grateful for all the details I've got jotted down in my notebook.'

107

'Do you confine yourself to descriptions of people, or do you notice cars as well?' Rutter asked idly.

'Well, of course I notice cars,' the old man said. 'Criminals are *allowed* to drive cars – more's the pity.'

Was it possible, Rutter wondered, was it just vaguely possible that . . . ?

'How often do you go out on patrol?' he asked.

'Never thought of what I do as going out on patrol,' Morrisson said. 'But you're damn right – that's exactly what I do.'

'How often?' Rutter asked patiently.

'I'm out for the greater part of the day. To tell you the truth, Inspector, my lady wife gets nervous if I'm in the house for too long at a time.'

'And do you patrol at night?'

'Usually. I like to do a final tour before I have my cup of Horlicks and retire for the night.'

'Were you out the night before last – in the fog?'

'I most certainly was. You probably wouldn't know this – not being a specialist in burglary – but criminals like the fog. They think it means they can move about without being spotted.' Morrisson puffed out his chest. 'But, of course, they haven't reckoned on me.'

'There can't have been many people, or cars for that matter, about on a night like that.'

'There weren't. Very few, in fact. But it only takes one bad apple, as the old saying goes.'

'I wonder if you happened to notice a green car, some time between nine and ten o'clock,' Rutter said.

'I saw a green *Ford Cortina*, if that's what you're asking about,' the old man said.

'At what time?'

'Couldn't say precisely. I'd guess it was some time between nine and ten o'clock.'

He's throwing my own estimate back at me, Rutter thought.

'Could it have been a little earlier – or a little later – than that, do you think?' he asked.

'Suppose so,' Morrisson admitted reluctantly.

'What are the chances that this green Cortina was being driven by one of your neighbours?'

'No chance at all.'

'How can you be so sure?'

'Make it my business to know what everybody who lives in this area drives. Nobody owns a Cortina.'

The right kind of car, spotted at roughly the right time!

Bingo! Rutter thought.

'Cortinas are normally purchased by travelling salesmen and people of that ilk,' the old man continued, dismissively. 'No one from Bankside would be seen dead in one.'

But maybe Bradley Pine *had* been.

'Tell me more about it,' Rutter said.

'Not much more to tell. It was going slowly, but I expect that was because of the fog.'

'How many people were there in it?'

'Only the driver.'

'Could you describe him to me?'

'Afraid not. I only saw him from a distance, and it *was* foggy. He wasn't a midget, but he wasn't a giant, either, if that's any help.'

'Could the driver have been a woman?'

The old man sighed. 'I suppose so. In my time, ladies didn't drive, but anything's possible, these days.'

'You didn't happen to take down the registration, did you?' Rutter asked hopefully.

'Not all of it – fog, again – but I did manage the last part.' Morrisson opened his notebook and flicked through a few pages. 'Here it is. 732 B. Is that any help to you?'

It was a perfect match with Pine's car, Rutter thought, and whilst it was just possible that there was another green Cortina around with the same end-designation, it didn't seem at all likely.

'Could you tell me where the Cortina was coming from, and where it was going to?' he asked.

'It was coming from the centre of town,' the old man said, pointing vaguely in the direction of the railway station. 'And it was heading that way,' he continued, indicating the gently sloping hill which was all that separated Lower Bankside from *Upper* Bankside.

Eighteen

Beresford stood at the main gate of Hawtrey and Pine Holdings, trying to decide not only *who* he should ask if it was true that Mrs Hawtrey would have liked to see Bradley Pine dead, but also *how* he should phrase the question.

'Back again, lad?' asked a voice.

Beresford turned, and saw old Harry Ramsbotham standing there.

'That's right, I'm back,' he agreed.

The old man had a string bag in his hand which contained a packet of sugar and a bottle of milk, and now he held it up for Beresford's inspection, as if it were some sort of prize.

'I've just been doin' my shoppin',' he announced.

'Is that right?' Beresford asked.

'Most people aren't allowed to nip out without permission durin' the course of the workin' day,' Harry continued, 'but I've been doin' it for close on to fifty years now.'

'That is a long time,' Beresford said, and he was thinking, *How could* anybody *do* anything *for nearly* fifty *years?*

'It was old Mr Hawtrey who first said that it would be all right, an' nobody's told me anythin' different since. It's a bit of a tradition, you see, and even Mr Pine didn't want to go against tradition.'

'I can imagine he wouldn't,' said Beresford, who was starting to get some insight into what made the old man tick.

'Well, now I've been out an' got the makin's of it, I might as well offer you a brew,' Harry said.

'I'm not sure I can—' Beresford began.

'Come on!' the old man urged. 'You can't start work without a cup of tea inside you.'

Perhaps he was right, Beresford thought. And perhaps, over

the brew, he might learn something which would put his investigation into gear.

Beresford followed Harry down the steep concrete steps which led to the basement boiler room.

'I started workin' down here in 1915,' the old man said. 'Course, they didn't put me in charge of the whole thing right away – I was only a lad at the time – but my immediate boss died in 1924, an', right away, old Mr Hawtrey called me up to the office to see him.'

Some sort of response was obviously expected.

'Did he, indeed?' Beresford asked.

'*Called me up to his office*,' Harry repeated. 'An' there's not many workin' men from this factory who can say they've been in there.'

'I imagine not.'

'Well, Mr Hawtrey didn't ask me to sit down – I was in my workin' clothes, so that was perfectly understandable – but he did offer me a cigarette. Then, when we'd both lit up, he asked me if I thought I could handle the job of lookin' after the boilers on my own. I told him I thought I could, an' he said that were grand, an' that in future he'd be payin' me ten shillings a week more. Well, to be honest with you, I'd have taken the job for the same money I'd been earnin' before, but, of course, I didn't tell old Mr Hawtrey that.'

'Of course you didn't,' Beresford agreed.

They had reached the foot of the stairs, and were facing a large steel door, which was closed.

'It's locked, but I've got my own key to it,' Harry said complacently, reaching into his pocket.

The boilers were not half as large or impressive as Beresford – who was no great technical brain – had been expecting.

'They're all oil-fired these days,' Harry said, noticing the surprised expression on his face. 'It wasn't like that when I first started workin' here. Then, all the boilers ran off coke.'

'It must have been hard work, stoking them.'

'It was. You could lose pounds in sweat in this job. But still, I was sorry to see them old boilers go. I'd got to know them, an' all their little quirks, you see, whereas these new boilers have got no personality at all.'

111

He could almost have been talking about his last two bosses – Hawtrey and Pine – Beresford thought to himself.

Harry sighed, regretfully. 'Yes, I was sorry to see them boilers finally go, but I suppose we all have to move with the times, don't we? An' one thing you *do* have to say about these new boilers is that they do leave me a bit of space for myself.'

Harry had made good use of his space, Beresford thought. There were two battered armchairs, which stood on an off-cut of carpet in a flower pattern which had been fashionable just after the War. There was a kitchen table, on which had been placed a spirit stove, a kettle, teapot and two large enamel mugs. And there was a small black-and-white television, with a spider's web of wire which served as an aerial, resting on a packing case.

But it was the far wall which was most surprising. Shelves ran along it at waist height, and on those shelves were bits of junk which seemed to be vaguely connected with mattress manufacturing. Above the shelves, reaching almost to the ceiling, Harry had pasted a montage of newspaper clippings, publicity handouts and catalogue covers.

'I call it my museum,' Harry said proudly, seeing it had caught Beresford's attention. 'The Museum of the Mattress. When I've made us a brew, I'll show it to you.'

The old man pumped the spirit stove on the table, lit it, and then perched the kettle on top.

'Do you see much of Mrs Hawtrey these days?' Beresford asked, trying to sound casual.

'Not a lot.' Harry replied. 'She was always here, of course, when she worked in the typin' pool, but she's hardly set foot in the place since she married the boss – an' that must have been a good fifteen years ago now.'

The kettle came to the boil, and Harry Ramsbotham poured the hot water into the teapot.

'Still, she must have been a few times,' Beresford said. 'Like when she opened the new workshop.'

'That's right, she was here for that,' Harry agreed. 'Well, I suppose we might as well take a look at my museum while the tea's brewin'.'

Reluctantly, Beresford rose to his feet and allowed himself to be led over to the shelves.

Harry picked a wad of cotton-packing, which must once have been white, but had now gone brown with age.

'This was the flock we used for stuffin' the mattresses when I first joined the company,' he said. 'We bought it in big bales, from one of the mills. Of course, that mill, like most of the others, has closed down now.'

'Very interesting,' Beresford said.

Harry replaced the wadding reverentially on the shelf, and picked up a coil of metal.

'And this is one of the first springs we used. Looks a bit clumsy now, doesn't it? But it was very advanced for its time.'

'When Mrs Hawtrey opened the new workshop, how did she and Mr Pine seem to be getting on?' Beresford asked.

'That's Mr Hawtrey and the *first* Mrs Hawtrey on their weddin' day,' Harry said, pointing to a photograph in the middle of one of the faded newspaper articles that he'd pasted to the wall. 'An' that's old Mr Hawtrey – Mr Alec's father – standin' next to them.'

The two men in the picture were wearing morning suits, and the bride was dressed in an elaborate lace and silk gown. They stood as stiff as tailor's dummies, and though they were all probably very happy on this special day, the smile the photographer had demanded from them made them look almost manic.

His mother and father had been married at around the same time, Beresford thought, and though these people were dressed in a far grander style than his parents had been, he was still reminded of the wedding photographs which sat on the sideboard at home. Looking at his mother now – with that dead expression in her eyes – it was almost impossible to believe that she had once been young and vital, had probably danced with gay abandon and treated life as if it were a joy to experience.

'Have I lost you, lad?' Harry asked.

'What?' Beresford said, startled.

'This is an article about the house that the Hawtreys moved into just after they married. Caused quite a stir at the time, it did. To be honest with you, most people didn't care for it at all.'

Beresford could quite see why it hadn't been exactly popular. Whitebridge folk tended to be quite conventional when it came

113

to matters of design – and there was nothing at all conventional about this house. For a start, it was three storeys high, rather than the normal two. Then there was the fact that there was a veranda running along the front. (Why, people must have asked when they saw it, would anybody want a veranda in *Lancashire*?) And as if all that were not enough to cause outrage, there was a terrace running the entire length of the first floor, supported by eight thick pillars.

'They had an architect design it for them, but most of the ideas about how it should look came from Mrs Hawtrey,' Harry said.

'How did they feel when they learned that most people didn't like it?' Beresford asked.

'I don't know how Mrs Hawtrey felt, but Mr Hawtrey didn't really care. It was enough for him that it was what his wife wanted – an' he'd have done anythin' for her in them days.'

'Where is it?' Beresford asked, allowing his natural curiosity to divert him from the line of questioning he had been intending to persue. 'I know most places in Whitebridge, but I don't think I've ever seen it.'

'Ee, lad, it's long gone. The council slapped a compulsory purchase order on it, an' pulled it down. It stood in the way of redevelopment, you see, an' people's dreams don't matter to the planners. The one good thing about the whole sorry business was that the first Mrs Hawtrey wasn't here to see it bein' pulled down, because it would have broken her heart. But then, I suppose, her heart had *already* been broken, because she'd got divorced an' moved away by then.'

'That's certainly all very interesting,' Beresford said, 'but what I was wondering was—'

'Here's an article on Mr an' Mrs Hawtreys first holiday abroad. It wouldn't be exactly what you'd call news these days, would it?'

'No, it—'

'But back then, you see, most folk had been no further than Blackpool, so it had somethin' of a novelty about it.'

The picture in this article showed the Hawtreys standing on a beach, with camels in the background. They had their children with them, a boy of about thirteen and a girl a couple of years younger. The girl looked happy enough, but the boy had the worried look of someone with a lot on his mind.

'An' over here's an article on Mr Hawtrey's funeral,' Harry said, pointing out a page of newspaper which – being more recent – had yellowed less than most of the others. 'That's the *second* Mrs Hawtrey by the grave.'

'She's standing quite close to Mr Pine, but she's not really looking at him, is she?' Beresford asked.

'You don't have much interest in my museum, do you, lad?' Harry asked, in a tone which was mid-way between anger and sadness.

'Yes, I do,' Beresford protested. 'Honestly, I do!'

'I may be gettin' old, but I'm still a long way from senile – an' I can see what you're after,' Harry said.

'I promise you, I'm not—'

'My old dad never taught me much, but one thing he always said is that you should hold your employer in respect,' Harry said. '"It's the wages they pay you that puts food on the table an' keeps a roof over your head," he told me.'

'All I want to know is how Mrs Hawtrey and Mr Pine got on after Mr Hawtrey's death,' Beresford protested.

'An' do you know what else my old dad said?'

'No.'

'He said, "It doesn't matter what your boss does in his private life – it's not your place to judge him, an' it's not your place to criticize him." There's not many people still hold them views these days, but I do.'

'Mr Pine's dead,' Beresford pointed out.

'So he is, but that still doesn't give me licence to tear his good name to shreds. Anyway, I thought it was Mrs Hawtrey you were more interested in.'

'Yes, it is, but—'

'Now that Mr Pine *is* dead, she's the only boss I've got. That may have slipped your attention, but it certainly hasn't slipped mine.'

'I didn't mean to offend you, Harry,' Beresford said, remorsefully. 'I honestly didn't.'

'Didn't you?' the old man countered. 'Well, you succeeded, whether or not. I think you should go now – an' I'd rather you didn't come again.'

Nineteen

The public service bus did not actually pass *through* Upper Bankside – the residents would not have wanted their living space polluted by the intrusion of mass transportation – but it did skirt the area, and there was a bus stop just beyond the end of Lawrence Road, at which a number of women in cheap coats and thick stockings were just alighting.

Woodend, sitting behind the wheel of his Wolseley, turned to Paniatowski, who was in the passenger seat.

'Of course, what the women who reside around here – I beg your pardon, what the *ladies* who reside around here – would really like to have would be *live-in* servants,' he said. 'An' there'd certainly be plenty of space to accommodate them in those big double-fronted houses. But since the War, you can't get anybody to do that kind of job, however much you're willin' to pay, so they've just had to settle for a daily visit from the charwomen.'

'You can't be sure that Thelma Hawtrey has one though, can you?' Paniatowski pointed out, as the women crossed the street and began to walk down Lawrence Road.

'I'd be most surprised if she didn't,' Woodend replied. 'It'd be seen as lettin' the side down to actually do any of your own cleanin' yourself. Besides, I've had a look at the finger-nails on the woman, an' you don't keep your nails lookin' like that if you do any bloody work.'

He eased the car into gear, and began to drive slowly down Lawrence Road. The ragged column of charwomen was already beginning to thin out, as some of its number peeled off and made their way up the driveways to one or other of the big houses.

'We won't know which of them "does" for Mrs Hawtrey until she reaches the house, so you'll have to move a bit sharpish and catch her up before she reaches the front door,' Woodend said.

'What if she doesn't want to come with us?' Paniatowski asked. 'I mean, it's not as if we're arresting her, is it?'

'True,' Woodend agreed. 'So you'll just have to use your powers of persuasion, won't you?'

'And if she says she can't be late for work?'

'Tell her she's nothing to worry about, because we'll ring Mrs Hawtrey up, an' explain that she's helpin' us with our inquiries.'

'And will we really do that?'

'Really do what?'

'Ring up Mrs Hawtrey?'

'I don't see why we shouldn't.'

'Don't you?' Paniatowski asked. 'Suppose we *do* ring her up and tell her what's going on. What do you think is the first thing that Mrs Hawtrey will do when the charwoman does eventually arrive on her doorstep?'

'I imagine she'll ask her exactly what the police wanted to question her about.'

'And the charwoman will tell her that what we've been asking questions about is *her*.'

'Yes, she will.'

'And doesn't that bother you?'

'Not a lot.'

'You're not worried that when Mrs Hawtrey learns we're taking such a close interest in her, she might get rattled?'

'On the contrary,' Woodend said. 'Getting rattled is exactly what I *want* her to do.'

The nearest café to Upper Bankside – and it was not *that* near, because Banksiders would never demean themselves by entering such an establishment – was called The Cosy Corner. It had formica-topped tables, a linoleum floor, and a large metal urn which gurgled constantly and occasionally let loose a jet of steam. It was just the sort of place you might expect to find a woman in the heavy brown coat and knitted woollen hat, but the woman in question certainly didn't seem very happy to be there at that particular moment.

'I'd normally like nothin' better than to be sittin' in a nice café, sippin' a nice hot cup of tea,' she explained to Woodend and Paniatowski, 'but I do have a job to do, you know – an' I am paid by the *hour*.'

Woodend reached into his pocket, pulled out a ten shilling note, and laid it on the table.

'That should more than cover the time you'll lose, shouldn't it, Mrs Chubb?' he asked.

'I suppose so,' the woman agreed. 'But there's other things to be taken into consideration as well, aren't there?'

'Such as?'

'I don't want to get anybody in trouble.'

'Why should you even think that you would?'

'Well, you're the police, aren't you?'

'So we are,' Woodend agreed. 'But the questions we want to ask you are very innocent ones, an' if you feel uncomfortable about answerin' any of them, you don't have to. All right?'

'All right,' Mrs Chubb agreed, though she still sounded dubious about the whole idea.

'How long have you been working for Mrs Hawtrey?'

'Must be a good ten years now.'

'Which means that you were working for her long before her husband was killed?'

'Yes, I was.'

'How did she take his death?' Woodend wondered.

'How would you expect her to take it? She was absolutely devastated, as anybody in her place would be.'

'But I expect her family were very supportive of her in her time of need,' Paniatowski said.

'Her family?' Mrs Chubb repeated.

'Yes.'

'She hasn't got no family.'

'None?' Woodend asked.

'None at all.'

'That's very unusual, isn't it?'

'I suppose it is, if you don't happen to know the circumstances.'

'An' what *are* the circumstances, in her case?'

'Accordin' to what Mrs Hawtrey told me once, her family were big landowners somewhere down south, an' when her mum an' dad were killed in a tragic motorin' accident, the rest of the family – all the uncles an' aunts an' cousins – got together an' grabbed the land for themselves. Well, she couldn't stand to be anywhere near them after that happened, could she? So she came up north to start a new life for herself.'

'You don't sound as if you entirely believe the story,' Monika Paniatowski said.

'Well, I do and I don't, if you see what I mean,' Mrs Chubb replied. 'I believe her mum an' dad were killed, an' that the relatives grabbed what they could – because that's what *some* relatives do. My Auntie Betty had this lovely grandfather clock, which she'd definitely promised to me, but she'd no sooner passed on than my cousin, Vera—'

'What part *don't* you believe?' Paniatowski interrupted.

'The bit about them bein' big landowners.'

'And *why* don't you believe it?'

'Because I've worked for a lot of posh folk in my time, an' I could tell that Mrs Hawtrey hadn't been posh for that long.'

'So she didn't have any relatives to give her the support she needed,' Paniatowski said. 'Which means, I suppose, that she just had to rely on her friends instead.'

'Didn't have many of them, neither.'

'And why was that?'

'Lots of reasons,' Mrs Chubb said evasively.

'Tell me a few of them,' Paniatowski suggested.

'Well, like I may have hinted earlier, she wasn't quite posh enough for some of her neighbours.'

'What else?'

'I did hear that most of Mr Hawtrey's old friends wouldn't have anythin' to do with him after he married her. They're *Catholic*, you see,' Mrs Chubb said, mouthing the word 'Catholic' with much the same reverential dread as some women mouthed the word 'cancer'. 'They don't believe in divorce, you know. They're old-fashioned in that way.'

'So the neighbouring ladies didn't have much to do with her, and neither did her husband's old friends, but did she have any male friends of her own?' Paniatowski asked.

'That Mr Pine, the one who got himself murdered—' Mrs Chubb stopped suddenly. 'Hang on, is that what this is all about?'

'Don't go worryin' your head over that,' Woodend told her. 'Just carry on with what you were sayin'.'

'That Mr Pine came round to the house a few times in the first couple of weeks after Mr Hawtrey's funeral, but you could tell he wasn't really welcome, an' in the end, the visits stopped.'

'How could you tell he wasn't really welcome in the house?' Woodend wondered.

'Well, Mrs Hawtrey was very cold an' distant with him. Not that you can altogether blame her – he was with her husband when he died, you see, an' maybe he could have done more to save him.'

'Where did you get that idea from, Mrs Chubb?' Paniatowski asked. 'Did it come from Mrs Hawtrey?'

'What idea are you talkin' about?'

'The idea that maybe Mr Pine could have done more to save Mr Hawtrey?'

'No, I can't say I really got it from her,' Mrs Chubb said, slightly unconvincingly. 'It was more just what I was thinking myself.'

'You didn't really answer the question about Mrs Hawtrey's male friends,' Paniatowski pointed out. '*Does* she have any?'

'Not really,' Mrs Chubb replied – just a little too quickly.

'Lyin' to the police is a serious matter, you know,' Woodend said, in his gravest and most official voice.

'I'm not lyin'!' Mrs Chubb protested.

'Of course you're not. I know that. But maybe you're not quite telling us the *whole* truth?' Paniatowski suggested, gently.

'I don't actually *know* anythin',' Mrs Chubb told her, reluctantly.

'But you have *guessed* something?'

Mrs Chubb shrugged. 'I notice things.'

'Like what?'

'When I leave that house of an afternoon, it's in a perfect condition. Everythin's neat an' tidy, an' you could eat your dinner right out of the toilet bowl, if you were so inclined.'

'I'm sure you could.'

'So if anythin's changed between me leavin' the house one day an' comin' back the next, I notice it.'

'Would you care to give us an example?'

'There's always brown ale in the fridge, even though Mrs Hawtrey doesn't much like the taste of it herself – an' sometimes, I'll find empty bottles in the rubbish bin.'

'So she's had a visitor who drinks brown ale, and you think that must mean that's he's a man?' Woodend asked.

'Of course it's a man!' Mrs Chubb said scornfully. 'It's a man's drink, isn't it?' She turned to Paniatowski. 'How many women do you know who drink brown ale?'

'None that I can think of,' Paniatowski admitted.

'Well, exactly!' Mrs Chubb said triumphantly. 'And that's not all he drinks. He doesn't say no to a glass or two of wine, either.'

'How do you know that?'

'Mrs Hawtrey likes the odd tipple herself – not that there's anythin' wrong with that – and most mornin's I'll find a wine glass sittin' on the coffee table with her lipstick all around the rim.'

'Go on,' Woodend encouraged.

'But some nights, there's been *two* glasses used – an' she's washed up the second one.'

'How can you tell?' Woodend wondered.

Mrs Chubb turned to Paniatowski again.

'Men!' she said, with mild contempt.

'Men!' Paniatowski agreed.

'There's an art to washin' up, which is unknown to *all* men an' *some* women,' Mrs Chubb told Woodend, 'and Mrs Hawtrey is one of them women who doesn't know how to do it properly. How can I tell! What a question to even have to ask me!'

'What a question,' Paniatowski echoed obediently.

'I can tell because the glasses that she *does* wash up are always left streaky,' Mrs Chubb told Woodend.

'Anythin' else?' the chief inspector asked.

'He smokes.'

'How do you know? Doesn't *she* smoke?'

'Of course she does. *Everybody* smokes! But she smokes filter-tipped, and his are untipped. Mrs Hawtrey puts *his* fag ends in the bin, but when I'm emptyin' it out, I can't help noticin' them.'

I bet there's not much you can't help noticin', you nosy old bat, Woodend thought.

'Is that it?' he asked.

'That's it,' Mrs Chubb agreed.

'Are you sure?'

The charwoman fidgeted in her seat. 'Well, there is one more thing,' she admitted, 'but it's a bit personal, if you see what I mean, an' I don't like to talk about it.'

'You can say anythin' at all – however personal – to us,' Woodend assured her. 'We're a bit like doctors, in that way.'

'Or priests,' Paniatowski added.

'Well, Mrs Hawtrey doesn't really do anythin' at all around the house,' Mrs Chubb said. 'Even the simplest little job – one that she could finish in a minute, while she's waitin' for the kettle to boil – she leaves for me to do in the mornin'.' She paused. 'Not that I'm complain' in any way, shape or form,' she added hastily. 'If she did it all herself, she wouldn't need me.'

'Understood,' Woodend said.

'But every now an' then, she does strip down the bed. She doesn't actually put the new sheets on – that would be too much to ask of her – but she takes the dirty sheets an' puts them in the washin' machine, so they're already half-way through their cycle by the time I arrive. An' why do you think she does that?'

'Because she doesn't want you to see that the sheets are stained?' Paniatowski guessed. 'Because she doesn't want you to know that she hasn't spent the night alone.'

Mrs Chubb jutted out her chin in a prim and righteous manner. 'What people do in their own homes is their own business,' she said. 'But I still think they could have some standards.'

Twenty

Rutter spread the map of the Whitebridge area across the table in the public bar of the Drum and Monkey.

'The green Ford Cortina was spotted here,' he said, indicating a point in Lower Bankside. 'It's unfortunate that my witness can't say for sure exactly what time he saw it – and doesn't know who was driving it – but in my mind there's no doubt at all that it was Pine's car.'

'Nor in mine, either,' Woodend agreed.

'Now, the car was coming from the centre of town, which is here, and the body was found here, on the dual carriageway,' Rutter continued, pointing to two spots on the map. 'Does the fact that it was ever in Bankside make any sense to either of you?'

'No, it doesn't,' Paniatowski said. 'If it was the killer behind the wheel, and he was taking Pine's body to be dumped, why would he go that way? The quickest route out to the dual carriageway from the centre of town is in completely the opposite direction.'

'And if Pine himself was driving the car, what was he doing going towards Upper Bankside?' Rutter wondered. 'We know from what the charwoman said that his relations with Mrs Hawtrey have been distinctly chilly since her husband's death, so why would he even be thinking of calling on her?'

'No reason at all,' Woodend said. 'But I can think of somebody else who might have had a very good reason for payin' her a visit.'

'Her lover?' Paniatowski asked.

'That's right,' Woodend said. 'Her wine-drinking, untipped-cigarette-smoking, bed-staining lover.'

He paused, to take a drag on his own untipped cigarette.

'I can see two possible ways that this whole thing could have developed,' he continued. 'The first is that Thelma

123

Hawtrey makes the decision to take a lover simply because she's lonely, or because she's missin' the sex. But later, when the affair's been goin' on for some time, she suddenly realizes that she can use this lover of hers to kill Bradley Pine.'

'And the other way it could have developed is that the *only* reason she takes a lover in the first place is *so* she'll have someone to kill Pine,' Monika Paniatowski said.

'That's right. She has no relatives she can turn to – they're either dead, or she's lost contact with them years ago. She has no male friends to speak of, either. An' even if she had, it'd be stretchin' friendship a bit too far to ask that friend to kill for her. So she has to find some other way to recruit her accomplice. An' where would be a better place for recruitin' him than in bed! I don't imagine that findin' a man willin' to sleep with her would have been much of a problem, because she *is* a good-lookin' woman.'

'And once she's got him into bed?' Paniatowski asked.

'She'll have played the poor bugger like a violin for months – maybe even years. An' just when he's so hopelessly in love with her that he can't bear to live without her – when he's prepared to do anythin' at all to keep her – she tells him exactly what her price for stayin' with him is.'

'That would explain why she's been keeping him a secret from everyone else all this time,' Paniatowski said. 'She will have seen that we couldn't possibly suspect the man of murder if we didn't even know he existed!'

'I'm still more than a little bit troubled about the *nature* of the attack,' Bob Rutter said.

'In what way?'

'Dr Shastri said there'd been a lot of anger – as well as a lot of force – behind the fatal blow.'

'So?'

'Why would the lover have been angry with Pine?'

'He wasn't angry with Pine,' Woodend said. 'He was angry with Mrs Hawtrey, for talking him into carryin' out the murder. Or maybe he was angry with himself – for agreein' to it. Whichever was the case, it was Bradley Pine who bore the brunt of the anger.'

'Perhaps,' Rutter conceded. 'But even allowing for that, I still don't see why he would have driven the Cortina – presumably with Pine's body in the back – up to Mrs Hawtrey's house. Surely, once he'd done the deed, he'd have wanted to dump the corpse as soon as possible.'

'You'd think so, wouldn't you?' Woodend said. 'But remember that the body wasn't just dumped – it was mutilated as well.'

A look of pure horror came to Rutter's face. 'And you think that she . . . that she . . . ?'

'I think she wanted to do that part of the business herself. I think that once he'd killed Pine, her lover went to her house to pick her up, and they *both* drove out to the dual carriageway, where Mrs Hawtrey first smashed Pine's mouth in, and then slit his stomach open.'

'If that's true, she's not just a murderer – she's a complete bloody monster!' Rutter said.

'If that's true, she certainly is,' Woodend agreed. 'An' once we've got a warrant from a friendly magistrate to search her house, we just might have the evidence to *prove* she is.'

Woodend stood in the centre of the large living room of the house in Lawrence Road. He had hardly moved at all for several minutes. Thelma Hawtrey, in contrast, seemed unable to keep still, and was continually pacing from one end of the room to the other, then back again.

'This is bloody outrageous!' she said angrily, as she passed by Woodend for fifteenth or sixteenth time. 'You have absolutely no right to invade my house in this manner.'

'We've got every right,' Woodend replied evenly. 'An' since you've seen the search warrant for yourself, you *know* we've got every right.'

There was the sound of banging overhead.

'They're in my bedroom now,' Thelma Hawtrey said bitterly. 'They're destroying my home, and I still have no idea what you're looking for.'

'If it'll make it any easier for you to bear, I'll *tell* you what we're lookin' for,' Woodend said. 'We're lookin' for evidence.'

'Evidence!' Mrs Hawtrey repeated. 'Evidence of *what*?'

'Any kind of evidence. But it would be especially nice if we could find somethin' that would not only reveal your lover's identity to us, but also give us an indication of where we might find him.'

'My lover?' Thelma Hawtrey said. 'You want to find the identity of my *lover*?'

'You don't really think that the trick to soundin' innocent is simply to repeat everythin' I say, do you?' Woodend asked. 'Because I'll tell you right now, it doesn't work.'

'Is that really what you said? That you're looking for my lover?'

'In fact, Mrs Hawtrey, the more you try that particular trick, the less effective it becomes.'

'Even if I did have a lover, why would you want to find him?' Thelma Hawtrey asked.

'Oh, that's an easy one to answer. We want to find him because we think he helped you murder Bradley Pine.'

Thelma Hawtrey laughed, hysterically. 'That really is too funny for words, you know,' she said.

'Well, I certainly hope you'll still be findin' it amusin' when you're both standin' in the dock,' Woodend countered.

Rutter had started by searching the area around the part of the driveway which was closest to the house, and was gradually working his way towards the point at which it let out on to the road outside. He had chosen this particular task himself, not because he expected to find anything out there – he was sure that he wouldn't, since Pine had almost certainly been killed elsewhere – but because rummaging through other people's homes had always been one of the aspects of police work that he most disliked.

His aversion to it came, he supposed, from his childhood. His father had run a small greengrocer's shop in London, and the family had lived above it. His mother had loathed the business, and loathed the area in which it was located, and her solution had been to pretend that none of it existed.

The flat had provided her with an escape from the real world. She had treated it almost as if it were sacred – a kind of holy hot air balloon, which allowed her to hover above, and remain totally untouched by, all the distasteful things which were going on at street level. It gradually became her life, and she would rather have lost an arm or a leg than give up even one tiny corner of it.

Thus, though Rutter could – and did – force himself to execute search warrants, he often felt, when he left the premises, as if he had been raping his mother's dream, and so generally avoided it whenever he could.

He had reached the big double gates. Large rhododendron bushes grew on either side of them, giving this part of the garden a rather funereal air – and him something of the creeps.

He was on the point of widening his search – perhaps following the progress of the walls round the small estate – when a sudden burst of sunshine hit the bushes, and he saw that, from under the foliage, something was glinting at him.

It could be anything – the silver foil wrapper of a discarded chocolate bar; a bottle which some thoughtless drunk had thrown over the wall on his ambling way back home; a coin or cheap brooch dropped by a hapless magpie and never retrieved – but he supposed that now that he was there, it was probably worth investigating it more fully.

He crouched down in front of the bush, pushed one of the branches to one side with his hand – and saw the watch. He picked it up carefully in his handkerchief, straightened up again, and moved away from the shadow of the bushes so he could examine it in better light.

He could tell immediately that it was a very expensive timepiece – far better than he could ever have afforded on a detective inspector's salary. There was a little dirt on it, but it bore none of the signs of deterioration which it would have acquired if it had been lying there a long time. Besides, it was still working perfectly. In fact, the only damage which seemed to have been done to it was that the leather strap was broken.

Rutter turned the watch over, hoping to find an inscription on the back of it, and was disappointed to discover that there wasn't one.

He took another step back, and considered how the watch might have got there.

It could, he supposed, have fallen off a man's wrist when he was opening the gates. But would it then have flown far enough to have landed where he'd discovered it? And even if it had, surely the owner would have noticed the loss of such an expensive watch before too long, and immediately gone searching in the places he might have dropped it.

Rutter wrapped the handkerchief around the watch and

slipped it into his pocket. Then he knelt down again, in order to see if the rhododendron bush had any more treasures it might be willing to yield up.

'You've been here for over an hour,' Mrs Hawtrey said. 'If there *was* anything to find, don't you think you'd have found it by now?'

'This is a big house,' Woodend reminded her. 'There's lots of places in it where you could have hidden things.'

'But I *have* nothing to hide, for God's sake!' Mrs Hawtrey protested. 'My life's an open book.'

'Oh, I sincerely doubt that,' Woodend told her. 'I doubt, to be honest with you, that anybody's is.'

A door to the hallway opened, and Bob Rutter entered the living room. 'Could I have a word, sir?' he asked.

'Certainly,' Woodend said. 'What's on your mind?'

'Not here,' Rutter cautioned. 'I think it would be much better if we talked outside.'

'Whatever you say,' Woodend replied, following him to the door.

It was five minutes before Woodend returned to the living room, and when he did he was holding his hands palm upwards, and carrying a handkerchief in them.

'What's that?' Thelma Hawtrey asked. 'The Holy Grail?'

'No,' Woodend said. 'But for my money, it comes pretty damn close to it.' He carefully unwrapped the package, and held it out for the woman to see. 'Does this look familiar to you?'

'Oh, my God, it's Brad's watch!' Mrs Hawtrey gasped.

'Do you know, I rather thought it might be,' Woodend said.

'Where did you . . . where was it . . .'

'Where was it found? Near the gates. Just about where the struggle must have taken place.'

'The struggle? What struggle? I have absolutely no idea what you're talking about.'

'I've told you before that just repeatin' my words won't do you any good,' Woodend said.

'But I really *don't* have any idea,' Mrs Hawtrey protested.

'Oh, I think you do,' Woodend said confidently. He cleared his throat, as he always did on such occasions. 'Thelma

Hawtrey, I am arrestin' you for the murder of Bradley Pine,'
he continued. 'You do not have to say anythin' but anythin'
you *do* say may be taken down an' used in evidence against
you.'

Twenty-One

There were three interview rooms in Whitebridge Police Headquarters. They were all rather depressing – and deliberately so – but Interview Room C, which had the smallest window and the least natural light, was the dreariest of the trio. And Interview Room C was the one in which Woodend had chosen to conduct his interrogation of Thelma Hawtrey.

Woodend looked across the table, at the woman who he had already charged with murder.

She looked very calm, he thought. No, that wasn't it at all. She didn't just *look* very calm – she *was* very calm.

'You may as well make a clean breast of it right from the start, you know, Thelma,' he said.

'I've done nothing wrong, and I've nothing to come clean about,' Thelma Hawtrey said firmly. 'And I would prefer it, Chief Inspector Woodend, if you would address me as either Mrs Hawtrey or Madam.'

Woodend sighed. 'Look, Mrs Hawtrey, you know we found Bradley Pine's watch in your garden, don't you?

'I know you *say* that you did. But I've no proof you didn't put it there yourselves.'

'Now why should we have done that?'

'I should have thought that was obvious.'

'Not to me, it isn't.'

'Then I'll explain it to you. I've seen Henry Marlowe on the television. He's desperate for *someone* to be arrested for Bradley's murder, and you've decided that I'm the perfect candidate. But before you could arrest me, you needed some kind of proof, and *that's* why you planted the watch.'

'Your argument might sound a bit more convincin' if it had been only the watch that we found,' Woodend said. 'But it wasn't. We also retrieved a button that matches the ones

130

on the jacket that Bradley Pine was wearing when his body was discovered.'

'You could have planted that, too.'

'An' what about the bloodstains, Mrs Hawtrey?' Woodend asked, exasperatedly. 'Because you do know that we found bloodstains on the ground, don't you?'

'None of which has anything to do with me.'

'Up until now, we've been assumin' that Pine was already dead by the time he reached your house, and that he was only taken there so that you could accompany him on his last journey to the lay-by,' Woodend said.

Thelma Hawtrey smiled. 'You almost make it sound like a funeral cortege,' she said.

'But he wasn't dead at that point, was he?' Woodend asked, ignoring the interruption. 'He was killed in *your* garden, by *your* lover, who'd been waitin' for him in the bushes. How'd you get him to come to your house on a night when he must have had lots of other things to do, and there was thick fog which made goin' anywhere a bit of an effort? Exactly what tale did you spin him, Mrs Hawtrey?'

'I didn't spin him any tale, as you put it, and, *as far as I know*, he didn't come to the house.'

'Maybe you didn't know anythin' about it, after all,' Woodend conceded. 'Maybe it was all your lover's idea, an' he kept you completely in the dark about the murder until after the deed itself was actually done.'

He paused, to give Thelma Hawtrey time to speak, but it was clear that she wasn't going to.

'If that is the case,' he continued, 'then the worst thing that you can possibly do, from your own viewpoint, is to take the fall for him. So why not tell us his name, then we can go an' pick him up? I promise you, Mrs Hawtrey, that the moment he's confessed, all charges against you will be dropped, an' we'll have you back in your own home within half an hour.'

'There is no lover, and though you have charged me with Bradley Pine's murder, you'll never make the charges stick.'

'Won't I? What makes you think that?'

'I still have faith in British justice. I still believe that the guilty will be punished, and the innocent will go free. And I'll go free, Mr Woodend – because I didn't do it!'

131

'What about all the evidence which seems to say different?' Woodend asked quietly.

'Look, maybe I was being unfair to you to even suggest that you planted the watch,' Thelma Hawtrey said. 'Perhaps you've behaved properly throughout this whole sorry business, and you really did find the watch in my garden, after all. And maybe Bradley Pine was killed there, too. I honestly don't know. But it still had nothing to do with me.'

What had happened to bring about the change in her, Woodend wondered. While they'd been searching her house, she'd seemed as nervous as a kitten. Now, in the intimidating atmosphere of the interview room – and after she'd actually been *charged* – she seemed perfectly in control of herself.

Woodend reached into his pocket and pulled out a packet of Capstan Full Strength.

'Would you care for a cigarette, Mrs Hawtrey?' he asked, offering them across the table.

Thelma Hawtrey shook her head. 'No, thank you.'

'Go on,' Woodend urged. 'I'm only offerin' you a smoke, you know. It's not all part of some kind of clever trick to get you to lower your guard, I can promise you that.'

'I never thought it was a trick,' Thelma Hawtrey said – still calm, still very much in control. 'But it just so happens that I don't smoke untipped cigarettes.'

'No, you don't, do you?' Woodend agreed quietly. 'There were half a dozen opened packets of cigarettes lyin' around your house at various points, but not a single one of them was untipped. So where did all the untipped butt ends come from?'

'What untipped butt ends?'

'The ones that kept appearin' in your rubbish bin.'

Thelma Hawtrey's left eye suddenly began to twitch.

That question had shaken her, Woodend thought. Finally, he'd been able to come up with a question that had bloody shaken her!

'Who . . . who was it who told you about the untipped cigarette ends?' she asked.

'If it's true – an' I believe it is – then the source doesn't really matter, does it?'

'It was that awful Chubb woman, wasn't it?' Thelma Hawtrey demanded. 'The nosy bitch!'

'Aye, it was her,' Woodend admitted. 'An' we got a lot more

information from her, as well – the brown ale that got drunk, when you never touched the stuff yourself; the one wine glass you washed up, while you left the other for Mrs Chubb to deal with; the bed sheets that you stripped off personally, so she wouldn't find out what you'd been doin' between them . . . Need I go on?'

Thelma Hawtrey was looking more than rattled – she looked as if she'd gone into shock. With what obviously took her a huge effort, she managed to fold her arms across her chest.

'Well, *do* I need to go on?' Woodend asked.

'I'd like to talk to my solicitor now,' Thelma Hawtrey said.

'You can certainly do that if you want to,' Woodend agreed, 'but once we put things on a formal footin', that's how they have to stay, an' I think you might be better off just tellin' me—'

'My solicitor,' Thelma Hawtrey said. 'I demand to speak to my solicitor.'

'She's asked for Foxy Rowton,' Woodend told the rest of the team as they sat over steaming cups of industrial-strength tea in the police canteen.

Paniatowski consulted the background notes she'd started making the moment that Thelma Hawtrey had been arrested.

'Rowton?' she said. 'But he's not the solicitor that she normally uses to handle her affairs.'

'No, he isn't,' Woodend agreed. 'But maybe somebody's told her that he's the feller you go to when you're in such deep shit that it's starting to spill over the top of your wellingtons.'

'What I don't understand is why she didn't ask for him when you first charged her,' Rutter said.

'I think I've got an answer to that,' Woodend told him. 'When we brought her in, she was confident that she could beat the murder charge. An' maybe she was right about that. If her lover did everythin' – killed Pine, took his body to the lay-by an' carried out the mutilation – then there'd be no *physical* evidence to tie her to the killin' at all.'

'And so what if the murder was committed in her garden?' Paniatowski added. 'When we find a body, we don't automatically arrest anybody who happens to be living near the scene of the crime, do we?'

'So what was it that panicked her?' Rutter asked.

'It was when I talked about the untipped cigarette ends that

133

Mrs Chubb had seen in the waste bin,' Woodend said.

'Why should that have done it?'

'Because, although she already knew that we thought she had a lover who'd helped her to carry out the murder, she didn't think we'd ever be able to trace him. But when I mentioned the cigarette ends, she began to get some idea of the extent of the resources we've got at our disposal. From that, it was a short step to convincin' herself that if we really wanted to find him, we would. An' maybe she thinks he's the weak link in the chain. Maybe she thinks that the second we slap the cuffs on him, he'll tell us everythin' we want to know.'

'You could be right,' Rutter said.

A uniformed constable entered the canteen, and walked straight over to their table.

'Excuse me, sir,' he said to Woodend.

'Yes?'

'Mrs Hawtrey and her solicitor would like to see you now.'

Woodend nodded. 'Well, that's it then,' he told his team. 'It's all over bar the shoutin'.'

Foxy Rowton had a thin, pointy face and restless, searching eyes, but his nickname came not so much from his looks as from the manner in which he conducted his business. Half the serious criminals in Whitebridge had his telephone number either memorized or tattooed on their arms, and there were any number of men who, thanks to his efforts, were still walking free when – if justice had been allowed to run its course – they would have been banged up long ago.

Rowton was sitting in the interview room, next to his client, with his hand resting reassuringly on her arm. He gave the briefest of nods when Woodend entered the room.

'Please sit down, Chief Inspector,' he said, as if this whole encounter was taking place on his *own* territory.

Woodend sat, without comment. After all, why not let Rowton have his moment at centre stage when, in the few moments, he'd become no more than a minor character in the drama which was being played out.

'My client wishes to make a short statement, then is prepared to answer any questions you may care to put to her,' Rowton said. 'Is that acceptable to you, Chief Inspector?'

'Aye, as long as she *does* eventually answer my questions.'

134

'She will.'

'Then I'm all ears.'

'I was not expecting Bradley Pine to come to my house that night,' Thelma Hawtrey said, almost as if she were reading – badly – from a prepared script. 'But though I was not expecting him, I would not have been at all surprised if he had turned up unannounced. He often did that – especially late at night.'

'Hang on!' Woodend said. 'You told me you'd hardly seen him at all since your husband's funeral – an' even then it had been mostly by chance.'

'First the statement, then the questions, if you don't mind,' Foxy Rowton said, rebukingly.

'Oh, all right! Just get on with it!' Woodend replied.

'That is precisely what my client was attempting to do when you interrupted her,' Rowton said. He turned to that client now. 'Do please carry on, Mrs Hawtrey, whenever you feel ready.'

'I heard a few cars that night, but not as many as usual, probably because of the fog,' Thelma Hawtrey continued. 'Two of them even stopped quite close to my house, but since no one rang my door bell, I assumed they were either neighbours themselves, or were visiting neighbours. I was drinking wine as I watched the television, and without really noticing I was doing it, I finished a whole bottle. I suddenly realized I was quite drunk, and decided to go to bed. When I got out of my chair to turn the television off, the nine o'clock news was just starting.'

Woodend waited for her to say more, but she had plainly reached the end of her tale.

'Is that it?' he asked.

'What more do you want?' Rowton asked. 'What more *can* Mrs Hawtrey tell you than what actually happened?'

'Well, she could give me the name of her lover, for a start.'

Rowton looked pained. 'Is that really absolutely necessary, Chief Inspector?' he asked.

'You bet it bloody-well is!'

Rowton nodded to his client. 'Go ahead.'

'For the past three years, since shortly after my husband's death, I have been having an affair with Bradley Pine,' Thelma Hawtrey said.

'What!' Woodend exploded.

'That was clear enough, surely,' Rowton said.

'You were havin' an affair – an' nobody else knew about it?' Woodend asked, incredulously.

'We were very discreet,' Thelma Hawtrey said.

'But why, for God's sake? You were both free as birds. You could have done what you liked.'

'This is Whitebridge, where we are ruled not by a monarch and her government, but by the tyranny of public opinion,' Foxy Rowton said.

'An' what's that supposed to mean, exactly?' Woodend asked.

'It means that in some circles, though not perhaps the ones that you move in, Chief Inspector, there is a very keen sense of what is appropriate behaviour and what isn't.'

'I haven't had much of a social life since my husband's death,' Thelma Hawtrey said, 'but if it had become generally known that I'd started an affair so soon after his funeral, I would have had no social life at all.'

'But it's now three years since your husband died,' Woodend said. 'Surely there was no need to keep it a secret any longer.'

'Not from my side, no,' Thelma Hawtrey agreed. 'But there was from Bradley's. The electors of Whitebridge would not look favourably on a candidate who had a mistress.'

'Then why didn't you get wed?'

'We could have done that, I suppose. Bradley wanted to. But I have no wish to be married again to anyone – and certainly not to Bradley.'

'No?'

'No!'

'Why not?'

'Mainly because I didn't love him. In fact, I'm not sure that I even *liked* him that much.'

'Then why . . . ?'

'But he was a stallion in the bedroom, and – in some strange way – that helped to ease the grief I was feeling for Alec.'

'This is bollocks!' Woodend said. 'You think that you can keep your real lover hidden away from me by confessin' to an affair you never had. Well, I'm not buyin' it!'

'Mrs Hawtrey and Mr Pine were not always as discreet everywhere else as they had to be in places where they were both well known,' Foxy Rowton said.

'Meanin' what?'

'We found excuses for us both to be away from Whitebridge at the same time,' Thelma Hawtrey said. 'Bradley would say he had to attend a mattress conference somewhere, and I would come up with some other convenient reason to explain my absence. Then we'd spend a few days in a hotel together, as man and wife. London was one of the places we went to. Brighton was another.'

'An' I suppose you're about to tell me you can prove that, are you?' Woodend asked sceptically.

'Yes, she is,' Foxy Rowton said. 'The last time they went away together was only three weeks ago, just before the start of the election campaign.'

Mrs Hawtrey smiled. 'Bradley said he needed a break before the campaign started to hot up,' she said.

'They stayed in the Grand Hotel in Great Yarmouth for the weekend,' Rowton continued. 'You'll find Mr Pine's name down in the register, and I'm sure that if you show Mrs Hawtrey's photograph to the hotel staff, they'll be more than willing to identify her as the woman they knew as *Mrs* Pine.'

Woodend had a sinking feeling in the pit of his stomach. Both Thelma Hawtrey and her solicitor sounded so sure of what they were saying that it simply had to be true.

'So the only way Mrs Hawtrey could have got her lover to kill Mr Pine was if she'd persuaded Mr Pine to hit himself over the back of the head, and then drive himself out to the lay-by, which – considering he was already dead – would have been no mean feat,' Rowton said.

'You're a very funny man,' Woodend told the solicitor. 'You should be on the stage.'

Rowton looked suitably modest. 'I bet you say that to all the solicitors who manage to run rings round you,' he said.

Twenty-Two

Holy Trinity Catholic Orphanage for Boys had been established in a large country house which stood shivering at
the foot of the Pennine Hills. Its design had been grand in
concept but crude in execution, and the result was a heavy
sandstone structure which squatted instead of soared, and had
probably once been a Victorian wool-millionaire's misguided
idea of gracious living.

The director's office, to which Woodend was shown, was
panelled in dark oak and filled with heavy furniture which
had been out of style long before the Second World War. There
were photographs of groups of boys on the walls, and a display
case holding sporting trophies and thus proclaiming to the
whole world that even orphans can sometimes win prizes.

The director himself, Father Swales, was in his late sixties.
His face was heavily lined, and his gnarled hands gave evidence
of advanced arthritis, but his pale eyes suggested kindness as
well as authority, and his welcoming smile was that of a man
who was far from giving up on life.

'You wanted to ask about Bradley Pine,' he said.

'That's right,' Woodend agreed.

The director shook his head sadly. 'Poor Bradley. To have
come so far and yet have died in such a violent manner.'

'You remember him well, do you?'

'Oh yes, even after twenty-five long years, I remember him.
But I must admit, it is far from clear to me how my memories of him will help you to catch his murderer.'

'I'm not sure, either,' Woodend admitted.

But apart from the line of inquiry he was now following,
what other options were open to him?

There was no disputing that Thelma Hawtrey's revelations
had been a blow, and that they'd unravelled what he'd thought

was a cast-iron case as if it were no more than a ball of string. So now he was like a gambler, who puts his last pound on the outsider in the last race of the day – or a centre-forward who hopes against hope that his misplaced shot will magically rebound into the goal-mouth in the few remaining seconds of the game.

'I like to build up a picture of the victim in my head,' he explained to the director. 'It helps me to see the world as he might have seen it – and sometimes, it leads me to his killer.'

The director nodded. 'Very well, if you think it might help you, I will do my best to paint a picture for you of the boy I knew,' he promised. 'Bradley was eleven when he came to us, and had already known more despair, at that tender age, than most of us will experience in a lifetime.'

'You're sayin' he'd had a rough childhood?'

'He had a *vile* childhood. His own mother died when he was just a baby. His father married again, and he and his new wife had another child – a little girl. It could have been a shining bright new start for all of them.'

'But it wasn't?'

'His father and his stepmother had skills by which they could have earned a very decent living – he was a motor mechanic, she was a ladies' hairdresser – but they were hopeless alcoholics, and so neither of them held a job down for very long. Bradley and his little half-sister were both badly neglected by them, and sometimes – when the drink took one of the parents the wrong way – they were actually physically abused.'

Woodend remembered what Monika Paniatowski told him about cigarette-burn scars on Bradley Pine's arms.

'How did he come to be an orphan?' he asked.

'Bradley's parents died in a car crash – doubtless they were both drunk at the time – and since he had no other relatives able or willing to take care of him, he was sent here.'

'An' how did he settle in?'

'Remarkably well. The orphanage is, by its very nature, a highly structured society, and structure was something that had been sadly lacking in Bradley's previous life. He embraced the order he found here. His locker was the tidiest and best set-out that I think I have ever seen.'

'An' that was a habit which stayed with him,' Woodend

said, thinking of the arrangement of both Pine's office and his home.

'He also developed a remarkable self-discipline,' the director continued. 'Once he had decided there was something he wished to achieve, he would work towards that goal with a slow, single-minded determination. He exhibited absolutely none of the impatience that most children – and indeed, a great many adults – would have shown in his situation.'

'In other words, he was a bit cold an' ruthless,' Woodend suggested.

'I suppose you could apply that term, if you feeling unchar-itable,' the director said, with a hint of mild rebuke in his voice, 'but I would much prefer to describe him in the way I just have. At any rate, I was not at all surprised to learn that he had risen to be a partner in the company we placed him in as a fifteen-year-old boy. Of all the orphans who have passed through this institution, he was the one of whom I expected the most.'

'What can you tell me about his friends?' Woodend asked.

'He didn't have any,' the director replied, without a second's hesitation. 'And that was not because the other boys wouldn't accept him, but because he wouldn't accept them.'

'Why was that?'

'I suspect it was because he thought he didn't *need* them.'

'Everybody needs somebody.'

'Indeed they do, and in his case, the person he seemed to need was his sister, who had been placed in St Claire's Orphanage, in the care of Sister Martha and her nuns.' The director paused for a moment. 'I think that little girl was the only person in the whole world who Bradley ever really cared about.'

'What was the age difference between them?'

'Round about four years. I suspect Bradley had to be both mother and father to her, almost from the moment she was born. And it was perhaps because of that – and perhaps because of what they had had to endure together – that they had devel-oped an amazing bond with each other.'

'An amazin' bond,' Woodend repeated, musingly. 'How would you know that? Did he tell you?'

The director laughed. 'As if he would have confided in me! As if he would have confided in *anybody*! No, Chief Inspector, he didn't tell me – I observed it for myself.'

'So you allowed Bradley Pine an' his sister to see one another sometimes, did you?'

'Not at first. Sister Martha and I discussed the matter when the children arrived at our respective orphanages, and we came to the conclusion that to allow them to meet would have a disturbing effect on both of them. We even feared that, in order to be together, they might contemplate running away. It wouldn't be the first time something like that had happened with orphans who'd been separated.'

'So what eventually made you change your mind?'

'Bradley did. Not so much from what he said, as by the way he behaved – by his general approach to life. I soon came to understand that he would never do anything which might upset his sister, and that he was far too much of a realist to ever think that running away would be a solution to their problems. He was prepared to wait, you see – he was *always* prepared to wait.'

'How do you mean? Prepared to wait.'

'He never complained about the amount of time we allowed them to spend together when he was still living here, nor about the number of occasions on which he was permitted to visit her once he had left the orphanage himself. But the second she was old enough to leave St Claire's, he found her a job which ensured that they would see each other every day.'

'An' where was this job?' Woodend asked.

'In Whitebridge, of course,' the director replied, sounding slightly surprised that Woodend even needed to ask the question. 'He found her a position in the typing pool of the company he himself was working for.'

Woodend, Rutter and Paniatowski were sitting around their usual table in the Drum and Monkey. It had been obvious – from the moment he had entered the pub – that the chief inspector had something of significance to tell his team, and once the drinks had arrived, he launched straight into it.

'The story that Thelma Hawtrey told her charlady about her life before she came to Whitebridge had some truth in it, but not a lot,' Woodend said. 'Her parents were killed in a car crash, but they weren't big landowners – not by any stretch of the imagination. What they actually were was a pair of drunks who'd never amounted to anythin'.'

141

'You can't blame her for lying about that,' Rutter said. 'It isn't something anybody would find it easy to admit to.'

'Agreed,' Woodend said. 'But the other thing she forgot to mention to Mrs Chubb is that Bradley Pine was her half-brother.'

'You're sure about that?' Rutter asked.

'I'm sure. The only reason she came to Whitebridge at all was that her brother made all the arrangements.'

'Then she was lying when she said that Pine was her lover!' Rutter exclaimed.

'Was she?' Woodend asked.

'Of course. If she was his sister—'

'She changed the bed-sheets after he'd visited her,' Monika Paniatowski interrupted. 'And when they went away together, they booked into hotels as husband and wife.'

'I asked her why they didn't get married, an' she said it was because she didn't want to,' Woodend continued. 'But now we know the truth, don't we? They didn't get married because they *couldn't*.'

'But that's monstrous!' Rutter said.

'They've loved each other from the time they were little kids,' Woodend said. 'I don't know when they started to crave for each other sexually, but whenever it was, they held back until they'd both left the orphanage. An' I think that's all down to Pine's determination. The director told me he always knew what he wanted, but would wait patiently until the time was right to get it. That's what he was doin' in that case – waiting patiently until the time was right.'

'How can you be so sure they didn't have a sexual relationship while they were still in the orphanages?' Paniatowski asked.

'Their meetings were always supervised. If there'd been any hint of physical attraction passin' between them, Thelma would never have been allowed to come to Whitebridge when she'd just turned fourteen.'

'So when do you think their affair *did* begin?' Rutter asked.

'My guess would be that it began the second she started workin' in the typin' pool.'

'And did it carry on, even after she'd begun seeing Alec Hawtrey?'

'Oh yes! In fact, I think she only made her play for Hawtrey because Pine told her to.'

'That doesn't make sense,' Rutter protested. 'If he loved her, as you say he did—'

'He wanted to get on in life. He wanted them *both* to get on in life. He hadn't earned enough money from his patent to buy his own factory, but he could just about scrape together a sufficient amount to buy his way into Hawtrey's Mattresses – if Alec Hawtrey was willing to let him. And once Hawtrey had made the settlement on his first wife – a settlement made necessary by his affair with Thelma – he didn't have a lot of choice *but* to take on a partner in the long term.'

'I still don't get it,' Rutter said. 'I can just about see Pine encouraging Thelma to split up Hawtrey's first marriage, but why would he then agree to letting her become the second Mrs Hawtrey?'

'To make sure that when Alec Hawtrey *did* take on a partner, that partner was Bradley. It was like havin' a spy right in the middle of the enemy camp. Besides, why would he object? He couldn't marry Thelma himself, could he? And if she was married to a good friend, who eventually became his partner, he'd have all the excuse in the world for bein' in her company.'

'But knowing he had to share her—'

'Maybe he didn't,' Woodend argued. 'Maybe she stopped sleepin' with Alec the moment they were married. Maybe that's why Alec went mountain climbin' – because he thought that might excite her, an' make her want him back in her bed again. But even if Pine did have to share her, it's possible it didn't bother him overmuch. Not everybody places as much of a premium on sexual fidelity as . . . as . . .'

Oh shit! he thought, as he felt his words dry up in his mouth.

Caught up in making his case, as he had been, he'd inadvertently wandered back in Rutter's emotional minefield again – for though he hadn't actually been going to say, '. . . as Maria did,' he was sure that Bob was perfectly capable of burning those words on to his own brain himself.

'Besides, even if he had to share her body with Alec Hawtrey, he had her heart all to himself, and that was probably all that mattered to him,' Paniatowski said, coming to the rescue.

'Exactly,' Woodend agreed gratefully.

'I don't really understand why we're still discussing Pine's relationship with his sister,' Rutter said, eager to move away

143

from the subject as soon as possible. 'After all, that's not going to help us to find our murderer, now is it?'

'Not *that* murderer, no,' Woodend agreed.

'What other murderer *is* there?' Rutter wondered.

'Think about it,' Woodend said. 'In carryin' on as they always had, Pine an' Thelma were playin' a very dangerous game. An' what would have happened if Alec Hawtrey found out about it?'

'At the very least, they'd have become social pariahs,' Monika Paniatowski said, embracing Woodend's line of argument. 'There's absolutely no doubt in my mind that Alec Hawtrey would have divorced Thelma, and Bradley Pine would have lost any chance of pursuing his political ambitions.'

'The business partnership would have broken up – there's no doubt about that, either – and the business itself would probably have collapsed,' Woodend continued. 'An', very possibly, both Thelma Hawtrey an' Bradley Pine would have gone to prison.'

'But why should Alec Hawtrey have started to suspect what was going on?' Rutter asked. 'They'd been getting away with it for years.'

'An' maybe they thought that their luck couldn't hold for very much longer,' Woodend suggested. 'Or perhaps Alec Hawtrey was *already* startin' to get suspicious.'

'So they killed him?'

'It's a possibility.'

'It's pure speculation!' Rutter protested.

'Speculation is what we do, lad,' Woodend said patiently. 'It's how we work. We're presented with numerous strands of life, an' the way we narrow them down to leads which are worth followin' is by *speculation*.'

'Even so—'

'Say we're right – Monika an' me. Say Thelma an' Pine *had* decided they had to get rid of Alec Hawtrey. What better way would there be to go about it than by stagin' an accident on a mountainside?'

144

Twenty-Three

It hadn't taken Beresford long to prepare his mother's evening meal, for though she had once been a wonderful cook herself, she would now very rarely eat anything other than baked beans on toast.

Watching her eat it – since even this simple task could sometimes be something of a challenge for her – he found himself wondering what he would do when the increasing demands of his job eventually made it impossible for him to look after her any more.

'You don't have to sit there like a stuffed owl, you know, Colin,' Mrs Beresford said. 'I'm sure there are any number of things that you'd rather be getting on with.'

Beresford smiled, sadly.

There were times when his mother seemed so lucid – so aware of the world around her. On such occasions it was almost possible to believe that her Alzheimer's had been no more than a bad dream from which he was just waking up. But if that were really the case – and sometimes he found himself questioning what *was* real and what *wasn't* – the period of wakefulness did not last long, and soon he was back in his nightmare again.

'You never talk to me much about your work, these days,' his mother said, between mouthfuls of baked beans. 'Why is that?'

'I didn't think you'd be interested,' he said weakly.

'Didn't you? Well, I can assure you that I am. So why don't you tell me about it now?'

'There's this murder case that we're investigating at the moment,' Beresford said, feeling his mental floodgates burst open, and the words come spilling out. 'My boss, Chief Inspector Woodend, has been letting me carry out a lot of inquiries on my own. I think that's because he's impressed

145

with the work I did on the Judith Maitland case.'

'That's nice,' his mother said, encouragingly.

'It is,' Beresford agreed. 'In fact, it's a lot more than just nice. He's giving me a chance that no other chief inspector on the Force would even think of giving me. The thing is, I'm not sure he's right to have so much faith in me. There are times when I think that any success I had with the Maitland case may have been no more than a fluke.'

'Oh dear! That must be very worrying for you, son,' his mother commiserated.

'Very worrying,' Beresford agreed. 'You see, Mum, I don't want to tell him just how unsure of myself I am, in case he stops trusting me to do the job. On the other hand, I'm terrified that I might miss a vital clue, and let him and the rest of the team down.'

'It is a problem,' his mother agreed.

'I suppose I could ask Sergeant Paniatowski what to do,' Beresford continued. 'She's not *that* much older than me, so she probably remembers what it was like to have doubts about herself. Of course, there's always the danger that if I do that, she'll go straight to Mr Woodend and tell *him* exactly what I've told *her*. So what do you think I should do, Mum?'

His mother pushed her plate of beans to one side.

'Didn't you . . .' she began. 'Didn't you . . . I'm sorry, I've forgotten your name for the minute.'

'Colin,' Beresford said dully. 'My name's Colin.'

'That's right,' his mother agreed. 'Didn't you used to be a policeman, Colin?'

It was easier to walk through the church door this time, Monika Paniatowski thought. It was getting easier every time she did it.

But why should it ever have been *hard*? She was no longer the frightened little girl she'd been the last time she had attended church on a regular basis. She was a grown woman – a detective sergeant in the Central Lancs Constabulary. It had been nothing but an act of cowardice on her part to ever allow her past to intimidate her as she had.

Father Taylor was standing near the main door, almost as if he had been waiting for her to arrive.

'Now that's what I call a quick response,' he said. 'Not only has it only been missing for a little over half an hour, but I haven't even got around to reporting it gone yet.'

'What's missing?' Paniatowski asked, mystified. 'What haven't you reported?'

'My bicycle. I left it outside the church, and when I went back – no more than five minutes later – it wasn't there any more.'

'Was it chained up?'

'No.'

'You should have a chain, you know.'

'I do, but I never bother to use it.'

'Did you see anybody suspicious hanging around at the time you parked the bicycle?'

Father Taylor laughed. 'Monika, Monika, Monika . . .' he said, shaking his head.

'What's so funny,' Paniatowski demanded.

'It was just a *joke*, dear Monika. I thought you'd have seen that long before now.'

'So you didn't have your bicycle stolen after all?'

'Yes, I did. Or, at least, it's gone missing. But the point of the joke was in my pretending to think that a detective sergeant – with much more important things on her mind – would even be *interested* in a stolen bicycle.'

Paniatowski smiled weakly. 'I get it now,' she admitted. 'But if your bicycle has been stolen—'

'Monika, Monika, Monika,' the priest repeated, shaking his head again. 'My bike doesn't *matter*.'

'Of course it does. There are laws—'

'If it's only been borrowed, it will be returned. If it's been stolen, then perhaps whoever took it needed it more than I do.'

'Still, you do need the use of your bike, if you're to visit your parishioners and—'

'If I don't get it back, Father Kenyon will probably give me a little money from the parish funds to buy another one. And he doesn't, well, I've been blessed with strong legs, and I can always walk.' Father Taylor's face grew more serious. 'You must learn not to focus your attention on the small matters whilst the larger matters are still left unresolved. You must not use the *little* picture as a way of escaping having to deal with the *big* one.'

'Is that what I was doing?'

'Yes, I truly think it was.'

'And what big picture am I attempting to escape from?'

'The state of your spiritual health, of course.'

'I didn't come here to talk about that.'

'Then why *did* you come here?'

A good question, Paniatowski thought. *Why* did *I come here?*

'I had a little free time on my hands, and I thought the walk up the hill might be good exercise,' she said aloud.

'Of course! That would explain everything,' Father Taylor agreed. 'Can I ask you another question?'

'If you want to.'

'If I were to suggest that we walked over to the confessional together, would you turn me down?'

'Not at all.'

'You wouldn't?'

'No. I'd be perfectly willing to walk over to it with you. It's going *into* it that I'd object to.'

'Then let's go somewhere else,' Father Taylor suggested. 'I know a little spot, not far from here. I can't say it has a pretty view to look at, or a brilliant band to listen to. I can't even claim it serves the best food in town – because it doesn't have a kitchen.'

'You're talking about the vestry, aren't you?' Paniatowski asked, with a smile slowly creeping across her mouth.

Father Taylor laughed again. 'Yes, you're quite right, Detective Sergeant, I'm talking about the vestry,' he admitted. 'Are you willing to accept my less-than-dazzling invitation?'

Paniatowski shrugged. 'Why not?' she said.

There was still what Woodend would have called, 'a good two hours suppin' time' left in the day, but Bob Rutter had had enough of pouring beer down his throat, and told his boss that he'd decided to have an early night.

The moment he'd reached his car, he began to think that he'd made a mistake. True, he hadn't wanted to spend any more time in the pub, but there was nothing else that he particularly wanted to do either.

For an hour or two, he drove around, thinking about the past and fretting about the future.

He was so lonely, and there was a part of him that wanted to ask Monika if they might pick up again where they had left off. But he understood – deep within himself – that he could never do that. However much he missed her – and he did – however much he wished he could take her in his arms again – and he ached to do just that – he knew that the shadow of his wronged, dead wife would always be hanging over them like a poisonous cloud.

So what was he to do? What was he to *bloody* do?

Still unable to bring himself to move into the house he had once shared with Maria, he had taken a room in a moderately priced boarding house on the edge of town, and it was to there that he finally decided to head.

It was already after eleven when he pulled up in the street outside, and most of the houses were in darkness. He hoped that once he was in bed himself, he would eventually drop off to sleep.

He was slipping his key into the lock when he heard a voice just behind him say, 'Bob!'

He turned around, and saw a blonde woman standing by the gate.

'Monika?' he asked.

Then he realized that it was not Monika at all, and when he spoke again, his voice had hardened.

'You've got a nerve,' he told the woman.

'I know I have,' Elizabeth Driver replied.

'How did you know where to find me?' he asked.

Elizabeth Driver laughed, but it was a nervous laugh rather than an amused one.

'I'm a reporter,' she said. 'It's all a part of my job to know where to find people.'

'You haven't been following me, have you?' he demanded angrily.

Elizabeth Driver shook her head. 'No, I haven't been following you, I promise you that.'

'Then how did you know I was going to turn up here at just this time. Until ten or fifteen minutes ago, I didn't even know it myself.'

'I had no idea when you'd arrive. But I knew you had to come eventually, and I've been waiting.'

'For how long?'

Elizabeth Driver shrugged. 'A couple of hours. Maybe more. I don't really know.'

'*Why* have you been waiting?'

'Because I needed to talk to you, and I knew if I approached you anywhere else, you'd probably refuse to speak to me.'

'I should refuse to speak to you now,' Rutter said.

'I know you should. But please don't!'

Rutter sighed heavily. 'Say what you've got to say – and then get the hell out of here.'

'I wanted to say how sorry I am for ever telling Maria about your affair with Sergeant Paniatowski,' Elizabeth Driver said.

'Why should you want to do that now?' Rutter demanded angrily. 'Is it because she's dead?'

'No, it's not at all because she's dead, though that only makes it even worse than it would have been otherwise. I should never have told her at all – even if she'd been going to live to a hundred.'

'Then why did you?'

'Because I thought there'd be a story in it. Because, at the time I did it, I thought that getting stories was the only thing that really mattered in life. But I don't think that now.'

'Why are you telling me all this?' Rutter asked.

'Because I want your forgiveness.'

'I don't know if I *can* forgive you.'

'Thank you.'

'For what? Did you hear what I said?'

'You said you don't know if you can forgive me – but that's not the same as saying you know you *can't*, is it, Bob?'

'No,' Rutter agreed. 'It's not the same.'

'Think about it,' Elizabeth Driver told. 'Search your soul, to see if you can find a little charity somewhere in it for me. If you can, it will be a great weight off my shoulders.'

'And if I can't?'

'If you can't,' Elizabeth Driver said, 'I suppose that's no more than I deserve.'

Then she turned on her heel, and walked quickly away up the street.

Henry Marlowe had been drinking steadily since late afternoon, and now he was unquestionably – demonstrably – drunk.

'Bloody Woodend!' he growled.

'It was your decision to assign him to the case,' Bill Hawes, his political agent, pointed out.

'I know it was my bloody decision, but what choice did I have? I needed a quick result, and Woodend, of all the officers serving under me, was the man most likely to get me one. But I never thought – not for a second – that he'd arrest Thelma Hawtrey.'

'I fail to see why you're getting so het up about it,' Dawes said. 'So what if he arrested her? He let her go again, didn't he?'

'Yes, he let her go.'

'Well, then?'

'But you don't know the bastard like I do. Once he's got a scent in his nose, he won't let go until he's sunk his teeth into something.'

'But is there anything there for him to sink his teeth into? Is Thelma Hawtrey aware of what happened up that mountainside?'

'How the bloody hell am I expected to know that?'

'I thought perhaps you might have asked her.'

'I might have *asked* her,' Marlowe repeated bitterly. 'Oh, absolutely! I could just have gone up to her, and said casually, "Do you know what your boyfriend did to your husband on that mountainside?" That would have been a brilliant stroke, wouldn't it?'

'The only reason I raised that particular point is because, if he *didn't* tell her, then the secret died with Bradley Pine, and you're in the clear.'

'Died with him?' Marlowe repeated, slurring his words. 'How could it have *died with him*, when all those top bobbies up in Cumberland know about it?'

'They'll say nothing, because they're almost as guilty as you are.'

Marlowe shuddered. 'Guilty?' he repeated. 'Am I guilty?'

'What else would you call it?' Hawes asked practically. 'But, as I said, it's as much in their interest to keep it quiet as it is in yours.'

'And then there's that other bugger, who knows *exactly* what happened,' Marlowe said.

'Jeremy Tully? The company's accountant? But he's in Australia now, isn't he?'

'It doesn't matter where he is,' Marlowe moaned. 'If Woodend decides he wants to find him, that's just what he'll bloody-well do.'

Twenty-Four

Had Bradley Pine still been alive, the letter would have been delivered to his home address, but since he was now occupying a refrigerated drawer in the police morgue, it was diverted instead to Whitebridge Police Headquarters, where it was waiting on Woodend's desk when he got into work the next morning.

It was postmarked 'Western Australia', and contained a single sheet of paper. Even before he started to read it, Woodend could tell from the wild handwriting that the sender had been very agitated.

> I know you are no worse a man than most of us, Bradley. The Devil tempts us all. He tempted Jesus Christ on a mountainside, just as he tempted you. But Our Lord resisted – and you did not. Before I went away, I begged you to confess your sins, but you would not listen. And now, I beg you again to confess. There will be no rest for either of us until you do.
>
> What if you die, Bradley? What if you have a fatal accident before you cleanse your soul? Confess! For the love of God, confess.
>
> Jeremy

Woodend lit up a Capstan Full Strength, and took a deep and thoughtful drag of it.

'Speculation' was what Bob Rutter had called the theory that he'd been propounding in the Drum and Monkey the previous night. Well, this was more than speculation – this was proof positive!

But so what?

'Stop thinking about it, Charlie!' he said aloud. 'It's nothin' but a waste of time.'

A *complete* waste of time, in fact!

A *bloody* waste of time!

Because if Bradley Pine *had* killed Alec Hawtrey, then any chance of bringing him to justice had ended with his own murder. And if Thelma Hawtrey had assisted Pine – or at least, strongly encouraged him to go ahead – there was absolutely no way of proving it now.

Woodend took another drag on his cigarette. 'Focus on the matter in hand,' he ordered himself. 'Focus on Pine's death!'

And then, completely ignoring his own sound advice, he picked up the phone and asked to be connected to Superintendent Springer of the Cumberland Constabulary.

It was ten minutes before Springer could be tracked down, but when he finally came on to the line he seemed more than delighted to be talking to an old colleague from his days in Scotland Yard.

'It's really quite absurd that we don't see much more of each other, Charlie,' he said.

'It is,' Woodend agreed.

'How far is your patch from mine, would you think?' Springer asked. 'Sixty miles, more or less?'

'Somethin' like that.'

'So it's two hours at the most – even in bad traffic. There's no reason at all why we shouldn't get together. You and Joan should come up for dinner. Soon! And rather than drive back to Whitebridge, you could spend the night with us. The house is plenty big enough for you to bring your Annie, too, if she's available – though if she's anything like my kids, she won't want to be spending her time with old farts like us.'

Woodend chuckled. 'She probably wouldn't, but she couldn't even if she wanted to, because they're keepin' her very busy in that nursin' school in Manchester – or so she'd have me believe.'

'But you an' the missus could certainly come up?'

'I'll have to check with Joan first, but I'm sure she'd enjoy it as much as I would,' Woodend said.

He meant it. A lot of the bobbies who he'd worked with in the Yard had got right up his nose most of the time, but Ron Springer never had. He was a bloody good bobby, and a thoroughly decent feller.

154

'Anyway, that probably isn't why you're calling me now, is it?' Springer asked.

'No, it isn't,' Woodend agreed. 'I'm ringin' you about a feller called Alec Hawtrey, who was killed in a mountaineerin' accident on your territory about three years ago.'

There was a pause at the other end of the line, then Springer said, 'Why would you be asking about that, Charlie, after all this time?'

'Any reason why I shouldn't?' Woodend countered.

'I suppose not. But that's all over and done with, isn't it?'

'Well, yes, in a way, I suppose it is,' Woodend agreed. 'But, as it happens, I'm investigating the murder of a man called Bradley Pine, who was standin' as Conservative—'

'I read the newspapers, Charlie,' Springer interrupted. 'I know all about that.'

'An' Pine, in case you haven't made the connection, was the *same* Bradley Pine who was with Alec Hawtrey when he died.'

'And did everything he possibly could to keep him alive. But Hawtrey was in his fifties, and had a broken leg.'

'You seem to be remarkably well informed about the incident,' Woodend said.

'I was there,' Springer told him.

'Why was that?'

'Policing up here's not at all like it is down there in Lancashire. We have to get involved in all kinds of things that you lot never even have to bother your heads about.'

'Which means what, exactly?'

'One of our jobs is to provide tactical support to the mountain rescue teams, and, during the particular incident you're asking about, I was the one who happened to be co-ordinating it.'

'An' did you notice anythin' out of the ordinary?'

'What do you mean – out of the ordinary?'

'I wouldn't have thought the phrase was too difficult to understand,' Woodend said, wondering exactly what was going on at the other end of the line. 'I mean strange! Unusual! Not quite the norm!'

There was another pause from Springer.

'Listen, Charlie,' he said finally, 'I've known you for a long time, and chancing your arm because you think you've finally

155

got Henry Marlowe out of the way is just the sort of thing I'd expect you to do.'

'Pardon?' Woodend said.

'But he may *lose* the election, you know, in which case, he'll be back with you as chief constable.'

'So what?'

'And even if he wins, he might still have some considerable influence – even at a distance – over how the Central Lancs Force is run. So if I was you, I wouldn't even think of crossing him.'

'I've no idea what you're talking about,' Woodend confessed.

'Pull the other leg, Charlie – it's got bells on,' Springer said.

'You really *have* lost me,' Woodend protested.

'Three years ago, there was a climbing accident in the mountains involving two experienced climbers and a novice,' Springer said, as flatly as if he were reading it off a piece of paper. 'The novice broke his leg, probably through his lack of experience. The other two climbers did all they could to save him, but it was a losing battle from the start, and, weakened as he was by his injuries, he died of exposure. That's not only all you *need* to know – it's all there *is* to know.'

'Then why is this phone in my hand almost frostin' over?' Woodend wondered.

'Now *you're* the one who's not making any sense at all, Charlie,' Springer said.

'You say you've known me for a long time. Well, I've known you for a long time, an' all,' Woodend said. 'Three or four minutes ago, you sounded just like my old mate Ron. Then I mentioned Bradley Pine and Alec Hawtrey, an' suddenly you turn as cold as a Siberian blizzard. What's it all about?'

'It's not about anything,' Springer said. 'If I seem a little strange to you, it's probably because, at the moment, I'm under a lot of pressure at work.'

'Fair enough,' Woodend said, though he didn't sound entirely convinced. 'But to get back to that other matter—'

'What other matter?'

'Me an' Joan comin' up there, havin' dinner with you, an' maybe stayin' the night. By the middle of next week, the case I'm workin' on will either be solved or completely in the doldrums, so I can't see any reason why we shouldn't at least pencil in Friday or Saturday—'

'Listen, about that,' Springer interrupted.

'Yes?'

'I'll . . . err . . . have to talk to Mary, and see when we can fit it in,' Springer said. 'We'll definitely do it, but I can't promise it will be all that *soon*, because, as I've just explained, I've got a lot of work on.'

'I see,' Woodend said thoughtfully, 'So maybe we'll wait until things have eased off a bit for you.'

'Yes, I think that would be the best idea.'

'But in the meantime, if anythin' does occur to you about what happened to Alec Hawtrey on that—'

'Leave it, Charlie!' Springer urged. 'Alec Hawtrey's dead and buried. Let him rest in peace, for God's sake!'

And then he hung up.

Rutter and Paniatowski were in Woodend's office, studying a detailed street map of Whitebridge.

'If the boss and I are right, then the only reason that the killer drove the car back into Whitebridge is because he needed to get back here himself,' Rutter said. 'An if we work on that assumption, then it's only reasonable to also assume that he doesn't live more than a mile away from Greenfields. Would you agree with that?'

'Probably,' Paniatowski replied. 'Chances are that, however careful he'd been, there was probably some blood on him – and the longer he was out on the streets, the more chance there was of someone spotting that.'

Being in such close proximity to Bob Rutter again was a bit like forcing yourself to walk into the church after a long absence, she thought – you were probably never going to be entirely comfortable with it, but it got a little easier every time you did it.

'So let's see just what falls within that one-mile area, shall we,' Rutter suggested.

He picked up a compass, set it to scale, and drew a circle on the map, with the spot where the Cortina had been found at the centre of it.

To the south of the centre were the old cotton mills, the *raison d'être* for Greenfields ever having been built. To the east was the city centre, and the beginnings of the access road out to the dual carriageway. Council estates lay to the west, and private housing estates to the north. St Mary's Church – the last place that Pine had been seen alive – was well outside the circle, but Bankside – where he met his death – was neatly dissected by it.

Rutter and Paniatowski gazed down at the line for a moment, then Rutter said, 'Maybe we've been overlooking the obvious solution.'

'That the killer could have been one of Thelma Hawtrey's neighbours?' Paniatowski asked.

'Exactly. A neighbour wouldn't have known exactly when Pine was planning to visit Thelma, but that wouldn't have mattered – because he could have seen him arrive through his front window.'

'But if that had been the case, he wouldn't have had time to set his ambush in the shrubbery.'

'If he was a neighbour, there'd have been no need for an ambush.'

'No?'

'No! Just put yourself in Pine's position for a minute. He's very careful about when he visits Thelma, because he doesn't want to be seen to be doing it. But with the cover provided by the fog, he probably thinks he'll be safe enough that night. Then, just as he's parking, he sees somebody coming out of one of the other houses. What's he going to do now? Is he going to walk straight up to Thelma's door, even though he knows that he's been spotted?'

'No, he isn't,' Paniatowski said. 'He's going to wait until the neighbour draws level with him, and then produce some kind of story which will explain why he's there.'

'Like what?'

'He'll probably claim that he's got lost in the fog.'

'Exactly. So he's standing there – worried, but not the least suspicious – as the neighbour approaches him. Now all that neighbour has to do is to get him to turn his back for a second, and the job's done.'

'So the neighbour says something like, "I thought I saw somebody moving around outside Mrs Hawtrey's front door"?'

'Yes. And Pine turns to look. He's already standing in the gateway, so when the blow is struck he falls straight into the rhododendron bushes.'

'And if the killer *was* a neighbour, he might also have been

158

a friend of Alec Hawtrey's,' Paniatowski said, with growing enthusiasm. 'Living where he was, he could have worked out what was going on between Pine and Thelma, and been outraged that Thelma was dishonouring his friend's memory.'

'But would he have been outraged enough to *kill* Pine?' Rutter wondered. 'Enough to *mutilate* his body?'

They had been building up a bubble of excitement between them, but these last few words from Rutter quite punctured it.

'It's hard to imagine anyone hating Pine enough to do that,' Paniatowski agreed.

'If I could have got my hands on the bloody bastard who killed Maria . . .' Rutter said.

An awkward silence followed, as it always did when Maria's name accidentally came up.

Then Paniatowski said, 'Would you have killed Maria's murderer for what he did to her – or for what he'd done to you?'

'You can be cruel,' Rutter told her.

Had she *meant* to be cruel, Paniatowski wondered.

Had *she* been punishing *him* for what *he'd* done to *her*?

And if that was the case, did she have any right to do it?

'I'm not being cruel,' she said, pushing self-analysis to one side. 'I'm just doing my job.'

'Are you?'

'Yes.'

'Is that *really* what you're doing? And if it is, would you like to explain *how*?'

'The boss says we have to try to get into the heads of murderers, and if we need to use our own experiences to do that – however painful they might be – we just need to bite on the bullet and go ahead.'

'You're right,' Rutter said, somewhat pacified, 'and I apologize for taking it the wrong way.'

'And I apologize for pushing you like that,' Paniatowski said. 'You don't have to answer the question if you don't want to.'

'But I *do* want to, because you're spot on when you say that it might help,' Rutter told her. He thought for a moment. 'If I'm honest,' he continued, slightly shakily, 'I think I'd have to say I would have killed him for my own benefit, because however much pain I could have caused Maria's murderer, it wouldn't have helped her at all.'

'So we think this murderer did it for himself, and not to avenge someone else?' Paniatowski said.

'That's what we think.'

'And because he was so full of hatred, he wanted to humiliate Pine even in death?'

'Yes.'

'Then what I still don't understand is why the murderer put Pine in the back of the car,' Paniatowski said.

'You've lost me,' Rutter admitted.

'If he was so keen to rob Pine of his dignity, why not cram him in the boot? Putting him on the back seat instead seems ... I don't know ... to be almost *cherishing* him.'

'And even with the thick fog, placing him on the back seat increased the risk tremendously,' Rutter said. 'It would have been *much* safer for him to hide the body away in the boot.'

There was a discreet cough behind them, and they turned to see Sergeant Dix standing there in the open doorway.

'What can I do for you, Sergeant?' Rutter asked.

'I just thought you'd like to know that me an' the lads are about to set off for Upper Bankside, sir,' Dix told him. 'Will you be coming with us?'

'Yes I will,' Rutter replied. 'Just give me a minute to finish off here, will you?'

Dix nodded and left.

'I think we might have hit on something important with this question of why the killer didn't put the body in the boot,' Paniatowski said. 'Do you want to bounce it around some more, later?'

Rutter smiled. 'That's a good idea. Bouncing ideas off each other was what we used to do in the good old days, wasn't it?

Paniatowski returned his smile. 'Yes, it was. That's exactly what we did in the good old days.'

'And there's no reason we can't get back into the habit.'

'None at all.' Paniatowski took a deep breath. 'We could perhaps discuss it over lunch,' she suggested.

Rutter shook his head. 'That's not on, I'm afraid. I've already got a lunch appointment booked.'

'With the boss?'

160

'No.'

'Then who with?'

'That's really none of your business, is it?' Rutter asked, an angry note suddenly present in his voice.

'I didn't mean to pry,' Paniatowski replied, surprised by the unexpected vehemence.

'I don't have to justify my movements to you,' Rutter said. 'You're not my wife, you know!'

'Thank you for taking the trouble to remind me, but I was already quite well aware of that,' Monika answered quietly.

Rutter slapped his forehead – hard – with the palm of his hand. 'Oh God, Monika, I didn't mean . . . I wasn't trying to say . . .'

'I know,' Paniatowski said.

'We'll meet up sometime this afternoon,' Rutter promised. 'There's . . . there's a lot to talk about, and I do think we're making progress.'

Then he stood up and strode quickly out of the office.

When Henry Marlowe put down the telephone, the look on his face was one of almost blind panic.

'That was the Cumberland Police on the line,' he told Bill Hawes. 'They've just had a phone call from Woodend. He wanted to know all about Alec Hawtrey's accident.'

'Who did he talk to?'

'Superintendent Springer.'

'And what does this superintendent know about it?'

'Everything! He was there on the mountainside at the time. It couldn't have been done without him.'

'"I am in blood stepp'd in so far, should I wade no more, returning were as tedious as go o'er,"' Bill Hawes said.

'What in God's name are you talking about, Bill?' Henry Marlowe demanded.

'It's a quote.'

'A quote!'

'From Shakespeare's *Macbeth,* or, as actors prefer to call it, the Scottish Play.'

'Oh, well that's a very bloody useful thing to know, isn't it, now?' Marlowe said.

'It is, as a matter of fact,' Hawes told him. 'It reminds us, in case we need reminding, that there's no going back – that once we've done something wrong, we have to *keep on* doing wrong in order not to be found out.'

'So what's the point?'

'The point is that once you'd told me this Superintendent Springer was involved in the incident, I ceased to be in the least bit concerned. Not only will he not shop you, Henry, he'll continue to tell lies – perhaps even bigger ones than he's told already – in order to protect you. He has no choice. He can't protect himself, if he doesn't first protect you.'

'I hope to God you're right,' Marlowe said.

So do I, Hawes thought. Because the last thing I need at this stage in the election is to have to come up with a *third* candidate.

Twenty-Five

The weather was still not quite warm enough for Dr Shastri to have abandoned the trademark sheepskin jacket which she wore over her sari, but, as she climbed down from her Land Rover, Woodend saw that her small delicate feet were now clad only in elegant thong sandals.

Actually, the chief inspector thought, 'climbing down' was not the right way to describe the motions she'd just gone through. Other people – ordinary people – climbed down from their Land Rovers. Dr Shastri seemed to float, and though she was not, in fact, bathed in a cloud of swirling rose petals as she descended, it almost *seemed* as though she were.

The doctor saw him standing there next to his Wolseley, and favoured him with a wide smile.

'Ah, my dear Chief Inspector!' she said. 'How thoughtful of you to drive all the way over here with the sole purpose of providing me with an escort from my vehicle to my place of business.'

Woodend grinned. 'Your place of business! Sometimes, you know, you talk just like my bank manager.'

'Yes, I suppose I do,' the doctor agreed. 'And is there not good reason for it, considering that, in many ways, the resemblance between the bank manager and the police surgeon is quite remarkable?'

'How do you figure that out?'

'I should have thought it was obvious. Both of us deal with customers who would never come to see us if they weren't already dead men.'

'True.'

'And though the bank manager may use only cutting words, whereas I use a very sharp scalpel, we are both intent on draining whatever is left of those poor customers' blood.'

'You really should go on the stage,' Woodend said, and –

163

unlike when he'd used almost the same words to Foxy Rowton, the solicitor – he meant it as a compliment.

'You seem very eager to move me into another line of work,' Dr Shastri said. 'But ask yourself this, my dear Chief Inspector – if I were gone, seduced by the glamour of a life in the lime-light, who would then be here to perform those miracles that you demand of me on almost a daily basis? And it *is* another miracle that you have come here to request, is it not?'

'Not quite a miracle,' Woodend said.

'No?' Dr Shastri asked sceptically.

'It's more like a small favour.'

'Now I am becoming most concerned,' Dr Shastri told him. 'To ask me for a favour is one thing, but if you go out of your way to soften your request by calling it a *small* favour, I can only assume it is, in reality, the size of an elephant. Am I not right?'

'Perhaps,' Woodend agreed. 'But not a *full-sized* elephant. At most, it's a cute little baby.'

'My concern is mounting by the minute,' Dr Shastri told him. 'But let us see this beast of yours anyway.'

'Do you happen, by any chance, to know the Cumberland police surgeon?' Woodend asked.

'We have met.'

'An' would you say that you're on good terms with him?'

'Of course I'm on good terms with him. All doctors are on the best of possible terms with each other – just as all policemen are on the best of possible with their own colleagues.'

Woodend thought of his own relationship with Henry Marlowe, and grimaced.

'Does that mean that he'd send you a copy of an autopsy report, if you asked for it?' he asked.

'I should think so. What is the name of this deceased person you have suddenly developed a morbid interest in?'

'He's a feller called Alec Hawtrey,' Woodend said.

The woman who answered the door of the house directly opposite Thelma Hawtrey's was called Mrs Comstock. She was somewhere in her mid-fifties, and had enough rings on her fingers to open a jewellery store.

'It's absolutely appalling that there was a murder just beyond my gate,' she said to Rutter, with tears in her eyes.

164

'Yes, it's always a shock when something terrible like that happens so close to home,' Rutter replied, sympathetically.

'I don't know how I shall bear it,' Mrs Comstock continued. 'All my friends will be laughing at me.'

'Laughing at you?'

'I can almost *hear* them telling one another that perhaps their houses didn't cost quite as much as ours did, but at least the streets in front of them aren't running with blood.'

'I can't begin to describe how deeply, deeply, sorry I feel for you,' Rutter said.

'We always thought we were above that kind of thing,' Mrs Comstock said, not even noticing the sarcasm. She sniffed. 'Of course, Mr Pine wasn't actually a resident,' she continued, brightening a little, 'so in a way, it doesn't really reflect on us at all, does it?'

'Did you see anything?' Rutter asked.

'When?'

'On the night of the murder.'

'No, we didn't. We only got back from our holiday – from our *vacation*, I should say – yesterday afternoon. We went on a cruise, in the Caribbean, you know. Very expensive, but absolutely delightful.'

'Do you have any holiday snaps that you could show me?' Rutter asked, and then, before the bloody woman could reply that she had, he quickly added, 'No, you won't have, will you? They won't be back from the chemist's yet.'

'Our *photographs* of the excursion are being developed in a professional laboratory, to the highest possible standards,' Mrs Comstock said, missing the point yet again.

'Well, much as I'd love to stay and chat some more, Mrs Comstock, I do have a murderer to catch,' Rutter said, before turning and starting to walk back down the drive.

'We used to go to Spain for our vacations, you know,' Mrs Comstock called after him. 'But we had to stop that, because every Tom, Dick and Harry goes there now.'

'My chief inspector went to Spain himself, last year,' Rutter said, over his shoulder.

'Well, that just goes to prove my point, doesn't it?' Mrs Comstock asked, stepping back into her expensive hallway and closing her polished oak door behind her.

Rutter walked down the driveway, then paused at the gate to look up and down the street.

This was not a promising area to trawl for eye-witnesses, he thought. The distance between the houses – the separation of one property from the next – was far too great for that. But when you really *needed* to find someone who'd seen what happened, you just had to hope – against the odds – that someone actually had.

Twenty-Six

'We've stumbled across somethin' very big here, Monika,' Woodend said gravely to his sergeant, 'somethin that goes far beyond the boundaries of a single murder. What we've got here is a conspiracy – an' I've absolutely no idea why it should have happened.'

Paniatowski nodded, but said nothing.

'I can understand why Bradley Pine killed Alec Hawtrey,' Woodend continued. 'He did it in order to protect the life he'd built up for himself and his relationship with Thelma. But what I simply can't get my head around is why Ron Springer – who used to be a bloody good bobby – should have allowed himself to be involved in the cover-up.'

'Hang on, aren't you getting a little ahead of yourself, here, sir?' Paniatowski asked. 'You can't say for certain that Pine *did* kill Hawtrey.'

'Can't I?' Woodend asked. 'Not even after Jeremy Tully's letter? What was that about, if it wasn't about murder?'

'Fair point,' Paniatowski conceded. 'But I'm still a long way from being convinced that whatever happened on that mountainside in Cumberland – even if it *was* murder – has anything to do with us.'

'We're *police officers*,' Woodend said.

'Yes, we are,' Paniatowski agreed. 'And our job at the moment is to catch Bradley Pine's murderer.'

'So if I was a surgeon who'd cut somebody to remove his appendix an' found he'd got stomach cancer, I should ignore the cancer an' just finish the job I'd originally set out to do, should I?'

'It's not the same thing,' Paniatowski said.

'It's exactly the same thing,' Woodend insisted. 'If we're in the process of investigatin' one crime, an' see another bein' committed, we don't just turn the other way.'

'But the crime you're talking about isn't being committed *now*. It happened nearly three years ago. The trail's cold.'

'You might be right that the murder trail's cold,' Woodend countered, 'but the trail leadin' to the cover-up is anythin' but. That stays hot for as long as the cover-up exists. I want to follow it, Monika. I *have to* follow it. And I'm not sure I can do it without your help.'

'But it didn't even happen on our patch,' Paniatowski protested. 'Following that trail would be just like advancing into enemy territory under heavy fire. And if anything went wrong, we could take a real fall for this, Charlie.'

'So you're sayin' you don't want anythin' to do with it?' Woodend asked disappointedly. Then he shrugged. 'Well, I can't entirely blame you for that, lass,' he continued, 'an' I want you to know that I won't hold it against you in the future.'

'I'm not saying I don't *want* anything to do with it,' Paniatowski told him. 'I'm saying I shouldn't *have* anything to do with it.' She paused for a second. 'But if you're going to stick your head above the parapet, I don't suppose I have any choice but to stick mine up next to it.'

'I appreciate it, Monika,' Woodend said. 'You're a good friend an' a good colleague.'

'I'm a bloody fool, is what I am,' Paniatowski replied. 'So what do you want me to do? March straight into Cumberland Police Headquarters and demand to know the truth?'

'No,' Woodend said. 'If I thought that would work, I'd do it myself rather than sendin' you. What you need to do instead, Monika, is to approach the whole matter from a completely different angle.'

'And what angle might that be?'

'Superintendent Springer assured me that there was absolutely nothin' abnormal about Alec Hawtrey's death – that, in fact, it was absolutely typical of the sort of thing that could happen to folk if they didn't take sufficient care on that mountainside.'

'So?'

'So I'd like you to go up there yourself – an' find out if the mountain rescue team agrees with him.'

The house next door to Mrs Comstock's was called 'Xanadu',

though there was nothing of the 'stately pleasure-dome' about its very conventional frontage.

The man who answered Rutter's knock on the door was in his late sixties. He had a shiny bald head and a large nose, under which rested a trim military moustache. He was dressed in a blue blazer with a badge on its pocket which depicted crossed rifles. He had stout brogues on his feet, and a silken cravat expertly knotted around his neck.

In some ways, he immediately reminded Rutter of Mr Morrisson – the vigilante with the notebook who patrolled Lower Bankside – but whereas Morrisson *hoped* other people would take him seriously, this man had the definite air of someone who clearly *expected* it.

The man ran his eyes quickly up and down Rutter, almost as if he were standing on parade, then said, 'Got the look of a policeman about you. Is that what you are?'

'That's right, sir,' Rutter began, reaching into his jacket for his warrant card. 'I'm a detective inspector in the—'

'Don't bother fetching out your papers, as if I was some sort of office-wallah,' the other man said dismissively. 'You say you're a policeman, and I believe you. What's your name?'

'Rutter.'

'It's a pleasure to meet you, Inspector Rutter. My name's Thompson. Lieutenant Colonel Thompson, to be strictly accurate, though I suppose you may as well forget the rank now I've left the Army. I've been expecting you since you took away that awful woman from across the road. I suppose you did *have to* let her go again, did you?'

Rutter smiled, despite himself. 'Yes, I'm afraid we did, sir. It turns out she hadn't done anything wrong.'

'Poppycock!' Colonel Thompson said.

'Poppycock?'

'Bound to have done *something* wrong – we all have – but if she didn't kill that Pine chap, you were probably quite correct to release her.'

'You said, a moment ago, that you'd been expecting me, sir,' Rutter said. 'Why was that?'

'Because I saw both the murderer and his victim.'

'Where?'

'Where do you think? Over there. Right in front of the awful Thelma's house.'

Was Thompson the sort of witness that bobbies conducting an investigation would give their eye teeth for, Rutter wondered. Or was he simply a nutter? At the moment, he was putting his money on the man being a nutter.

'If you *did* see them over there, why didn't you report it immediately?' he asked.

'Didn't know *what* I'd seen at the time, did I? Until I read in the morning paper that Pine had been croaked almost on my own doorstep, I thought that I'd been witnessing no more than the tail-end of a drunken party.'

'Go on,' Rutter said cautiously.

'I was out in the garden the other night, when I saw a green Cortina parked in front of Thelma Hawtrey's house.'

'What were you doing out in the garden?' Rutter wondered.

'Can't a man stand around on his own property when he wants to?' Thompson asked.

'There was a thick fog that night. It wouldn't have been very pleasant to be outside.'

Thompson snorted. 'Don't know the meaning of unpleasant weather till you've served in India.'

'Even so . . .'

'You're not going to let go of this until I give you an explanation you're happy with, are you?' Colonel Thompson asked.

'No. I'm afraid I'm not.'

'All right, I suppose I'd better come clean. My dear lady wife's quite a sweet old thing in her own way, but she does have some very strange ideas.'

'Like what?'

'Doesn't like me smoking in the house. Says it makes the place smell. Can you believe it?'

'It is a little unusual,' Rutter admitted.

'But be that as it may, one of the first things you're taught as a young officer is that you should never become involved in a battle that you know you can't possibly win, and if there was ever a perfect example of that dictum, this is it. So if the memsahib wishes to enforce a policy of no smoking in quarters, that's the way it has to be.'

'Quite,' Rutter said.

'And it's not such a high price to pay, considering that the woman's allowed herself to be dragged halfway around the world and back over the last thirty or so years,' Colonel Thompson said.

'So you came out into the garden for the purpose of having a smoke?!' Rutter said.

'Took you long enough to get there, didn't it?' Colonel Thompson said. 'Lucky you weren't facing wild tribesmen, or you'd have been dead by now. Anyway, the point is, I *did* come out into the garden, and that's when I noticed the car parked on the street in front of the Hawtrey residence.'

'Was there anybody in it?'

'I'll tell this in my own way, if you don't mind,' Colonel Thompson said sharply.

'Go ahead,' Rutter agreed.

'There was nobody there at first. Then a chap appeared out of the driveway. Can't give you much of a description, I'm afraid. In the fog, he was little more than a black shape. At any rate, he opened the boot of the car and—'

'You're sure he opened the boot?'

'Of course I'm sure. Wouldn't have said it if I hadn't been. He opened the boot, then he disappeared up the driveway again. And at that point, I must admit, I wandered off to the other side of the garden.'

'So you didn't see any more?'

'If you can stop interrupting for a moment, I'll tell you what I saw and what I didn't see.'

'Sorry,' Rutter said.

'By the time I returned to my original vantage point, the man had reappeared from the driveway, and this time he was holding another man up. I assumed the second man was drunk, but from what I've read in the papers, the other man was probably Pine – and he was dead.'

'That's more than likely,' Rutter agreed.

'The murderer . . . we are agreed that it was probably the murderer, are we?'

'We're agreed.'

'The murderer opened the back door of the car, and bundled Pine into it. He had a certain amount of difficulty doing it, but no more than he'd have had if Pine been dead drunk instead of simply dead.'

'Can I ask a question now?' Rutter said.

'Yes, *now* you may,' the Colonel conceded.

171

'Did it, at any point, look as if he might be thinking of putting Pine in the boot?'

'No, it didn't – though the boot was still open.'

'So what happened next?'

'Once he'd crammed Pine into the car, he slammed the door closed. It made quite a noise in the still night air, and I remember thinking that I hoped the poor drunk was well tucked inside the car, because if his arm had been hanging out, the force would have broken it.'

'What did the murderer do next?' Rutter asked. 'Did he get into the driver's seat?'

'No, he didn't. The boot was still open, remember.' Colonel Thompson paused for a moment. 'That wasn't some kind of test you were putting me to, was it?' he continued.

'A test?'

'To try and establish whether or not I'm gaga?'

'Of course not,' Rutter replied, hoping that he wasn't blushing.

'The killer went round to the back of the car, and closed the boot. And this time, he was much more careful about it. I thought at the time it was because he was showing some belated consideration for the residents.'

'But you don't think that now?'

'Chap who's just smashed another chap's head in isn't going to worry about causing offence to the local rate-payers, now is he?'

'So why *did* he close the boot so carefully?'

'I haven't the foggiest idea.' Colonel Thompson chuckled. 'That was rather good, wasn't it? It was foggy, and I haven't the foggiest idea.'

'Very droll,' Rutter agreed. 'I'll be sending a man round to take down your statement later, sir. That should be no problem, should it?'

'No problem at all,' Colonel Thompson agreed. 'I'll do my duty, as I always have.'

Twenty-Seven

Dr Shastri entered Woodend's office without knocking. For once there was nothing in her movements to suggest the gentle gliding of a butterfly. In fact, she came much closer to resembling an enraged wasp.

'In case you wish to keep a record of it for posterity, I should inform you that your little deception was effective for exactly one hour, thirty-five minutes and twenty-eight seconds, Chief Inspector,' she said.

'I beg your pardon?' Woodend replied.

'That is precisely how long it took me to discover I have been wasting my time. For a moment, it seemed to me just like a return to the bad old days, and I was very angry indeed.'

'The bad old days?' Woodend repeated, completely mystified. 'What bad old days?'

'The bad old days when I first came to this country of yours.'

'You're not makin' a lot of sense, lass.'

'Then I will explain further. Many of the English people with whom I worked at that time thought it might be most amusing to hold me up to ridicule. And so they talked in my presence about diseases I had never heard of – which is hardly surprising, since they had just invented them – and they sent me off on countless pointless errands. Nor did it stop there. They hid medical records from me, and sent me friends of theirs who claimed to be suffering terrible symptoms, but were only really *pretending* to be ill.'

'Why did they do that?'

'Because they considered it great sport to confuse the poor, unsophisticated Indian doctor – to make a complete monkey out of her, in fact. And it seemed to me that you were doing exactly the same thing yourself.'

'Come off it, Doc,' Woodend protested. 'First of all, if one of us is unsophisticated, it certainly isn't you. An' secondly – an' more importantly – I've got too much respect for you to try an' make you look a fool.'

Dr Shastri nodded. 'Yes, that is the conclusion I had already almost reached myself, and I am pleased to have you confirm it,' she said. 'So I am no longer angry. You are far too nice a man to ever deliberately insult me, so if it is not an insult it must be an example of your strange English sense of humour, which you expected me to share. Very well, then, I must learn to develop this strange sense of humour, too, and when the opportunity arises, I will play a similar joke on you.'

'I still don't have the slightest idea of what you're talkin' about, Doc,' Woodend confessed.

'Of course you don't,' Dr Shastri replied, smiling knowingly. 'Would you care to hear what is in the autopsy report?'

She might *say* she wasn't angry any more, Woodend thought, but anger was still there, bubbling just below the surface.

'Yes, I'd like to hear what it,' he told her. 'An' I must say, you've got hold of it very quickly.'

'Indeed I have. But then, you always knew that I would, didn't you, Chief Inspector?'

'Did I? How?'

'Very good,' Dr Shastri said. 'Very nicely played. You kept your face perfectly straight, and you *almost* convince me that you had no idea what I was talking about. But to return to the report – Mr Alec Hawtrey broke his leg when he was climbing. He sustained no other injuries, but the broken leg alone was enough to make him less resilient than his companions in the face of the blizzard, and he died of exposure.'

'You still haven't told me how you managed to get hold of the report so quickly?' Woodend pointed out.

'I called my colleague in Cumberland, and reminded him of the jolly times we had spent together at medical conferences, playing "Pass the Vital Organ" and "Pin the Appendix on the Cadaver",' Dr Shastri said, regaining some of her normal good humour. 'Once I had him eating out of my hand, I asked him if he wouldn't mind sending me the autopsy report. He said that wasn't necessary, because we already had a copy of it.'

'What?'

'He did not perform the autopsy himself, you see. He was

intending to perform it, but then a Police Superintendent, by the name of Springer, informed him that it would instead be carried out by another medical examiner from outside the county.'

'Isn't that unusual?' Woodend asked.

'Very unusual indeed. But Superintendent Springer told him that the decision had been taken at the *highest levels* of the police authority, so he saw no point in arguing.'

'An' who *was* this medical examiner from outside the county, who actually did the job?'

Dr Shastri smiled again. 'So you continue with your little joke right through to the bitter end,' she said. 'I must make a note of that, so that when you become the victim of my revenge-joke on you, I can sustain it with equal ferocity.'

'I honestly don't know who he was,' Woodend said.

'If it pleases you so much, I can see no harm in going along with your game,' Dr Shastri said. She put her hand to her forehead, as if thinking very hard. 'Who *could* it be?' she continued. 'If the death occurred in Cumberland, why would we have a copy of the autopsy report here in Whitebridge?'

'Because the medical examiner who carried out the autopsy was from Whitebridge himself?' Woodend asked, finally grasping the point.

'Exactly! It was my predecessor who actually performed the autopsy – Dr Pierson.'

Doc Pierson! Woodend repeated to himself.

The last case that he and Pierson had worked on together had been the murder at Dugdale's Farm. And Pierson really *had* made a monkey out of *him*, because in order to conceal a whole stinking level of municipal corruption, he had deliberately distorted the medical evidence – and almost allowed the killer to escape.

The doctor was still serving time in HM Prison Saltney for that particular betrayal of his Hippocratic oath. But who could say how many more times before then he had fudged the evidence, in order to protect some rich or powerful member of the Whitebridge élite?

And given that Bradley Pine had been both rich *and* powerful, was the autopsy report really worth the paper it was printed on?

* * *

Constable Colin Beresford did not feel entirely comfortable about entering a Catholic church, and there was ample reason for this. When he had to fill in any forms which asked about his religion, he always wrote down 'Church of England', but his church-going was largely confined to christenings, weddings and funerals, and if he thought about God at all, it was only to wonder why He had chosen to inflict a mind-decaying disease on a woman who was still in her early sixties.

Still, once he was actually inside St Mary's, he could not help but be fascinated by what he saw. The place might not be holier than any of the churches he was used to, but it was certainly much more elaborate.

Looking around at the statues and paintings, smelling the incense which lingered in the air from the last service, he got the distinct impression that this was a religion which took itself very seriously indeed.

The priest's appearance came as something of a surprise, too. All the vicars who Beresford had come across had been old men – in their fifties, at least – but this man couldn't be more than thirty.

'Can I help you?' the priest asked.

'I'm looking for someone,' Beresford said.

The priest smiled. 'And is that someone God?' he asked. 'Because if He is who you're looking for, you've come to the right place.'

'No, I'm . . . I'm looking for a police officer,' Beresford said, starting to feel a little confused.

'Then might I suggest you would be likely to be more successful if you began your search at a police station?'

'This officer – this *female* officer – is working on a case at the moment, and I thought she might be here.'

'You're talking about Monika, aren't you?'

'Yes, that's right. Sergeant Paniatowski.'

'She's not here,' Father Taylor said. 'Nor, as far as I know, is she expected in the near future. But if you'd care to leave a message with me, I'll deliver it to her the next time I see her.'

'No, that's all right,' Beresford said. 'I should be seeing her myself before too long.'

'Is what's troubling you something that only Monika can help you with?' the priest asked, with a concerned and sympathetic look on his face. 'Or might I, possibly, be of some assistance?'

'No, I'm very sorry, but it really does have to be Sergeant Paniatowski,' Beresford said.

'There's no need to apologize,' Father Taylor said softly. 'We all have the right to choose our own guides.'

'You're very understanding, Father,' Beresford said.

'I try to be,' the priest replied.

Once outside again, Beresford cleared his head of the slightly intimidating atmosphere of the Catholic Church by greedily sucking in the contaminated air of a Northern industrial town.

The priest had asked him why he had been looking for Sergeant Paniatowski. Well, the answer to that was simple enough.

He was a lost soul – though in an investigative, rather than a religious, sense.

He was a man out of his depth, wondering if he could keep treading water until he learned how to swim, or whether it might not be better to be hauled on to the shore and content himself, henceforth, with wearing a uniform.

Sergeant Paniatowski would advise him. Sergeant Paniatowski was the only person he could think of who would be *able* to advise him – which was why he had spent the best part of two hours aimlessly scouring Whitebridge for her, instead of simply waiting until they met up in the pub later.

He fully realized that this urge to talk to her immediately was nothing more than a sign of his own desperation, but there was nothing he could do about that. He was *so* desperate, in fact, that he'd almost poured out his troubles to the priest – and now he was beginning to wonder why he hadn't.

It was true that Father Taylor was not a bobby himself – and so would have had an imperfect grasp of the sorts of problems bobbies had to face – but he had appeared to be a kind man, an understanding man. And though Beresford was sure they had never met before, he'd seemed strangely familiar.

Though the Dirty Duck was rather a come-down for a woman used to living off a more-than-generous expense account, Elizabeth Driver was glad that she had chosen it as the place to have her lunch with Bob Rutter. She could see, just by looking at him from across the table, that he was far more at home there than he would have been at one of Whitebridge's more expensive restaurants – and it was very important that he *did* feel at home.

'I can't tell you how gratified I am that you said you'd meet me today,' she told him. 'I'm *especially* grateful because I know I don't deserve it – because we *both* know I don't deserve it.'

'There was a time when I'd have agreed with you,' Rutter replied. 'But not any more.'

'So what's changed?'

'My life has changed. And because of that, the way I look at everything else has changed, too.'

'Do you want to tell me about it?' Elizabeth Driver asked, only just resisting the temptation to reach across the table and place her hand softly on top of his.

'The one thing in life that everybody needs is forgiveness,' Rutter told her. 'I wanted my wife to forgive me, but now I'll never know whether she would have or not.'

'I'm certain she would have,' Elizabeth Driver said. 'I'm convinced she would eventually have come to see that what happened was all Monika Paniatowski's fault.'

'It wasn't all Monika's fault!' Rutter said, with a hint of rising anger in his voice.

'No, of course it wasn't,' Elizabeth Driver said hastily. 'I phrased it badly. What I meant to say was that the affair would never have happened if Monika hadn't been around – that you'd never have strayed from your marriage vows with any woman but her.'

'I think that's true,' Rutter said.

'I'm sure it is,' Elizabeth Driver said, reassuringly.

'Everybody makes mistakes, and everybody needs forgiveness,' Rutter said, returning to his earlier theme. 'That's why I'm trying as hard as I possibly can to forgive you.'

'And is it working?'

'I think I'm almost there.'

'You're so kind,' Elizabeth Driver said, in a voice she hoped sounded both deeply touched and deeply sincere.

Rutter shook his head vehemently. 'I'm not kind at all. I'm doing it for purely selfish reasons. If I can't learn to forgive you, then how will I ever learn to forgive myself?'

'I've been wondering how *I* could make amends,' Elizabeth Driver said. 'And I think I may have found a way.'

'How?'

'Through using the only real talent I have. I want to write a book on you and Maria.'

'What kind of book?'

'An inspirational book. One which shows how bravely you both coped with her blindness.'

'Until I betrayed her,' Rutter said.

'I wouldn't go into that.'

'You'd have to!' Rutter said fiercely. 'It wouldn't be an honest book if you didn't.'

'I'm not sure that's necessarily—'

'And if it wasn't an honest book, then it wouldn't be worth writing at all.'

'I can quite see that,' Elizabeth Driver lied. 'But have you thought about what it might do to your reputation if that part of the story appeared in print?'

'I don't care about my reputation.'

Elizabeth Driver pursed her brow thoughtfully. 'I suppose I could always protect you by changing the names,' she suggested.

'I don't want the names changing. Maria has the right to be admired under her own name – and I deserve to be vilified under mine.'

'And what about Monika?'

'Monika's name *would* have to be changed,' Rutter admitted. 'And she couldn't appear as she is – real flesh and blood. She'd have to be no more than a shadow.'

'That shouldn't be too much of a problem,' Elizabeth Driver said. She paused for a second. 'You sound as if you're almost ready to give me permission to go ahead with the project.'

'I *am* almost ready.'

'Though I must say, the way you've outlined what you want, it won't be quite the same book as I'd thought of writing. You make your agreement to it seem almost like a penance.'

'It's not *almost like* a penance at all,' Rutter told her. 'It *is* a bloody penance.'

Twenty-Eight

The Last Drop Inn was a squat stone building, with thick walls to repel the drifting snow, and ceiling heights designed with the much shorter men of earlier generations in mind. A large open fire burned brightly in the grate of the bar parlour, and its flames were reflected in the copper pots which hung on the walls.

It had already been a thriving pub when John Hancock had been the first man to sign a document containing what he and his fellow delegates considered to be self-evident truths. It had served pints of fine and frothy Lake District ale to passengers on the London mail coach on the very day that Louis XVI of France had lost his head. And when Victoria had ascended to the throne of England in 1837, its regular drinkers had shaken their heads and wondered just how a young, inexperienced girl like her could ever be expected to act like a monarch.

Monika Paniatowski quite liked the place herself, and knew that Woodend would have absolutely loved it.

She was sitting at a table with Brian Steele, leader of the mountain rescue team, and his nephew Craig. Brian struck her as a man who made decisions quickly, and probably didn't appreciate being questioned on them. Craig had an appealing innocence which reminded her a little of Constable Beresford's.

'To be honest with you, Sergeant, I don't see how what happened on the mountain over three years ago can have anything to do with a murder that's only a few days old,' Brian Steele was saying.

'Neither do I,' Paniatowski replied. 'But my boss wanted the questions asked, and I wasn't going to turn down the chance of spending the day up here among your lovely lakes.'

Craig Steele positively beamed with pleasure. 'I'm glad you like them, Monika.'

'That's *Sergeant Paniatowski* to you,' his uncle told him.

'I don't mind being called Monika, honestly I don't,' Paniatowski said, being deliberately girlish.

'Please yourself, then,' Brian said, taking slight umbrage at his ruling being overturned.

'Tell me about the rescue,' Paniatowski suggested.

'It was one of the worst blizzards I can ever recall experiencing, and I've been part of one mountain rescue team or another for nearly twenty-five years now,' Brian Steele said.

'Was it actually forecast that it would be such bad weather?' Paniatowski asked.

'Now why would you want to know that?' Brian Steele wondered, with the slightly suspicious tone to his voice that all men of action seemed to have when confronted with people who write up reports of their conversations with them in warm offices.

I want to know because, if I were planning any funny business on the mountainside, I might decide that bad weather would provide me with the perfect cover for it, Paniatowski thought.

But aloud, she said, 'I'm just trying to build up a general picture of how things were.'

'The blizzard came out of nowhere,' Brian said. 'It took *everybody* by surprise.'

'Especially those three poor buggers who were stuck up the mountain,' Craig added.

'Watch your language when there's a lady present,' his uncle warned him. 'Now, where was I? Oh yes, Pine, Hawtrey and Tulworth were staying at the Bluebell Hotel and—'

'Tully,' Craig interrupted. 'His name was Tully.'

'Pine, Hawtrey and *Tully* were staying at the Bluebell Hotel,' Brian said, flashing a look of annoyance at his nephew. 'Before they set out that morning, they left all the details of their planned expedition at the reception desk, just as they were supposed to do, so when they hadn't returned by nightfall, the hotel naturally phoned us.'

'We knew roughly where they were, but there was no way we could get to them in those conditions,' Craig Steele said.

'What the boy means is that we have one golden rule that we always operate under,' Brian explained. 'We're more than willing to put our own lives at risk in order to carry out a rescue, but that's not the same thing at all as being prepared to *throw* our lives away.'

'Getting *yourself* killed doesn't help the people who you're trying to save one little bit,' Craig added.

'Anyway, we got ready to go, and waited for the weather to lift,' Brian said. 'But it didn't lift the next day, nor the day after that. It wasn't until the fourth morning that it started to improve, and by then, the three of them had been stranded on the mountain for at least eighty hours.'

'It was when it *did* finally did start to lift that your feller actually turned up,' Craig said.

'Our feller? You mean Superintendent Springer by that, do you?' Paniatowski asked.

'No, not him,' Brian said dismissively. 'Ron Springer may have worked down in London once upon a time, but over the years he's got all that out of his system, and now he's one of ours.'

'Then who—'

'The feller that I'm talkin' about was a Lancashire bobby. What was his name, Craig?'

'Marlowe, I think,' Craig Steele replied.

'Marlowe?' Paniatowski repeated. '*Henry* Marlowe?'

'That's him,' Brian agreed. 'You sound as if it's news to you that he was ever here.'

'It is,' Paniatowski replied, thoughtfully. 'But please don't let me interrupt you.'

'It's not the first time that some bigwig or other has turned up at the scene of one of our rescues,' Craig said. 'They think it's glamorous, you see – a bit like putting a Stetson on and pretending you're a cowboy.'

'And we tolerate them poncing about like that because we have no choice in the matter,' Brian said.

'No choice?' Paniatowski repeated.

'You have to understand that we're a voluntary organization, and it's people like your Mr Marlowe who help to raise the funds we need to keep our operation going.'

'Of course, it doesn't take them long to realize that there's very little glamour in what we do – and a lot of hard slog,' Craig said. 'And it's usually at that point that they start saying that while they'd love to come along on the final stages of the rescue, they think they've pulled a muscle.'

182

Brian laughed. 'That's exactly what they say,' he agreed. 'Not that we'd have *let* them come along with us, anyway. It's a dangerous job we do, and there's no room for passengers.'

'You did let that Marlowe feller come along,' Craig pointed out.

'That was the exception to the rule,' Brian said, giving his nephew another warning glance. 'And there were two very good reasons for making it an exception. The first one was that he'd done some mountain climbing himself, and when he was talking to me, he managed to convince me that not only would he not be a hindrance in the rescue, but he might actually be some help.'

'And what was the second?' Paniatowski asked.

Brian looked a little sheepish. 'Superintendent Springer wanted us to let him come with us. He said that Mr Marlowe was considering entering politics, and it would sort of give him a leg up if he could be associated with the rescue.'

'I've never met a feller quite as keen to get himself in the limelight as Marlowe was that day,' Craig said. 'He'd hardly arrived at the rescue centre before he was asking my permission to use the radio telephone.'

'*I'd* put Craig in charge of that,' Brian said. 'It's a very responsible job, but I thought he could handle it.'

'So, since we didn't need the channel open for anything else, I said it would be all right,' Craig told Paniatowski. 'He made more than one call, and from the bits of the conversation that I happened to overhear, I'm almost sure he was talking to the newspapers.'

'Let's get back to the main point of the story, shall we?' Brian said. 'Springer asked me if we'd take Marlowe along, and I said yes. If anybody else had asked me, I'd have turned him down, but since Ron Springer's been a good friend to our unit, I decided to oblige him. But I want to make it perfectly plain to you that I'd *never* have agreed – however much pressure Springer had put on me – if I hadn't thought Marlowe was up to it.'

'Understood,' Paniatowski said.

'It was the helicopter that spotted them,' Brian continued. 'But there was no way it could have landed where they were, and even using a winch would have been difficult, so it was decided that we'd do the job from the ground. When we finally

183

reached the three fellers, we could see straight away that while the others were in a pretty bad way, Hawtrey was beyond any kind of help we could give him.'

'He'd had a fall off the rock and broken his leg, hadn't he?' Paniatowski asked.

'That's right. And Pine had fashioned some rough splints for it, from the frame to his rucksack.'

'Had Hawtrey sustained any other injuries?'

'Wouldn't they be in the autopsy report?' Brian asked, with a hint of suspicion again.

'I suppose they would be, but I was just wondering if you'd noticed anything yourselves.'

'He'd injured his arm,' Craig volunteered. 'It was quite a nasty wound as well.'

'Did you see it yourself?' Paniatowski asked.

'Not personally, no.'

'Then how do you know it was nasty?'

'I could tell from the amount of blood there was on his trousers and his boots.'

'But that could have come from anywhere,' Paniatowski pointed out. 'How can you be so sure the wound was in his arm?'

'Because that's where he was bloodiest of all. The blood on his boots and trousers was just spattered, but on his arm – where it had soaked through the sleeve of his jacket – it was a thick stain.'

Paniatowski lit a cigarette, to give herself time to think.

'If he was still wearing his jacket, how was it possible that some of the blood had spattered on other parts of his body?' she asked, once she'd inhaled.

'It probably happened when they stripped off his jacket in an attempt to staunch the wound,' Craig replied.

'This is getting *less* like an interview, and *more* like an interrogation,' Brian said.

Paniatowski laughed. 'Sorry! I do tend to get carried away, don't I? I'll be asking you if you've paid your television licence fee next!'

Craig joined in her laughter, but Brian just said, 'I have paid it. I can show you, if you like.'

'What sort of state were Pine and Tully in when you found them?' Paniatowski asked.

'Pine had frostbite in one hand, but otherwise he didn't seem too bad,' Brian said. 'And he was certainly glad to see his mate.'

Bradley Pine, lying on the ground, looks up at Marlowe.
'Henry!' he gasps. 'Thank God you're here.'
'It was the least I could do for a friend,' Marlowe replies.
'If you'll just step aside, Mr Marlowe, I'd like to examine Mr Pine now,' Brian says, crisply and businesslike.
'No!' Pine says, raising an arm weakly into the air, as if that will ward off a fit mountain rescuer. 'No!'
'You have to be examined, Mr Pine,' Brian says firmly.
'Henry will do it.'
'I'm the one with the qualifications.'
'Henry . . . will . . . do it.'

'It's sometimes better to give way in these matters,' Brian Steele told Paniatowski. 'I was right, wasn't I, in assuming that, as a serving police officer, Marlowe would have kept himself up to date with the latest First Aid techniques?'

'Undoubtedly,' Paniatowski replied, with as straight a face as she could muster.

'And when a patient is as distressed as Pine obviously was, you can often do more harm than good by forcing the issue.'

'What state was Tully in?' Paniatowski asked.

'Tully was a mess,' Brian replied. 'Not physically – he was in better shape than Pine, in that respect – but mentally.'

Tully's eyes are wide and wild and filled with pain. He looks as if he were watching his own ghost walk before him. He doesn't even seem to realize that anybody else is there.
'We're the mountain rescue team. We're here to help you,' Brian Steele informs him.
'Asperges me,' Tully intones. 'Domine, hyssopo, et mundabor: lavabis me, et super nivem dealbabor.'
'You're not making any sense, man,' Brian tells him.
'Ab homine iniquo, et doloso erue me,' Tully says, and it is clear that it is not his rescuer he is speaking to.
'Pull yourself together!' Brian says sharply. 'When you've been through an ordeal like yours, you've got to pull yourself

together as soon as possible. You've got to come back to the real world.'

'Munda cor meum ac labia mea, omnipotens Deus, qui labia Isaiæ Prophetæ calculo mundasti ignito,' Tully replies.

'Most of what he said was in a foreign language,' Brian Steele told Paniatowski. 'German or French, or something like that.'

'It was Latin,' Craig corrected him.

His uncle looked at him sharply, as if annoyed that Craig knew something that he didn't.

'Who told you that?' he demanded.

'Tommy O'Donnell,' Craig said. He turned to Paniatowski. 'Tommy was another member of the team,' he explained.

'And how would somebody like *Tommy O'Donnell* know whether it was Latin or just gobbledegook?' Brian asked scornfully.

'He's a Catholic,' Craig said.

'Oh, is he?' Brian said. 'Well, that would explain it, I suppose. Is this Tully feller a Catholic, an' all?' he asked Paniatowski.

'I believe he is.'

Brian sniffed. 'Well, there you are, then. People are entitled to follow any faith they choose, even if it is Papist.'

'Did he say anything that *wasn't* in Latin?' Paniatowski asked.

'Not that I heard. But then I didn't have much opportunity to hear it, did I? Because that's when your Mr Marlowe decided to stick his oar into the proceedings again.'

'I thought he was taking care of Bradley Pine.'

'He had been. But he seemed to lose any interest in Pine, and from then on, all he cared about was Tully.'

Marlowe has stuck close to Tully all the way down from the mountainside, and now, when the ambulances arrive at the rescue centre, he announces that he will travel in the same ambulance as the man.

'You'll be in the way of the paramedics,' Brian Steele says.

'I'll be assisting the paramedics,' Marlowe tells him.

'Have they agreed to it?'

'They will. And anyway, what happens between them and me is no concern of yours. Your part of the rescue operation is over.'

'I don't want people falling down and kissing my feet for what I do for them, but I don't like being spoken to like that, either,' Brian Steele said. 'If the bugger hadn't been a policeman, I'd have dropped him where he was standing.'

'I wish you had,' Paniatowski said.

'Pardon?'

'I wish you had . . . had pointed out to him how ungrateful he was being,' Paniatowski quickly corrected herself. 'But there's one thing I still don't understand about this whole affair.'

'And what might that be?'

'I don't understand why I've never heard anything about any of this before today. Surely, if Mr Marlowe had rung the papers, as Craig says he did, his part in the rescue would have been splashed all over them.'

'So it would,' Craig agreed, 'if he hadn't had second thoughts about the whole thing on the way back to town.'

The ambulance carrying Jeremy Tully arrives at the hospital ahead of the one carrying Bradley Pine, and Marlowe is the first person to climb out of it. He sees the half a dozen news photographers who are gathered around the door which leads into the main hospital building, and visibly blanches.

The paramedics are already in the process of lifting Tully's stretcher out of the vehicle when Marlowe swings round to face them again.

'Wait!' he says.

'What do you mean?' one of the paramedics asks.

'Isn't plain English good enough for you?' Marlowe demands. 'I want you to wait until I tell you it's all right to bloody-well unload him.'

'Now just a minute—' the paramedic begins.

'And if you don't do exactly what I say, I'll personally ensure that the local police make your life a bloody misery from now on,' Marlowe hisses.

The mountain rescue Land Rover and Superintendent Springer's car pull up behind the ambulance. Craig Steele gets out of the one, and Springer out of the other. They reach the ambulance at roughly the same time.

'What's the delay?' Springer asks.

'Get rid of them,' Marlowe says, gesturing towards the pressmen.

187

Superintendent Springer looks puzzled. 'But I thought you told me that you wanted them to—'

'I want them out of here!'

Springer walks over to the reporters, and explains that his colleague has decided that it would be best for the injured men if they weren't bothered by reporters at this point. He apologizes for the inconvenience, and promises them he'll find a way to make it up to them in the near future.

The journalists readily agree – this is, after all, nothing more than a common or garden mountain rescue, and now Springer's in their debt, he'll throw them something really juicy next time.

Marlowe waits until the reporters are well clear of the area, and only then does he allow the paramedics to get on with their job.

'So why do you think there was a sudden about-face on Mr Marlowe's part?' Paniatowski asked.

'Who knows?' Craig Steele replied. 'I was right there, and I certainly don't. Maybe it was something that Mr Pine had said to him. Or maybe it was what Mr Tully wanted.'

'I thought you said Tully was speaking in *Latin!*' said his uncle, still smarting over the earlier revelation of his ignorance.

'Perhaps he'd switched back to English,' Craig suggested. 'Or perhaps Mr Marlowe knows Latin.'

Mr Marlowe doesn't know his arse from his elbow most of the time, Paniatowski thought, but she kept it to herself.

'What happened after that?' she asked.

'We wouldn't know,' Brian Steele told her. 'Our job was done. And unlike your Mr Marlowe, we didn't want to get in the way of other professionals who were trying to do theirs.'

'So we all went straight to the pub and got absolutely legless,' his nephew said.

'So we stood down from duty,' Brian Steele corrected him.

'But I do know that Mr Marlowe didn't leave immediately, because I saw him in town the next day,' Craig said.

Twenty-Nine

'They may well be livin' in the so-called "Permissive Society" down in London, an' possibly they are in Manchester an' all,' Woodend said, gazing into his pint of bitter as if he suspected that the answer to all the mysteries of the world were contained in a single glass, 'but the idea of "doin' your own thing" is still an alien concept to Whitebridge.'

Bob Rutter grinned. 'And what do you think the reason for that is, sir?' he asked.

'It's because the glue that's always held industrial towns like this one together is *conformity*. The mills dictated the pattern of life, you see, lad. Everybody started work at the same time, everybody left work at the same time – and everybody went on holiday at the same time, usually to the same place, while all the mills were closed down for maintenance. An' even though the mills have gone, we're still livin' in their shadow.'

'I don't see that should necessarily stop the *middle* class from "doing their own thing",' Rutter said.

'That's where you're wrong, lad. They don't have to conform to the same things as the workers, but they still *do* have to conform. There's as much a proper way to dress – an' a proper way to behave – up at that Golf an' Country Club as there is down in the cobbled streets. There's rules which are not written down, but everybody still knows. An' if you want a good example of what happens when you break the rules, you've only got to look at the case of Alec Hawtrey.'

'Yes, I can imagine he was somewhat shunned by some of his old Catholic friends, because they didn't recognize that his second marriage was—' Bob Rutter began.

'From what I've heard up at the Golf Club, he was shunned by nearly every bugger – because if you can't fit in with one part of the Establishment, you'll find yourself unwelcome in *any* part of it.'

'Poor devil,' Rutter said.

'Poor devil, indeed,' Woodend agreed. 'Alec Hawtrey seems to have sacrificed a great deal by givin' into the temptations of the—' He stopped abruptly, and made great show of checking his watch. 'I wonder where the devil young Monika's got to?' he continued. 'She should have been back from her trip to the Lakes by now.'

'He sacrificed a great deal by giving into the temptations of the *flesh*,' Rutter completed. 'Isn't that what you were about to say?'

'Aye, I was,' Woodend admitted. 'However careful I try to be, I always seem to be puttin' my foot right in it on that particular question, don't I? I'm really very sorry, lad.'

'There's no need to apologize. We can't make what's happened go away by just ignoring it.'

'Monika said pretty much the same thing to me. An' you may well both have a point. On the other hand, there isn't much to be gained by constantly draggin' it into the spotlight, is there?'

'As a matter of fact, there is,' Rutter said. 'It's only by frankly and openly confessing our sins that we can ever hope to put them behind us. That's why I'm seriously considering Elizabeth's idea of—'

He stopped himself speaking mid-sentence, just as the chief inspector had done earlier.

'What was that?' Woodend asked.

'Nothing.'

'Which Elizabeth are we talkin' about? Do I know her?'

'Let's change the subject,' Rutter suggested forcefully. 'What do you make of what the old colonel told me this afternoon?'

'Well, he pretty much confirmed what we already suspected, didn't he?' Woodend said. 'That the killer was actin' on his own.'

'True. But Colonel Thompson also confirmed that the killer made no effort to put the body in the boot, and I still haven't been able to work out why that should have been.'

'It was a foggy night, an' there weren't many people about on the streets,' Woodend pointed out. 'Maybe the killer thought puttin' him on the back seat would be safe enough.'

'There weren't *many* people about, but there were *some* – which meant there was still an element of risk,' Rutter countered. 'Say he'd been pulled up at a traffic light, and a passing pedestrian had just happened to look into the car. Say there'd been an accident somewhere on his route, and the traffic patrol sent to deal with it had flagged him down.'

'There'd only have been a slight possibility of either of those things actually happenin'.'

'Agreed. But why run any risk at all, when he didn't have to?'

'You're right, of course,' Woodend agreed. 'An' since, accordin' to your pal the colonel, he *had* opened the boot, his initial thought *must have been* to put Pine in there.'

'And then there's the difference between the ways he closed the door and closed the boot,' Rutter said. 'Colonel Thompson says that he *slammed* the back door, but he shut the boot very gently.'

'Almost as if he didn't want to damage whatever – or *whoever* – was inside it,' Woodend mused. 'Perhaps he *did* have an accomplice after all, an' the accomplice was hidin' in the boot.'

The bar door swung open, and Monika Paniatowski walked in. Even from a distance, both men could see that her face was flushed with excitement, and as she strode across the room it looked as if she could hardly wait to tell Woodend and Rutter what it was that she'd discovered.

'Did you know that Mr Marlowe was in the rescue party that brought Pine, Hawtrey and Tully down from the mountainside?' she asked, the moment she'd reached the table.

Woodend frowned. 'No, I certainly bloody didn't! An' perhaps more to the point, *why* didn't I know?'

'Because Marlowe didn't want to advertise the fact that he'd been there at all. Nor would I, if I'd helped to cover up a murder!'

'So you're comin' round to the idea that what Tully wrote in his letter was no more than the simple truth?'

'The evidence certainly seems to be pointing that way.'

Paniatowski quickly filled Woodend and Rutter in on her conversation with the mountain rescue men, including the details of the blood spatters on the trousers and boots, and the patch of blood on the sleeve of Hawtrey's jacket.

'Maybe all the blood *did* come from a wound in his arm,' Woodend suggested.

'The sleeve of his jacket wasn't torn!' Paniatowski countered. 'If it had have been, I'm sure either Brian or Craig Steele would have mentioned it. If it had have been, they'd have seen the wound on the arm for themselves, instead of just being *told* about it.'

'I still don't see why the sleeve *had* to be torn,' Woodend said.

'Neither do I,' Rutter agreed. 'As a kid, I was always falling down and grazing my knee without actually tearing my pants.'

'But this wasn't just a graze,' Paniatowski pointed out. 'Hawtrey must have lost at least a pint of blood.'

'Good point,' Woodend conceded. 'But if that's the case, why didn't these Steele fellers – who are experienced mountain rescuers – reach the same conclusion that you did?'

'Because they'd got plenty of other things to think about at the time,' Paniatowski argued. 'Hawtrey was dead. There was nothing more they could do for him, and they were well aware of it. So they paid him virtually no attention at all. Besides, conditions were still hazardous, even though the blizzard had lifted somewhat, and their main concern was to get the living – Pine and Tully – back to safety. But the *really* big difference is that they weren't looking for signs of foul play – why should they have been? – but I *was*!'

'So are you sayin' that you don't think Alec Hawtrey *was* wounded in the arm?'

'No, I'm not saying that at all. The patch of blood on the sleeve of his jacket would seem to indicate that he was almost definitely wounded there, possibly during the struggle.'

'Well, then?'

'But what I *am* putting forward is the idea that there was another wound – a *fatal* one – on some other part of his body. What I *don't* know is how Marlowe managed to persuade the local medical examiner to ignore the wounds.'

'He didn't have to,' Woodend said. 'It was good old Doc Pierson, our completely discredited police doctor, who carried out the autopsy.'

'Well, that explains everything!' Paniatowski told him.

'No, it doesn't,' Woodend contradicted her. 'We know Doc Pierson was willin' to bend the rules on other occasions – that's why he's in gaol now. But Marlowe had nothin' to gain by helpin' to cover up a murder. In fact, he had one hell of a lot to lose.'

'Maybe Bradley Pine told him there hadn't *been* a murder at all,' Paniatowski suggested.

'An' why would he have believed him, when, accordin' to you, there was clear evidence of foul play somewhere on Hawtrey's body?'

'Perhaps Pine managed to persuade the chief constable that he and Hawtrey had got into a fight over Thelma, and he'd killed Hawtrey accidentally.'

'Even if Marlowe had believed that – which would be stretchin' even *his* credulity to the absolute limit – he'd still be running one hell of a risk assistin' in a cover-up,' Woodend said dubiously. 'An', knowin' him as I do, I can't honestly see our Mr Marlowe sticking his neck out for *anybody*.'

'Perhaps he had no choice in the matter,' Paniatowski said. 'Perhaps Marlowe's got a guilty secret, and Pine knew all about it.'

'Now that is a possibility,' Woodend said.

It was more than a possibility, and it didn't even have to be a *big* secret that Pine had got hold of. Given that Marlowe was already planning to stand for parliament at the time, even a sordid *little* secret – for example, a liking for wearing women's underwear – would have been enough to sink his political ambitions.

'But we've still got a big problem, even if we're finally thinkin' along the right lines,' Woodend said, frowning deeply. 'Marlowe's never goin' to admit to his involvement, however much we try to pressure him. An' we can't have another autopsy carried out on Hawtrey, because – very conveniently for every-body involved in the cover-up, an' very *inconveniently* for us – the bugger was cremated.' He gazed down into the pint glass again, and when he raised his head he was looking consider-ably more cheerful. 'Still, we've got at least a couple of strings left to our bow, haven't we?' he asked the other two.

'And what strings might they be?' Rutter wondered.

'The first one is Jeremy Tully. He knows exactly what happened on that mountainside – because he was there.'

'And now he's in Australia,' Paniatowski said.

'Which is a long, long way, but that still doesn't mean he's beyond our reach,' Woodend told her. 'I've been on the phone to the Australian police this afternoon, an' they've promised to interview him as soon as possible.'

'Is the other string Doc Pierson?' Rutter asked.

'The other string's Doc Pierson,' Woodend agreed. 'I've made an appointment to visit him in Saltney Prison tomorrow mornin'.'

'Why should *he* be willing to tell you what you want to know?' Paniatowski asked.

'No reason at all, that I can think of,' Woodend conceded. 'So I'll just have to charm him into it, won't I? An' – let's be honest about this – I'm well-known for my charm.'

'Practically world-famous,' Rutter said, deadpan.

A waiter arrived with a vodka for Paniatowski, and the sergeant drained it in one gulp.

'I think I'll have an early night,' she said, placing the empty glass on the table.

'That's not like you at all,' Woodend told her.

And it wasn't. Normally Monika would rather do anything than go back to her lonely flat.

'I've done a lot of driving today, and it's rather taken it out of me,' Paniatowski explained.

And *that* wasn't like her, either, Woodend thought. She loved driving. It never seemed to tire her.

'I'd better be going, too,' Rutter said, standing up. 'I'm due to meet someone in half an hour.'

'About the case?' Woodend asked.

Rutter hesitated. 'No, it's a personal matter,' he said finally.

Woodend looked first at Rutter, then at Paniatowski, then back at Rutter again.

What the bloody hell was going on with these two, he wondered.

Thirty

Whoever had last been using the two chairs in the vestry had placed them much closer together than they had been previously, and though both Father Taylor and Paniatowski could have repositioned one of them before sitting down, neither of them chose to.

'This is becoming something of a habit of ours, isn't it, Monika?' Father Taylor asked.

'Is that some tactful way of saying that I'm taking up far too much of your time?' Paniatowski wondered.

'No, no, not at all,' Father Taylor said hastily. 'I meant that it was becoming a habit in the nicest possible sense of the word.'

'And what sense is that?'

'It's a rather *cosy* habit, if you see what I'm getting at.'

Yes, she did see what he was getting at, Paniatowski thought. It was becoming a cosy habit because, in many ways, he was a cosy *man.*

She could almost picture him – after a hard day's work in some office or other – sitting in his favourite armchair in his pleasant suburban living room. He would be wearing worn carpet slippers and an old cardigan – which was going at the elbows, but which he could not bear to throw out – and he would be listening happily while his children, gathered around at his feet, described their day's adventures to him.

'Why did you become a priest?' she heard herself saying.

'I thought I'd already answered that question the other night.'

'Maybe you did.'

'Well, then?'

'And maybe I wasn't entirely convinced by what you told me.'

'I assure you, Monika, I—'

'Or it could be that I'd like to hear it all again, just to make certain I heard it right the first time.'

Father Taylor hesitated for a moment, then said, 'I suppose the simplest way to explain how I came to be what I am is to say that I became a priest because I felt – I believed – that that's what God wanted me to become.'

'So you had no choice – no free will?'

'We all of us always have a choice. What would be the point in striving to become virtuous, if we didn't have the free will to choose not to be?'

'What made you so sure that this was what God wanted you to do?' Paniatowski asked.

'The gifts He appears to have bestowed on me.'

'Like what?'

'Even when I was very young, people seemed to have this urge to confide in me.'

'So you're a good listener. That doesn't mean—'

'And more than that, they took what I said in return very seriously. I had the power to comfort them – to lighten their burden. There was a time – in my teens – when I saw it more as a curse than a gift. But gradually I came to see God's purpose working through me.'

'In other words, you became a priest simply because you had a talent for it?' Paniatowski asked. 'In much the same way as you might have become a concert pianist if you'd had a natural aptitude for the piano?'

'Are you mocking me now?' Father Taylor asked, looking hurt.

Paniatowski shook her head, vehemently.

'No, I promise you, I'm not,' she said.

'Then what *are* you doing?'

'I'm trying to understand how a man like you could turn his back on a normal life. You *should* be married! You *should* have children. Even if they weren't your own. Even if you had to adopt them!'

'If it had been God's plan for me to fall in love before I entered the priesthood, then that is what I would have done,' Father Taylor said, simply.

'And once you had entered the priesthood, it was no longer possible?'

'If I feel any stirrings – and I have already confessed to

196

you that I do – I know it is only God's way of tempting me.'

'He must be a very cruel god, then.'

'No, He is a infinitely loving God, and He only does it to help me to strengthen my faith.'

They had strayed on to very dangerous ground Paniatowski realized – and it was all her fault.

'I have a problem you might be able to help me with,' she said, trying to sound more businesslike. 'And before you jump to any conclusions, Father Fred, it's professional – it's not about God at all.'

Father Taylor smiled. '*Most* things are about God,' he said, 'but if you wish me to keep Him out of the conversation, I promise to try my hardest. What is it you want to know?'

'Say that there were three men cut off by the weather on a mountainside, and that before their rescuers could get to them, one of them had already died,' Paniatowski began.

'Is this some sort of moral theoretical question, or is it real?' Father Taylor asked.

'It's theoretical,' Paniatowski lied.

'I see. Well, in that case, do carry on.'

'Say that when the rescuers do get there, one of the men who's survived is speaking in Latin. Why would he be doing that?'

'What is it he's saying?'

'I don't know. But he's not a classical scholar, or anything like that. He's an accountant and—'

'Are we *sure* this a theoretical example?'

'Does it matter if it isn't?'

'I suppose not. Is this man a Catholic?'

'He is.'

'So you think that he was speaking what, for want of a better phrase, we might call *church* Latin, do you?'

'Yes, I do.'

'And you're wondering what particular piece of church Latin might have come to his mind in the situation you describe?'

'Exactly.'

'Well, I suppose he could have been saying a prayer for the soul of his dead friend.'

'I don't think that was it at all.'

'No?'

'No. From the way he was described to me, he seemed to be more concerned about himself than his dead friend.'

'Then he could have been praying for forgiveness. Perhaps he felt responsible for his friend's death.'

'Responsible *how*?'

'I can't say. It would be impossible to say, without knowing more details. But perhaps – and this is *only* a suggestion – he felt guilty because he was the one who had come up with the idea of the expedition in the first place.'

'I don't think it *was* his idea.'

'Then I'm at a loss.'

'Is it possible that he felt guilty because he could have done something to *prevent* the friend's death, but chose not to?'

'Certainly,' the priest said.

Paniatowski stood up. 'Thank you, Father.'

'Are you going so soon?' Father Taylor asked.

'Well, yes,' Paniatowski said. 'You answered my questions – at least as far as you're able to – so I won't take up any more of your time.'

Father Taylor stood up, and placed his hands on her shoulders.

'Is that truly the only reason that you came here tonight, Monika?' he said. 'To ask me your theoretical questions which we both know were not really theoretical at all?'

'Yes. Well, mainly.'

'Are you sure about that?'

'Of course I'm sure.'

Father Taylor's hands ceased to merely rest on Paniatowski's shoulders, and instead began to grasp them. She could feel his fingers digging into her flesh with an urgency which demanded the truth.

'Look into my eyes – look *deeply* into them – and tell me again that you're sure,' he said.

Monika raised her head, so that their eyes met. 'I'm sure,' she said, unconvincingly.

And before either of them really knew what was happening, they were kissing one another.

Beresford still felt a desperate need to talk to Sergeant Paniatowski, and on the way to the pub he had been racking his brains for some ruse he might employ to detach her from the rest of the team. It was almost crushingly disappointing to find that she wasn't even there – and more than disturbing

198

to see that the only person who *was* actually sitting at the usual table was also the one person who he really didn't want to talk to at all.

He was already backing towards the door when Woodend spotted him, and gestured that he should join him.

Beresford walked reluctantly over to the table and sat down in the chair opposite the chief inspector's.

'What's the matter, lad?' Woodend asked. 'You look like you've lost a pound an' found sixpence.'

'I don't think I'm cut out for CID work, sir,' Beresford blurted out. 'I don't think I'm cut out for it all.'

There! He'd said it! It was finally out in the open!

Woodend shook his head slowly from side to side.

'Oh dear, it's the old crisis of confidence raisin' its ugly head, is it? Don't worry, lad, we all suffer from that now an' again.'

'That's easy enough for you to say, sir,' Beresford told him. 'When you have any doubts, you've got a rock-solid track record to reassure you. *You* can always remind yourself that you've arrested more murderers than I've had hot dinners. But what have I got?'

'You've had your own modest successes, even if you don't quite realize it yet.'

'Like what?'

'Well, for example, bringin' Thelma Hawtrey into the picture. Why did we go an' see her in the first place? Because of what you'd learned about her husband's death from the people in the factory!'

'But I didn't *want* us to go and see her,' Beresford pointed out. 'I didn't think Thelma could possibly have had anything to do with Pine's murder.'

'An', as it happens, you were quite right about that. But if we hadn't gone to see Thelma, we'd never have found the spot on which Bradley Pine was murdered, would we?'

'So if I helped the investigation at all, it was purely by accident,' Beresford said glumly.

'Half the time, *any* progress we make comes about as a result of a lucky accident,' Woodend told him. 'We stir up the pot, an' see what floats to the surface. Sometimes what bobs up is of no earthly use, but if we don't keep stirrin', we'll never get anywhere.'

'I don't think I'm even a very good stirrer, sir,' Beresford said.

'Of course you are. Tell me a few of the things that you've found that I probably don't know about yet.'

'I don't see that'll do any good, sir.'

'Humour me!'

'Well,' Beresford said, reluctantly, 'I found out that Alec Hawtrey had two children by his first wife, a boy and girl.'

'Which was news to me.'

'But is it news that's going to be of any use?'

'We won't know until we've finally closed the case. Were they a happy family before Thelma came along?'

'I think so. I saw this picture of them on their holidays. They all looked as if they were having a good time. Except for the son. He seemed miserable. Not, that's not the right word. What he seemed was *troubled*.' Beresford paused. 'Honestly, sir, I don't think this is doing any—'

'Tell me more.'

'Whatever happened later, Mr Hawtrey must have really doted on his first wife in the early years of their marriage, because he built this huge elaborate house for her, and—'

Woodend chuckled. 'Oh, aye. That house! "Tara"!'

'Sorry, sir?'

'"Tara". It's what other people used to call the house. An' they didn't necessarily mean it as a compliment.'

Beresford looked at him blankly. 'Tara?' he repeated.

'Aye, you know, after the house in *Gone with the Wind*?'

'I'm sorry, sir, I still don't—'

'You've never heard of a film called *Gone with the Wind*?'

'No, sir. When was it made?'

'Round about 1939, I think.'

'That was an awfully long time ago, sir.'

Woodend sighed heavily. 'Sometimes you do make me feel very, very old, lad.'

'I'm sorry, sir, I didn't mean to—'

'Oh, for God's sake, don't go apologizin',' Woodend told him. 'Anybody who says they don't envy you for your youth is a bloody liar – but that's their problem, not yours.' He paused to light up a cigarette. 'They pulled that house down in the end. I was sorry to see it go.'

'Why? I thought you said it was a bit of a joke.'

'Well, I suppose it was, in an way.'

'Well, then?'

'But it was rather like the odd characters you sometimes come across in the pub – they can irritate the hell out of you when they're there, but you quite miss them when they've gone. Still, that's progress for you. The town planners – in their infinite wisdom – decided that the people of Whitebridge needed a new road much more than they needed a good talkin' point, and so they . . . so they . . .'

'What's the matter, sir?' Beresford asked, slightly alarmed by the change that had suddenly come over his boss.

'"Tara" was pulled down because – like a lot of other properties – it stood in the way of the new Whitebridge to Accrington dual carriageway,' Woodend said. 'An' I may be wrong about this, but when I think about exactly where it was, I get the distinct impression it must have been very close to that lay-by we found Bradley Pine in!'

Thirty-One

The visiting room in HM Prison Saltney was large and square, and the table in the centre of it looked as lost as a small island in the middle of a vast ocean. It was perhaps not quite as depressing as the interview rooms back in Whitebridge Police HQ, Woodend thought, but it certainly ran a damn close second.

The door to the corridor swung open, and one of the prison officers escorted Dr Pierson into the room. The doctor had been incarcerated for a little over two years. He had the unhealthy pallor of someone who is rarely out in the open air, but otherwise looked better than might have been expected in a man who had seen his whole life disintegrate.

Pierson sat down opposite the chief inspector, and said, 'Have you got a cigarette, Charlie?'

Woodend slid a full packet across the table. 'You can keep them, Doc,' he said.

'So you think you can bribe me with a few fags, do you?' Pierson asked, but even as he was speaking, he was sliding the cigarettes into the pocket of his prison overalls.

'What makes you think that I was offering them as a bribe?' Woodend wondered.

Pierson shrugged. 'What else could it be, Charlie? This is the first time you've ever been to see me, and you wouldn't have come now if you hadn't wanted something.'

'Do you blame me for that?'

'Blame you for what? For wanting something? Or for not coming to see me before now?'

'For not coming to see you before now.'

Pierson thought about it. 'No, probably not. We wouldn't have had much to say to one another if you had come. We could hardly have reminisced about old times, could we, when the "old time" that really stands out in both our minds is the one when you arrested me?'

'Given what you'd been involved in, you didn't leave me much choice about that, did you?' Woodend asked.

'No, I suppose I didn't,' Pierson agreed. 'When all's said and done, you were only doing your job. But *you* can't blame *me* for wishing that you hadn't done it quite so well.'

'Why don't you tell me about the autopsy you performed on Alec Hawtrey?' Woodend suggested.

'Alec Hawtrey,' Pierson mused. 'So that's what this is all about. As I recall, Hawtrey fell off a mountainside in a blizzard, and broke his leg. His death was the result of exposure.'

'Was it really exposure which killed him?'

'Yes, it was.'

'You're sure about that?'

'I know I've often lied to you in the past, Charlie, but please believe me when I say that, this time, I'm telling you the truth.'

I do believe you, Woodend thought. I don't want to – because that means we've been following another false trail – but I *do*.

'Why did Marlowe go to all that trouble of ensurin' you were the one who carried out the autopsy?' he asked.

'You'll have to ask Henry that.'

'I'm askin' you.'

'I suppose it's possible he did because he had no faith in the Cumberland medical examiner.'

'Now you *are* lyin' aren't you?' Woodend asked.

'Maybe yes, and maybe no. But *if* I am lying, what are you prepared to offer me for telling the truth, Charlie?'

'What do you want?'

'My freedom!'

'Come on now, Doc! You know I couldn't get you released at this stage in your sentence, even if I wanted to!'

'Then perhaps I'd be willing to settle for something a little more modest. A cell that I didn't have to share with anyone else would be nice. I'd also like unlimited supplies of the finest old malt whisky. And if you could round off the package with a promise of gourmet meals which have been cooked especially for me in the finest restaurant in the area, you just might have yourself a deal.'

'Aye, there should be no problem with any of that,' Woodend said. 'An' while I'm at it, why don't I see if Brigitte Bardot, Elizabeth Taylor and Sophia Loren are free at the moment – because I'm sure if they are, I can arrange for them all to visit you on the long winter nights.'

Dr Pierson smiled wanly. 'In other words, you can't get me anything at all that will make my life in here a little pleasanter,' he said.

'Got it in one,' Woodend agreed. 'But I promise you this – if you committed any illegal acts durin' the course of the autopsy on Hawtrey, I'll personally guarantee that you won't be prosecuted for them.'

Pierson laughed. 'All that boils down to is a promise that if I put my head in the noose, you won't pull the handle and open the trapdoor. But why should I even think of putting my head in the noose *at all*?'

'Because it's the right thing to do.'

'And do you seriously think I *care* about "doing the right thing"?' Pierson asked, with derision.

'Yes, I do,' Woodend said seriously. 'I was talkin' to the Governor before I came to see you , an' it seems you've been an exemplary prisoner.'

'Well, of course I have. If you want to earn time off for good behaviour, that's exactly what you have to be.'

'He also told me that you've often volunteered to work extra hours in the prison hospital.'

'Why wouldn't I? The hospital's a pleasant place. Certainly a great deal more pleasant than my cell.'

'An' you've been holdin' classes – teachin' some of the worst educated prisoners to read. Now why, I ask myself, should you have bothered to have done all that?'

'Because it helps to fill in the time?'

'I don't think so. I think you're doin' it because you're tryin' to redeem youself.'

'Redeem myself!' Doc Pierson repeated with a contempt which didn't quite ring true. 'What kind of language is that to use about me? I'm not a Catholic, you know.'

'Doesn't matter whether you are or whether you're not,' Woodend said firmly. 'You don't have to belong to the Church of Rome to understand that you've done wrong in the past, an' to want to try an' compensate for it in any way that you can.'

'And are you saying that my telling you what happened at that autopsy will be part of the redemption process?'

'Yes, I think it will.'

'Why should it be?'

'Because it'll be one more secret that you'll no longer have to keep locked up inside yourself – one less weight of wrong-doin' that's pressin' down on your shoulders.'

Pierson laughed again. 'Perhaps you should have become a priest instead of a policeman,' he said.

Woodend shook his head. 'There'd have been no chance of that. I didn't have the Latin, you see, and you'll never get anywhere in the priesthood if you don't have the Latin.' He paused for a moment. 'So are you goin' to tell me what happened, Doc?'

'Why not?' Pierson asked. 'If for no other reason, it'll be worth it just to see the look on your face when you finally learn the truth.'

The house was located on the cliff-tops, in a seaside town about sixty miles from Whitebridge. It was not quite grand enough to have been called a mansion, but most of the people with whom Rutter rubbed shoulders would have thought all their dreams had come true if they'd had the title deeds to it in their own pockets.

Its present owner had lived there for fifteen years. She had bought it with the money she'd been awarded in the divorce settlement which had left Alec Hawtrey feeling so poor that, in the end, he'd had no choice but to take Bradley Pine into the business as his partner.

The first Mrs Hawtrey was in her late fifties, and was inclining towards becoming stout. She had resisted the temptation to dye her hair – which was now almost white – but it was well cared for and recently permed. She was wearing a sensible tweed skirt, a plain blouse and strong walking shoes – and she had insisted that Rutter accompany her in her daily stroll along the cliffs.

They stood quite close to the edge for a while, watching the seagulls swoop over the sea, then the first Mrs Hawtrey turned to Rutter and said, 'It is truly remarkable how long bitterness can linger, isn't it? It's sixteen years since the divorce, you know.'

'Yes, I'd worked that out for myself,' Rutter said.

'You'd have thought, wouldn't you, that we would have been able to build ourselves a new life during all that time? But the sad truth is that none of us have quite managed it.'

'None of you?' Rutter repeated. 'None of who?'

'Oh, I'm sorry, I wasn't being very clear, was I? I meant myself and the children. I suppose that if you asked other people's opinion of us, they'd say we *had* changed, but believe me, the change is only on the surface. Both children lead their own independent lives now, and I'm very highly thought of as a result of the hard work I've put into several local charities. But there's something missing in all of us, you see – and that something is Alec.'

'I understand,' Rutter said, though he was not entirely convinced that he really did.

'If Alec had died – I mean, if he'd died back then, rather than thirteen years later – it might have been different.'

'How?'

'We'd still have been grieving for him even now, of course, but I think that sense of loss would have been a much easier thing to bear than this feeling of betrayal which still clings to me like a thick layer of dirt. We were such a happy family, you see. His life was built around us, and our lives were built around him. Other people called our house "Tara" – in a sneering sort of way – but we didn't care, because we all loved it. And then Alec became involved with that woman – and he simply deserted us.'

'Do you blame her entirely for what happened to your marriage?' Rutter asked.

'Oh no, I don't blame her at all.'

'Really?'

'Really! I'd know her for years before it all happened, you see. In fact, since she came to us from the orphanage, as little more than a child. That was Bradley's doing. Being an orphan himself, I think he felt sorry for her.'

She really didn't know the half of it, Rutter thought. She had no idea of the *planning* that had gone into the destruction of her idyllic life.

But he said nothing – because it would have been incredibly cruel to tell her the truth now.

'Even in those early days,' the first Mrs Hawtrey continued,

'I could clearly see that she was nothing more than a scheming little bitch – pardon my French, Inspector Rutter, but it happens to be true – and I always thought she'd try to get her claws into some poor unsuspecting man eventually. I just never imagined that man would be my loving husband.'

'But *still* you don't blame her?'

'No, I promise you I don't. I happen to believe in free will, and whilst I'm sure that she used all the pretty little tricks she could to win him away from us, Alec could have resisted the temptation if he'd really tried.'

Just as I could have resisted Monika *if I'd really tried*, Rutter thought.

And he didn't even have any of the excuses that Alec Hawtrey had, he told himself. Monika hadn't been anything like a 'scheming little bitch'. And he hadn't been going through a mid-life crisis which had made him feel the need to have his vanity massaged.

'I'd like to ask you about your husband's friends, if I may,' he said, pulling his thoughts back to the main purpose of his visit.

'His friends? I saw nothing at all of Alec in the last thirteen years of his life. So I have absolutely no idea if he made any new friends or not – though I rather suspect that he didn't.'

'It's his old friends I'm more interested in,' Rutter told her. 'Friends he'd known for so long that they'd become almost like brothers to him.'

'Can I know why you're asking that particular question?' the first Mrs Hawtrey said thoughtfully. 'Does it, in some way, have anything to do with Bradley Pine's death?'

'We think it may.'

'And what way might that be?'

'We think that there may still be people around who were very fond of your husband and blame Bradley Pine for his accident,' Rutter said, picking his words very carefully.

'So what you're actually saying is that you think that Pine's murder may have been a kind of revenge killing?'

'It's a possibility we're certainly not dismissing.'

'If you don't mind me saying so, I think you're barking up the completely wrong tree,' the first Mrs Hawtrey told Rutter. 'Alec simply didn't have close friends like that.'

'Everybody has at least *one* close friend.'

'Not my Alec. He worshipped his father and he loved the spring mattress business – and from quite an early age that seems to have been more than enough for him.'

'Until he met you.'

'Until he met me. You can't even imagine what our courtship was like. He was so shy and awkward – characteristics his son has inherited from him – and I almost went into shock when he plucked up the nerve to propose to me. But he *did* propose and I accepted, and we had the lavish wedding which his father insisted on.' She paused, and frowned. 'I think it was the wedding which really brought home to me just how isolated he'd been.'

'Why was that?'

'Well, there were quite a lot of my friends there, but very few of his – and even the ones of his who did turn up were really more like acquaintances. So, you see, Alec simply wasn't the kind of man who inspired that kind of loyalty. The only person who'd ever have cared enough about him to avenge his death was me, and since the betrayal, even that's not true.'

'Thank you for being so open with me, Mrs Hawtrey,' Rutter said. 'I know it can't have been easy for you.'

'Actually, it was easier than I thought it would be,' the first Mrs Hawtrey told him. 'You're a good listener. In that way, you quite remind me of my son. Are you shy, too?'

'Shy?'

'You are! I can see it now. I suspect that's why you decided to become a policeman.'

'Do you really think that "shyness" is a word most people would ever think of applying to bobbies?' Rutter asked, wondering, even as he spoke, why he should have suddenly started to sound so defensive.

'Not to all policemen, no, but certainly to some. I would imagine that your work gives you both a sense of certainty and a sense of purpose that would otherwise be lacking. It forces you to be a part of the world, whereas your natural tendency would be to withdraw.'

She was talking total bollocks, Rutter thought. So why had her words made his stomach turn over?

'If you'll excuse me, I think I should be getting back to Whitebridge,' he said hurriedly.

He shook hands with her, and began to walk away.

He had only gone a few yards when she called after him, 'Will you be writing a report on this meeting?'

He stopped, and turned around. 'A report? Yes, I suppose so. But I don't imagine it will be a very long one.'

'It doesn't matter how long or short it is,' the woman said. 'When you write it, don't refer to me as you did just now?'

'I beg your pardon?'

'You called me Mrs Hawtrey.'

'Yes?'

'For years, I thought of *myself* like that. But it wasn't true. Even if the Catholic Church refused to recognize the divorce – even if we were still married in the eyes of God – I wasn't Mrs Hawtrey any longer. At best, I was Used-To-Be Mrs Hawtrey. So I finally cut myself adrift from the past, and reverted to my maiden name. That probably seems like nothing to you, but for me it took a great deal of courage. So when you refer to me in the report, please use my maiden name, which is the name I go by now, even if it does mean putting "Mrs Hawtrey" in brackets after it.'

'I'd be glad to,' Rutter said. 'But I don't know what your maiden name is?'

'Don't you?' the woman asked. 'Well, I suppose there's no reason why you should.'

And then she told him what name she would prefer him to use.

Thirty-Two

Henry Marlowe was standing in the back room of a village hall – the latest in a long string of village halls which the strategists behind his election campaign were requiring him to visit.

The caretaker – who seemed inordinately proud of the place – had informed him it was known as the Green Room, since it was where the 'actors' changed when the village put on one of its entertainments.

And what pathetic spectacles *they* must be, Marlowe thought sourly, picturing half a dozen overweight middle-aged women thumping around the stage and fluffing their lines.

Once he was in London, he'd go to *real* plays in *real* theatres, and return to Whitebridge as little as possible, he promised himself.

He looked around him again. When the 'Green Room' was between productions, it seemed to serve as nothing more than a general store room for all kinds of unwanted junk. There was a sink – with a mirror above it, and a tap which at first gurgled and then reluctantly released a thin stream of water – but there were no chairs, since these had all been taken into the main hall.

It was a sordid little space at best, Marlowe thought, and he really had no wish to be there.

He'd been booked to address the Women's Institute. He didn't want to face them. In truth, he couldn't see why he should have to face them. He was the Conservative candidate – why didn't they just vote for him?

His political agent, Bill Hawes, had failed to see his point of view on the matter.

'So what if you have to humiliate yourself by rubbing shoulders with the riff-raff once every four or five years?' he'd asked. 'In between elections, you're in clover, aren't you?

210

You've got a job which is comparatively well-paid, yet requires no more work than you're prepared to put into it. You've an expense account which most businessmen would give their personal assistants' right arms to have. And companies will be falling over themselves to offer you directorships. Isn't all that worth having to crawl on your belly for, just once in a while?'

'But the WI!' Marlowe had complained.

'Oh, they're a bunch of scatty old bags, who I'd probably end up garrotting myself if I had to spend too much time with them,' Hawes had admitted cheerfully, 'but they can usually be trusted to put their cross in roughly the right place, if they're handled properly.'

And so there he was – in this run-down village hall, practising sincere expressions in the mirror over the sink, and wondering if it was too early to uncork his hip flask – when the door opened and Woodend walked in.

'What precisely are you doing here, Chief Inspector?' Marlowe demanded, irritably.

'I just came to wish you the best of luck with the meeting, sir,' Woodend said.

'Is that right?' Marlowe asked, unconvinced. 'And you will be voting for me come election day, will you?'

'No, I'm afraid I just couldn't quite bring myself to do that, sir,' Woodend said.

He looked around for somewhere to sit, upended an empty milk crate, and lowered himself on to it.

'Why are you *really* here?' Marlowe asked.

'I'm really here because of Alec Hawtrey,' Woodend replied, lighting up a cigarette and inhaling deeply. 'I was quite convinced, for a while back there, that Bradley Pine had murdered him, you know.'

'That's a quite ludicrous assumption for anyone – even you – to make!' Marlowe said.

'Thanks for the vote of confidence, sir,' Woodend said dryly. 'But there's more.'

'More?'

'I was also convinced that Bradley Pine knew some nasty little secret of yours, an', because of that, he was able to blackmail you into helpin' him to cover up the murder.'

'How dare you even have such thoughts?' Marlowe

211

demanded. 'I'm a chief constable! I'm *going to be* a member of parliament. It would never even occur to me to become involved in a sordid cover-up.'

'Now that's not strictly true, is it?' Woodend asked mildly. 'You didn't cover up a murder, but you did cover up somethin' sordid – somethin' pretty horrific, in fact – that Pine did on that mountainside.'

'I must tell you that I have absolutely no idea what you're talking about!' Marlowe said hotly.

'What made you do it?' Woodend mused. 'The only explanation that I can come up with is that you saw it as no more than a natural extension of the mutual back-scratchin' that you Golf Club types have made a way of life. But it was a rather *big* favour he was askin' on that particular occasion, wasn't it?'

'I've heard quite enough of this, Chief Inspector Woodend. I don't know where you get your—'

'Of course, your lot never do anythin' without expectin' somethin' in return. So what were you expectin' from Pine? That he'd support your application to be the next Tory candidate? Because if that *was* what you were after, he let you down quite badly, didn't he?'

'I should never have trusted the man,' Marlowe said bitterly. 'I should never have taken him at his word.'

He was talking to himself, rather than to Woodend. In fact, in his anger at the dead man, he seemed almost to have forgotten that the chief inspector was even there in the room.

'I don't see you had much choice *but* to take him at his word,' Woodend pointed out. 'After all, it wasn't the kind of deal that you could ever have put down in writin', now was it?'

'Deal? What deal?' Marlowe asked, suddenly conscious of the other man's presence again. 'There was no *deal*. And I can assure you that there was absolutely no *cover-up*.'

Woodend shook his head slowly – and almost mournfully – from side to side.

'That really won't wash any more, you know,' he said. 'You can go on denyin' it till you've turned blue in the face, but I talked to your old mate Doc Pierson earlier this mornin' – an' so I'm never goin' to believe you.'

'You talked to Pierson? And he told you . . .?'

212

'He told me everythin'.'

'What Pine did wasn't a crime, you know!' Marlowe said. 'They'd never have locked him up for it.'

'Possibly you're right, though I think I could find half a dozen lawyers who might disagree with you,' Woodend replied. 'But that's not really the point, is it, sir? Even if it wasn't strictly a *criminal* act, it would have ruined him socially. It wouldn't have done much for his business, either. People tend to be a bit squeamish about havin' dealin's with a man like that.'

'What was so wrong with it, when you look at it objectively?' Marlowe asked. 'Strip away all the sugary emotionalism behind it, and what are you left with? The fact that Bradley Pine found himself in a difficult situation, and did no more than he needed to do to ensure his own well-being!'

'That's certainly one way of lookin' at what happened,' Woodend agreed. 'But since I'm not one of the élite of Whitebridge society – like you are, an' Pine was – I don't think I'd look at it that way myself.'

He stood up and walked towards the door.

'What are you going to do?' Marlowe asked, with a strong hint of panic in his voice.

'Do?' Woodend repeated. 'I'm goin' to do what I get paid to do – which is to try my hardest to find Bradley Pine's murderer.'

'That isn't what I meant, and you know it,' Marlowe said.

'Oh, you mean, am I goin' to tell anybody else what Pierson told me?' Woodend said.

'Listen, Charlie, I'll still have considerable influence in the Central Lancs Constabulary once I'm elected, you know.'

'I'm sure you will.'

'I'll still have a say in who gets promoted and who doesn't. Would you like to be a superintendent? Or even a *chief* superintendent? That can be arranged – as long as you're prepared to keep quiet.'

'There's no need to offer me a bribe,' Woodend told him. '*I* won't tell anybody your nasty little secret.'

Marlowe mopped his sweating brow with his handkerchief.

'Thank you, Chief Inspector,' he said. 'Thank you so much.'

'But whether or not it leaks out from some *other* source will depend, I would imagine, on who killed Pine, an' *why* he killed him.'

Thirty-Three

Since his mother appeared to be having one of her more lucid mornings, Colin Beresford had decided to take off a couple of the hours that his recent spate of overtime entitled him to, and spend them with her.

Why bother going into work anyway, he asked himself, when – despite Woodend's pep talk the previous evening – he was far from convinced he was contributing anything of importance to the investigation.

It was true, he argued, putting the case from the other side – as Woodend had done the previous evening – that the chief inspector would probably not have realized, had it not been for him, that Bradley Pine's body had been dumped on the site of what had once been 'Tara' – the old Hawtrey family house.

But how did that particular piece of knowledge help them advance the investigation?

Even if it were more than a coincidence – and that was a long way from being firmly established – neither he nor Woodend had any real idea of *what* it signified.

The inside of his poor mother's head must be a little like this case, he thought. There was so much information – so many memories – floating around in there.

But no structure at all.

No system.

No coherent whole.

'Why don't we look at the old photograph albums, Colin?' his mother suggested.

Why not, Beresford agreed.

Leave it a couple of hours, and all the faces smiling up at her would mean nothing to his mother. So why not grab the opportunity to have her live in the real world while she still could?

She even remembered where they *kept* the albums, he thought, as he watched her open the drawer.

But he shouldn't let that fool him, even for a moment, into thinking she was getting any better. She would *never* get any better. All he had left to hope for was that her decline would not be too rapid.

His mother placed one of the albums on the table, and opened it.

'This was the holiday we all spent in Blackpool, when you were just a little boy,' she said. 'Do you remember?'

'I remember.'

'There's your dad in front of the Tower . . .' Mrs Beresford paused and looked around the room. 'Where *is* your dad, by the way? Has he gone out?'

'Dad's dead, Mum,' Beresford said.

Mrs Beresford blinked, then tried to pretend that she hadn't.

'Of course he's dead, I knew that,' she agreed. 'And there's you, on the sands,' she continued, hastily. 'Weren't you a lovely little boy?'

Beresford examined the faded photograph. The boy in it looked serious – almost brooding.

Had he sensed, even then, what lay ahead of him, he wondered. Could he already see into a future in which his father was dead and his mother was slowly going gaga?

The picture began to remind him of another photograph – though it was not one of him.

And suddenly, he realized why the priest had seemed so familiar!

Woodend had only just got back to his office when the phone on his desk began to ring.

He picked it up, and heard the operator say, 'I have a long-distance phone call from Australia for you. I'm connecting you now.'

Australia?

'Chief Inspector Woodend?' asked a cheery voice down the crackling line. 'G'day! It's Sergeant Archie Boon of the Western Australia Police here. I'm told you've been making inquiries about Jeremy Tully.'

'That's right,' Woodend agreed.

'Then I'm the bloke you need to speak to. He works on one of the farms on my patch.'

'He works on a *farm*!'

'That's what I said. He's a sheep-shearer. An' for a beginner, he's a damn good one.'

'Are you quite sure that we're talkin' about the same man?' Woodend wondered.

'Jeremy Nathan Tully?' Boon asked. 'Moved here from Whitebridge, Lancashire? Used to be an accountant?'

'That's him. What's he doin' shearin' sheep?'

'There's not much choice in the matter, since the sheep can't shear themselves,' Boon pointed out. 'An' old Jerry tells me he quite likes the work. Says he's found peace at last – whatever that means.'

'D'you mean to say you've already talked to him?' Woodend asked.

'Talked to him? I've done more than that. I've *interrogated* him.'

'You done *what*?'

'Interrogated him. But not like you might have done over there in the Old Country – shining bright lights into his face and tapping your truncheon menacingly against your trouser leg.'

Woodend grinned. 'You've been watchin' too many old films, Sergeant,' he said.

'You're probably right,' Boon agreed. 'Anyway, since he's one of my closest neighbours – which means he only lives a couple of hours drive from where I live – I thought I'd better leave the lamp and truncheon at home, and interrogate him the *Ozzie* way.'

'An' what way's that?' Woodend wondered.

'I turned up at his place with a case of beer, and suggested he light up the barbie and throw a few thick juicy steaks on it. We had a real good chin-wag once he'd done that – especially after we'd drained a few tinnies of the amber nectar.'

'What did you talk *about*?'

'Mainly about why he came to Oz. Seems he had a bit of a rough time up a mountainside in old England. Must admit, I didn't know you even had mountains over there.'

'They probably don't look much in comparison to yours,

216

but we're used to them,' Woodend said. 'And I know what happened on the mountainside, so you can skip that bit.'

'Oh, all right,' Boon agreed easily. 'Well, after he came down from the mountain, he was having trouble sleeping, and when he did fall asleep he had these terrible nightmares. He's a Catholic. Did you know that?'

'Yes, I did.'

'Anyway, he went to his priest, and confessed. I don't understand how these things work – not got much time for religion myself – but I think that was supposed to make everything all right again. Only it didn't work out like that. He was still getting the sweats and the trembles. So he went to see the priest again, and the priest suggested that he moved to Oz.'

'The *priest* did?'

'Yeah, that's right. He told Jerry he should put his past behind him – get as far away from England as he could, and make a new start. And you can't get further away from England than Oz. Turns out it was a real beaut of an idea, because he has no trouble at all sleepin' now.' The sergeant chuckled. 'Course, that *could* have something to do with the fact that he's shearing sheep from dawn till dusk.'

'Did he happen to tell you the name of the priest who gave him this advice?' Woodend asked.

'Can't say that he did. But he did tell me that it was a very *young* priest.'

Paniatowski crossed herself awkwardly and self-consciously. 'Bless me, Father, for I have sinned,' she said.

'You shouldn't have come here, Monika,' the voice hissed from the other side of the grille.

'Isn't this the right place to talk about what happened last night?' Paniatowski asked.

'Yes, but—'

'Well, that's why I'm here.'

'—but not with *me*.'

'I want to know if I did wrong,' Paniatowski said firmly.

'We *both* did wrong,' Father Taylor said. 'But though I know there are no degrees of difference within mortal sin, I still believe that I did more wrong than you – and that I will burn in hellfire for eternity as a result.'

'Not if you confess! Not if you get some other priest to absolve you from your sins!'

'I *can't* confess,' Father Taylor said, agonized.

'Why?'

'Because there can be no forgiveness without true repentance – and I cannot bring myself to repent.'

'So what will happen to *us*?'

'That is in God's hands.'

'Don't give me all that crap!' Paniatowski said angrily. 'You still have your free will, don't you? You can still go where you want to, and be with who you want to be with.'

'Perhaps you're right about that – for the moment,' Father Taylor said. 'But I don't think it will be the case for very much longer.'

'Why?'

'Because events – circumstances – are closing in on me.'

'And just what's that supposed to mean?'

There was the sound of two sets of men's footsteps, crossing the floor of the church and approaching the confessional.

'In the name of the Father, Son and Holy Spirit, I absolve you of your sins,' Father Taylor said.

Though he spoke hurriedly, it was not with the uncertain voice of the man she had been with the previous evening, but with the authority of an ordained priest of the Holy Catholic Church.

'But I can't be forgiven, because I don't repent *either*!' Paniatowski said angrily.

'You will repent,' Father Taylor told her, sadly. 'And perhaps sooner than you think. You have to go now.'

'I don't *want* to go!'

'You must,' Father Taylor insisted.

There were tears in Paniatowski's eyes as she stepped out of the confessional, but through those tears she still managed to see Charlie Woodend and Bob Rutter standing there.

And suddenly, everything Father Taylor had said to her started to make sense.

Thirty-Four

'This is all a complete waste of time, you know,' Father Taylor said, quite calmly, as he looked at Woodend across the table in Whitebridge Police Headquarters' Interview Room B.

'*Why* is it a complete waste of time?' Woodend asked. 'Because you're innocent of the crime with which you're charged?'

'No. Quite the contrary. Because I'm guilty of it. I killed Bradley Pine, and I'll willingly sign any confession that you care to put in front of me. Isn't that enough for you?'

'No, it isn't,' Woodend told him. 'The Crown Prosecution Service will want a comprehensive report, which means that I need you to flesh out some of the details for me.'

Father Taylor laughed. '*Flesh* out some of the details!' he repeated. 'Is that really what you said? Don't you think that's a rather macabre use of the word under the circumstances?'

'Possibly it is,' Woodend agreed. 'But then I've found this whole investigation a little macabre, because we don't get a great many cases of mutilation in Whitebridge.' He paused for a moment. 'Would you like to give me a full statement now?'

'No, I wouldn't. I've said all I intend to say.'

'Come on, help me out a bit here,' Woodend cajoled.

Father Taylor folded his arms across his chest, and kept his mouth tightly closed.

'Then how about this as an alternative suggestion?' Woodend said. 'I'll tell you everything that I *think* happened, an' if I'm goin' wrong at any point, you'll let me know.'

Father Taylor considered the suggestion for what seemed to Woodend like a long time. 'You do understand that there are some things I can neither confirm nor deny,' he said finally.

'Yes.'

'Then if what you propose will bring about an end to all this in the shortest possible time, please go ahead.'

'An hour or so before Bradley Pine was murdered, he paid a visit to St Mary's Church,' Woodend said. 'He knelt down in one of the pews an' prayed for a while, and then he took confession with Father Kenyon. By the time he left the church, you'd already gone yourself.'

'That is correct.'

'You cycled up over to Thelma Hawtrey's house in Upper Bankside – which is a good two miles from your church. Once you got there, you hid your bicycle, and waited in the bushes for Pine to arrive. Is that right?'

'Yes.'

'What did you use as your murder weapon?'

'A large spanner.'

'Where did you get it from?'

'The church boiler room.'

'*When* did you get it?'

'Just before I cycled to that woman's house.'

'So, if you took it with you, you must already have been planning to kill Pine when you left the church?'

'Yes.'

'How did you know where to lie in wait for him?'

'I'm not sure I understand the question.'

'Yes, you do. Bradley Pine could have gone off in any direction once he'd left the church – so what made you so certain that he would be going to see Thelma Hawtrey?'

'That is one of the things that I cannot say.'

'Ah, I see! You knew where he'd probably be going because you learned of his affair with Thelma in the confessional. Was it Thelma herself who told you? Or was it Jeremy Tully?'

Father Taylor said nothing.

'You killed him in the driveway of Thelma's house, then you put your bicycle in the boot of his car. You might have been planning to put his body in there as well – I don't know about that – but anyway, there was no room. So you squeezed the corpse on to the back seat, instead.' Woodend paused to take a drag on his cigarette. 'What happened to the bike, by the way?'

'I threw it into the canal.'

'Why?'

220

'I thought there might be some forensic evidence on it which would link me with the crime.'

'I see.'

'And once I'd safely disposed of it, I told Monika that it had been stolen from outside the church, so I'd be covered if there were any questions about it later. Isn't it terrible?'

'Isn't what terrible?'

'The way that we use other people – even the people that we love?'

'We're gettin' off the point,' Woodend said awkwardly. 'You killed him, and then you put his body in the boot—'

'And drove out to the lay-by on the dual carriageway,' Father Taylor supplied.

'And drove out to the exact spot where your home had once stood, Mr Hawtrey,' Woodend corrected him.

'Taylor,' the other man said firmly. 'My name is *Taylor*.'

'But you were born—'

'When my mother changed her name back to what it had once been, she changed mine and my sister's as well.'

'Mr Taylor, then,' Woodend agreed.

'And I would be grateful if you call me *Father*. Whatever I might have done, I was anointed as a priest. The hands were laid upon me, and I will be a priest until the day I die, whether I wish it or not.'

'All right, Father Taylor it is,' Woodend agreed. 'When he was making his confessions to you, Jeremy Tully didn't know you were Alec Hawtrey's son, did he, Father Taylor?'

'Nobody knew, except for Father Kenyon. I went away from here as a boy, and came back as an adult. Besides, when people look at a priest, it is only the cassock they see, not the man inside it. Except for Monika. *She* saw the man.'

'Why take the body to the lay-by?'

'I'm truly not sure,' Taylor admitted.

'But you have your suspicions?'

'Perhaps, in some strange, unexplainable way, I thought I was doing it for my father.'

'Because it was Bradley Pine – using Thelma as his instrument – who broke up your family? You did *know* all about that, didn't you, even if your mother didn't? It's another one of those things you learned in the confessional.'

'I have nothing to say on the matter,' Father Taylor told him.

'Pine destroyed the father you'd known as a child, and turned him into someone else entirely. So it somehow seemed appropriate to place Pine's body on the spot where that other man – that other father – had lived before the Fall?'

'Again, my lips are sealed.'

'You didn't blame Thelma, in any way, for what happened?'

'Mother said we shouldn't, and Mother was right.'

'Because Thelma was no more than Pine's creature?'

'My father must bear a part of the blame,' Father Taylor said, side-stepping the question. 'And so . . . and so must I!'

'You think it was partly *your* fault?'

'Yes.'

'Why?'

'Because I wouldn't listen to him.'

Young Fred is sitting in the garden of the house which has always represented a picture of true happiness in his mother's mind, but is now a reality – because his father has had it built out of love for her.

He is thinking about how confusing life is for most people, and how – even at his age – they seem to want to confide their confusion in him.

Why should that happen, he wonders.

Perhaps it is because he's more of a listener than a talker. Perhaps it is because of something else entirely – something he doesn't even understand, yet feels himself in the grip of.

But whatever the reason, it is beyond doubt that he has the gift of being able to help guide these unhappy people through all the complexities of their earthly existence.

He looks up to see his father standing there. They have never spoken much – it is hard to overcome your own shyness with someone who is also very shy – but Alec plainly wants to speak now.

'It's a horrible thing,' he says.

'What is?'

'Getting old.'

'You're not old, Father!' Fred tells him.

'But I'm older than I once was,' Alec says. 'My body aches in places it never used to. I don't have anything like the same amount of energy I had ten years ago.'

'Of course, you don't. That's the way that—'

'There are things I can no longer do – and other things which are starting to slip away. I feel the urge to reach out for some of those things that are still within my grasp – while I still can.'

'You shouldn't worry yourself about such matters,' Fred says. 'A gradual decline, as we get closer to our graves, is no more than the human condition as God intended it to be. Ashes to ashes, dust to dust.'

His father looks at him strangely, as if seeing him as he really is for the first time. 'Don't you ever worry about anything, Fred?'

'Of course I do. Everybody does.'

'And how do you deal with it?'

'I go to church, and pray for guidance.'

His father nods. 'I used to think I was a good Catholic myself,' he says, 'but I seem so unworthy when I compare my faith to yours.'

'We're all unworthy,' Fred tells him.

Alec pulls up a chair, and sits down next to him. 'I want to talk about love,' he says.

'All right.'

'Love is a very strange thing. I love your mother with all my heart—'

'I know you do.'

'—but I no longer feel the same passion for her that I used to.'

'As you said yourself, you're getting older.'

'But the passion's still there within me, Fred, even if your mother can't arouse it! I can feel it whenever I—'

Fred gets to his feet so quickly that the chair he has been sitting on goes flying off behind him.

'I have to go,' he says, in a complete panic. 'There are matters I must attend to. Now!'

'Please, son, I need to explain,' his father says, with an agonized expression filling his face.

But Fred is already striding back to the house.

'You mustn't blame yourself for that!' Woodend said, horrified.

'Why mustn't I? If I'd stopped and listened to him, our lives might have turned out quite differently. Through me –

through my words and encouragement – he might have found the strength to resist temptation.'

'You were just a kid at the time!' Woodend protested. 'You can't possibly be held responsible.'

'When I first came back to Whitebridge as a priest, I used to dream that one day my father would walk into my church and ask for forgiveness,' Father Taylor said wistfully.

'Ask forgiveness from whom?' Woodend wondered. 'From his confessor? Or from his son?'

'It wouldn't have mattered which of those two he chose to talk to. He would have said he was sorry for what he had done, and I would have said I was sorry for what I had *not* done. But he never came. And then he died, and so I knew he never would. But I still loved him. And I still wanted his forgiveness.'

'What about Pine? Did you hope he'd confess to you, too?'

'Yes.'

'About how he'd used Thelma to get what he wanted? Or about what happened on that mountainside?'

'Once more, I cannot say.'

'But if he had chosen to confess to you, do you think he might still have been alive today?'

'It's a possibility.'

'What was it that finally drove you to kill him?' Woodend wondered. 'What was the straw that broke the camel's back? Was it seein' his face in the paper nearly every day – bein' constantly reminded that the man who'd committed so much evil was goin' on from triumph to triumph?'

Father Taylor maintained his silence.

'An' which of his evils did you most hold against him?' Woodend continued. 'Was it destroying your parents' marriage? Or was it what he did to your father on the mountain?'

'I killed him. That is all you need to know.'

'Given that you smashed in his mouth, an' slit open his stomach, I'm inclined to believe it was the latter.'

'There is nothing I can do about what you choose to believe.'

'Bradley Pine didn't kill your father, as I once thought he must have done,' Woodend said, 'but it's more than possible that he lived on *because of* your father. It must have been very hard for you, seeing him leading a full and happy life, sleeping with the woman who he'd used to break up your parents' marriage – and knowing all the time about the pain and misery he must have caused your father in his dying moments.'

'Do you still expect me to break the seal of confession? Even now?' Father Taylor asked.

'No, I don't,' Woodend replied. 'You've given me ample proof that you'd never do that.' He paused to light up a fresh cigarette. 'My chief constable, Mr Marlowe, doesn't really see the harm in what Bradley Pine did,' he continued. 'As far as he's concerned, the man needed food to stay alive, and if that involved cutting the flesh off a dead man's arm and eating it, then that was what he should have done, however repugnant it might sound to other people.'

Father Taylor had fallen silent again, though now tears were beginning to appear in his eyes.

'But Mr Marlowe's not bein' entirely honest about the matter, is he?' Woodend asked. 'He's deliberately overlookin' certain important facts – because that way he can avoid facin' the truth. But *we've* both faced the truth, haven't we, Father Taylor?'

Tears had begun to stream down the young priest's cheeks, but still he said nothing.

'You know it because of what Jeremy Tully told you in the confessional,' Woodend continued, 'an' I know it because my sergeant questioned the witnesses who were at the scene. An' *what* do we know? We know that when Pine took his knife an' sliced into your father's arm, the blood spurted everywhere. Because his heart was still pumpin' it round! Because your father might have been dyin' – but he certainly wasn't dead.'

Thirty-Five

Woodend and Beresford sat at the team's usual table in the public bar of the Drum and Monkey.

'Now do you see what I mean about stirrin' up the pot an' seein' what floats to the top, lad?' Woodend asked. 'Most of the stuff you learned at the factory *was* a waste of time, as you suspected it might be, but if you'd never gone there, you'd never have seen a photograph of young Fred Hawtrey – on holiday with his mum an' dad – on the wall of the boiler room. An' if you'd never seen the photograph, you'd never have realized that Hawtrey an' Taylor were the same man.'

'Inspector Rutter came up with exactly the same information from talking to the first Mrs Hawtrey,' Beresford pointed out.

'That's true,' Woodend agreed. 'But he might not have done. We could have decided we didn't need to talk to her at all. Or she might never have mentioned her maiden name to Inspector Rutter. That's why we need as many spoons in the pot as possible – as long as they're good, solid spoons. An' that's what you are – a good solid spoon.'

'You're very kind, sir,' Beresford said.

'I'm very practical,' Woodend replied. 'I need men I can rely on, an' once I've got them, I try not to let go of them.'

Beresford checked his watch, and then drained his pint. 'I think I'd better be going,' he said.

'It's my round,' Woodend said. 'Why not let me buy you one for the road before you go?'

'That's very kind of you, sir,' Beresford replied, 'but I'd better not.'

'If it's your mam you're thinking of, I don't imagine she'd begrudge you an extra half-hour in the pub, tonight of all nights,' Woodend said.

The second the words were out of his mouth he realized

he'd made a mistake. And from the black look Beresford was giving him, it was clear the remark had not gone unnoticed by him, either.

'What's that supposed to mean?' Beresford demanded. 'That you think I'm tied to my mother's apron strings?'

'No,' Woodend said heavily. 'It means I know about your mam's condition – an' I know that you're doin' your best to try an' look after her.'

'Who told you?' Beresford asked.

'That doesn't really matter, does it?' Woodend said soothingly. 'The important thing is that you didn't want me to know – an' you're far from chuffed to learn that I do.' He paused for a moment. 'Why *didn't* you want me to find out, lad? It can't be because you're ashamed of her, can it?'

'Of course not,' Beresford said angrily. 'She can't help it, any more than she could help having cancer.'

'So what is the problem?' Woodend wondered.

'I don't want you making excuses for me!' Beresford told him.

'Pardon?'

'If I do something wrong, I want you to give me a first-class bollocking for it. I don't want you holding back, because of what I have to put up with at home. I don't want you making *allowances* for me!'

'What you really mean is, you don't want me to start *pityin'* you,' Woodend said.

'Maybe that is what I mean,' Beresford agreed.

'You're doin' neither me nor yourself justice, lad,' Woodend told him. 'Pity's somethin' that's reserved for people who can't handle what life throws at them, an' from what I've seen of you, you're not one of them. You'll cope with your mam's deterioration – probably better than I would have done in your place.'

'And if I start to screw up the job, because of the pressures at home?'

'I tell you, just as I've had to tell Bob an' Monika in their time.'

'Honestly?'

'Honestly. I'll have no choice in the matter, because the job's got to be done, an' if you can't do it, somebody else will just have to take your place. But there's no point in worryin' about somethin' that hasn't happened yet, now is there?'

Beresford was silent for a moment, then he said, 'We seem to have spent so much time talking over my problems that I could have had that pint you offered me after all. But now it really *is* time I went.'

Woodend nodded, sympathetically. 'I can't do anythin' to make what goes on at home any easier,' he said, as Beresford stood up and turned towards the door, 'but what I can do is offer you a job that'll at least distract you while you're at work. Think about that, when you're making up your mind whether you'd rather direct traffic or track down murderers.'

On the previous occasions when Monika Paniatowski had walked through the main door of St Mary's Church, she had done so warily, and perhaps a little deferentially. There was no evidence of deference this time – she strode in as if the church counted for nothing, and she was all that mattered.

'I've come to collect a few things that Fred Taylor might need,' she told Father Kenyon.

'Things?' the old priest repeated. 'What kind of things?'

'Toiletries. Tooth brush, nail brush, electric razor . . . all the stuff a well-groomed man will need when he's banged up in gaol.'

'Did they have to sent *you*, of all people, on this errand, my child?' Father Kenyon asked, pityingly.

'You've got it all wrong,' Paniatowski told him. 'Nobody *sent* me. I'm here because I *wanted* to do it.'

And to prove to myself that I could, she added silently.

The priest nodded, almost as if she'd spoken those last words aloud, and he'd heard them.

'Give me a moment to deal with matters here, and then we'll go together and get whatever you think Father Fred will need,' he said.

'You don't seem the least surprised that he's been arrested,' Paniatowski said.

'Don't I?' Father Kenyon asked.

'You haven't even asked me *why* he's in gaol.'

'That's true,' the priest agreed. 'I haven't.'

'But then you don't *need* to ask, do you? He'll have told you all about it when he made his confession. Isn't that right?'

'What a man says in the confessional is between him and his God,' Father Kenyon said.

'What about what Pine said when he was in that holy box of yours?' Monika demanded. 'Did he confess to you that he'd eaten living flesh in order to save his own miserable life?'

'I must answer as before,' the priest said calmly.

'Mind you, that probably didn't shock you half as much as it would have shocked most people, did it?' Paniatowski said. 'Eating living flesh is what you're supposed to be doing every time you take Communion.'

'You are very bitter, my child, and I can understand that,' the priest said gently. 'But I hope and pray that what has happened will not turn you against the Church.'

'You are joking, aren't you?' Paniatowski asked.

'I never joke where matters of faith are concerned.'

'I've tried your religion twice, and it hasn't worked out for me either time,' Paniatowski said. 'It doesn't get another chance.'

'My child—'

'Listen, I really don't need any of this,' Paniatowski said. 'In fact, there's only one thing I really need – and that's a bloody drink. So if you want to make sure that Fred gets his stuff, you'd better take it to the station yourself.'

She turned, and began to walk towards the door.

'However you may feel about Him, God will always give *you* another chance,' the priest called after her. 'And another. And another. That, above all else, is what makes Him God.'

'Well, the next time you talk to Him, tell Him I don't need another chance,' Paniatowski called over her shoulder. 'Tell Him I've decided to go it alone from now on.'

When Paniatowski arrived at the Drum and Monkey, she found her boss sitting there alone.

'Bob's just rung to say he's still got a bit of private business to wrap up, but that he should be here shortly,' Woodend said.

There was a vodka already waiting for her on the table, and Paniatowski downed it in one.

'So that's what he calls it, is it?' she snorted, as the alcohol hit her nervous system. 'A bit of private business!'

'Is something wrong?' Woodend asked.

'Why should anything be wrong?' Paniatowski demanded. 'Does something always have to be *wrong*?'

'No, but you sound a little—'

'Can't we forget Bob Rutter for a while? Can't we talk about something else for a change?'

'I wasn't aware we *did* normally spend that much time talkin' about Bob,' Woodend said mildly. 'But if you want to change the subject, that's fine with me. What shall we talk about?'

'I don't know. Anything at all, as long as it's not Bob-bloody-Rutter! How's the election going?'

'Not all that well – at least for Henry Marlowe,' Woodend said. 'He's withdrawn his candidature, which was probably very wise, considerin' that what he did on that mountainside will soon be public knowledge.'

'So who'll blow the whistle on him? You?'

'No, not me.'

'Then who?'

'Father Taylor's defence lawyer. When it comes to the sentencin', he'll put forward what Bradley Pine did to Taylor's dad up that mountain as a mitigatin' factor.'

'Fred will never allow that. He can't – because it was told him under the seal of confession.'

'But the man who *made* the confession can say what he likes, and I'd be very surprised if I don't see Jeremy Tully – the reborn Australian sheep-shearer – up there in the witness box.'

'Do you think Marlowe will go to gaol?'

Woodend shook his head. 'Not unless the age of miracles has finally come to pass. He's got too many friends in high places – friends who follow the same code as he does, an' will understand that he only did what was necessary to protect one of their own. They won't exactly pin a medal on him – that would be too much, even for them – but if you ask me, all that's likely to happen is that he'll get a slap on the wrist an' then be given his old job back.'

'Which won't be good news for you,' Paniatowski said. 'He's bound to hold you responsible for his having to withdraw from the election.'

'Of course he'll hold me responsible,' Woodend agreed. 'He holds me responsible when a stray dog craps on his front lawn. But I'll get by.' He lit up a cigarette. 'Now we've exhausted the subject of local politics, do you want to tell me what's been on your mind ever since you walked in here?'

'No.'

'I really think you better had, Monika. It's doin' you absolutely no good at all keepin' it bottled up inside.'

Paniatowski sighed wearily. 'I stopped on the way here to buy a packet of cigarettes. There's a café just next to the off licence I went to. I just happened to look in through the window and I saw Bob. He was sitting at one of the tables – with Elizabeth Driver.'

'Was he, now?' Woodend said, thoughtfully. 'Still, it probably doesn't mean anythin'.'

'Yes it does. They seemed very . . . close.'

'What are you sayin' exactly? Did he have his hand up her skirt or somethin'?'

'No, he didn't.'

'Well, then—'

'But it's only a matter of time before he does.'

'This investigation's been a big strain on you, lass, an' I think you're overreactin' a bit,' Woodend said.

'Am I?' Paniatowski demanded. 'Why do you think she changed her hair colour from black to blonde?'

'I don't know.'

'Because Maria's hair was black!'

'I still don't see it.'

'Then you're a fool! Now that Maria's dead, she's become some kind of saint in Bob's eyes, and Driver knows she can never compete with her, however much she tries. But I'm still alive – so I'm fair game.'

'Come on, lass,' Woodend said uneasily.

'Don't you see what she's offering him? She's offering another version of me – but without the guilt.'

'Do you want him back?' Woodend asked gently.

'No!'

'Truthfully?'

'I *want* him back – of course, I do – but after all that's happened, I know I can never have him. What I *really* don't want is for Elizabeth Driver to have him – because she'll destroy him.'

'You could be quite wrong about the whole thing, you know, Monika,' Woodend said.

'I'm not wrong! And before too long, you'll see for *yourself* that I'm not.'

* * *

231

Elizabeth Driver had tried to talk Rutter out of going for an end-of-investigation drink with Woodend and Paniatowski. She had done so for no other reason than to see how strong a hold she had over him, but she had not been too disappointed when her efforts failed, because it was still early days yet.

Alone again, now that Rutter had gone, she was on the phone, talking to her literary agent in London.

'I've had a wonderful idea for a book,' she said. 'I'm going to base it on one of the regional police forces.'

'That's not a very good way to go, if you're aiming at it being a blockbuster,' the agent cautioned. 'It might sell well in the area where it's set, but that's about the extent of it. Most people – and Londoners especially – aren't really interested in how the police work in other parts of the country.'

'But you see, it *won't* be about how this police force works,' Elizabeth Driver said.

'No?'

'No! It'll be about how it *doesn't* work – and it will be sensational!'

'You might have trouble getting enough information to fill a whole book,' the agent said, still dubious. 'Police forces tend to be tightly-knit, and, as you know from your own experience, they're very good at keeping reporters like you at arm's length.'

'Not this time,' Elizabeth Driver said confidently. 'This time I've got a man on the inside, and he'll give me everything I need.'

'What rank is he?'

'An inspector.'

'Not bad, providing he has contacts in the higher ranks.'

'He does. His *chief inspector* thinks he's wonderful, and would never dream of hiding anything from him.'

'And does this inspector of yours know exactly what it is you're planning to do?'

'Of course he doesn't,' Elizabeth Driver said. 'He hasn't got a bloody clue. And he'll continue to have no bloody clue – at least until the whole thing collapses in on him.'

Other Books by Joey Green

Hellbent on Insanity
The Gilligan's Island Handbook
The Get Smart Handbook
The Partridge Family Album
Polish Your Furniture with Panty Hose
Hi Bob!
Selling Out
Paint Your House with Powdered Milk
Wash Your Hair with Whipped Cream
The Bubble Wrap Book
Joey Green's Encyclopedia of Offbeat Uses for Brand-Name Products
The Zen of Oz
The Warning Label Book
Monica Speaks
The Official Slinky Book
You Know You've Reached Middle Age If . . .
The Mad Scientist Handbook
Clean Your Clothes with Cheez Whiz
The Road to Success Is Paved with Failure
Clean It! Fix It! Eat It!
Joey Green's Magic Brands
The Mad Scientist Handbook 2
Senior Moments
Jesus and Moses: The Parallel Sayings
Joey Green's Amazing Kitchen Cures
Jesus and Muhammad: The Parallel Sayings
Joey Green's Gardening Magic
How They Met
Joey Green's Incredible Country Store
Potato Radio, Dizzy Dice